DIARIES OF A CASANOVA
BOOK 1
LEGEND AWAKENING

by

Randi Alexander

and

Leo J. Canyon

Randi Alexander

"LEGEND AWAKENING,
DIARIES OF A CASANOVA, BOOK 1"

~~*~*

Edited by E. Felder

~~*~*

Cover Art by Diana Carlisle

~~*~*

Cover Model: Jackson Young

~~*~*

Lyrics to *Get a Little Rain On Ya'* courtesy of
Jackson Young

~~*~*

Table of Contents

Chapter One	1
Chapter Two	11
Chapter Three	18
Chapter Four	29
Chapter Five	39
Chapter Six	52
Chapter Seven	62
Chapter Eight	73
Chapter Nine	84
Chapter Ten	93
Chapter Eleven	104
Chapter Twelve	116
Chapter Thirteen	131
Chapter Fourteen	139
Chapter Fifteen	150
Chapter Sixteen	161
Chapter Seventeen	172
Chapter Eighteen	181
Chapter Nineteen	193
Chapter Twenty	203
Chapter Twenty-One	215
Chapter Twenty-Two	226
Chapter Twenty-Three	241
Chapter Twenty-Four	251
Chapter Twenty-Five	261
Chapter Twenty-Six	274
Chapter Twenty-Seven	286
Chapter Twenty-Eight	297
Chapter Twenty-Nine	306
Chapter Thirty	313
Chapter Thirty-One	321
Chapter Thirty-Two	332
Connect With Me	340
About the Author	341

Chapter One

Liam Jackson stepped out of the raucous locker room into the quiet, sultry air of a Southern Friday night. A cicada buzzed in a tree as he walked toward the closed concession stand. Groups of high school students, parents, and teachers stood talking, but he didn't have to look to see if Kaylee was still here. He could sense her, almost smell her like a pheromone in the air. A scent he couldn't place, but one that kind of reminded him of a spring rain. As he turned in her direction, he checked the sky to see if a rain cloud marred the evening sky, but, as usual when he smelled her unique scent, there were no clouds in sight.

"Hey, Liam." His buddy, Travis Hackers, caught up to him, still wearing his baseball uniform. "Krenshaw's got a keg, and we're gonna meet out at the old Dorster farm at nine."

They'd lost their game tonight, and a consolation beer would help wash away the taste of defeat, but Liam shook his head. "Can't tonight. I've got plans already. With Kaylee."

"Aw, damn, buddy, I almost forgot. Your grandparents are gone, ain't they?" Travis grabbed the crotch of his baseball pants. "You're gonna get some tonight."

A blast of anger shot through Liam and he faced his friend head-on, squaring his shoulders, wide and heavily muscled from his hours working on the family farm. "Keep it to yourself." His eyes narrowed and he leaned his six-foot-three-inch frame closer to Travis's shorter body. "Kaylee is someone special. I don't want her name thrown around school."

Stepping back, Travis's brown eyes widened as he held up his hands in surrender. "Not a word from me, bro. You got my promise."

Liam didn't mean to offend his only friend, but he had it bad for Kaylee. He cooled his temper and winked at Travis. "It's okay. Guess you hit a nerve, there." He ran his hand through his dark brown hair. "Yeah, I'm hoping I'll be gettin' some tonight."

"Good luck." Travis grinned and wandered away.

Two months ago, since he'd turned eighteen, Liam had lived a wild ride of emotions. Anger and confusion warring day and night. And daydreams. Visions that ran like movies in his head. Things that startled him, but at the same time fascinated him. Even though he couldn't remember them exactly, they made him crave something he couldn't quite put his finger on.

Whatever was happening, or at least felt like it was happening, was big, strange, even monumental. And she was somehow part of it.

"Hi. Looking for me?" Kaylee walked up beside him, tan and confident, tall and leggy in her cut-off jean shorts. A strand of her blonde-streaked brown hair blew across her face and she tucked it behind her ear. Her finger stayed at her earlobe to play with a gold loop earring.

Kaylee. Inside his head, her name sounded so beautiful. Her olive-green eyes found his deep-blue ones. The smile that spread across her pretty face made his breath catch for a moment. On an exhale, he breathed the word, "Tonight."

"What?"

He held out his hand and Kaylee slid her palm onto his. That familiar race of awareness caught him, seemed to catch her, too. They stared at each other as the scent of her peach perfume drifted in his direction. It definitely was not the same as the spring rain scent that had lured him to her. That was a special connection, both chemically and emotionally, which ran between them, wild as a March thunderstorm.

Kaylee. There wasn't another girl he knew who made him feel whole, like he belonged to someone. Before he met her, he'd never desired a woman this much. Thank heaven she'd moved here to Liberation, Tennessee in March. Before he met her, he'd begun to wonder if he'd be a virgin forever.

He leaned down and whispered in her ear, "Are you ready?" Pulling back, he watched her cheeks color. Obviously, she'd understood exactly what he asked.

"I am." Her Midwestern accent still sounded odd, but cute. She squeezed his hand. "Let's go." Her voice purred softly, making her inflection seem sexy.

Was it the anticipation of being with her, looking at her beautiful curves, or was it something else that made his blood rush through his body, heading south, making him dizzy? Could she tell that he'd grown hard as steel in his jeans? "C'mon, let's go." His request sounded over-eager to him. They skirted the crowd to avoid having to talk with anyone

Beside him, her flip-flops smacked her feet, and her breasts bounced in her peach tank top. Her hips swayed to the beat of his pulse racing in his ears.

They found his car parked alone in the overflow lot. After tugging open the passenger door, he automatically reached to flip the front seat forward so they could sit in the back like they usually did. Shaking his head, he pulled back his hand. What was he thinking? Tonight he had the house to himself, and he planned to make good use of it.

"Cherry." Kaylee's voice came from behind him.

"What?" She didn't know this was his first time. Did she? He leaned back to look at her.

Kaylee skimmed her hand along the quarter panel of his grandpa's old 1967 Chevy Malibu. Using the same hand, she brushed her fingers across his stomach. "I want to name your car Cherry."

"Whatever you say, sweetheart." No way in hell would he call his car Cherry, but Kaylee could do whatever she wanted tonight. He ushered her into the seat before closing the door and jogging around the front end, smacking his palm on the hood. Hiding his smirk, he pressed his lips together as he imagined them sharing a night of passionate, hot sex. "Damn."

As he opened the door, he felt high, like a two-beer kind of buzz mixed with the sure knowledge that tonight would be monumental.

He dropped into his seat and started the engine. The 327 roared to life and he snapped on the radio and switched from rock to the pop country she liked so much. It didn't do anything for him, but he could tolerate whatever made her happy.

Kaylee fastened her seatbelt. "Hurry, Liam." She bit the corner of her full lower lip, her eyelids drooping. In his head, he heard her command, *I can't wait much longer.*

He broke nearly every traffic law getting her to his grandparents' farm as she quietly sang along to her favorite song, but Liam couldn't help but reduce his speed the way he always did to check out the bean field he'd planted last month. In the moonlight, he made out the rows of soybeans. Turning down the driveway to the house, he looked out where the green shoots had just started to emerge on the other side of the dirt road. Should they be taller by now?

They'd had two bad years in a row, the crops barely producing the minimum yield they needed to pay the taxes and keep food on the table. Would this year be better?

In the midst of his distraction, a vision overtook Liam. Kaylee, between his legs, her lips wrapping around his hard length.

Smacking his hand on the steering wheel, he laughed. Why was he thinking about the crops when he had the most amazing woman sitting right next to him?

She looked at him from the corner of her eye, sexy as a goddess. "What's so funny?"

"Not a thing, sweetheart. Not a thing." He stopped the car by the front steps of the weathered Southern colonial and looked at her.

Kaylee turned to him. "Liam, I just want you to know that whatever happens tonight, happens." She made an "O" with her hand. "Zero expectations." Without warning, she grabbed his T-shirt and pulled him to her. With an open-mouthed kiss, she pressed hard into his lips. Wild and unrestrained, her tongue tangled with his, making a lie out of the words she'd just spoken.

As she pulled away, she sighed. "Okay, wow."

Her kiss, her touch, sent shockwaves of desire to his loins "So, whatever happens happens, huh?" He smirked at her, jumped out of the car, and strode around to open her door. That kiss, hell, where had that come from? It wasn't anywhere close to the ones he'd shared with her before. As he helped her out, his hand brushed her breast.

She sucked in a breath, and her nipple rose to a point under her shirt.

He circled his tongue in his mouth, wanting a taste of her.

Blinking, Kaylee leaned closer to him. "And whatever that magic is that happens when we touch..."

He nodded once. He couldn't explain it any better than she could. It was just there between them, their own magic. With his hand on her back, he guided her up the steps and in through the kitchen door. She'd been to the house before but had never seen his bedroom. That would change tonight.

His grandparents had seemed to like her pretty well when she'd met them. Of course, they were probably just relieved that he'd finally taken an interest in one special girl.

Liam turned on a small light under the kitchen cabinet. "Would you like anything?" He pointed to the refrigerator.

She shook her head and tugged him against her. "Show me your bedroom." Her breasts pressed tightly to his chest, her belly soft and hot against the ridge of his shaft. Was this the same girl he'd been dating? "You sure about this, Kaylee?" They'd only been seeing each for a little over a month, but she seemed more experienced, and definitely older, so he assumed she'd been with other guys before. He didn't want to rush things tonight, but something inside him drove him to complete this. Whatever this intense link was between them, he wanted it to last, to grow, to bind them together.

"I'm sure, Liam." Her eyes grew bold as she wrapped her arms around his neck and kissed him deeply.

He let the urge to be with her take over inside him. He ran his tongue along her lips, tasting her peach lip gloss, then plunged inside to twine with her tongue and tickle her cheeks. Walking her backward, he guided her down the dark hallway to his bedroom. He'd left on a lamp with a low wattage bulb. He didn't want her to notice the scars on his body, souvenirs of a terrifying childhood.

His extra-long double bed had a new black quilt, pillows, and sheets, the cost having wiped out half this month's spending cash.

Kaylee ended the kiss to look around. "Just like I pictured it." The wood floor needed refinishing, but his grandmother had scattered a few rugs around on the worst spots. Sports trophies and team pictures sat on shelves above his cheap pressboard desk, but his tall dresser held only one picture; a framed photo of Kaylee and him at the amusement park on senior skip day. "Aw, Liam." She smiled at the picture. "That's so sweet."

Sweet? Great. He wanted her to think of him as her big, hulking stud, not the sweet guy she'd throw away once some real bad-boy caught her eye.

Maybe he just needed to show her his bad side. "Let's get naked." He tugged up the bottom of her tank top.

She smiled and that pheromone she gave off thickened like ecstasy in the air. To his brain, it flowed sweet, the scent of a gentle rain. When she lifted her arms over her head, he pulled off her top. Her breasts popped free. They looked as beautiful as he'd imagined them. Large and round, with peach-colored nipples and dark areolas.

His mouth watered.

She shivered.

He leaned in for a taste, pulling one nipple into his mouth while his hands cupped and massaged her breasts. Supple and warm. He flicked her nipple with soft, then fast, tweaks of his tongue. Amazing. Circling it, his tongue tickled the tight bud, then he sucked greedily, wanting all of her that he could get.

He became so consumed with the longing to please her that he barely noticed when she cried out. When she gasped, he eased the pressure, reminding himself to treat her with the gentleness she deserved.

She grabbed his hair, staring deep into his eyes. “No, harder! Don’t stop!”

Filled with wanting, craving, needing her unqualified approval, he devoured her breasts, moving from one nipple to the other, repeating the same technique in time with her heartbeat on his tongue.

Her fingers fisted in his hair, pulling him in roughly. “Yeah, yes, Liam. Oh, wow. Just wow.”

His hands slowly glided along her back, He wanted to suffocate himself in her passion. Although his thoughts raced wildly, there was only one thing he was absolutely sure of. He wanted, craved, needed, to be inside her.

His erection had grown so large that he couldn’t take the gentle lust of the moment any longer. The desire to feel himself deep inside her throat rattled him. To curb the direction of his thoughts, he dropped to his knees.

“Yes, whatever happens, happens.” She ran her fingers through his hair.

Liam looked up at her. Her pupils had widened in her green eyes, her face almost glowing. What was happening to her? To both of them. Had his eyes changed, too? He shook away the thought as he unbuttoned and unzipped her shorts. Tugging them down, he revealed her pink thong embroidered with the word "Cherry." He spotted the two stemmed cherries set right over the spot he longed to taste, and he nearly laughed out loud.

His mouth watered. "Too cute." He drawled the words as he pulled her thong down and she stepped out of the remainder of her clothes. As he moved closer to her, even in the dim light of his room, he could see her juicing for him. His heart pounded and his mind raced. He couldn't remember a word of the how-to books he'd read a hundred times, couldn't visualize any scenes from the porn that had satisfied him before her. He had no clue what came next, but he did know one thing for sure; he didn't want to make any mistakes. The need to please her grew inside him, swelling and shifting around his heart.

His big, work-roughened hand skimmed softly up her thigh to her hip, taking pains not to move too fast. He needed to be careful. In his mind, he fought the urge to devour her in lust. He'd always been taught it was best to respect a lady.

He leaned forward and kissed her sweet lips, sliding one finger slowly but instantly deep. As his strokes moved steadily in and out of her, wet cream coated his digit. For a moment, he could almost taste the spring rain, and his whole body jerked, setting both his hands shaking. Mentally he paused, calming himself. He needed to resist the temptation to take her fast and hard.

As Kaylee's hands cupped his face, through her touch he could sense her strong anticipation. "Liam, everything is fine. Just take your time."

"I'm sorry, Kaylee. Don't tell me to stop—"

She shoved his face into her sweetness, cutting off his words.

He hated the submissive behavior he exhibited, but right now, he would bow down and be her slave just as long as she'd let him continue.

As she ground herself into his face, she shuddered. "Liam, babe, you don't have to be nervous. I know this is your first time." Her mouth said one thing while her body communicated something else. She tugged at his T-shirt, and didn't allow him to help her take it off. Kaylee became more aggressive by the minute.

Somewhere in the back of his mind, a sense of insecurity arose. An almost childlike panic. Did she feel he wasn't man enough to control the situation?

She insisted on taking off his boots.

Seeing the sexy small of her back giving way to her heart-shaped bottom, he almost lost control. With the clomp of the second boot dropping, he found the confidence he'd been lacking. He unzipped his pants and stood. In one quick jerk, he pushed his jeans and briefs down to his knees.

"Taste me, Kaylee."

His turgid thickness, free in the cool air, bobbed and bounced with each heartbeat.

Kaylee just stood and stared.

Chapter Two

"Kaylee. Sweetheart?"

Her mouth watered for a sample of Liam's essence. She grasped him with both hands and he scorched her palms, feeling like satin over red-hot iron. She immediately pushed him down on the edge of his bed, her fingers nearly losing their grip.

He leaned back, bracing himself with his hands. The irresistible allure he gave off grew stronger, blanketed her, as she loved him with her mouth.

He stopped breathing for a moment.

Giving him her most mischievous grin, she licked her lips, then found the hot spot on the bottom side of his shaft, right at the head. She looked at him, showing him with her eyes how lust had totally possessed her.

He groaned, his eyes rolling back into his head, then closing completely.

Flicking her tongue right there, she felt him jerk, as if bolts of electricity coursed through his body.

"Mmmm. Is that your favorite?" Her voice purred.

Liam opened one eye.

In the palm of her hand, she could feel his heartbeat, and moaned as a shiver of excitement zinged through her. She liked running the show.

Tugging his shaft down, she tried to slip her lips around his head, but it just wasn't happening. She backed away, licked him a little more, then tried again. She'd never realized she had such a small mouth until being faced with this amazing challenge. When she got most of it in, it immediately slipped out of her mouth.

Liam smiled, kissed her head, and reached over, opening the nightstand drawer. He pulled out a condom packet, opened it and sheathed himself, grinning at her.

****

Liam reached for Kaylee and helped her to her feet, then guided her to sit on his lap facing him. He had an almost overwhelming urge to want her mouth back on him. Any guy would want more, but it distracted him, becoming an instinctual need in him. More than just a sexual desire.

She kissed him, quick and wild, her tongue lashing against his. Ending the kiss, she shoved him back on the bed.

Liam just looked at her, trying to continue behaving as a gentleman. "You're beautiful and sexy." Romance was quickly turning into lust.

Wiggling her hips, she moved forward, rubbing her sweet honey all over his hungry manhood. She lowered herself, adjusting her trajectory until the head of his shaft touched her outer lips.

A blast of heat raced through his loins, engulfing him in fire. He slid his palms along her firm thighs.

She grabbed the base of him and rubbed his tip into her sex, pushing it into her soft, ready warmth.

A big, Texas-sized grin spread across his face as epiphany hit him. Holy fricking hell, he was about to have sex. With *his* hot, amazing woman.

"Liam, oh wow, babe, it's...so...oh, wow." She dropped herself a few inches, taking his head deep into her slick depths.

Energy flooded his bloodstream, tingling raced along his skin. His hands dropped to his sides, his heart began to pound. This felt indescribable. He'd come by his own hand, but nothing like this had ever charged through him.

Kaylee moved slowly, up and down, taking his length deeper and deeper.

It felt too slow for him. The urge to grab her and shove her balls-deep on his shaft became nearly uncontrollable.

She leaned forward and put her palms on his chest. Her unfocused eyes stared at his chin as she panted, as if she'd become possessed by more than just the moment. "Liam, it's so, so…so fucking marvelous."

This was the first time he'd ever heard her cuss.

Her body worked, tipping and circling, as her tightness relaxed just a little and shifted, making room for him.

His hips jerked and she made a small noise. He had to hold on, couldn't risk hurting her. Grabbing the quilt on each side of him in tight fists, he fought back, holding his hunger at bay by sheer force of will.

When she sat up again, he slid inside her those few last inches. Her thighs pressed on his hips. She shuddered and cried out, her face flushed pink, her eyes barely slits.

His blood roared in his ears like a squadron of jets flying over. Insatiable desire, so strong it would not be restrained, took over his body, and he gave in to the compulsion.

Liam pulled Kaylee into his arms and flipped her under him on the mattress.

"Oh my God, I—"

He dug the fingers of one hand into her hair and pressed his lips to her perfect mouth, his tongue plunging, their teeth tapping with the intensity of the kiss.

Running his free hand down to her luscious bottom, he lifted her hips, impaling her with everything he had. What the hell happened to treating her like she was breakable? He paused, looking at her face.

She smiled up at him and made a moaning sound that amped up the lust inside him. Then, she grabbed fistfuls of his hair. "Yes. Hard. Do me hard."

Liam had no doubt Kaylee was not acting like herself, and there was no question that he wasn't himself either. What was going on here? He jerked his hips back, pulling nearly all the way out of her, then slammed back in, pulled out and slammed back in harder. The pleasure flowing into his swollen member coursed through his body like an explosion of molten lava.

Her indrawn breath made her nipples cut hot trails along the skin of his chest. Her eyes went wild as she wrapped her legs around him, opening herself wider for him, urging him further inside her with her calves.

He growled, a sound he'd never made before, and he let the intense craving drive his hips. Pistoning his shaft into her, he took her hard and fast, moving his hand from her hair to her shoulder to hold her under him. His other hand slid between their bodies and his thumb found her "oh my God" button and began circling it.

She screamed his name and her tightness contracted around his shaft, her whole body tensing. Her nails scraped along his back as she cried out with each sure thrust of his powerful hips.

He couldn't get deep enough inside her, he couldn't pump hard enough, fast enough. The feral need spun his thoughts until all he knew was the drive to mate.

Slamming into her, her body melted beneath him as her climax slowed, dropping her back to Earth with a quiet cry. She sucked in air. "Liam, holy fuck, I've never had anything like that..."

He pistoned faster, asking her with his eyes, *"Again?"*

Her eyes shone as she smiled. "Yeah, again."

He pulled out of her and knelt. Flipping her over onto her knees, he propped her amazing ass in the air. Sweet and tight, her round cheeks sparked another frantic blast of heat through him. He nibbled her right butt cheek, bringing a laughing cry from her, then did the same to her other cheek, but harder.

"Liam, yes. Anything you want." Her head rested on the bed, her hands on each side, gripping the quilt. "Own me, Liam."

In the front of his mind, there was nothing he desired more. "You want me to own you, Kaylee? You scream my fuckin' name, woman." His hand smacked her ass cheek, stinging his hand. Had he just cussed in front of her? He knew that wasn't right, but nothing about the last ten minutes was normal for him.

Guiding himself into her, he gripped her hips with both hands. "You want me to take it all?" He jerked his body forward, stretching her tight muscles, feeling her clench around him.

She screamed and circled her hips around his shaft. "Take it, hell yes, take it."

The roaring in his head intensified, the heat

flowing through his body kicked up a notch, and he pulled back and rammed into her, over and over and over.

He'd never imagined it like this. Never knew it'd be this rowdy. Every daydream he'd had about sex with Kaylee was slow, sweet loving.

Instead, they rutted like animals. For being so inexperienced, this seemed natural to him. It turned him wild, and he couldn't get enough.

"Push up, woman." His voice didn't sound like his own.

She lifted her torso, holding herself up on shaky arms.

"Arch your back for me. You like it like that, don't you. I'm about to tear you up, all night long."

Her breath rushed from her lungs on a sexy laugh, as she threw her head back and her spine curved downward in a graceful arch.

Liam reached for her long hair, gathering it in his fist and tugging.

"Yes, ride me, Liam." Her body shimmied and races of goosebumps puckered along her skin.

He jackhammered into her, unable to get enough of her, needing more with each thrust.

Sucking in ragged breaths, she stiffened and her hips shook. She screamed and her muscles tightened around him, sending jagged blasts of lightning up his spine to radiate through his brain. When her arms collapsed, he withdrew and turned her over once again, her body limp and her smile pure ecstasy.

It became a compulsion, needing to make her come, taking pleasure in the act of racing her to orgasm after orgasm. More important than the satisfaction of his own completion.

Bracing himself over her with one arm, he wrapped his other arm under her, lifting her hips to the perfect height. Pushing his throbbing shaft inside her hot opening, he worked his hips, tightening his ass with each thrust into her. Physical warmth built inside him with each thrust. He knew he was close. He needed more. Deeper.

Charges of electricity shook through his groin and shot up his spine to click each brain cell off, turning his mind into a black hole spinning in space as he erupted.

A picture flashed into his head, then disappeared. A woman? It came again. For a few seconds, he saw a young woman, dark red hair. She reached out to him, her lips moving. He didn't understand the words she spoke, the phrase she repeated, but he spoke them with her, again and again, as if they were a prayer. When she touched his chest with one fingertip, a completely surreal feeling filled him soul-deep and all thought drained from his mind. For a moment, he knew nothing but true love, but as reality set back in, it disappeared.

The roaring sound quieted, his heartbeat returned to normal, and tingles raced along his spine. His thrusts slowed. Damn, he hadn't even noticed if Kaylee had come or not. Squinting through the last spins of his orgasm, he caught her shiver as her insides clenched around his thickness.

"Liam, babe..." She swallowed and licked her lips, her breath racing in and out of her lungs. "Don't you even try to tell me that was your first time."

Chapter Three

Liam lifted Kaylee's leg and kissed her calf, then slid his arms under her to pick her up. His knees wobbled, threatening to buckle and send him into a heap on the floor. He scooped her into his arms and lay her the long way on the bed, tucking himself in next to her.

She hummed for a few seconds then closed her eyes.

Absolutely beautiful. Her face, her body, her soul. He found it difficult to draw in a full breath. An urgency wrapped itself around his heart and he tucked his face into her neck. Nothing had ever felt so right, so perfect.

The sex had been phenomenal. As if the sexual knowledge of the ages flooded his brain and guided his movements. When he'd come, it had been like planets collided and...he jerked. Wait, what had happened just as he'd come? Something...

Liam's eyes darted frantically, his breath coming fast and shallow. What had he seen? Shit, he couldn't remember. It was important, vital, that he recall exactly—

"What language was that?" Kaylee rested her hand on his hip, drawing a pattern with her finger.

"Language?" He knew English and the few phrases he'd retained from sophomore Spanish.

"When you came, you kept repeating something, but I didn't recognize the language."

He'd spoken out loud? He couldn't recollect anything from those few minutes.

"Don't get me wrong, it was sexy." She kissed his jaw.

He had to figure out what the hell had

happened to him. “Hang on to that thought.” Liam jumped up and strode down the hall to the bathroom. He closed the door and left the light off. The yard light shone through the window, and he used a few tissues to clean up.

“Concentrate.” He pressed his palm to his forehead. Why couldn’t he remember?

Three light taps sounded on the door. “Liam, babe? Are you okay?”

The memory wouldn’t come back. He’d try again later. Right now, he had a hot, willing woman to please. He snapped on the light and pulled open the door.

Her sweet face twisted with concern. She’d pulled on the T-shirt he’d been wearing, looking cute as a button.

Liam grinned. “Yeah, I’m okay.” Nothing in his life had ever looked better than his woman, wearing that shirt, with her hair sex-snarled from his hard lovin’. He tugged her close and stared into her eyes. He could be with her forever. The explosion of emotion hit like buckshot. Was this love? How had he lived without this incredible emotional connection until now?

“You should have seen your eyes. They were this amazing green while you were taking me, but now they’re back to blue again.”

He slid his hands down to her ass, cupping her cheeks. “Are you ready to see them turn green again?”

She gave him a wicked smile. “You betcha, farm boy.”

To his right, the clawfoot bathtub stood behind a striped shower curtain. Liam got a picture in his mind of what he wanted to do to her. For her.

He'd read directions for it in books, had been absolutely fascinated with the porn he'd seen of it. But could he get her to do it for him? He pushed aside the curtain and backed her against the tile wall. "Sit on the edge."

Her eyebrows rose. "Oh, yeah? What's going through that valedictorian mind of yours?"

He could visualize giving his graduation speech for the whole school, looking down from the stage and seeing Kaylee, the woman he loved, watching him with pride. He shoved that picture to the back of his mind. "Here's something I didn't learn in school, darlin'." As he laid on his accent, thick and slow, he spread a towel on the wide corner ledge of the bathtub. Tugging up her shirt, he pulled the front up and over her head but left it on her. That tile would get too cold on her bare skin.

She laid her hand on the edge, and he took her other wrist and guided her fingers to wrap around the metal towel rod.

"Hang on, beautiful. This is going to turn you wild."

Liam stood over her, softly rubbing her, easing his finger into her swollen lower lips. When she moaned, he slid his two middle digits in deeper. His big, rough fingers gentled as they warmed inside her velvet opening. Liam moved his hand lower, sliding his fingers all the way inside her.

Her body jerked, stiffened a little. Was she surprised he could go that far in?

Now that he had her positioned correctly, his free hand caressed her stomach, just over her belly button. He looked into her eyes. "Now, sweetheart, I want you to relax. Just focus on the rhythm of my hand." He stroked inside her a few times. "You may feel like you want to pee, and that's okay. But trust me, it won't be pee. Everything is all good, just trust me. It's important to push out, no matter what. Push harder, the closer you get to orgasm. Do you understand?"

She nodded submissively.

As Liam started to stroke his fingers in a 'come here' motion inside her, she immediately began to drip. Again, the strong scent of spring rain flooded his nostrils. Why did that scent randomly appear?

She moaned with the beat of the motion of his fingers.

He became obsessed with wanting to do this for her, like he was possessed by his own body to do so. The inner sides of her walls tightened around his fingers, her lower body stiffened.

She did exactly what he'd told her to do, and her body pushed out harder, the closer she got.

His hand on her stomach pressed in and down, moving in sync with the motion of his fingers inside her. He created a rhythm with his hands, a strong motion with his fingers, pushing up and sliding back inside her. A rush of excitement started his heart pounding. It was as if he knew exactly what to do and could sense what she was feeling.

His fingers became completely saturated in her erogenous cream.

She began to pant hard as his fingers moved more firmly.

Feeling the spongy circle against his fingertips, he pressed firmly against her G spot, right inside and under her pubic bone. This was the place that would send her over the edge, according to everything he had heard.

The 'come here' motions of his fingers quickened, and her panting turned into louder moans. Her knuckles turned white as they gripped the bathtub and towel rod and her face flushed. A small trickle of sweat rolled down her forehead and into the furrows between her brows.

He could sense her holding back slightly. His actions taking her to a place she had never been before. Would her anxiety keep her from reaching her peak?

Pressing firmer on her belly, he willed her to let go of her reservations, to give in to what her body craved. Instantly, the lines between her brows smoothed away and her lips softened into a sweet smile.

His motions continued, almost like he played her song with his fingertips. The space inside her grew smaller and smaller as she pushed out harder and harder. With his fingers, he focused on the spongy spot, and started moving his wrist in tandem with the motion of his fingers.

Her legs began to shake. Her body convulsed. Against his palm, her rain slowly trickled out. His anticipation had him panting along with her. He was headed in the right direction, and she would explode any time now. He quickened the motions of his wrist and caressed with a firmer press of his fingers on her spongy spot, his wrist buckling backward and forward.

His hand on her belly pressed down.

Her body bucked with the motion of his hand. Almost tribal, savage. Beautiful lust.

Her moans turned to shouts. "I'm going to come." She screamed the words with thunderous conviction.

He removed his hand from her belly, transfixed by the site of her orgasming. She looked so beautiful as the sweat trickled down her forehead.

With a few more quick motions of his wrist, she released sprays of the most beautiful element Liam had ever seen. As the light hit the streams, it looked like a series of rainbows expelling from the petals of her beautiful core.

Liam had created a storm of ecstasy which had brought forth a flooding orgasm of epic proportions. His sense of accomplishment outweighed anything he'd ever achieved before. Chills raced through him as a smile broke on his face. Had he really done this? "Amazing."

As the last drops dribbled down her thighs, Liam rubbed his fingers in the sweet offering dripping down his chest, and lifted his hand to his mouth and sampled it. It was definitely not pee, in fact, it was the strongest he had ever smelled the spring rain scent, and it tasted sweet, like fruit candy.

She gasped in a breath. Her body slumped, completely limp on the edge of the bathtub. Her eyes, now nearly black from her dilated pupils, appeared unfocused, as if she couldn't see him, as though she'd slid into a state of euphoria.

Like a lightning strike, all his strength left him, and Liam fell to his knees.

What seemed like binding chains of sorrow clenched Liam's soul. The room darkened until he couldn't see anything but black. A flame burst into his vision, screams echoed in his ears. Beyond the consuming fire, people raced past, some wearing buckskin. A woman dropped, crimson staining her back, her long, midnight hair covering her face as she lay in the dirt.

"What the hell just happened?" He blinked and the strange vision receded.

He sat on the floor, resting his arm on the bathtub, dropping his head onto it. Whatever that was, it had seemed too real.

Kaylee cried out, lifting her hand as if reaching for something. Or someone?

She shivered and mumbled.

"Sweetheart?" He struggled to his feet. She didn't respond, just stared blindly ahead. "C'mon, let's get you into bed."

As his strength came back, he sat her up and pulled the T-shirt off her. He picked her up in his arms and she hung limp, a dead weight, still mumbling and staring off into space. Was she having the same vision he'd had? No, she was smiling. He'd been terrified. He stopped. Hadn't he? Shit, what had happened in that vision? It'd just been in his thoughts, and now it was gone.

On the way out of the bathroom, he grabbed a towel. He laid her on his bed, dried her thighs, between her legs, and his chest.

How could something so beautiful create such a dark moment inside him? How and why did that happen? He turned off the light, plunging them into darkness. Lying next to her, he arranged her, half on top of him, her head under his chin, then covered them both with the quilt. She slept, waking occasionally to mumble, sometimes thrashing, sleeping restlessly for nearly an hour before she quieted and drifted off. For the next hour, he stared into the dark, wanting to remember his visions, but failing. Finally, with his woman melted into his arms, he closed his eyes, and fell asleep.

The bed moved, his chest cooled, and he

dragged himself out of the depths of slumber.

"Kaylee?" He switched on the light.

She sat on the edge of the bed. "What happened?"

"Before or after you squirted for me?" He rolled on his side with a huge smile on his face, propping his head up on a bent arm.

She turned to face him. "That was the first time I ever did…that." She spoke slowly, quietly.

"It's okay, you can say it. Squirted. And I'm glad I could be your first."

"It wasn't…you know, weird or anything?" She wouldn't meet his eyes.

"It was beautiful, Kaylee. I've never seen anything that sexy."

"Really?" Her gaze met his, her brows drawn together.

"Yes, really." He reached over and took her hand. "The way you responded to me, the lovely rain that flowed from you. Perfection."

"Rain?" One side of her mouth curled up. "When you put it that way, it's not so..." She shrugged.

"It's nothing but natural and sensual, sweetheart."

She rubbed her thumb on his hand. "I've never experienced anything so freeing."

How was it that she felt freed, while he felt like an anchor dragged him further and further down?

Kaylee chattered on about how the experience gave her insight into the direction she needed to take. She clasped her hands on her chest. "I realize now, just how self-defeating my actions have been."

"Good for you." He'd give anything to feel the same right now. Confusion filled his thoughts.

"I'll be right back." She slid off the bed and padded down the hall. The click of the bathroom door closing hit him like the slamming of a jail cell door. No, he wouldn't panic. Nothing was wrong, she just needed her privacy. He stacked his hands behind his head and stared at the ceiling. The rest of the night would go smoothly. He'd make sure of that.

He awoke with a gasp. Something was wrong. Kaylee wasn't beside him. He sat up and spotted her clothes still on the floor. Sliding out of bed, he pulled on his briefs and walked to the bathroom. After knocking twice, he pushed open the door.

Kaylee stood naked in front of the sink, staring at herself in the mirror.

Her behavior seemed strange. He walked into the room and she held out her hand to him. "Look at me. Do I seem different?" She blinked at her reflection.

Pressing his body against her back, he snugged his arms around her belly. "You look more beautiful than you ever have. You look like a woman who's been satisfied by her lover in almost every way possible. Almost." He kissed her neck, breathing deeply of her perfume. But something was missing. He caught the reflection of her eyes in the mirror. That rain scent, the feeling of ecstasy, the one that always attracted him to her, that lured him in like a fish on a line? It was gone. Yet, he experienced a need to know everything. Even though he didn't feel what he imagined loving tenderness should feel like, he wanted to hear her every thought, know her every move, gain her approval.

The intensity of his need lasted for long moments, then finally faded, disappearing into the background.

"Did you shower?" He wanted to know why things had changed, why her scent had changed.

She shook her head. "No." She went back to staring at herself.

Would the scent come back? It was his favorite thing about her, that connection they shared. He needed to grab onto whatever was left between them, needed to have her approval, to make sure the connection remained. "Kaylee, I think I'm falling for you." He let his heart lead, but felt off-center, unbalanced. Why had these feelings emerged all of a sudden?

She glanced at him in the mirror. "That's sweet of you, but I don't know how I feel. I'm so confused. Let's not do this right now, okay?"

Panic clenched his chest. "I don't want to push you, and I…I don't expect an answer with the same words. I just want to know how you're feeling." He realized he needed to regain his composure, to stop acting like less than the man he needed to be. Putting on a show for her, he smiled as she turned in his arms.

She pecked a kiss on his lips. "You're amazing, Liam. Tonight was the best ever, babe."

Liam nodded, but deep inside, he knew something had been lost between them. He wagged one brow at her. "Let's go back to bed and see what else I can do to impress you."

She patted his chest. "You go ahead. I need a few more minutes."

Hell, this was not how he'd expected the rest of the night to go. What would she do if he grabbed her, threw her over his shoulder, and stomped down the hallway? He stared at her, his mind acting out the scene.

"Liam?" Her gaze met his in the mirror and a wrinkle formed between her brows.

He kissed her. "You take all the time you need."

"You're hard to read tonight. One minute you're caring, and gentle, then you get this look in your eyes like you want to devour me." She shivered. "You've got a lot of intensity inside you."

Intensity? Is that all it was? It felt like his plans for Kaylee and him were taking a detour.

****

Kaylee watched Liam walk down the hall toward his room. He was still darn sexy, but there didn't seem to be anything drawing her to him now. The energy they'd shared since the day they met had completely disappeared.

She looked into the mirror again. Whatever had happened on the bathtub ledge had renewed her, as if she'd been born again. She was a different person. How could she be exactly the same outside, but completely changed inside?

A sensation grew in her, she could feel it increasing like a flooding stream during a hard rain. Whatever this pure joy was, it manifested itself in the need to seek out her own happiness

And the vision she'd seen... Her entire future had flashed in front of her eyes. Marriage, career, babies. Elation and sorrow, joys and disappointments. They'd rolled in front of her like a silent movie. She clasped her hands together at her chest. She hadn't prayed since she was a child, but she sent up words begging that she be granted that glorious future.

Strangely, it was the perfect life, but a life without Liam.

Chapter Four

Liam woke with the sun on his face. Rolling over, he plopped his hand on the spot next to him. Cold. Had she ever come back to bed? He'd planned to remain awake, wait for her, but once he'd closed his eyes, exhaustion took him.

"Kaylee?" He got to his feet and pulled on a pair of shorts. Her clothes were gone, the bathroom was empty, and he was the only one in the house. Damn, he'd scared her away, trying to get her back to bed right after he'd told her how he felt about her. In the driveway, his car sat where he'd left it. How had she gotten home? She had an early shift at the gas station this morning, but he'd assumed she'd wake him when she needed to get to work.

He had to go see her, to tell her he wasn't lying about how he felt. He loved her, wanted her in his life. And he'd apologize for not getting up and driving her in.

After he dressed, he grabbed his keys and headed to town. He rolled down the windows and let the earthy smell of late spring rush through the car. The sun shone bright and hot, shining green off the leaves of new growth in the fields. Everything had changed from yesterday. Whatever he'd imagined happening last night must have been due to the fear and anxiety of losing his virginity. He had performed an amazing feat that he never thought he could make a woman experience, then the realization that he was crazy about Kaylee had washed over him. The bizarre visions had to be his imagination. After all, stress could do that to a guy, and the first time being with a woman, especially one as beautiful and sexy as Kaylee, had definitely been stressful.

Liam pulled into the Pump and Run but didn't spot Kaylee's car. Whoever had picked her up must have dropped her off. He strode into the convenience store.

Her boss, Ray, stood behind the counter. "Where's that girlfriend of yours, boy?" The man scratched his round belly. "She's blocked my calls and her mother's not answering her phone."

Liam's gut dropped. That wasn't like Kaylee. He turned and walked out, pulled out his phone, then thought better of it and slid it back into his jeans' pocket. Face-to-face would be the best way to do this. Pushing the speed limit, he turned into Kaylee's driveway in less than five minutes. Her beat-up Toyota wasn't outside the garage. He ran up to the front door and knocked.

Kaylee's mother pulled the door open. She blinked through watery red eyes and wiped her nose with a tissue. "Liam, why?"

Had Kaylee been injured? Killed? "Where is she?" He could barely draw breath.

The older woman pulled another tissue from her pocket.

He wanted to shake the information out of her.

"She left." A burst of tears swamped her. "She said she realized she'd let go of someone who she should have hung on to."

Liam's brain spun for a second. "Gone?" Without telling him she was leaving? They'd dated for over a month, then last night... Oh, God, last night. Whatever crazy shit was going on inside him, she'd seen it and run like her life depended on it. "Did she go to her dad's?" He had to find her, explain... Explain what? Hell, he didn't know what had happened to him last night.

"No." Kaylee's mom mopped her face and leaned on the door handle. "She wouldn't tell me. She promised to call once she got there, but Liam?" She frowned.

He braced himself.

"I'm so sorry, but she made me promise not to ever tell you where she was." She reached for him.

He took a step back. Why would Kaylee go to such extremes to get away from him? "I don't know what I did wrong."

The woman shrugged. "Kaylee didn't say anything about you...well, except that she didn't want you finding her. She was focused on whatever had gotten her all whipped up to go see her ex-boyfriend."

He squeezed his eyes shut for a moment. His woman was in her car right now, driving to see another man, the morning after Liam had made love to her for the first time. Pain gripped his chest, forcing a groan from him as he concentrated on putting one foot in front of the other toward his car.

Kaylee's mother followed a few steps, her flip-flops smacking behind him. "I'm sure it's not you, Liam. She really liked you. She's just confused after this divorce, and by my dating again."

Sliding into his seat, he nodded at her politely, and backed out of the driveway, laying rubber on the street as he sped away. What could he do to make her come back? He had to figure out a plan, a way to convince her she needed to be with him. Maybe he'd offer marriage. His head told him that was psycho, but his heart thudded wildly at the prospect of making a life with her.

He took a right and headed for the lake. They'd spent a lot of nights parked there, steaming up the windows from the back seat. That's where he'd call her.

Filling the ten-minute drive with a dozen different variations on his speech, he settled on the direct approach. He'd tell her he needed her, that he'd take it as slow as she wanted, or as fast as she needed, but she had to give him another chance. For some reason, he felt absolutely desperate.

Parking in the empty lot, he crossed the sandy beach, stood at the water's edge, and took his phone out. With a deep breath, he pressed dial. A recorded voice told him Kaylee wasn't accepting calls from his number.

She'd blocked him.

He opened a text window. *Please talk to me.* Seconds after he hit send, an "unavailable" message popped up.

He sank to a squat and dropped his head forward. His eyes burned with unshed tears, his stomach roiled with fear. His heart sunk lower into a bottomless pit. She didn't want him. In one quick motion, he stood and whipped the arm holding his phone back behind his head, ready to throw it into the water. It took sheer will not to let loose with the throw but eventually he stuck his phone back in his pocket.

Anger, hot and bitter, boiled up and took away all hope, all happiness. It was all her fault. She'd used him, walked away without a word. "Bitch!" He shouted the word and a flock of birds cried out as they flew out of a tree. He raised his fist.

Oh shit. He stared at his hand, his knuckles white. His stepfather had liked to use his fists. On whoever got in his way, or tried too hard to stay out of his way.

Liam opened his hand and looked at his palm.

He would never hurt a woman. Never do anything to harm Kaylee. Sliding his hands into his pockets, he slowed his breathing, bringing himself back into control, pushing away the rage that had surfaced without warning.

Across the lake, a fish jumped, flopping against the surface of the water, creating ripples that grew and spread.

Was this break in his mind the beginning of mental illness? After all, his mom had been sick, and he'd heard a rumor it could be hereditary. Would it only grow and spread inside him? Would that mental illness one day make him as evil as his step-dad, the man who'd tortured his childhood? But why now? Why, after making love to Kaylee, did these symptoms manifest themselves?

He had to talk to someone, needed to go over everything that happened last night, to figure out why shit was falling apart. Pulling his phone from his pocket, he dialed Travis's number.

"It's fucking nine in the morning, asshole." Travis's voice sounded like a rock grinder.

"Sorry. I need to talk to you, bro."

His friend cleared his throat. "What's up?"

"Not on the phone. Can you head out to the house?"

"You don't sound so good."

Fear clutched at him. His world spun for a few seconds and he stumbled. "I don't know what's happening to me."

"Be there in half an hour. Hang on, okay?" The sound of water running came through the phone.

"Yeah." He hung up. What choice did he have?

Taking the back roads, he reached the farm in

five minutes. This morning, the fields on each side of the driveway had glowed emerald green with new life. Colors seemed faded now as he walked into the house. The kitchen hadn't been remodeled since the '70s, and Kaylee had commented on the cute retro gold appliances. He looked in the refrigerator. His grandparents didn't drink, but he wished they did. A beer would taste damn good right now. Maybe a whole bottle of Jack. He slammed the door shut.

He needed to forget her, but how? All he wanted was to hold her. He banged the side of his fist on the front of the refrigerator, then checked to make sure he hadn't left a dent. How did he get past this?

Grabbing a box of cereal, he leaned on the counter and ate it dry by the fistfuls. Dumping the empty box in the trash, he pulled a gallon of milk out of the refrigerator and drank from the container.

He walked to his room and flopped down on the bed. Her perfume wafted from the sheets, reminding him what a failure last night had been.

The photo of the two of them taunted him from his dresser. Turning his head away, he glanced at his trophies. Sports, academics, community service. His life should be moving forward. A scholarship to the local agricultural school, taking over the farm in a few years. He wasn't rich like Travis, but Liam had it good since his grandparents took him in when he was fifteen, and he'd done everything he could to make them proud. To never make them regret their decision to take on a scared kid who'd nearly been locked away in juvenile detention and forgotten. Below the shelf, one of his notebooks leaned up against the wall, open to a blank page. Wait, was there writing on it?

Getting to his feet, he walked over and picked it up.

Liam, I'm sorry to leave you this way. Somehow, being with you last night released me. I've never felt this way. I hate having to cut you out of my life, but it's for the best, for both of us. Thank you for whatever you did for me, but now I need to follow my heart. Kaylee. She'd drawn a small heart after her name.

His knees buckled and he braced his hands on the desk. Pulling out his chair, he sat and crossed his arms on the desktop, dropping his head on them. "Why, Kaylee? Am I so damaged that you couldn't find anything redeemable in me?" Maybe it had been too much to hope she'd love him back, but to leave town to get away from him…how fucked-up was that?

He sat up and grabbed the notebook, started ripping out the page, then stopped. As he set down the book, he composed a reply to her in his mind, came up with a hundred questions for her, hundreds for himself. He smoothed the page and chose a pen to use.

Today I will start this journal or, I suppose, a diary of a would-be Casanova, it seems. I'm the one who was left wanting more, wanting you. Have I confused lust with love?

Last night, I loved you so much, it wasn't sex for me, it was an awakening. I swore it was so strong...I thought you felt it too, sweetheart, felt our souls align.

What do I do now...who am I now...what have you done to me? You left me with the worst part and you took the best! Now, I'm just obsessed. Someday, I will find you, and I will get answers... Until then, I'll exist, go on living, go through the motions, but the ache in my soul for you will remind me every minute of what I've lost.

Until next time...I pray to escape this pain and to find you, find the answers, find our love...Our "true" love.

Liam tossed the pen onto the tablet. What good had that done him? She'd never see it. Kaylee had cut him off cold. He stood and walked to the window, slapping his palms on the frame and staring out over the endless fields.

What had he done wrong? The question had no answer, and every time he told himself it was something she did to him, anger rose in him. He needed to forget her. For now. He had to finish school, graduate, and take a job in town this summer to pay for the tuition and books that weren't covered by his scholarship. Shit, he'd been so wrapped up in Kaylee the last month or so, he hadn't applied anywhere.

A spot of red followed by a roostertail of dirt came over the horizon. Travis, and his new pickup truck. His graduation gift from his parents. The guy had it all, but still hung out with Liam—the dirt-poor kid whose clothes came from the tractor supply store.

As Travis turned into the driveway, Liam headed out to the side porch.

His friend jumped out of his pickup, pulling on a seed cap to cover his curly blond hair. He grabbed a small cooler from the bed. "Found an old six pack in the tree fort."

Liam nodded. They'd reinforced Travis's childhood fort a few years ago so they could hole up and drink whenever they found someone who'd buy liquor for them.

Travis plopped into one of the old rocking chairs, opened the cooler, and dug through the ice until he pulled out a can. Tossing it to Liam, he sat back. "Listen, I called Penny."

Penny and Kaylee were best friends. Whatever was about to come out of Travis's mouth would not be good. Liam held the beer, the cold seeping into his palm, as he stared out at a cluster of trees across the road. "Yeah?"

"She picked up Kaylee this morning. Here." Ice shifted as he searched for a can, then a tab popped open with a hiss. "Man, she said Kaylee was talking crazy. Like she was on a mission, or something. All she talked about was some other guy she'd broken up with."

Opening his own can, Liam took a long pull. "That's what her mom said."

Travis rocked in the chair a few minutes. "That had to be rough."

Rough didn't cover it. Didn't even come close. "I don't know what happened." Shit, he sounded like a child caught lying.

"Talk to me." The rocking stopped. "I got your back, I won't say shit to nobody."

Liam turned to look at him. They'd been friends for three years, since the day four assholes ganged up on Liam his first week of school. *City boy*, they'd called him. *Shit show.* His jeans hanging low, his boxers showing, his cap on sideways, about five fake-gold chains hanging around his neck.

After the seventh or eighth hit Liam had taken, Travis had jumped into the fight and the two of them had been friends ever since. Of course, Liam's taste in clothing had quickly countrified.

Friends, but could he share what was happening inside him without scaring away the only guy Liam trusted? "It's fucking messed up, Trav. You're gonna think I'm ready for the psych ward."

Chapter Five

Travis stared at his buddy. Could this be real, or was Liam losing his mind? He opened another cold one and started his chair rocking slowly.

Liam's head rested against the back of his own rocking chair. He'd been silent for nearly twenty minutes.

Some kind of visions...that he couldn't remember. Then whatever happened in the bathroom that made him feel like his world was ending—and made Kaylee run to some other guy. Fucking hard to believe.

"Maybe you just need to get away." Travis gulped a few swallows. He wasn't any sort of a shrink, but a few days of hard labor might take Liam's mind off all this shit. "I gotta go to Dad's cousin's farm up in Juniper, Thursday. You should go ahead with me."

Liam let out a loud breath. "I got a game Friday." He turned his head to look at Travis. "You do, too."

"We're not going to make state this year. Fuck it. Come with me. It's an hour's drive, and away from all the shit going on around here."

Liam's head swiveled back and stared at the porch ceiling. "I don't know."

"You realize, the talk about you and Kaylee is gonna be all over school."

Liam lifted his hands then dropped them. "I don't care. Maybe some chick will feel sorry for me and I can start over."

Travis finished his beer and checked the time on his phone. He had to get back to the farm to help his dad with a stock buyer.

Sitting forward, Liam rested his forearms on his thighs. “If I find somebody to buy us a case, want to hang out here tonight and get plowed?”

His buddy sure didn’t need to be stuck on a dirt farm drowning his hurt with cheap beer. “Let’s go to Schaefer tonight. Hit that drive-in where everybody hangs out.”

“No.” He dropped his head. “I’m not much good company.”

“We don’t have to talk to anybody. We’ll just take your car for a drive, blow some carbon out of the carburetor. Get a decent burger.”

Liam glanced at him then stared back out into nothing. “Maybe.”

Setting down his empty can, Travis got to his feet. “Okay, well, just promise you’ll think about riding with me to the cousin’s place Thursday. Get away from here.” Otherwise, the guy would just sit and fixate on whatever strange shit had gone on with him and Kaylee.

“I’ll think about it.” Liam rocked slowly, his boots tapping on the painted wood floor.

Travis didn’t know what else to say. What else to do for his friend. He’d just be there for him. “Pick me up at seven tonight.” He jogged down the steps. “Gotta go work some.” He jumped into his truck and took off, spinning the wheels, fishtailing along the gravel driveway.

His buddy was in sore need of a good time. He’d make sure he found it. Pulling out his phone, he called his cousin who lived in Schaefer. “Hey Jesse. I need you to fix me up with a couple girls.”

****

Just after sunset, Liam pulled his Malibu into the parking lot of the Schaefer Drive-up ‘N Dine. The low, glass, 1960s building glowed brightly, spotlighting the dozens of cars parked at the drive-up spaces. There had to be at least fifty people standing in groups outside the building.

Shifting into neutral, he revved the motor as he coasted by.

Heads turned.

"Looking for some attention tonight, huh?" Travis unbuckled his seatbelt. "There's a spot." He pointed to the row of cars on the opposite side of the driveway.

Yes, he was looking for attention. Maybe just someone to talk to, take his mind off Kaylee for a while. He backed in between two lift-kit pickup trucks.

As he and Travis stepped out of the car, a guy walked over, carrying a cup. "Hey. How you been?" He went right to Travis and shook his hand.

"Good, man." He gestured to Liam. "Jesse, this is Liam. Jesse's my cousin."

Walking around the grill, Liam shook the other guy's hand. Not as tall as Travis, Jesse had the same smile and brown eyes, but his hair was short and brown. "Good to meet you."

"Come and meet some friends." Jesse turned and headed back toward the building.

"You arrange this?" Liam used his fingers to comb his hair.

"I told him we were coming over. Figured it'd be easier."

Liam should have known Travis would set something up. Being from one of the founding families of the county, Travis was related to half the population.

"Wait." He stopped and waited for Travis to

come back. "I don't know if I'm ready for this."

"Bro, you are. This is what you need." Travis squinted. "After all the crazy shit you said happened with Kaylee, plus her just taking off on you, this is exactly what you need."

Liam glanced to where Jesse walked up to a circle of girls. "To hook up with some chick?" It didn't feel wrong, necessarily, but he couldn't get over the feeling that he was betraying...Kaylee. "Yeah, okay." Kaylee was gone, and Liam needed to wipe her from his memory. "Let's go meet the girls."

Jesse stood in front of three young women, who all smiled expectantly at them. He introduced the girls. "Sarah, Angie, and Maureen, this is my cousin Travis and his friend, Liam."

They nodded to each other and Liam looked them over, wanting to find that attraction, that pull that had connected him with Kaylee. Breathing deeply, he tried to catch that essence that he craved. Nothing.

They all talked for a few minutes, their chatter relaxing him. Sarah's long, curly red hair reached to nearly the middle of her back. What would that hair feel like in his hands? A vision of him holding her head to his erection as she went down on him popped into his mind.

Just then, she reached up and touched the side of her head, her fingers twisting into her curls. When she glanced at him, her cheeks turned a sexy pink.

He smiled. Funny, almost like she'd read his mind.

Travis asked Angie a question, and she just nodded, staring at him as he rambled on about something.

Liam's gaze traveled down Angie's long legs

to her sandals and shiny purple toenails.

She curled her toes.

He looked at her face, but she still watched Travis.

Jesse said something to her and she turned her head toward the guy and spoke a few words.

Liam glanced at where her shirt bared a couple inches of skin at her belly. Would she have an inny or an outie belly button?

Her hand pressed against the middle of her stomach.

He looked at her face, but she stared at Jesse.

Strange. Wherever his thoughts went, the girls seemed to respond accordingly.

"Liam?" Maureen spoke to him. "Are you going to the concert at the fairgrounds next weekend?

"No. I'm not really into country music." He looked into her sky blue eyes. Tall and curvy, her shoulder-length blonde hair swung like strands of silk as she looked at Travis and asked him the same question. Her nose, a bit too long and pointy for her face, gave her a quirky look.

With the back of her fingers, she rubbed her nose a couple times.

Was he doing that? No. Couldn't be. Could it? Shit, with all the bizarre things that had happened to him in the last twenty-four hours, why wouldn't he be able to control people's minds?

He stared at Maureen's sweet round ass. In seconds, her hand brushed over the back of her shorts.

Damn freaky shit.

Liam stared at Travis and gave his buddy a half-dozen suggestions, but the guy didn't go for any of them. Staring at Jesse's jeans, Liam concentrated on making him put his hand in his pocket. Nothing.

"Liam." Jesse's voice snapped.

Liam looked up at the guy's frown. Great. He'd just gotten busted staring at Jesse's groin. "Yeah?"

"The girls want a coke." Jesse winked at the three ladies. "We'll be right back." Jesse gave Liam a strange look and shook his head. He and Travis followed him inside the building. They got in line and Jesse turned to them. "Sarah's a pastor's daughter, so she's pretty fuckin' wild."

Travis grinned. "I could tell." The redhead had stared at and flirted with Travis, giving him body language no one could miss.

"Angie's a little shy, but she puts out." Jesse tapped his pocket. "I brought a joint so we can get them loosened up."

The guy was serious about getting them hooked up tonight.

"What about Maureen?" Something about her was different from the other two.

"Yeah, I could tell you liked her." Jesse ordered six cokes and they each threw money onto the counter. Taking two cups each, they followed Jesse out the back door and around to a dark corner of the building.

Jesse pulled out a flask and poured some kind of liquor into each cup. "She's known as The *Sub-Maureen* around town 'cause she likes to go down."

"That's rank." Travis chuckled.

A burst of swelling flooded behind the zipper in Liam's jeans. Was that what he needed? Someone to take him deep, take every inch of him down her throat. The urge nearly overwhelmed him. "I want her." Shit, he sounded like a fucking Neanderthal.

Travis and Jesse looked at him then laughed.

"Glad you know what you're looking for." Jesse slipped his flask back into his pocket, picked up his cups, and headed toward the front of the building. They followed him.

Liam handed one cup to Maureen. "What're ya doing after graduation?"

They talked a while as couples. Jesse nudged Liam. "Angie and I are going for a drive on up to Barker Lake. Y'all want to follow?"

Maureen leaned into Liam. "I'd like that." Her eyes locked with his, her wide mouth curving into a smile.

All he had to do was say yes, and she'd be like putty in his hands. The need to forget Kaylee made up his mind for him. "Yeah." Liam looked at Travis.

His friend shook his head. "Sarah and I'll stay here."

Maureen handed Sarah a set of keys. "You can use my car."

Travis took Sarah's hand. "Let's sit and talk a while. Let me buy you a burger or something."

Sarah looked a little confused, then she nodded and they headed into the building.

Liam had never known Travis to turn down the opportunity to go parking. Either he didn't like the girl...or he liked her a lot. Either way, it was his loss. Slinging his arm around Maureen's shoulder, he smiled down at her. "C'mon darlin'. Let's go have some fun."

He downed his drink, warming with the rush of whiskey in his bloodstream.

Maureen chatted the whole way to the lake while all Liam could think of was the hard throbbing between his legs. And getting it relieved by an experienced woman. Sub-Maureen. Crazy shit.

This was just rebound sex for him, but she didn't seem to be looking for anything more serious either. They'd make each other happy for one night.

They parked in a dark spot next to the lake and stood by Jesse's truck, sharing the joint. Crickets chirruped as a breeze off the lake cooled the air.

He leaned against the truck and pulled Maureen into his arms. "What do you want to do now?" He figured she'd want to walk along the shore, or sit at a picnic table and talk.

"Let's check out your backseat, sugar."

The flare of lust enticed him. "Yeah, that sounds good." Between the alcohol, weed, and blood rushing south from his brain, it all made him dizzy.

Jesse opened the driver's door on his truck. "We're gonna move down a ways. We'll see y'all back at the drive-in." Angie climbed in and Jesse followed.

Maureen grabbed Liam's T-shirt and walked backward.

For a moment, he flashed back to being with Kaylee.

As Maureen pulled him toward his car, she said, "You're a big, sexy guy."

He grabbed her shoulders and stopped her, almost saying Kaylee's name, he caught himself and said, "You're gorgeous, Maureen." He slanted his lips over hers, breathing deeply of her floral perfume, the marijuana, and whiskey. Desire took over and he slid his tongue into her mouth, playing with hers, sucking and nibbling.

She pressed her belly against his erection and moved slowly, teasing him.

He had to concentrate hard not to call her Kaylee. But everything seemed different, not raging the way it had been with Kaylee. Not overwhelming.

They made it to his car and he opened the passenger door, flipping the front seat forward. "After you, ma'am."

"Thank you, sir." Her drawl curled thick and sexy. Definitely southern, nothing like Kaylee, but somehow, everything going on made him think of Kaylee.

She scooted in and slid over, he followed, closing the door. Before he could put an arm around her, she cupped his shaft through his jeans. "Wow, you're a big one."

The warmth of her fingers sent chills through his body. "Take a closer look, darlin'." He sounded like a bad porn film, but didn't give a shit.

Maureen unbuckled his belt and tugged his zipper down.

Liam lifted his hips and she slid the denim to his knees, then grabbed for his briefs. "You sure now, Maureen?" He'd asked Kaylee the same thing and...hell, why did that woman's name have to pop into his brain right now?

"You're quite the gentleman, Liam Jackman." She licked her lips as she tugged on the waistband of his underwear.

"Jack*son*."

"What?" A wrinkle puckered her forehead.

"Ah, nothing." He lifted off the seat and let her slide his shorts down his thighs. He popped free, pulsing hot and bouncing wildly.

"Lord on High, you're huge." Her eyes widened and her mouth opened, her jaw cracking.

"But not too big, right, darlin'?" He winked at her as he smoothed her hair back from her face. The craving to be deep down her throat made him pray that she could take all of him.

Her cool palm gripped the base of his shaft. "I can't touch my fingertips together." Pressing her lips into in a devious smile, she wiggled her whole body. "Damn, boy, this is fabulous." Leaning over him, she took his entire head into her mouth and hummed.

Fireworks shot from his groin up his spine, blasting multi-colored in his brain. "Yeah, darlin' girl, that's what I like."

Her tongue ran in wild circles around his head, first one direction, then the opposite. The tip of her tongue flicked over him slowly. She backed off, kissing the top of him.

What was wrong? Had she changed her mind? It'd kill him if she couldn't finish him off inside her mouth.

Shifting onto her knees, Maureen tucked her hair behind her ears and glanced at him. "I need to get on top of this bad boy."

A pump of pure lust sent pre-cum from his balls up through his shaft.

Her breath caught. She leaned over and licked the drip off of him. "You taste so sweet."

Hadn't Kaylee said that, too? He gritted his teeth. Fuck Kaylee. Setting his hand on the nape of Maureen's neck, he eased her down. "Taste it again."

She let out a little moan and wrapped her hands around the base of his cock. Her tongue flicked the sweet spot at the bottom of his head.

A rocket blast raced from her mouth all the way up his shaft, jerking his hips with the need to pump into her.

"Take it, darlin'." He pushed her a little closer.

"We a little impatient, sugar?" She nipped

softly at his head. “I’ll get you there, just hold your horses.” Her mouth opened and she slid her lips over his head and halfway down his shaft.

The tip hit the back of her throat and she eased off of him, sucking strong. Bobbing her head, she worked herself along his length, taking him a fraction deeper each time. After a minute of hitting the back of her throat, she shifted her body, pulled his shaft toward her, and took him deep.

It didn’t work. Something kept him from going down her throat.

She backed off, still bobbing and sucking along his length, then tried again. Her breathing stopped and she rammed her throat against him, but he wouldn’t slide in any further.

Pulling her mouth from him, she gave him a frustrated frown. “It just won’t go.”

“Keep trying?” His only goal in life right now was to be deep in her throat, her face pressing against his belly.

“I will, hun, but you are really, really big.” Licking her palms, she grasped his cock, slid her hands down, and followed them with her mouth. Her sucking coordinated with her hands, moving up and down his shaft. Every few strokes, she tried shoving him deep.

Shit, it wasn’t going to happen. He let go of the frustration and just enjoyed the feeling, the slide of her hands, the slick wetness of her mouth, the occasional flick of her tongue. He closed his eyes as his mind imploded for a second, then burst as cascades of hot color rained through his body, shimmered in his head. As massive amounts of his load pulsed from his balls and shot down her throat.

She tried again to take him deep, but settled

for swallowing around his head, squeezing the last of his orgasm from him.

The colors receded, a fast aftershock rattled through him, and he tightened himself, pumping one last squirt of cum up his shaft.

She sucked and squeezed, sliding off him, taking his last drop.

Liam's eyes popped open. No vision? With Kaylee, he'd seen the...whatever it was he'd seen. But not this time. The joint they'd smoked blurred the sharp edges of his thoughts and he ran his fingers through Maureen's hair.

When she leaned back and smiled at him, he pulled her against his chest and kissed the top of her head. So talented, but she couldn't give him what he desired most. "You're amazing, darlin'." He drifted, lethargic and content.

She shrugged and snuggled closer. "I'm genetically predisposed to give head."

That jarred him awake. "You're what?"

"It's true. My nose is long and pointy, and I've got really big nostrils so I can breathe even with my mouth full of your lusciousness."

"I've never heard that one before." Her openness impressed him.

"And..." She shifted and opened her mouth. "I have no gag reflex."

"Oh yeah?" He hooked a finger under her jaw and tipped her head up for a kiss. Her lips felt swollen, warm and soft. As he kissed her, his mind spun. *Genetically predisposed*. Did he have the same thing? His urges, his emotions, the hurt that occupied the center of his core, were they something inherent to his DNA?

His hand slid over her shoulder and down to

the side of her breast. "You've definitely got skills."

"I've got a reputation, too. But I don't really care." She moved his hand to cover her breast, circling it, her nipple hardening against his palm. "My last boyfriend gave me a T-shirt that said, *Bad Girls Suck, Good Girls Swallow.*"

Liam should feel anger at the insensitivity of a man labeling a woman that way, but it felt like his emotions were becoming desensitized. He forced a frown for her benefit, but she started laughing. "It's kinda cool." She'd accepted her sexual proclivity and made the most of it. Was that something he'd need to do himself? He focused on Maureen. Fuck all the head chatter, it was time to return the favor.

"Yeah, you know what my motto is?" He gave her a wicked smile. "Both good and bad girls...squirt."

Chapter Six

Liam tweaked Maureen's nipple, and she bucked around on the back seat of his car. He looked out the windows in every direction to make sure they were the only ones parked at this spot at the lake. Besides giving pleasure to this hot, sexy thing, this would be the test. Liam would make Maureen rain all over his back seat, and see if that same odd feeling invaded him as when Kaylee had released her storm for him.

"Squirt? Yeah, right." She rolled her eyes. "That's an urban legend. Women don't squirt, silly boy."

Sliding her shirt up and off her, he wagged his brows. "Darlin', I know from experience, they do."

She unhooked her bra, grabbed her shirt, and tossed them into the front seat. "Well, big boy, I'm always game for an adventure. Bring it on!"

Pulling off her sandals, Liam set them on the console between the seats.

Together they tugged off her shorts and thong panties.

Her bare peach looked tasty in the moonlight, and her full breasts jiggled as she ran her hands up from her tight stomach to cup the bottom of her breasts.

Just watching her, ignited his lust.

Her thumbs flicked her tight pink nipples and her hips rotated in perfect rhythm with his moans.

Hell, he'd better get in the game, or she'd hit a home run without him.

Laying her on the seat, he propped an elbow beside her, his hand at the nape of her neck. He leaned back against the upholstery. Her bottom hung off the edge of the seat and he eased his hand between her legs.

She spread her thighs for him, propping one foot on the front seat. Hot and wet, her tiny peach didn't give off the spring rain scent he'd smelled before. As a matter of fact, he hadn't smelled the scent at all since Kaylee left. He would lick her next, but right now, he wanted to give her an epic orgasm she'd never forget.

"You are so pretty, Maureen." Taking her nipple into his mouth, he eased his middle two fingers into her, finding that special spot.

She cried out and bucked against his hand. She was primed and ready. This would go real fast.

Slowly working his fingers inside her tight opening, his breath came faster as he explored her slick heat. This was so different from Kaylee. *Her again?* He shook his head and concentrated on Maureen.

As he kissed a path to her other breast, his fingers inside her began massaging the soft spot at the front of her willing openness. Sliding his fingers from top to bottom, then releasing and starting again at the top, he coaxed her body to give him what he wanted.

A quiet tune sounded from the front seat. He figured it must be her phone, but she ignored it. Her breath panted from her lungs, her eyes closed, and her head rolled from side to side.

When he took her nipple between his teeth and flicked it with his tongue, she braced her hands, one on the front seat, one on his shoulder.

Increasing the speed of his fingers inside her, he pressed more firmly into her softness. His lips surrounded her breast and he sucked hard each time his fingers pushed against the soft, walnut-sized area inside her. “Press down, darlin’. Like you’re gonna pee.”

Maureen shifted, following his instructions. Her body began to shake, and she pulled in a deep breath and held it.

Moisture burst from inside her and she screamed full-throttle, the sound ringing in his ears.

Liam released her nipple and looked out the windows. Not seeing anyone near, he concentrated on Maureen again, easing his finger movements inside her. His chest swelled as excitement flooded him. He’d done it again, given this beautiful woman an orgasm she’d never forget. Liam held the thrill deep inside him, concentrating on Maureen.

Her shaking slowed as she caught her breath and blinked her eyes open.

He froze. This was it. Would he experience that jolt again? Hear the roaring in his head? Feel the ache surrounding his soul? Staring at her, he waited, his body tense.

She looked into his eyes, her blue irises turning lighter as her orgasm waned.

Nothing. He felt...nothing.

Maureen smiled. “I don't believe it. You were right. I had no idea I could do that.” She looked down at her belly and struggled to sit up.

He helped her, keeping his wet hand between her thighs. The relief of not having to live through another episode of heartache, plus the crazy excitement of his purely unselfish talent, made him nearly giddy. “Darlin’, every woman I’ve been with has experienced the rain ceremony with me.” Technically true. But then it hit him; he’d said the words “rain ceremony” without conscious thought. He lifted his hand to his mouth and tasted her juices.

"Sweet. Just like a peach. Just like you, darlin'."

She blushed and ran a finger over the moisture on his hand, then rubbed it between her fingertip and thumb. "Amazing that this came out of me." She sniffed it.

"Taste it. It's beautiful."

Meeting his gaze, Maureen licked her finger. "Mm. It *is* sweet." Her smile lit her face. "That orgasm, Liam." She let out a dramatic sigh. "I've never been that high before."

Her phone chimed, and she ignored it again.

It had been life-changing for him, watching her climax, even watching Kaylee shatter the night before. If this was something he could do to help women grow sexually, he'd make it his mission in life. "You're a sexy woman." He kissed her, soft and slow.

He pulled a plastic bag containing a roll of paper towels from under the front seat. He dried her, kissing her belly and her thighs as she pulled on her bra.

Her phone sounded again, this time loud and thumping.

"Shit. I've got to get that." She lurched forward, nearly laying out over the console to grab her purse. "Hi." She grabbed her clothes, shimmied into the back seat, and started dressing one-handed. "I'm at the drive-in with Sarah. Where are you?"

Liam pulled up his pants and stepped out of the passenger door, breathing in the fresh night air as he fastened his jeans.

"No, I'm not." She sounded defensive. Was it one of her parents?

She jumped out of the back seat, her shorts on, barefoot, trying to pull on her top.

He stepped closer to help her and saw bruises on her back. Mostly faded, but one looked recent. He knew all about how long it took for bruises to fade. Tugging her top in place for her, he kissed her neck and heard an angry male voice coming through the phone.

Maureen backed away from Liam. "I'll be home in a few minutes." She spoke into the phone as she walked away. "I'll call you from there."

He'd like to go a few more rounds, but maybe another night this week. Liam walked around the car and got in the driver's seat.

A few seconds later she slid into her seat, shut the door, and dropped her phone in her purse.

He turned the ignition. "Who was that?" He shifted and they headed back to town. Maureen grabbed his phone from the console. "I'm going to put my digits in." She thumb-typed. "My boyfriend lives a couple towns over, and he works weekends a lot, so I have free nights. You'll call me, right?"

Boyfriend. He hefted a long sigh. Of course. A girl like her wouldn't be unattached. You'd think Liam would feel the slightest bit jealous, but he felt nothing inside.

After a moment, she set down his phone then lifted hers, pressed a button, and put it to her ear. "Sarah, we're on our way back. Y'all be ready when I get there." She listened, giggled, then hung up. "Your friend Travis is kind of shy, huh?"

He wasn't as much shy as he was intense. He dated, but didn't have casual sex often. His life was his family's farm, and he hoped to be married by twenty and start a pack of young'uns by twenty-two. The two of them were going to ag college together in the fall. Somehow, those plans didn't feel as exciting as they once had.

Maureen sat quietly. Probably because Liam hadn't answered her questions.

A million questions rolled through his head. Why hadn't Maureen's squirting orgasm triggered the vision and the darkness inside him? Had it just been Kaylee? Was she somehow evil? Had her sinfulness crept into him?

Biblical shit? He shoved away the apocalyptic theory. It had to have been a one-time thing, something Kaylee had manifested. And when he found her, he'd get the truth from her.

He pulled into the drive-in parking lot. Maureen leaned over for a quick kiss. "Call me." She jumped out of the car, closed the door, then leaned in the open window. "Hey." Maureen looked into Liam's eyes. "Thank you for tonight. I'll never forget it. Not ever, sugar."

Behind her, Travis strolled toward the car.

She blew Liam a kiss and turned away, giving Travis a finger wave as she passed him.

His friend jumped into the car and closed the door. He sniffed. "What is that smell?"

He grinned. "Sex, Trav. If you don't recognize the scent of it, you ain't gettin' enough of it." Liam pulled onto the highway.

Travis laughed as he fastened his seatbelt. "At least whatever went down has got you smiling again."

Smiling. Almost hopeful. Just then the specter of Kaylee slowly started creeping back into his mind.

****

Sunday afternoon, Liam walked out to greet his grandparents as they drove their old blue pickup toward the house. He opened the passenger door for his grandma. "How was the wedding?" A couple they knew from church had renewed their vows at Graceland.

"Just lovely." Emma Jackson struggled to get her legs out, her coral polyester pants and coordinating floral top matched her purse, and she'd curled her short, black and gray hair. She looked younger than her seventy years. "The Elvis minister was so authentic."

Stepping from the other side of the truck, Herschel Jackson coughed out a laugh, his brown eyes twinkling. "Craziest shenanigans I've ever seen." In his red western shirt and bluejeans, Liam's grandpa looked older than his sixty-eight years. He was a worrier, and it had taken its toll on his face. He'd trimmed the small fringe of gray hair he sported around the back of his head shorter than usual.

"They tried to feed us fried peanut butter and banana sandwiches." Herschel shut the driver's door and reached into the back of the truck.

"Let me get the bags, Grandpa." Liam reached for the suitcases from his side.

"They had other food." His grandma coughed and headed for the house.

Herschel watched his wife walk away. "She wasn't feeling well." He met Liam's gaze. "It's been off and on for a while now."

Liam toted the bags and met his grandpa in front of the truck. "I know she's been sleeping a lot. Has she seen the doctor?" His grandmother was the light of Liam's life, his savior and therapist and mentor, ever since she'd brought him home with her. Before he'd come to live here, he'd never known how powerful love could be. He needed her in his life for a long, long time to come.

"Ah." Herschel headed for the house. "She

says it's nothing. I'll get her to make an appointment this week."

Liam brought the bags into his grandparents' bedroom and set them on the cedar chest at the foot of the old iron bed. The scent of Emma's lily-of-the-valley perfume hit him; the same stuff she'd used since Grandpa had given her a bottle while they were dating.

His grandmother walked in behind him and tugged him around for a good, strong hug. She gripped his arms and pushed him away, smiling up at him. "What did you do this weekend?"

"Nothing." Other than lose his virginity, experience visions and become temporarily possessed, scare away the woman he loved, then try to replace her with a girl known as The Sub-Maureen. "Travis and I went to Schaefer to the drive-in last night."

She scrunched up her nose and released him, sitting on the edge of the bed, running her hand over the antique quilt. "Good for you. You need to get out more and have fun."

He'd heard that from her for three years. "I'm working on it, Grams."

Herschel walked into the room. "How was your game, Friday?" He sat on the other side of the bed and pulled off his boots.

"We lost. We're statistically eliminated from the state tourney." A few days ago, that would have bothered the hell out of him. Today, it was just a splattered bug on the cracked windshield of his life.

"Ah. You'll get 'em this week." His grandfather yawned.

Time for their afternoon nap. Liam stuffed his hands in his pockets and made a decision. "I'm gonna miss Friday's game." A few days away from here would feel good. Every minute he spent in his bedroom reminded him of Kaylee. "Travis asked me to go up to Juniper with him Thursday. Some relative needs help on the farm."

His grandparents looked at him. True, he'd never missed a baseball game, rarely missed a day of school, but the way they stared, you'd think he'd just announced his decision to become a serial killer.

"Well, that's nice of you." Emma got to her feet and trudged toward him, narrowing her hazel eyes as she stared at him. "Is there anything else you want to tell us, sweetie?" Grams was so good at reading his moods.

He may as well get it out. They'd hear it in town sooner or later. "Kaylee and I aren't together anymore."

"Oooh." His grandmother tipped her head and rubbed his arm. "Did you have a disagreement?"

"No. She had to move. Back to her dad's or something."

"Too young to get tied down, anyway." Herschel pulled back the quilt and unbuckled his belt.

Emma planted her fists on her hips and glared at her husband. "Let the boy have his feelings, Hersch."

His grandfather mumbled under his breath as he dropped his jeans.

"If you want to talk about it, I'm always here." Emma leaned in and Liam bent to press a kiss to her cheek.

"Okay. I'll let you two get some rest." Liam backed out, pulling the door closed after himself.

Their voices followed him as he strode back to his room. Closing his door, he toed off his boots. On his desk, his open calculus book taunted him to finish his homework, but he picked up his notebook and a pencil, propped pillows against his headboard, and sat, staring at the words he'd written the day before. He wrote the day's date on the next line, then words began to flow.

Words escape my mouth but landing this ink on this paper, it's like baring my soul. Since Kaylee left, I feel colder inside, deep, deep inside like my soul is...never mind, that's crazy. And talk about crazy, I feel like I can suggest things to women. I mean, what did Kaylee do to me...what am I doing to myself? It will pass, right? I'll be better, right?........right? I thought Travis was genius when he suggested using sex to get over her, but now I know I'm obsessed with Kaylee...I need help.

Chapter Seven

Thursday morning, Travis pulled up in the yard before sunrise. Liam toted his duffle bag and tossed it in the back seat of the shiny red truck. Sheetrock, lumber, toolboxes, and shingles filled the truck bed. He slid into the leather bucket seat. Travis slugged the last few inches from a bottle of Mountain Dew. Another bottle sat in the cup holder on Liam's side of the console.

"Fucking early, asshole." Travis had called Liam the night before to arrange the pre-dawn pickup.

"My old man just told me the whole story last night." Travis's brown eyes went wide as a grin broke over his face. "The cousin is laid up. She broke her wrist Friday and had surgery in Nashville today. She's staying there until Monday when she has to see her doctor." He shifted and headed down the driveway. "We've got the place to ourselves."

"Oh yeah?" Liam sat back, closing his eyes.

"Yeah. Good thing, too. She scares the shit out of me."

"Mm." Liam drifted closer toward sleep.

"Dad didn't tell me before because he knew I'd try to get a party together."

Liam smirked and opened his eyes. "And?"

"And...the party's Friday night." Travis turned onto the road. "A couple guys are bringing a keg, some of the girls are going to get food. Everyone will either sleep in their cars or in the hayloft."

"I bought a bottle of JD from Krenshaw." The only guy in school who carried a fake ID.

"Yeah!" Travis laid on the horn a couple times. "Fucking barn party, man. This is gonna rock." He smacked the back of his hand on Liam's shoulder.

"Why aren't you pumped?"

"Give me an hour of shut-eye. Then I'll give you pumped." Liam drifted off to sleep.

The truck stopped and Liam blinked awake. The morning sun glared at him through the windshield. How long had he slept?

"Pit stop." Travis grabbed both empty bottles of Dew and hopped out of the truck. He jogged into the building, probably in urgent need of the john.

Liam got out and stretched, looking around. He didn't recognize the place. When his stomach rumbled, he headed into the convenience store.

Travis stood leaning on the counter, giving the cutie in the red apron his sexiest look and smoothest lines.

Liam hit the bathroom then wandered around the store, picking up a jumbo bag of jerky, a coke, and a box of donuts. Travis could get his own breakfast.

His friend went outside and shoved the gas pump nozzle into his truck's tank. Liam set his items on the counter, and a sensation rattled into his brain. He jerked his head up, staring down into the wide green eyes of the redheaded cutie. His skin tingled, and he smelled it. The rain scent, the same ecstasy he'd sensed coming from Kaylee. More than a physical thing, it pulled at him like a connection, a link.

Her mouth dropped open an inch and her breath came faster. She felt it, too?

Blood pumped through him, fueling him from inside.

Her lips quivered for a second and he clearly visualized sliding his shaft between them, into her mouth, finding himself down deep in her throat.

"Y…you..." She swallowed, drew a long breath, then licked her lips. "Do I know you?"

He shook his head. "Not yet." She was the one, he could feel it in every cell in his body. "I'm Liam."

"Amanda."

Travis walked in and headed for the junk food aisle. Neither of them looked away from each other's eyes.

"Are you in high school?" He hoped she was older than she looked.

"No. I graduated last year. I worked this year, saving for college. How about you?"

"Where you keep the beer?" Travis's voice carried from somewhere in the store.

She dragged her gaze from Liam's and leaned to look around him. "It's all in the back cooler." She pointed toward her right.

Behind her red corporate apron, the nipples on her small breasts peaked hard. He took a glance at her ass. Round and high in her tight shorts. She stood about five-six, but her legs were thin and long.

He didn't want to tell her he was still a high school kid. "Going to ag college in Mortonson."

She nodded then rang up his purchases, took his cash, and gave him his change without meeting his eyes again.

"What town is this?"

Amanda handed him a bag with his food in it. "This is Rogers Corners." She glanced behind him, then into his eyes. Her cheeks turned pink. "Liam." The way she said his name brought back that hot still-frame of her tasting him.

Travis hauled an armload of food and set it on the counter. "This should get us to Juniper."

"You know, I'm supposed to card you for the beer." Amanda started ringing up his purchases. "But I won't if you tell me what's in Juniper?"

"Party. Friday night." Liam leaned on the counter. "Are you free?"

Travis gave him the stink-eye. "She told me she's working Friday night."

Liam nodded. Travis had claimed this one. "I'll be in the truck." He headed toward the door.

"You sure you can't get Friday off? The party's at a haunted farm." Travis's voice went low, mysterious.

Liam smiled and put his hand on the door.

"No!" Amanda squealed. "You mean Old Hag Hackers's place?"

Liam looked at Travis.

His buddy grinned at Amanda, lost in her smile.

He'd damn sure like to trade places with Trav right now. As he walked out, he heard his friend promise to call her that evening. Shit, he'd missed out by a few minutes

Once they got on the road again, Travis pulled a slip of paper from his pocket. "Got those digits, bro."

"She's cute. Are you gonna go for it?"

"I don't know. It's a forty-five minute drive up here." He peeled open a garlicky beef stick and bit off half of it.

Liam pulled his coke out of the bag and a piece of paper clung to the moisture on the can. His receipt? He started to crumple it, then saw writing. *Call me any time, Liam. Amanda.* Her phone number followed.

Glancing at his friend, he knew the right thing

to do would be to throw the damn thing out the window. But what if Travis didn't call her? Would he ask his buddy first, or would he just jump in and take her for his own?

That rain scent he'd caught coming from her. The dark promise of more than just sex, the lust that turned him into a rutting bull. It ate away at his conscience, blurred the lines between right and wrong. Kaylee had taken a back seat in his thoughts now that he'd met Amanda.

Fuck him for an asshole, Liam straightened out the paper and slid it into his wallet.

"What's this B.S. about Old Hag Hackers?" Liam opened his box of donuts and offered one to Travis.

"She's one scary chick." He took the donut and stuffed it into his mouth. "Last time I saw her, I was about twelve. We went out to her farm to help fix the roof on her house." Travis let out a grunt. "I went into the house, didn't know I wasn't supposed to. Shit, she went all..." He held his hands up like claws, and made a screeching sound.

"Was she a widow then?"

"No." Travis helped himself to another donut. "Her husband rodeoed, and he was gone a lot. He died last year around Christmas, and rumor has it, she's been gettin' crazier by the day."

After they'd polished off their beef products and two boxes of donuts, Travis looked at him. "School was shitty this week, huh?"

Liam shrugged his brows. "Shitty ain't even close." Monday morning, everyone had stared at him as if he'd gotten a bloody start on his serial killer job.

"You knew it would be like that. Everyone liked Kaylee."

Liam crushed his soda can. “That Raylene chick told me she’d called Kaylee. Said she’d left because her heart belonged to some guy in the oil fields in North Dakota.”

“Seriously?” Travis laughed. “She drove all the way up there?”

“I don’t know. Kaylee told her it wasn’t anything to do with...Friday night.”

The GPS’s feminine British voice spoke and Travis turned right onto a two-lane highway. “You don’t sound so sure of that.”

“You know what, Travis, honestly, who cares? What can I do about it, anyway?”

“Not a damn thing, hoss.” Travis rolled down his window and stuck his head out. “But party, motherfuckers!” He shouted, making the last word go on forever.

Liam chuckled. “Yeah. I’m ready, man.” It’d take his mind off shit, and if he found a cutie of his own for the night, he’d do what he did best: be a Casanova.

Travis pressed a button on the dashboard and staticky country music filled the truck.

Liam looked over at him. “Seriously, dude?”

“You still don’t like country?” Travis jammed a finger on the scan button until he found a channel that came in clear.

“My grandparents listen to that shit.” Even though Liam wouldn’t admit it to Travis, he sometimes listened to the late night soulful oldies on the local country channel.

“Just give it a chance, man. It talks to you, sometimes.” Travis tipped his seat back a ways.

“Yeah, I know. Lost my trailer, lost my dog, lost my woman, found a jar of moonshine.”

Travis laughed. "Used to be. It's different, now."

When a commercial came on, Liam punched the scan button, going around the numbers twice and finding only country and religious channels. He stopped when a hard-driving, funky song poured from the speakers. Soulful, it had him tapping his hand on the wheel.

The lyrics, sung in a low male voice, struck him as relevant. *"So what do you say, baby, let's get as wet as we can get."* This he could listen to. The chorus had him singing along. *"Get a little rain on ya."* The picture of a soaking wet woman in his arms made him hotter than sin.

Liam stared out the side window at the rich farmland, cooling his lust. His body wasn't his own any more. Neither was his mind. Confusing visions and bizarre cravings blasted through him at the worst possible times. Why was Kaylee's allure dulling in his mind? Now it was all about Amanda from the gas station. He thought of her every five minutes. He could have taken her right there, the urge, the connection had been that strong.

The GPS showed another eight miles before the next turn.

He let his mind wander where it shouldn't go. Amanda's body, naked against his, her breasts pressed hard against his chest, her nipples tight. His shaft hard, pushing into her mouth, into her soft opening, then her back door. Making her rain for him, then feasting on her for hours.

The GPS directed a turn and they swung onto a dirt road.

"Gotta piss." Travis eased to the side of the road near a stand of trees.

"Ain't you got no control over your bladder?"

Travis shoved open the door. "Just never mind my bladder."

Liam looked around. Fields of young green plants stretched to the horizon, growing in the hot sun. He loved the wide open spaces. Loved working his grandparents' farm. *His* farm. They'd made legal arrangements when he'd turned eighteen. It'd be all his when they passed.

Pain gripped his heart. They weren't doing as well this year. Liam had done most of the digging and planting. And whatever was making Grams so tired, he'd be sure to get her in to the doctor's next week.

Travis jumped back into the truck. "Listen to this." He dug his iPod out of the glove box and plugged it in. He played a list of songs, trying to prove that his music wasn't as crappy as Liam thought it was.

Liam rated the songs, shrugging, but that rain song he'd heard earlier kept coming back to him. The feelings it evoked in him hit a primal nerve, made him restless.

After a few minutes, they turned onto a rutted driveway. The farm didn't seem as rundown as Liam had expected. A big old white two-story house sat on a rise a ways off the road, a covered porch wrapped all the way around it.

"Can't go near the big house." Travis did the claw thing again, accompanied by the screeching noise. "We're bunking in the hired hand's shack."

Liam stared at the house. "You sure she's not home?"

"I'm sure. Dad would have called if she was coming home early."

Did a curtain move? The creepy feeling

reminded Liam of an old horror movie.

A red barn and white metal pole shed stood in the distance, and an old grain silo listed to the left. "That silo needs to come down."

"Not this weekend." Travis turned off his music. "But I'll let Dad know." Travis drove past the buildings to a small house down by the creek and shut off the engine.

The smell hit Liam. Manure. Next to the barn, a fenced-in wallow held a dozen swine. "You didn't mention hogs."

His buddy shrugged. "Hogs, cattle, and chickens. That's why we had to be here so early. They haven't been fed yet."

Liam grabbed his bag out of the truck. "Glad I brought my old boots."

The place looked clean but ratty. The furniture dated back to the last century, and the metal kitchen table and chairs looked like a movie set from the '60s. The kitchen appliances were about as old as the ones at Liam's place. The big picture window overlooked the creek and acres of fields.

He picked up a note with square printing on it from the table. *Left food in refrigerator. Six pack of beer for you—don't tell your father. Feed the stock twice a day—directions are in the barn. No one else on the property. No exceptions*. She mentioned she'd be home Sunday morning, told them they could leave before she got here. She'd signed it, *Cousin Grace.*

Grace. Pretty name. Liam grinned. For an old hag.

Travis trudged past him to the bedroom. "She's had a hard time of it since her husband died. The asshole cashed out his life insurance when he found out he was terminal. Spent it all on whores and booze and left her with nothing."

The squeak of old bed springs sounded from the bedroom as Liam grabbed a beer from the refrigerator and drank it in a few long pulls.

A few minutes later, Travis came out wearing bib overalls and crusty old knee-high boots.

Liam laughed. "Well, howdy, Junior Samples." His grandparents loved the old reruns of Hee Haw.

Flipping him the middle finger, Travis clomped across the kitchen to the refrigerator.

The living room held an old couch covered with a sheet, a scarred coffee table, and a worn cloth recliner covered in a blanket. Liam changed there, folding his clothes and tucking them into his bag. He sat on the couch then spread out on it. Not too bad.

"Beer?" Travis called from the kitchen.

"No, thanks." He sat up and dug in his bag, found his bottle of Jack Daniels, and wandered into the kitchen, setting the bottle on the table. "Where're the shot glasses? I'm gonna want a buzz on if I'm gonna be sloppin' hogs."

Travis laughed. "Shit, yeah! Pour me one, too."

With a few shots of sour mash in him, Liam followed Travis to the barn. A few of the boards needed replacing, wet spots darkened the floor from where the roof leaked, but she'd kept the place clean. The horse stalls stood empty, but the small tack room at the back of the building had the remnants of horse equipment, but no saddles.

Had she sold her horses to keep up with the mortgage payments?

After slopping the hogs, putting out grain and hay for the cattle, and Travis making a fool of himself crowing like a rooster while feeding the chickens, they headed back to the hand's house.

Travis stomped on a loose step. "Gotta fix this."

While Travis checked out the plumbing in the bathroom, Liam wandered into the bedroom. The double bed's mattress and box spring looked new, still sealed in plastic sheeting. A big galvanized tub sat in the middle of the bed.

Liam looked up. A chunk of the ceiling was missing, and a dark stain surrounded the hole. The tub must be to catch the water leaking in. "Trav, wanna work on this first?"

The toilet flushed. "Yeah." His footsteps sounded behind Liam. Travis walked up next to him and stuffed his hands into the big pockets of his overalls, looking up. "We can fix this easy."

"I'll get a ladder." Liam assumed there would be one in the metal pole barn.

"I'll get the tools out of the truck." Travis took off and Liam walked to the white corrugated-metal shed and pulled open the door. Flipping the light switch, he heard scurrying sounds. Some kind of critters were getting in here. They'd have to fix that.

The small tractor looked to be in good shape, and the implements scattered around the building weren't all that modern, but they'd get the job done. Climbing the tractor's ladder, he looked into the cab. Liam tried to imagine Grace bouncing across the field, planting corn to feed her livestock, or harvesting and baling hay, while cackling hysterically, as old hags liked to do.

But shit, she had to be a strong woman to tackle all this alone.

He found a ladder and stepped out into the sunshine. Half-blinded for a second, he thought he saw something moving at the big house.

Chapter Eight

When Liam's vision cleared, he watched a rocking chair going back and forth on the porch of the big house. The wind? He looked at a cluster of trees. The leaves weren't moving.

"Creepy." He hiked back to the little house, carrying the ladder. "You sure nobody's here but us?"

Travis laughed as he tugged a piece of sheetrock to the edge of the tailgate. "You seein' ghosts?" They slid the sheetrock out and hauled it into the house.

"How long has her hired man been gone?"

Travis shrugged as he stared at the ceiling. "I don't know. Looks like a while from the size of this water damage."

Liam went back outside. Had she run out of funds to pay him, or had he quit and she hadn't found a replacement yet? Why the heck did he care?

He set the ladder against the roof's overhang and climbed up to see the damage.

The roof had a shallow slope, and he could see all the way down into the bedroom. He poked at the rafters with a screwdriver. They felt solid. Stuck in one of the joists, a piece of paper caught his eye. He reached down and tugged it free. It looked like a photograph, torn in half. The blurred face of a woman with dark hair filled most of the picture. Was that Grace?

Along the jagged edge, part of a man's face showed, smiling at her. Dark hair, prominent brow bone. Was that her husband? On the back, drawn in marker, were some kind of symbols. A circle, some lines, dots, then part of another circle, maybe? What was this?

Should he know this? His head spun for a couple seconds.

Too much sun. He stuffed the paper in his pocket and climbed down the ladder, digging a bottle of water out of the cooler. Something about that drawing...

"Hey." Travis came out of the house. "You havin' a break already?" He grabbed a toolbox from the truck bed.

"Yeah. Take the time off my paycheck."

"Son, your payment is the skills you'll be learning just watching me." He smirked.

Liam snorted. "I'll be lucky if I don't end up haulin' you to the emergency room."

Travis flipped him off with a grin and headed back inside.

Two hours later, they'd patched the roof, nailed a piece of sheetrock in place on the ceiling, and taped and mudded it. They'd sand and paint it in the morning.

Liam sat on the top step of the porch, looking at the big house up on the hill. Something about it made the hairs on the back of his neck rise. Was it haunted? It felt like something inhabited the place.

Beeping came from the kitchen. Liam got up and walked in. The smell of beef made his mouth water. Travis took a plate out of the microwave and set it on the table. "This is mine." He pointed to an identical plate wrapped in plastic on the counter. "That's yours. Roast, potatoes, and green beans, compliments of my cousin."

Liam tossed it in the machine and got it heating.

With his belly full of really good food, he yawned and stretched. "Ain't no TV here, so I guess we keep working, huh?"

Travis looked at him. "Guess so. What next?"

"Saw some fencing that needs repair." He looked at the angle of the sun. Early afternoon. "Then a trip to Juniper to scrounge up some supper?"

Travis stood and set his dishes in the sink then headed toward the door. "Best idea I've heard all day." He turned and looked at Liam. "And I'm paying."

Liam stood, dishes in hand. "Damn right, you are. I'm free labor, here. You want to keep me workin', you'd best feed me."

****

The next day, Liam kept eyeing the big house as they fed the livestock, patched buildings, and repaired fencing.

"You need to stop doing that." Travis rubbed the back of his neck. "I'm getting the creeps."

Liam bit back a smile. Travis was one of those guys who screamed like a little girl at horror movies. Liam couldn't pass up a chance to taunt him some. "I'm going up to the big house." He set down his hammer. "Someone...or something...is in there." He took a step.

"No!" Travis grabbed his arm. "There's no one there. Just don't look at it." His voice rose in pitch.

Liam laughed. "Hell, that woman really freaked you out, huh, boy?" He went back to driving nails.

Travis looked at the house. "I'm just glad we'll be gone when she gets home Sunday."

That night as the sun neared the horizon, a caravan of trucks and cars rolled into the farmyard. Travis and Liam had cleaned the barn, strung some

Christmas lights they'd found in a box in the hayloft, and set up speakers running off Travis's truck radio.

Liam hefted the keg out of the back of one of his teammate's pickup truck, and they set it in a plastic barrel surrounded by ice. Using plywood Travis had in his truck, they set up a makeshift table for food. One of the girls brought a red checkered tablecloth and spread it under the bags of chips, buckets of chicken and all the fixin's, plus tubs of salads and fruit.

Holding his red plastic cup full of beer, Liam took his first sip and leaned on a stall. Some couples slow-danced, a few people stood at the table and ate, and Travis climbed the steep steps up to the hayloft behind a cute, black-haired junior from their school. Vanessa...something.

Knowing every one of the girls and their dating histories didn't give him much hope of finding one of his own to head to the hayloft with, but he'd give it a try.

Kevin, the shortstop from his team wandered over. "Hey, Liam. How's it going out here? Travis says you're fixin' up the place, huh?"

"Yep. Just a few things that need repair."

Kevin made a face. The guy was a townie "Stinks, don't it."

"What, the animal shit?"

Kevin nodded.

"Yep. But you get used to it."

Kevin glanced out the door as headlights from a vehicle turned into the driveway. "You don't have any stock out at your place, do you?"

He shook his head. "Just crops."

"I was meaning to ask you. Where do you buy your crop insurance?"

Liam's brows rose. Evidently, Kevin was going into the insurance business with his old man. He sure as hell didn't want to spend the night talking drought and hail damage. "My grandpa handles that." He nodded at someone across the room. "Be right back." He strolled off. Not coming back.

A girl with dirty-blonde hair who sat in front of him in chemistry opened a bag of chips and set it on the food table. She'd been friendly in school, shy, not flirty.

"Hi Tara."

She looked up at him, way up, a potato chip sticking halfway out of her mouth. How had he never noticed her eyes were different colors? One a murky green, and one grayish-blue. She looked deep into his and a soft pink blossomed on her cheeks. Chewing, she smiled and swallowed. "Hi, Liam. Travis said you'd be here."

Did that mean she'd come because he was here? He picked up her empty cup from the table. "Can I get you a beer?"

She nodded. "Just half-full. I don't like it warm."

Taking both cups in one hand, he put his palm on her lower back. Her long, straight hair brushed against the back of his fingers. "Who'd you drive up here with?"

"A couple of girls from the 4-H club." Her shorts curved around her big booty, showing off her heavy, tan, smooth legs. And her sandals showed her cute, plump little toes.

Why hadn't he noticed her before? "You live on a farm, right?" *Brilliant conversation, Liam.*

"Yes, we're out by the old dam on County 18." She smiled up at him. "I'm going to Mortonson to school this fall, too."

"Oh yeah? What classes are you taking?" He filled their cups from the tapper and guided her toward the barn doors as she went over a list of classes that sounded exactly like his. "I bet we'll be in a lot of classes together."

They stepped outside and he guided her upwind from the hog wallow. A soft breeze blew and the scent of earth and new growth drifted with it.

"I love frogs." She stopped and looked up at him.

"What?" He slowly glided his hand up her back then down again.

"Hear the frogs?" She tipped her head.

From the low spot across the creek, dozens of frogs croaked. "Uh, yeah, I didn't notice them with the music." He brushed his knuckles down her bare arm. He didn't really want to know, but he asked anyway, just to be polite. "Why do you like frogs so much?"

She sighed and stepped closer to him. "I think it's the beer making me brave, but I'd like you to kiss me, Liam."

Her words moved through him like a steamroller. "I'd be honored to, Tara, darlin'."

She shivered as he pulled her close. He spread his legs to get lower and tossed his beer cup. With one hand on her back and the other smoothing her hair, he bent, tipped his head, and kissed her.

Moaning softly, she parted her lips and their tongues brushed quickly. He tasted potato chips and beer. He could get used to... "Wait." He pulled back an inch. "Do you have a boyfriend?"

She stared into his eyes. "No, not yet."

He waited for her to blink, but when she

didn't, he looked away and swallowed. A skitter ran down his spine. Weird chick. He pulled her closer. As her round breasts pressed tight against his chest, he instantly reengaged. He traced the soft curve of her upper lip with his tongue, then slid it inside for a deeper taste.

She kissed him back tentatively, as if she didn't do this often. He sucked her tongue into his mouth, tangling it with his until she ran her tongue along his teeth, sucking them like they were Chicklets.

He pulled back, debating whether sex would be worth putting up with her strange behavior.

She rotated her hips, pressing herself along his hardening shaft.

Yeah, he could do this.

"Little darlin', you are the sweetest thing I've ever tasted."

"Liam. I knew we'd get along well." Her voice rose in pitch, as if she was about to cry.

He stood and took her hand. Maybe if they didn't talk so much. "Walk with me?"

"Uh huh."

He'd take her along the creek, end up at the farmhand's house. Do a little more kissing, and possibly a few other things. His anticipation had him walking fast.

"Wanna know why I thought we'd get along well?" She held his hand a little too tightly.

The more she said, the less he wanted to hear. "Sure." He cleared his throat. "But listen to those frogs, now. It's like they're getting louder or—"

"We're both good students." She skipped to keep up with him. "And I was almost Valedictorian, but you were instead, and I'm glad you were."

He slowed down a bit. "You should have gotten it."

"No, no, you. You're so smart." She rubbed against him like a purring cat.

He looked down at her. Was this worth it?

The music from the barn came to an abrupt halt.

"Your class load was much heavier, plus you have sports on your—"

"What the hell is going on?" A female voice screeched from inside the barn.

Liam's head jerked in that direction. "Ah, hell. Come on." He started to run for the barn, but Tara slowed him to a fast walk.

"Somebody's mother?" She puffed, breathless.

"Could be." Or had Old Hag Hackers come home early?

Liam heard Travis's voice, the tone sounding like he tried reasoning with whomever it was.

They reached the barn and he set Tara behind him and peeked into the building.

On the other side of the barn, backlit by the yard light, a short woman with wild hair stood in the small doorway. She put her hands on her hips. "Fuck." She dropped one casted hand, must have forgotten her broken wrist. "Don't call me cousin, Travis." Her voice screeched louder. "My no-account husband was your dad's cousin. And don't think your father won't hear about this party, boy. I specifically told you, nobody on my land."

That had to be Grace. Liam couldn't make out her face, but he could see Travis edging away from her.

"Pack up your shit..." She turned and pointed

out the barn doors where everyone had parked. "And get the hell off my property."

People started scattering, grabbing food, chugging their beers, and heading outside.

Definitely Grace. For a little thing, she had a big voice, and an even bigger temper.

Travis held the hand of the girl he'd brought up into the hayloft. "I'm sorry, I didn't think it would be a problem. I'll get everyone out of here and Liam and I will clean up and—"

"You leave, too. All of you. Just leave."

Two guys grabbed the handles of the barrel holding the keg.

"Oh no." Grace stormed toward them. "You leave that here. None of you are old enough to drink."

Liam couldn't take his eyes off her. Gesturing wildly, her hair flew around her like a dark halo.

Krenshaw walked toward her, pulling his wallet from his jeans. "I am, ma'am."

"Don't even show me your fake ID, boy." She pointed to the doors again. "Out."

Liam flattened back against the outside wall. "Better go. I'll call you." Liam gave Tara a push in the right direction.

Travis glanced at Liam as he walked past him with his girl. "Can you grab a ride with Bridget and them?" He smiled at the girl at his side. "We're going to go somewhere and get to know each other better."

Liam held in a snort. "Sure. I'll get our bags from the house. Tell them to wait for me."

The cutie staring at Travis like he was a god, nodded. "I will."

Liam jogged to the small house and went into the bathroom for his kit. He grabbed Travis's too and walked into the bedroom. "Fucking pig." Travis had spread his gear all over the room. He shoved it all in the bag, grabbed his own bag, and ran back to the barn.

Every car was gone. “Son of a bitch.”

He pulled out his phone and dialed Travis’s number. No answer. Shitty reception.

Something jabbed him in the back. “I told you to leave!” Her raised voice sounded hoarse.

He dropped the bags and held his hands up. “They left without me. Don’t shoot.” He was only half-joking.

The woman snorted. “This isn’t a gun, you idiot. It’s a shovel.” She leaned it against his arm. “Since you’re stranded here, you can clean up.”

He grabbed the handle and turned slowly, bracing himself for the worst. His first glimpse of her took his breath away. She was beautiful.

Her tan skin looked flawless. Her gray eyes were fringed by thick lashes. Petite and well-curved, her long, brown hair reached the middle of her back. She gathered it up to put in a ponytail. She had trouble with the hand in the cast, but eventually got it all tamed. “Don’t just stand there and stare. Get to work.”

“I’m Liam, Travis’s friend.” Something about her made him want to be friends. Was it her sad story? Or her smokin’ hot body?

“I know who you are.” She reached for a string of lights and yanked it down.

Liam used the shovel to gather up the hay they’d scattered on the floor to soak up the puddles. “You do?”

“I’ve been watching you.” She hauled a barrel and a bucket over and started dumping food in the bucket, and the containers in the barrel. A few things she set aside.

He leaned the shovel in a corner and went back to the food table. "You came back early."

She gathered the food she was keeping in her arms. "Yep. This morning. Damn hotel was so loud, I couldn't get no rest."

If she'd just come back today, who had he seen on the porch yesterday? Liam swore someone had been watching him. He broke down the makeshift tables. "Anyone else live here?"

She froze for a second, then looked at him. "Did you see him? He's been creeping around here since... Damn him." Grace shook her head. "Close them doors, would ya?" She nodded toward the big barn doors.

He brought the two duffle bags inside and closed the doors, securing them, then turned back to her. "What do you want me to do with the keg?"

She stared at it a few seconds. "Guess we'd better drink it up." She sighed. "There's a hand truck in the tack room. Haul that sucker up to the porch."

We'd better drink it up?

She glared at him. "Close your pie hole. You're drawin' flies."

Chapter Nine

Sitting on the top porch step of the big house, Liam refilled Grace's plastic cup with beer from the keg. She reached for it, bumping it with her fingers before she got a hold of it. Was it her fifth beer? He gulped from his sixth.

"And then, the damn horse stepped on my foot." She straightened her leg, the yard light shining on the crescent-shaped scar on her arch.

He laughed. "You can't ride horses barefoot."

"You sayin' I deserved this?" She almost smiled.

The woman was rough on the outside, but a lot of fun once she had the right level of alcohol in her.

He unbuttoned his shirt down to his belly and peeled open the left side. "Baseball." He touched the red scar. "A bat broke, I was on deck and it came right at me, sharp edge first."

"Hell, that had to hurt." She leaned closer, narrowing her eyes.

"Seven stitches."

She pointed to another scar, lower on his torso. "What's that from?"

He shrugged and pulled his shirt closed. "Something from when I was a kid." He chugged his beer and refilled the cup.

She sighed. "Something you want to talk about?"

Liam looked at her. Her head wobbled a little. She was probably more than halfway to sloshed.

Setting her beer down, she pulled up the back of her shirt with the hand in the cast. "My asshole husband used to like to swing his belt at me when he got pissed at life."

He looked at the red scar that resembled his. She was too beautiful to deserve that. Too strong to put up with it. "Sorry."

She dropped the edge of her shirt and picked up her cup. "He's dead. I'm alive. Guess I won that fight."

He struggled to catch his breath. "Yeah, guess you can look at it that way." Like a lioness, she bore her scars with pride.

She sat silently.

The urge to confide in her built like steam in Gram's pressure cooker. "My stepfather had a mean streak."

She looked down then shook her head. "Fucking no good rat bastard."

"Yep." Liam took a slug of beer. "He's all that and then some." He let the memories go. "No big deal."

"Yes, it's a big deal." Her gray eyes stared into his. "You still see him?"

"Naw. My grandparents pulled me out of there. Saved me, I guess." He looked down into his beer, wondering about his brother who had stayed behind.

"That's why I never had kids with Judd. I knew he'd be a shitty father." She shivered and some of her beer sloshed over the rim.

Liam's heart skipped a beat. The lioness without cubs. Sad, she would have made a great mother, too. "Some men shouldn't even be allowed around kids."

Grace leaned toward him, their shoulders touching. "Aw, kid. It'll get better." She tipped her head up and smiled at him.

Damn, she was lovely and kind and... Before he knew what he was doing, he leaned down and pressed his lips to hers.

Soft and warm, she kissed him back with a tiny moan.

“Shit.” She scrambled back from him, her beer cup hitting a step and tumbling down to the ground, spreading alcohol abuse in its wake. She stared at him, wide-eyed. “What the fuck do you think you’re doing?” Her face contorted into a frown. Hauling back, she smacked him in the face. “Damn you!”

His beer went flying, landing between his legs, sloshing beer on the stairs. “Sorry, I...” What? He wasn’t sorry. Massive pressure grew down low, in his Wranglers. The swelling was becoming unbearable.

Liam looked at Grace, his jaw tense, his body primed with wanting this woman. He growled.

She blinked a couple times, her face losing its ferociousness. Her mouth dropped open and her lip quivered. “You make me want...”

Letting out a sharp cry, she grabbed his shirt in her fists and shoved him backward. His shoulders hit the porch. Her mouth moved, but no words came out.

He didn’t dare move.

As she ripped his shirt apart, buttons popped and bounced along the sloping porch.

Her mouth pushed so hard into his lips, it was nearly painful, but what a sweet pain, it hurt so good.

She rose from the kiss and a drop of saliva fell from her chin down onto his chest. The moonlight behind her gave her a predatory look.

Grace ripped open her flannel shirt, exposing

her bare, tan breasts to the cool night air. Her nipples hardened immediately. So aroused, and he hadn't even touched her. Yet.

He lifted his hands and she slapped them away.

"Oh damn, Liam." Before he could say a word, she plunged her tongue down his throat, shoving his head back onto the wood planks.

Despite the way her aggressiveness caused physical pain, Liam let his body enjoy the bittersweet ecstasy. Blood flooded immediately to the pulsing member in his jeans.

With her shirt half-open and her nipples begging to be tasted, she stood astride him and pulled her pants down to her thighs.

Her small, calloused hands took his big hands, guiding them to where her jeans had caught on her athletic thighs. She forced him to rip them down her legs, a pleasure he would have enjoyed even without her guidance.

He lifted one leg, then the other out of her jeans and plain white underwear, exposing her beautiful body and the sweet juices already flowing down between her thighs.

Her gray eyes piercing into his, she licked her lips. "I'm going to smother you with my lust."

Before he could toss her jeans aside, she crouched down over Liam's face.

Her sweet taste enraged the blood flow to the rock steel needing to be freed.

Grabbing the back of his head off the porch, she shoved him hard into the begging sex between her legs.

Not sure of what he was doing, he fought back nervous anticipation, opened his mouth, and bared his tongue, pressing it outward to be her saddle.

Feverishly, she began rocking, slowly at first as she felt the tip of his tongue caressing both holes lightly. Increasing the length of her movement, he glanced a lick over her swelling clit. It hardened to the point where he could feel it throbbing on his tongue.

Even with no experience, Liam suddenly knew exactly what to do. He grasped it with his lips and began sucking wildly, never letting up, pleasing her over and over and over again.

His jaw felt like it might break from the pressure of her grinding herself into a frenzy on top of him.

Sweet juices came from her, dribbling down his throat before he could even swallow.

All he could think about was how turned on he was by her confidence, her expressing her need in so physical a manner.

This empowerment of hers, taking exactly what she wanted from him, nearly pushed him over the edge into a climax. How had this gorgeous woman, a goddess long forgotten, lived without a man in her life for so long?

Liam submitted to her every nuance, the harder she pushed down, the faster he would push back. When she tilted her hips forward, pressing his face into her glorious opening, he forced his tongue from his mouth, as deep as he could get inside her.

Could he get so deep, he could find her deepest pleasure point? He groaned, imagining the wicked satisfaction.

Her slow grind suddenly became an eight-second ride, she bucked, ground, shoved, and thrust while low growls came from her throat.

The motion of her hips moving backward and forward became so fast, he thought she might spin off of his face.

She panted hard, fast, the echoes of her moans so loud, they rattled the windows of the old house.

He'd never felt as empowered, as sexually high as he did right this second, giving her everything she needed, but in the back of his mind, he imagined it was Amanda.

She ground into him hard and fast, he rolled his tongue around so quickly, his mouth almost went limp.

When every part of her body tensed up in one instantaneous shift, her contractions expanded and tightened around his tongue.

She came, then, hard and wild, and her body shuddered on his face for long moments.

Liam could no longer contain himself. He grabbed her by the hips and threw her off his face.

She landed on her hands and knees, doggie style, favoring the wrist with the cast on it and looking back at him. He'd never seen a more beautiful specimen of pure feminine bliss. Her smile looked angelic, her eyes filled with primal fulfillment.

Stumbling to his feet, seeing stars from the blood flow returning to his face, he automatically unbuttoned his pants and pushed his jeans down to his ankles. No time to take off his boots, so the jeans would stay right there.

It hadn't been like this with Kaylee or Maureen. He worked at his shirt, his hands shaking, almost as if he was a virgin again.

The excitement pounded inside him and his eagerness to please her became overwhelming. So overwhelming, he couldn't catch a conscious thought as he tugged off his shirt.

As he fumbled to free his turgid member from his briefs, she posed, picturesque, not moving, watching him with anticipation in her eyes, waiting.

Her juices flowed so freely, they dripped from her beautiful nether lips.

The way she stared at him, Liam lost his confidence. He'd only done this once. It had been magnificent, but could he please this wildcat of a woman? He had to try.

Taking a step toward her, his foot caught in the jeans pooled around his ankles and he tripped, falling hard onto the porch next to her.

Their gazes met. She let out a loud, tinkling laugh.

He couldn't help but chuckle at his clumsiness. For a moment, the trance was broken.

Grace set her hand on his cheek. "You ain't done yet, boy." She laughed again, stood, and helped him to his feet, her small frame stronger than he'd imagined, controlling him like he was her pet.

She grabbed his broad six-foot, three-inch body and backed him against the table, then with another shove, threw him against the wall, his body leaning back over a narrow table. She held him by the neck like a woman on a mission.

She looked down his body, saying nothing about his large member, in fact, she said nothing at all out loud. When her gaze locked with his, her eyes said everything: fire, hunger, intensity, the starvation of needing him inside her.

The table that sat between Liam and the wall braced his backside just enough for her to climb up, mount him almost like they were attempting midair sex.

Her little frame straddled him, one foot on the left side of the table, the other on the right.

Liam braced her with his big hands, holding onto her at the small of her back.

Hanging in mid-air, only supported by her feet and Liam's hands, she plunged every single inch of her slick opening onto him at once.

Incredible sensations blared through his torso, shimmering hot and wild along his limbs. The urge to release everything into her in that one quick thrust spun his brain. It took everything inside him to refrain from giving in to his own orgasm.

Once he slid inside her as far as she could take him, there was no soft movement. She lifted herself and pounded down hard, taking him balls deep with every single thrust.

Her hands grasped around his throat, the cast digging into him, as if collaring him as her own. She moved relentlessly, taking every inch every time. Driving him into a frenzy, she stared at him, watching as his eyes rolled back into his head.

In this hypnotic state, all he could hear was the slapping sounds of her body, forcefully driving down onto him over and over and over again.

She screamed so loud and powerful, the sound made a tympani of white noise that lasted so long, it told Liam only one thing; she was having multiple orgasms.

The moments that seemed like an eternity of lust broke instantly when she raised off his thick base and squirted her long-imprisoned beautiful rain all over his chest.

Liam came to, out of his trance. Holy shit, he'd made her do that with just his shaft? The knowledge he'd done something so exotic fueled his desire and flooded his body with adrenaline. He picked up her small frame and placed her, doggy style, on the table.

She propped herself up, her ass high in the air, bracing herself, almost as if this wasn't her first rodeo on that table.

"I want you to put your two middle fingers into me, and I want you to do it hard and I want to you to do it fast, and I don't want you to stop." Her definitive directions told Liam he had better follow them.

Regaining his confidence, a smirk split his face. Even though the words weren't exchanged, he knew exactly what Grace wanted. And he knew a swelling of pride that he could give it to her.

Chapter Ten

Liam was not gentle as he plunged his fingers, over and over again, into Grace's wet pool. On her hands and knees on the porch table, she panted like she'd run a marathon.

His hard, fast motions made her legs shake uncontrollably. "Liam, damnit, Liam." Her words came out a shrill cry.

Almost instantly, massive amounts of fluid began to expel from the beautiful lips between her thighs.

Her rain fell so hard onto the table that it sounded like a downpour, flooding everywhere, down her calves, off her toes, dripping onto the floorboards.

Liam backed away a few inches, watching her gush. His jaw dropped, his eyes opened wide. Had he just died and gone to heaven? This ability he had, to give women this extreme pleasure, was something he knew would define his life. Why him? How had he been gifted with this powerful skill?

It took Grace a few seconds to regain her composure after her wild, hard orgasm. With a cry, she leapt off the table and sank to her knees in front of him, wrapping her lips around his shaft.

Yes, this was truly heaven. Trying to plunge every inch of Liam's hungry manhood as deep inside her mouth as it would go, she seemed as frustrated as he was that he wouldn't slide past her tonsils.

The force with which she sucked him, and the tug and jerks she performed with her hands at the same time, caused him to climax so hard, she couldn't swallow it all.

As the last drop drained out of him, he became lightheaded and fell back a step, tripping over his jeans again. He stumbled sideways, his pants hobbling him.

As his feet grappled for purchase on the steps, he reached for the railing but missed. The wood, slickened by the spilled beer, sent his feet flying out from under him. He found himself airborne, hitting the ground hard, his bare ass in the air.

Even with the wind knocked out of him, he couldn't help but force an embarrassed laugh from his lungs.

When he rolled onto his side, his small-framed lioness loomed over him, licking her lips with a prideful smile for the prey she had just devoured.

Reaching her small hand to him, she helped him up and they both laughed.

"We're lucky you survived that, son." She placed her palms on his chest.

As Liam pulled her in close, wrapping his arms around her in a soul-healing hug, he let the words flow from his brain to his tongue. "What the hell just happened?"

She laughed softly. "I can't believe it, either. That's only the second time I've squirted." Tipping her head back, she kissed his chin. "I'll be right back." She pushed out of his arms, jogged up the steps, grabbed her clothes, and scurried into the house.

Liam pulled up his briefs and sat on a dry step. He tugged off his boots and jeans and smacked at the denim, ridding them of the dust and dirt they'd accumulated in his ignominious fall. In the midst of everything that had just happened, for some reason, Amanda played strong on Liam's mind.

Behind him, the screen door squeaked, catapulting his mind back to the farm as a soft puff sounded and a breeze blew over his back.

He turned to see Grace in a long T-shirt, making a bed for them out of blankets and pillows.

Liam had imagined she'd invite him inside, up to her bed, but this worked. Before he could stand, she went back inside, and came out with an armful of candles.

She set them down, circling their makeshift bed as he laid his jeans over the railing and climbed the steps. Handing him a book of matches, she smacked his butt. "Help me, lazy ass"

"Yes, ma'am." He grinned as he bent to light the dozen candles in jars. Was this how she lit her house? Using candlelight to keep costs down? When he finished, he just stood watching her. The last fifteen minutes would forever replay in his memory.

She snuggled down onto the pile of blankets and patted the spot beside her. "Too late to be shy now."

He lay next to her, turning to face her. Something niggled at his subconscious. What had she said? "You squirted once before?"

Rolling onto her back, she sighed and stared at the porch ceiling. "It was right after Thanksgiving." Her lips curled down in a frown. "I don't know why I remember that, but my husband had been gone since Labor Day, and I didn't think I'd ever see him again." She remained silent for a few minutes.

Liam wanted to reach out, hold her, but the thought of her slapping his hands away stopped him cold. He waited.

"Judd was sick." She glanced at him. "I suppose Travis told you?"

"Yes. He mentioned your husband passed away."

She rolled her head again, staring at that same spot on the porch roof. "Last summer, he found out his cancer was inoperable. Terminal. I'd mentioned how violent he could become, but he was also a selfish bastard."

"The life insurance?" He said it quietly, needing her to know she didn't have to say the words out loud.

Grace turned on her side to face him, her palm resting between her cheek and the pillow. "Yep, he cashed in every penny and disappeared the beginning of September. Drove off one day in our truck, and never looked back."

Liam would have liked to kick the fucker's ass for her.

"At the time, I thought it was the best thing that had ever happened to me. The farm was paid off. Our hired man, Buck Waya, worked for practically nothing, and I had enough revenue coming in from the livestock that I could live comfortably."

He waited, needing to hear her story, wanting to understand this complicated woman.

She let out a quick laugh. "Here I'm pouring out my whole life history, and you're wondering why I don't just get to the point, right?"

Liam reached out and skimmed his hand from her shoulder to her wrist, pulling back when he touched the cast. "I'm not goin' anywhere. Talk as long as you'd like, Grace."

A soft smile curled her lips and she blinked a few times. "You're a good kid, Liam." She swallowed hard. "Anyway, Buck and I took up with each other and I kinda fell for the guy. He's a Native American, and has a way about him." She looked dazed. "I don't know. He just attracted me like no one ever had."

Liam glanced at his jeans, hanging over the railing. The photograph he'd found sat tucked in his pocket. That must have been Buck Waya with Grace.

"Right after Thanksgiving, this huge storm rolled in, and he built this elaborate lean-to by the river. Something about water and lightning, sun and moon awakening...I don't remember it all." She pulled a blanket over herself, up to her neck. "It was almost surreal, you know? He was so confident that we were in love, and he swore that somehow, something in this ceremony would prove our 'true love'." Her eyes narrowed. "He explained it as just a legend, but said he'd found clues in his great grandfather's belongings that proved it was real. He called them, The People, and evidently they've been performing this ritual for generations. There are psychics, mystics, in one line of the tribe, the men only. They're called The Givers, and the ceremony they perform is called The Rain Ceremony."

"You believe in all that?" Not that Liam could dispute strange phenomena.

"At first, I thought he was just trying to impress me, but there was something in the air. I can't explain it. We performed The Rain Ceremony, then he told me he loved me."

Liam stiffened. "Wait, what did you say, Rain Ceremony? Why were those words so familiar? He'd said them once, hadn't he? Blurred from alcohol and bone-melting satisfaction, he couldn't focus on it. "What was it like? The ceremony?"

"You know, I fell into such a trance I barely remember it." Grace sat up and pulled her knees to her chest, wrapping her arms around her legs as she stared out over the farm. "Then something snapped, and everything changed for me."

Liam's heart rate sped. Shit, this sounded a lot like what Kaylee had told him.

"In that moment, I knew I loved my husband. The shithead motherfucker who'd left me, cashed in his insurance policy, and was living in Las Vegas." She chuckled, a sour sound. "More like dying there."

"What did it feel like? After you released your rain, I mean?" Her story came too close to what he'd gone through that night with Kaylee.

She turned her head, looking at him. "I remember some strange dream, like a vision of the future. Now that I think of it, yeah, it came to me like a roadmap of what I needed to do. I just felt freed. Then, all of a sudden, it was morning, the storm had passed, the sun was out." Her brows rose. "So strange, like a time warp." She blinked. "Anyway, I left that day for Vegas."

"How did you know he was there?"

She lay down again, facing him. "He'd sold the truck, and the paperwork came here."

Liam's stomach knotted. This story paralleled Kaylee's. Too damn closely.

Grace's eyes drifted shut. "I found Judd in a roach-infested hotel, barely alive. I brought him back here, hired nurses to take care of him, got him the pain meds he needed." A tear slipped from her eye and trailed over the bridge of her nose. "He died just before Christmas."

She must have spent a lot of money to do that for him. Grace looked like she could fall asleep at any minute. "What happened to your hired man?"

Blowing out a breath, she snuggled deeper into the pillows. "He went a little crazy. I had to get the sheriff involved, get a restraining order, have

Judd's cousin—Travis's dad—come and threaten to shoot him if he didn't leave the place." Grace sucked in a choppy breath. "It wasn't good, and Buck is still holding a grudge." She shrugged one shoulder. "Or in love with me, or obsessed with me, or some kind of bullshit. He comes creeping around here once in a while, and I fire off a shotgun round or two to chase him off, but..."

She let out a long sigh. "After all this happened, I did some research on the ritual. I asked some friends who are members of the tribe. Evidently, if the mystic doesn't see certain signs, certain clues or roadmarks, he isn't supposed to do the ritual."

"Why? What happens?"

"No one would tell me." She yawned. "Sounded like something so bad, no one would ever talk about it. But if the ritual is done right, between the right people, it causes their love to grow into true love." Her eyes slowly drifted shut. "Crazy stuff, huh?"

Before she fell asleep, before the beer buzz wore off, Liam wanted to tell her what was stuck in his brain. "I'd like to stay, Grace. The rest of the weekend. So maybe we can talk more." He wanted to tell her what had happened to him with Kaylee, see what she thought.

Her eyes popped open. "I'd like that. Too much, I think." Reaching out, she ran her calloused fingertips over his cheek. "You need to go tomorrow morning."

Grasping her hand in his, he kissed her palm. "Let me stay a while."

"Liam." She squeezed his hand. "You're young, wild, and free. You need to get back to your life." Suddenly, she froze. "I sense a war within you. A fight between good and evil."

"What?" The wild look in her eyes turned his body cold.

"Be careful which you feed, wolf cub." Her voice came like an echo from another century.

Something stirred inside him, awakening flashes of memories, thoughts, visions that were not his own. Tribal conflict, fire, blood.

Grace's long breaths told him she'd fallen asleep, but Liam lay wide-eyed, trying to recapture the fleeting revelations.

****

His phone rang, startling Liam awake. He felt for his phone but his eyes wouldn't open. Bright light, warm on his face, bored painfully through his eyelids, past his eyeballs, and into his brain. Hell, how many beers had he downed last night? Liam grunted, "What?"

"Buddy, I'm ten minutes away." Travis's voice came through the phone. "Shit, I'm sorry. I didn't realize you never made it home until this morning."

Liam visored his hand over his eyes before opening them and sitting up. He was alone on the porch. Licking his dry lips, he looked around for Grace. He needed to say goodbye before Trav got here.

"Okay, I'll start walking." Liam disconnected.

Liam stood. "Hell." His jeans flew like a freak flag on the step railing. His shirt lay on the ground on the other side of the porch. The keg floated in the water from the melted ice. "Great."

He pulled on his pants, socks, and boots, balled up the blankets and pillow, and knocked on the door. Nothing. "Grace?" He knocked again and looked in the window. "Grace, I want to tell you how much last night meant to me."

Nothing.

"I want to come back, even if we just talk." He didn't have a pen or paper, besides the photo of her, and he wasn't giving that up. "I'll call you." He dropped the bundle behind a plant stand and stomped down the steps. Picking up his shirt, he headed for the barn to grab his bag and a new shirt with buttons.

Toting both duffle bags, he walked up to the house again and looked in every window. No movement. He hefted the bags on his shoulders and walked to the end of the driveway then turned toward town.

Travis pulled up a couple minutes later, Liam tossed the bags in the back seat and slid into the passenger seat, avoiding his friend's gaze.

After a few seconds, Travis smacked his palm on the steering wheel. "I'm a shitty friend, huh? Leaving you here. With *her*."

****

Travis stared at Liam. "You okay?" Liam's red eyes and blotchy face looked like ten miles of bad road.

His friend pulled at his seatbelt. "Rough night."

"I bet. When did she grab you?"

Liam jerked his head to look at him. "What?" He shook his head. "Oh, right away. We cleaned up the barn, had a beer." Liam shrugged. "She's not so bad."

Travis laughed. "For a batshit crazy woman." He u-turned the truck, hit the gas, and kicked up dirt. His dad constantly yelled at him for beating his truck, but Travis didn't care. If he blew the engine, his mom would just buy him a new one.

Liam almost smiled.

"Come on, man. I'm sorry I left you."

"How'd you know I was here?" Liam ran his fingers through his hair.

"She called my dad this morning." Travis had listened to his old man lecture the whole time he'd gotten dressed, found his truck keys, and left for Juniper.

Liam sat silently for a long time. "How'd that go?" Now his friend had a real smile.

"Like an ice pick to the brain." His dad had even threatened to ground him. Ridiculous. He was fucking seventeen.

"You deserve it." Liam turned the volume on the radio up a few notches. Country music filled the cab.

An old song Travis had heard a few times. "Yeah, I deserve it."

Liam leaned forward, listening to the words.

Was his buddy starting to like country? Garth Brooks could do that to you. Garth crooned about a woman alone on a farm, seducing her young summer-hired man.

Liam picked up the tune, hummed along, then sang with the chorus, a smile on his face.

"Buddy, you have a great voice."

Liam looked at him, his face turning red, his eyes shifting.

Travis laughed. "Don't be embarrassed. You've got talent."

"Talent." He turned the down the volume. "Talent for making a mess out of my life." He stared out the passenger window.

"Yeah, shit. Here I thought a few days away from everything at home, would help. But instead, I leave you stuck with a crazy woman."

"It's not your fault, man." Liam ran a hand through his hair. "I don't know what to think anymore. It's like the universe has got me in its crosshairs and is shooting karma bullets at me."

Reaching into the back seat, Travis hauled a plastic bag forward and dumped it on Liam's lap. "I stopped at the gas station and got you breakfast."

Liam pulled out donuts, sausage sticks, and a Mountain Dew. "Thanks." He twisted the cap off the Dew and chugged.

"Amanda said to say hi." Travis glanced at his friend, watching for his reaction.

Liam choked and dribbled soda down his chin. "Amanda?" He coughed a few times. "Oh, yeah, right. That redhead you liked."

Travis gritted his teeth so hard they squeaked. *Yeah, Amanda.* The redhead who'd remembered Liam's name. But not his.

Chapter Eleven

When they pulled up at the Jackson farm, Liam jumped out of Travis's truck and opened the back door, reaching in for his bag. "See you."

"Hey." Travis leaned over the seat. "Really sorry I left you, bro."

Liam nodded. "It happens." He shut the door and walked toward the house.

His grandmother sat on the porch, a bowl of asparagus in her lap. "You're home early, sweetie. Didn't expect you 'til tomorrow." She snapped the bottom off a spear and tossed it into a paper bag on the floor as she set the good part in a bowl on the table.

Tossing his bag toward the screen door, Liam sat in the rocking chair on the other side of the table from her. "What, did you and Gramps have a wild Saturday night planned?" He stole a spear. "I can make myself scarce." He chomped it into pieces and chewed, then went back for another one.

She gave a quick laugh and slapped at his hand. "No, your grandpa and I may share a bed, but it's all sleepin' and no sparkin'."

He laughed. "Sparkin'? I haven't heard that one before." It reminded him of the song he'd heard on the radio. The one that nearly brought tears to his eyes, remembering how Grace had jumped him. Like she hadn't eaten in a month, and he was a juicy slab of ribs.

"Are you a fan of Garth Brooks, Grams?" He snuck another asparagus spear when she wasn't looking. It grew wild in the old cemetery down the road apiece, and she spent hours there in the spring, cleaning the old headstones and picking asparagus.

"Who isn't?" She shifted her milky blue eyes toward him. "Besides you?"

"Do you have any of his records? Eight-tracks? Cassette tapes?"

"I'll have you know, upstart..." She tipped up her chin. "I have Garth's greatest hits on CD."

He held up his hands. "Wow. I should have known you'd be up to date with your technology."

She shook her head and snapped another piece of asparagus. "Not really. We have a CD player in the truck, so I can only listen when we drive."

Liam would love to buy her a CD player. Some day. The music on Liam's iPod, the one he'd stolen at the age of twelve, was old hip-hop from his city days. He didn't have the money to buy every new song that came out. He'd have to ask Travis to copy the CD onto his iPod for him. The guy would gloat like a fool, but Liam wanted to hear more of Garth's music.

"I'll get it for you when we go in. You can sit in the truck and listen." Grams smiled and stacked her empty bowl under the full one.

They rocked for a few moments and Liam thought about the legend Grace had shared with him. The ceremony, what had she said it was called? The Flower? No, The Rain Ceremony. A foggy memory of saying those words to Maureen came back to him. It all seemed too random to be anything more than a coincidence, but he had to know for sure. "Grams, what nationality are we?"

She stopped rocking for a couple seconds. "Well, your grandfather is English and Scottish. I'm a little German, a little Scottish, some Irish, and I think that's it. Your mother, bless her heart..." Grams's chair rocked faster.

Liam remembered the fights Grams and his mom would have about the asshole Mom had married when Dad died.

"Your mother's people are new arrivals. They came from somewhere in Eastern Europe in the '40s, from some country, I don't remember which."

That left them out. It couldn't have been his mother's side of the family who had Native American blood.

She glanced at him. "Why the questions?"

"I don't know. I've been wondering if maybe some of our ancestors mingled with the locals."

Her chair stopped again. "Oh yeah?" She got to rocking faster. "Liam, what's going on with you lately? You don't seem yourself." She focused on him.

"Just everything at once, I guess. Amand…I mean, Kaylee and other stuff."

"Personal stuff? You know you can tell me anything, Liam. I won't judge you. I'll give you advice, because Lord knows I can't help myself." She rolled her eyes heavenward.

Liam chuckled. "Your advice has always been good." Some things though, he couldn't tell her.

"We all have secrets." She took his hand in hers, the blue veins standing out under her thin skin. "But having someone to talk to is better medicine than any psychologist could prescribe."

He had to wonder what secrets she had. "I'll try to work through this before I unload my soul on you."

She smiled, a little sad. "It's going to be tough leaving high school and going to college. But you'll still be here every night. There's always a place for you."

Liam's breath caught. His first night here, after she picked him up from the police station, she'd told him that. "I know, Grams. And if I don't say thank you enough, know that I feel it every minute in my heart."

Her lip quivered and her eyes filled with moisture. "Liam, you're a poet."

"Yeah, well, this poet had better get his valedictory address written for Friday, or the graduating class will be hearing me ramble on about nothing." He tried to let go of her hand, but she hung on tight.

"I'm sorry we can't have a graduation party for you, son." She frowned and her eyes glistened.

He gently squeezed her hand. "I don't need a party. I told you that. I'll go to everyone else's, eat a ton of sub sandwiches and cake, and watch all the other guys' grandmothers put lipstick kisses all over their faces.

Grams laughed. "I'm still going to put lipstick kisses all over you Friday night, you know."

"I'd be disappointed if you didn't." He helped her from her chair and picked up the bowls and trash bag. "I need to get looking for a summer job, too." He'd probably end up driving halfway to Nashville to find anything at this late date.

"Oh, I forgot to tell you." Grams opened the screen door for him. "I talked to Travis's grandmother. Her nephew owns the Pump and Run, you know."

Liam walked in the door, setting the bowls on the counter. "Yeah?"

Grams smiled. "There's an opening. I told her you'd be interested."

His brows dropped. His grandmother got him

a job? Aw, hell, the Pump and Run...Kaylee's old job.

"You don't want it?" His grandma put the bowl of asparagus in the sink.

"No, I do want it. It's just..." Their gazes locked.

"I know, Liam. Kaylee worked there." She turned on the faucet and rinsed the vegetables. "Take it for now, and when something else opens—"

"Thank you." He spun her to face him and planted a smooch on her cheek. "If they hire me, I'll stay there all summer." He briefly thought taking Kaylee's old job should bother him more than it did. He bent to her eye level. "You're so good to me, Grams." His heart shuffled up his throat. "Love you."

"Liam...." she looked like she would say more, then patted his cheek with wet fingers. Her smile seemed forced. "I love you too, Liam, sweetie. Now go write your valedictory talk and do us proud."

Liam shuffled along the hallway. If only he could live by those words.

Crazy things have been happening in my life lately. It seems like, for some reason, a girl I don't know is always on my mind. Why? I can't really feel anything like what I felt for Kaylee before. Why?

I want to get this down right now so I don't forget it. Rain Ceremony? Givers, I think? Obsession? What does all of this mean? True love... Is it real, or am I just exaggerating these thoughts in my head. It's kind of strange that even while I was with Grace having this wild crazy sex, all I could think about was this Amanda chick. Come to think about it, when I was with Maureen, all I could think about was Kaylee. Spring rain scent? True love. What does it really mean?

Late Friday night, Liam sat on his bed, holding the graduation gift his grandparents had presented to him. A camera with a video recorder built in. He read the directions as he waited for the battery pack to charge.

To disable the recording indication light... So, he could disable the light if he wanted to record someone without them knowing it. Like... "Ah, fuck." Amanda's face, her scent, that hot link between them, flooded his brain, sending urges rolling through him, pulsing blood low into his groin.

He could record the sex, see if he spoke those words again. He adjusted his jeans to fit his swelling member. He could watch what it looked like when she squirted. Damn. It was Friday night. What was he doing sitting at home? He went to grab his phone off his desk, but sat down instead. Amanda weighed heavy on his mind.

Saturday morning, Liam started his training at the gas station. He'd be working the afternoon shift, starting the following week. At two that afternoon, the manager told him to grab one of the hot dogs off the rolling warmer for his lunch.

Liam shook his head. "Thanks, but I brought something to eat." He walked out to his car, which was parked on the side of the building, for his half-hour break.

Tara jumped out of the pickup parked next to

the Malibu. “Hi, Liam.”

“Hey.” Holy shit. How long had she been out here waiting for him?

Standing close, she smiled up at him. “I never gave you my phone number.”

He set his hands on her shoulders. “I’m glad you stopped by, then.” He wasn’t going to kiss her in public like this. “I’ve only got a half hour.”

“I don’t mind sitting in your car watching you eat.”

He laughed. “You want to sit in my car and watch me eat?”

She giggled, her eyes jerking around. “Sounds like more fun than getting drunk at home.”

Hell, she was odd. They slid into his car and he reached in the cooler and pulled out the sandwich Grams had made for him. “Bite?” He held the triangle out to her.

Tara leaned toward him and bit off a corner. “Mmm. Tuna salad.” She licked her lips.

His least favorite. He smelled it. Whenever money was really short, his grandma switched from bologna to canned tuna. The camera they’d bought for him had probably set them back a few bucks.

“What did you get for graduation?” She grinned.

“A camera and a stereo.” Travis had spent a few bucks too, giving him a fancy stereo system. He would have refused it, but Grams was so thrilled to be able to play CDs in the house, he’d accepted the gift. “How about you?”

“I got new tires for my truck.” She rolled her eyes. “Just what an eighteen-year-old girl wants.”

He laughed. “Could have been worse.”

“I don’t know how.” She leaned over the

console. “I have a present for you, Liam.”

“Oh yeah?” He leaned closer. “Something kinky?” He didn’t know why that came out of his mouth.

She blinked a few times. “Kinky, like naughty? Bad-ass naughty?”

What was she trying to tell him? “Like up-the-ass naughty?”

Her cheeks turned red. “Maybe up the ass. Are you into that?”

He blew out a breath. “I don’t...”

“Because if you are, I know some girls who are into that.”

“What?” Wasn’t she just offering him sex? And now she was offering to find anal partners for him?

“If you want...” She shrugged. “I know some really freaky girls.”

Tara the farm girl knew freaky girls? Hard to believe. But maybe, if she was serious, she’d be willing to help him find some girls who wouldn’t mind being recorded during sex. “I’m looking for girls—women—to help me with some experimenting.”

Tara nodded. “Okay. Like what kind of experimenting?”

“I want to record them. And me. Together.” He watched for her reaction.

She smiled. “Oh yeah, I know some people who are into that. When do you want to do it?”

He couldn’t believe she really would do that for him. “My grandparents are visiting relatives out of town Saturday night.”

Tara reached for the door handle. “Okay. I’ll ask around.” She slid out of the car. “The present I have for you is a bottle of JD." She reached into her truck and pulled out a long brown bag and handed it to him. "But I'll still help you find women to record, Liam." She winked at him. "'Cause it's kinda kinky."

Jumping into her truck, her smile went a little wild. She tore out of the parking lot, laying rubber.

"What the hell had just happened?" Was she really that freaky, or did he plant some kind of suggestion in her mind?

****

Saturday night, Liam sat home watching a show on TV. He'd been invited to go to the movies and out to a dance with Travis and a blind date he'd set up for Liam, but he had to buckle down and save every penny he could, so his grandparents didn't have to live on a diet of canned tuna to pay for Liam's education.

Lights shone through the living room window as a car drove up to the house.

He got up and turned off the TV, then walked to the door and opened it.

A short girl stepped up onto the porch in four-inch heels and a leather mini-dress. She looked like she was about his age, but he'd never seen her before. "Holy shit."

She fastened her gaze on Liam, her eyes an unreal green in her golden skin. She'd spiked her short, black hair around her head and her ruby lips curled into a smile. "Are you the guy who works at the Pump and Run?" She looked him up and down.

He swallowed. "Uh, yeah?"

"Tara sent me."

His jaw dropped. Tara. "Really?" Who was Tara, if she hung out with people like this? Definitely not the shy girl she behaved like in school.

The leather-clad female walked right up to him. "Only got an hour, honey. Let's get busy."

His pulse became rapid. "Yeah, okay." He stepped back, letting her in, closed the door, and stared at her.

Looking around the house, she pivoted on her heels. "Cute place."

Everything in the house was old, worn, but immaculately clean.

She swung to face him. "Where are we going to do this?"

"This?"

Sucking in a breath, she looked heavenward. "We're having sex, right?"

His body jerked to life. "Yes. Sex. Yes." He pointed down the hall. "First door on the right."

She swung around and sashayed down the hall, her whole body writhing and sexy.

He followed her and she sat on his bed. "Is this your place? Your farm?"

Shaking his head, he said, "Yes?"

She laughed. "Not sure, huh?" Crossing her legs, she grabbed one of her shoes, then looked up at him. "On or off?"

Liam stared at the shoes for a moment. "Leave them on."

Her smile turned wicked as she ran her hand from her ankle up the inside of her leg to rest just under the hem of her skirt. "I like kinky."

Hell, that did it. Liam was going to use the next sixty minutes like it was his last hour on Earth. He walked to her, standing directly over her. She was a tiny little thing compared to him.

She looked up into his face. "What do you want to do, big guy?"

"Tara explained everything to you? If she didn't, I'm wanting to record sex."

Her eyes dropped and she grinned. "Are you sure?" She shook her head. "I don't know."

Taking her chin between his finger and thumb, he tipped her head up. "I promise you'll enjoy it."

She placed her hand on the bulge in his jeans. "I'm sure I will."

"Wow." Tara wasn't lying. She did know some kinky chicks. Unless there was something else going on here. "I think it's best that we don't tell each other our names." Liam looked at her face, waiting for her response.

"Okay. I like that." Her words whispered through her sexy lips.

Something in the back of his mind warned that her acquiescence had come too easily. Shouldn't there be awkwardness between two complete strangers? The vibe he got from this girl said she was way too comfortable. Then his thoughts flew to the video camera. "Let me get set up."

In seconds, he had the tripod at the right height, and his camera locked into place.

The woman slapped her small hands on her well-toned thighs. "How do we get started?"

Liam grinned at her eager excitement. "I think we should start by turning on the power button."

They both laughed as he fumbled with the tripod. He turned his back to his anonymous friend, as he struggled to steady his suddenly trembling hand. Was he really going to do this? It felt a little surreal.

He tightened all three tripod legs, arranging them on the scratched wooden floor, and pressed the button on his camera. If everything went right, it wouldn't be long now before he'd be watching himself shout out those strange words.

Nothing happened with the camera. He popped the lens cap free, pressed the button again, but still no action.

"So, where..." He started to make small talk, but what could he ask someone he wanted to stay anonymous with?

"What was that?" Her voice came from the direction of the bed.

"Ah, nothing. I think we're about ready." Liam turned and nearly tripped over his own feet.

She sat on the bed completely naked, except for the shoes.

Chapter Twelve

For a moment, Liam couldn't move. Who was this girl? She'd stripped bare, and now sat on his bed as if she didn't care who saw her.

Liam proceeded to explain what he wanted to do, sounding like a director in a bad porn movie.

"Okay. Whatever you want." She leaned back on the bed, spreading her legs slightly.

The bare pink softness between her legs had his groin tightening and his mouth watering. "Stay right there so I can get the lighting right." He stepped behind the camera, pressing buttons. "Now if I can just find the power button." Damn, he must look like a fool to her. "I know it's around here somewhere." Great. Stupid jokes were really not going to help this situation.

The girl stood and walked toward him on her high heels, coming around the tripod to stand beside him. "I think it's right here." She clicked a button on top of the camera. "And this one..." She turned a dial on the side. "This'll change it from camera to video." She smiled at him.

"Thanks." It felt so fucking clinical. Like he was at the doctor's office. "Want to lay on the bed again for me?"

She wagged her brows at him. "You're the director." She swung her hips as she sashayed to the bed.

Damn, five minutes ago, he had been watching baseball on TV. Now, a beautiful woman lay naked on his bed, waiting to have sex with him. Could this be a dream?

A red light on the camera told him the thing was recording. On the display, her skin looked golden, like honey, her green eyes sparkled from the fragments of the daylight bouncing off the reflection of the windowpane. He turned on the ceiling light and rechecked the camera.

He hadn't noticed her short hair had different highlights of color in it. Tara hadn't done that bad of a job selecting a woman for him.

Walking toward her, his gaze dropped to her breasts. Small and perky, no more than an A cup, tipped by pierced nipples. Perfectly proportioned for her five-foot frame.

Liam looked over every inch of her body.

She lay patiently, sure of herself, and not a bit shy.

Punk-rocker girl. That's what she'd always be to him. Inside him, a sense of arousal filled him, but not inside his pants. Embarrassment flushed through him. He was nearly flaccid. But his heart pounded so hard, the adrenaline rush was indescribable.

Everything about her seemed awkward, unfamiliar, except when he looked into her eyes. Something seemed strangely familiar.

He didn't care about the sex, and, sadly, didn't care about this girl. All he cared about was his need to find answers.

Liam leaned toward her for a kiss, but before he could get close, she twisted away and unbuttoned his pants. Unzipping him, she pulled his jeans down, almost as if she'd done this a hundred times before. His underwear followed, her hands skimming them down his thighs.

She looked up at him. "You're not even hard yet."

"Make me hard." He tested this girl, wanting to see what her breaking point would be. He waited for her to touch him, maybe kiss him.

"You got it." She lay back on the bed, spreading her legs as wide as she possibly could.

Liam stepped aside, out of the way of the camera. He was torn, knowing he had to be inside her beautiful passage to have any chance of finding the answers he was looking for. Right now, he wanted to see her pleasure herself.

His eyes darted to the video camera, then back to her completely exposed body.

Her fingers found her clit as her lips spread open wider. A glint of silver showed a loop through her labia. Pierced there, too?

Liam's mind grew more excited than his body. What did he need to do to get himself out of his brain and into her?

She rubbed herself slowly and began to moan. "You can look, but you can't touch. Not until you're hard."

His manhood contracted for a moment, wanting arousal, but his thoughts about it were immediately replaced with a checklist of things he wanted to accomplish in his hour with her.

There was no rain smell, no mystic connection, between them. Would that make a difference? He hadn't experienced the visions with Maureen or Grace. Only with Kaylee. Of course, with Amanda, there was the rain smell, too.

Shit, his first attempt at videotaping sex was not going like he'd hoped.

On the bed, she rolled her eyes, still rubbing her clit, but her enthusiasm waned. "Really? Nothing yet?"

He had to do something before she put on her clothes and left.

Grabbing the base of his shaft, Liam squeezed hard, causing the head to enlarge immediately.

She wiggled her tight bottom on his bed. "Okay. Now we're talking."

Liam placed his other hand on his shaft, too. Using two hands to stroke himself, his head continued to swell.

"You've got a big dick. I like that." Her voice came out breathy.

Looking at the video camera, making sure it was still on, he nodded. "Uh huh." He finally felt physical arousal, but could he curb his fixation on the red light of the video camera? He couldn't get it out of his head.

"Good boy. You're completely hard, aren't you." She immediately flipped onto all fours, exposing herself. Laying her head on the bed, she grabbed her ass cheeks, spreading them for him. "You can fuck me now."

Walking to the edge of the bed, Liam licked his palm and rubbed the moisture around his semi-engorged head. Without thinking, he slid his semi-hard member right into her.

"Whoa." She jerked her body forward, off his length. "Condom, big guy."

Damnit, he needed to get his mind on what he was doing. He reached for his bedside table and pulled out a foil packet. Seconds later, sheathed, he pushed back into her. She took almost every inch of him with ease, very little resistance, compared to what he'd experienced before.

Pushing back hard, she looked at him over her shoulder. "Is that all you got?"

"What?" His embarrassment at being only half-there surged hot through him. With sweat trickling down his forehead, he glanced back at the damn camera. Pushing the red light out of his mind, he pulled out and slid back into her. "Take this, woman." Liam began to pound every inch of his half-flaccid self in and out of her with each thrust. He closed his eyes, begging for his mind and body to connect, to reach his full potential. He was coming up short until he thought about Amanda; her perky breasts pressing through that apron.

The woman's breath came faster. Was she feeling the fullness, the ecstasy he gave her with each thrust? Or did her sigh mean she just wanted it to be over. In confusion, Liam decided to just commit, to use anger to reach his physical goal.

"Fuck it hard." Her eyes look unfocused. "If you can't fuck it hard, then we're done."

"You've got a dirty mouth, girl." He grabbed her hips and thrust faster, banging her ass against his hips with each push.

Grabbing handfuls of his quilt, she pressed her face into it, moaning, grunting, then shouting, "Fuck it hard."

Liam's thrusts became so fast and wild that he could hear the sound of his balls slapping as he punched his hot member into her, over and over and over again.

Beneath his feet, the old wooden floor creaked, and the bed shifted, almost lifting up off of its legs as he thrust.

The tripod began to move too, one of the legs shortening with each vibration.

"Damnit."

She tightened around him, and a hot burn raced up his spine. He wanted to come, needed the release to be able to see what happened to him.

But if the video camera fell... He drove into her, reaching for the tripod. With it almost in hand, cool air hit the end of his erection for a second. He pushed back into her, grabbing for the tripod. This time, a much tighter sensation gripped him.

She cried out with a laugh. "Yes, fuck me in the ass. That's what I like."

He glanced at her. He'd just driven eight-and-a-half inches into the wrong hole.

Reaching behind her, she grabbed his arms. "I want every inch of you. Hard. As hard as you can."

Liam's brain shot him into an orgasm so strong, the room spun around him. The sound of the camera falling registered, but as he exploded, massive amounts of warmth pulsing from him, he let his body shudder and his lungs release a low shout.

The spinning increased, and he grabbed the base of the condom, falling onto the bed next to her, and closing his eyes.

It had to be just seconds later, but when he blinked his eyes open, she wasn't next to him.

Punk rocker girl stood at the foot of the bed, putting on her clothes. "Are you going to call me so we can do this again?" She waved a shoe in the air, laughing. "You don't even know my name. How can you call me?"

Liam sat up, searching for the reason he felt so frantic. "The camera." He lunged for the edge of the bed and looked on the floor where it had dropped. The tripod was there, but the camera wasn't. He jumped up and fell to his knees, looking under the bed.

"Hey, okay, you have a good life, then." She turned and walked out the door.

"Shit." He'd offended her. "I'm sorry." He

was an ass sometimes. "Wait."

The front door closed. She was gone.

He found the camera sticking out from beneath his dresser. As he picked it up, the battery compartment flapped open. Empty. The battery must have fallen out when it hit the floor. Before he came. The most important part of this experiment hadn't been recorded. But...

"Hey, Punk Rock." He looked out his bedroom door. She could tell him if he said anything when he came.

He ran buck-naked through the house, pulling open the front door just as her car turned from the driveway onto the road. Pounding his hand on the frame, he let the depression he'd been holding off all day fill him completely. He closed the door and went to the kitchen, picking up the bottle Tara had given him.

"Great work, Liam." He unscrewed the top and took a long draw. "Another monumental Jackson screwup."

Tonight was a disaster. But it also uncovered some answers. It seems like some girls have the rain scent and others don't. Then, there's Amanda. I can't seem to get her out of my mind. I think that this video camera, if I can figure out how to use it, will be a great investigative tool. I'm not saying I'm a part of some legend, after all...I'm just Liam Jackson, but what if...can you imagine the possibility of me being something big, significant? If I have these powers, what will I do with them? Who will I become? I need more answers, but who can I trust? Travis will think I'm crazy, I can't exactly explain to my grandparents that I'm going on a sex quest to find out if I'm special. So, for now, it's just me and my video camera. Things to think about: what language am I using or what am I saying when I orgasm? Who are The People? And if Buck Waya is still around, can I find him and get more answers about the ritual and its meaning? And why am I obsessed with Amanda? True love, what does it mean…?

Monday morning, Travis showed up early for their last intramural game. A mist hung over the diamond as he trudged to the pitcher's mound. His stomach ached from holding in his anger. He'd wanted to yell back at his dad, wanted to throw his plate of eggs and bacon against the wall.

Travis wound up and threw a curve ball from halfway to the mound, hitting the backstop. Why was he solely responsible for his team not making the playoffs? Why did his dad even care whether Travis got a spot on the college baseball team? He was going to study agriculture, and going into partnership with his dad in a few years.

"I pitched my college team to a national championship, back when I was a sophomore." His old man seemed to think there was only one perfect path in life, and his dad had cut the trail.

Travis backed up three steps and threw another perfect ball. It helped to imagine his father crowding the plate and taking a ball to the solar plexus.

The ass had called in a favor at the college and a scout would be sitting in the front row, next to the dugout, watching him. He threw another one, this time aiming low, clocking the ghost of his dad in the kneecap. He turned and walked up the mound, digging into his briefs for the tin of resin his dad had given him.

“Damn him.” Why was it important to win at all costs?

After stretching his arm and throwing a few more heaters, he smeared resin on the inside of his waistband, then transferred it to his fingers. His screwball this time sunk perfectly just before crossing the plate. Yeah, he’d throw some fucking amazing balls, make his dad proud, get the attention of the scout. But what about Travis’s pride? Did he have any left?

****

Liam stood at first base. Bottom of the eighth inning, and Travis was throwing a no-hitter. Best game of his life. But he’d developed some strange new ticks. Every few throws, he’d touch his waistband then hold his hand between his stomach and his glove. Something strange was going on with that boy.

Liam gazed around the diamond. This would be the last time they played here, and it hit him hard that so much was changing in his life. He loved the game, wouldn’t mind playing it professionally one day, if his college ball career went as well as he hoped. He savored the scent of the freshly-cut grass, the warmth of the sun on his back, the murmur of the few onlookers sitting in the stands.

He'd remember this moment. The pure adrenaline of the game clearing everything else from his mind, focusing his emotions on the joy of doing something he was good at. His hard work and natural talent being noticed by his coach and teammates.

The umpire examined the last ball Travis threw as if it was questionable seafood. He blew his whistle and gestured to their coach.

The catcher stood and threw a practice ball to Travis. Liam waited for Travis to toss it to him so they could throw it around the bases, but his friend stood frozen to the spot.

Coach and the ump walked toward the pitcher's mound, followed by the catcher.

Travis turned toward Liam, his hand in his pants, then flung something onto the grassy infield.

Their gazes locked, Travis's pleading. Then his friend threw the practice ball on the ground near the object he'd dropped.

What the fuck?

Liam jogged over, and as he picked up the ball, he scooped up the circular plastic container, about the size of a fifty-cent piece.

Walking back to first, he stuck the container down inside his underwear. He didn't have to open it to see what it was.

A half-hour later, in the locker room, Liam gestured for Travis to follow him. He stepped out into the empty hall, digging out the resin. He swung around on his friend. "Are you fucking crazy? Don't you give a shit if you play ball next spring? Or any spring after that?" He tossed the container to Travis.

"Honestly? No." His buddy threw the resin into a refuse bin. "I had to put on a show today for Dad's friend, the scout." Travis made a fist, staring at the glass trophy case. "Win at all costs."

Liam leaned back against the wall, staying ready to spring if his friend went to throw a punch at the plate glass. "Your dad's pressuring you?" Liam couldn't imagine having a parent—or grandparent in his case—encouraging a kid to cheat. How screwed up did that make a man?

"Wants me to be exactly like him." Travis's voice came low and bitter.

"You've got to push back, man. You're not that way. You're not...your dad."

Travis rounded on him. "Aren't I? How do you know?" He smacked himself in the chest. "Maybe I'm okay with falsifying breeding documents. Maybe I'm happy with the way we sell underweight cattle. Maybe I don't care if we're dumping untreated waste into the river."

Liam's brows shot up. The Hackers were doing all that shit? For how long? How did they get away with it? An ache hit his chest. How long had Travis been an accomplice?

His friend deflated. "Hell, you're right. If I don't start standing up to him now..."

Liam walked to his friend and laid a hand on his shoulder. "I'm working tonight, but if you want to talk this afternoon...or come in to the Pump and Run, we can shoot the shit."

Shrugging, Travis headed for the locker room door. "I need time to think." He held open the door for Liam, glancing at him, then away. "Gotta get my mind straight first."

Liam stood a few minutes. How could Travis have let himself be badgered into polluting their time on the field? It was the one thing he loved as much as Liam did. His gut hurt for the guy, and for himself.

For the loss of his esteem for his friend, especially if Travis was part of all the illegal activities he'd accused his father of perpetrating.

Liam followed him in, the voices of their teammates echoing off the walls. "Hackers's first no-hitter!" They cheered.

Travis looked at Liam, his face tight. His head dropped, then he turned toward their teammates. "Fuck, yeah!"

Liam joined the party. Would it help Travis if he narked on him? Dug the resin out of the trash and spoke to the coach? Liam would never turn over on his friend, but there had to be some way to get him back in the right gear.

Shaking his head, he walked to his locker. As if Liam's life were anywhere near on track. He opened his locker. Light glinted off the video camera in his duffle bag. Liam's plans for the evening included one crazy-ass detour from the path of righteousness.

****

Touch your thigh. Liam narrowed his gaze on the woman in the candy aisle and repeated the silent command.

There was a half-hour left before his shift ended at the Pump and Run, and Liam should be working through the closing list, but instead, he pinpointed his focus on her. With a quick glance, he double-checked the position of the video camera, partially hidden behind a display of chips on one side of the checkout counter. The red light wasn't on, but he knew it was recording.

Her hand slid into her pocket.

Technically, she'd followed his instruction. *Back up a step.* Concentrating, he jumped when the door opened.

An older couple came in, and the woman from the candy aisle strolled up to the counter. "Just this." She set down a bag of red licorice.

He rang it up, handled the cash, then stared at her. *Put your hands on the counter.*

Smiling at him, she reached for the licorice but hesitated a second...with her hands touching the counter. She left quickly. He probably would have too, if some late-night cashier was staring at him like a mad scientist.

Liam stepped behind his camera. Still running. He pressed pause. Since his shift had started that evening, he'd been attempting to use his mind control powers—or whatever the hell they were—to make women do what he silently commanded. He couldn't wait to get home and watch the video to see if what he thought he saw was really happening.

Liam picked up the laminated list of closing duties. *Clean the slushy machine*. Gross.

A minute later, his boss, Ray, walked in, followed by a woman with red hair.

An invisible force hit Liam like a bullet train. The rain scent. That indescribable emotional allure. The undeniable attraction.

"Liam." Ray walked toward him. "Meet our new employee. Amanda just transferred here from the Rogers Corners' store."

She stepped out from behind him, her gaze locking with Liam's.

Opening his mouth, Liam had to force sound from his vocal cords. "Amanda. Hi."

Her smile turned wicked as she licked her lips. "We've met before, haven't we?" She winked.

Liam's body went jittery and hot, spiking his

blood pressure a level higher with each breath he took. “You’re Travis’s friend, right?” He spoke the reminder more for himself than for her.

She tightened her lips. “I’m looking forward to being *your* friend, too.”

He couldn’t meet her gaze. There was too much potency in her stare. “Sure.” Looking at their boss, he tried to shift his body between the man and Liam’s camera. He stayed close to the counter, though, hiding the sudden swelling behind his fly.

Ray grinned at Amanda. “Follow me. We’ll get your paperwork.” They headed for the back office.

Liam shut his eyes as he wrenched his brain off his libido and focused on his mind control project, concentrated on the new muffler he needed for the Malibu, worried about the money to buy the books he need to have for school this fall. Nothing worked. It was Amanda. Whatever pheromone she gave off made him lose his ability to function, and made him need to have her under him. Naked.

“...by tomorrow when you come in for training.” Ray’s voice drew closer.

Liam stared at the buttons on the cash register as if he could make them follow his commands.

“I’ll walk you out, show you where to park.” Ray walked past. “G’night, Liam.”

“Good night, Ray.”

Amanda glanced at Liam as she followed their boss out the door. When she blew him a kiss, Liam’s knees nearly buckled. His mind wouldn’t stay focused on the store. Glancing out the window, he watched Amanda talking to Ray. Why had she transferred here? Would she be working the afternoon shift? Would he have to see her every day? Could he keep himself from giving in to the mind-blowing urge to bend her over the checkout counter and pull up her skirt?

After she slid into her rusty blue four-door sedan, she drove past the front of the store and their gazes caught. He could swear he heard thunder somewhere in his brain. "Crazy shit." He pulled at the front of his jeans to ease the pressure. Whatever she had, it felt just like Kaylee all over again—magnified by ten.

Chapter Thirteen

When the store emptied, he rewound his camera to the last woman, the licorice one, and played it, watching closely. It'd be easier to see when he hooked it up to their TV at home.

The door opened. A gorgeous woman, maybe in her early thirties, walked in. Her black hair curled wild around her shoulders, blue-eyed gaze piercing his as she smiled at him then sauntered toward the back cooler.

Shit, the stiff one in his jeans hadn't gone down from Amanda. Now, it pointed toward this sexy momma.

Liam fast-forwarded the camera so he could get it hidden and running before she came back up front, but suddenly, she appeared in front of him.

Setting a six-pack of cold cans on the counter, she pointed to the camera. "Nice equipment."

He met her beautiful eyes, her smile soft and...welcoming? Was she interested?

She drew in a deep breath, pressing her drop-shaped breasts tighter against the fabric of her T-shirt. Her nipples pebbled, inviting him for a taste.

"It takes video, too." Some insane flash of lust made him add, "Are you into that?" Yeah, he'd do her, record it, but this time, there'd be no faulty tripod, no unfocused attention. He'd be all over her. More blood raced to his groin and his breath came faster.

She tipped her head, frowning. "Into...video recording?"

He set down the camera and leaned closer, looking right into her eyes. "You bring the beer, I'll bring the camera."

Stepping back, she held up a hand. "Are you hitting on me?" She didn't look angry, just surprised.

"You're beautiful. I'd like to take you somewhere. Get to know you better." If Liam had ever spoken a cheesier line, he couldn't remember when.

She nodded. "And record it, right?" She pulled a bill from her wallet and tossed it on the counter. "You know, Liam Jackson, I'm on the prayer chain with your grandmother." Her eyes shot flames at him. "What would she say if she knew you were behaving like this?"

As if ice water filled his veins, his lust cooled. He dropped his head. Shit. "I'm sorry. Please don't...she hasn't been feeling well." He rang up the beer and counted out her change.

She picked up the six-pack and stomped toward the door. With her hand on the glass, she turned to him. "Watch yourself, boy. You're heading for trouble." She walked out into the night and jumped into the passenger seat of a pickup.

Smacking himself on the forehead, he cussed himself, cursed his overripe libido, his newfound talents, or powers, or whatever was going on with his body. He did a quick run-through of the items on the closing list, and locked up, slinging his backpack with his camera over his shoulder.

His Malibu sat back near the stinky dumpster under a pale yellow pole light. Pulling out his keys, he touched one to the door lock.

"Hi, Liam!" A woman's voice.

He jumped about a foot, his heart hammering.

From the shadows surrounding the dumpster, Tara walked toward him.

"Jeez, woman. Scare a guy." He fought to

steady his breathing. How long had she been out here waiting for him?

She giggled. "Sorry." She leaned on his car. "How did it go with Peyton?" She'd dressed in a low-cut top that showed off her large breasts, and shorts that showed a lot of smooth skin.

"Peyton?" Did he know anyone named Peyton?

Tara's mouth dropped open. "You know, Peyton. The...my friend? Saturday night?"

Somehow that name didn't fit Punk Rock Girl. Liam narrowed his gaze on her. "What, you want details?" It wasn't going to happen.

"No, thank you." She rolled her eyes. "Did you get what you wanted? On the video, I mean?" She looked at him a little strange, like everything hinged on his answer.

He set his backpack down and leaned back next to her. "No. The damn thing fell over just before..." He crossed his arms and shrugged. "Maybe it wasn't a great idea." Especially if he ran the risk of small-town gossip reaching his grandparents.

She straightened and faced him, her eyes wide and her body tense. "You want to try it again?"

What did this nutty girl have in store for him now? "Not with someone from Liberation. Somebody a ways out."

Tara nodded. "I know the perfect person. I talked to her about you. She's interested."

Too much going on in his life right now. "I'll think about it."

"It has to be tonight." Tara looked around, as if anyone else would be standing next to a rancid-smelling dumpster. "She's an exotic dancer."

An image of long, lean muscles, toned limbs,

and a tight ass flashed through his mind. "Oh yeah?"

"She's really gorgeous. You'll love her."

"I don't know. I need to work on the irrigation pipes with my grandpa tomorrow morning." It all seemed too sudden, too convenient, too freaky. Tara setting him up with another woman? What was she getting out of this?

"Liam, say yes. She's working tonight at that place outside Rogers Corners. Sugar Cherry. I told her we'd meet her there after her shift at midnight." Tara leaned closer. "But if we go now, we can watch her dance."

"We?" Why did Tara want to get in the middle of this?

Her face turned bright red. "I told her I'd be there to introduce you." She glanced to her left. Wasn't that a sign of a lie?

"How would we get in? I don't have a fake ID."

"She'll get us in." Tara watched him closely. "Come on, Liam. This will be great."

Could he do this tonight, after all the shit heaped on him in the last few hours? "Yeah, why not." It'd take his mind off his reaction to Amanda and the dark-haired woman he'd failed to seduce. He picked up his backpack and opened the driver's door. "Where's your truck?"

"I got a ride here." She slid into his seat and climbed over the console onto the passenger seat. Pretty agile for a heavier girl.

He got in and cranked the engine. "What if I'd said no?"

She attempted a sexy smile. "Then you'd get to drive me home. And if you want, we can skip the whole stripper thing and go park somewhere."

Liam didn't feel that strong of an attraction to her. Especially now that he knew how...twisted she was.

He pulled out of the lot. "Let's do the strip club thing. That sounds like fun." Damn him for doing this, but he would let twisted Tara pimp for him.

****

Tara's friend, Trinity, let them into Sugar Cherry through a back door. The petite woman looked amazing, but what shocked Liam and nearly sent him falling on his face was the connection he felt with her. It was there, the pheromone, the rain scent. Not as intense as with Kaylee or Amanda, but present, just lingering between them, waiting to be grabbed.

Trinity stared up at him through purple eyes that had to come from a costume shop. The woman didn't speak for long moments. "Wow, baby, what kind of cologne are you wearing?"

"Sexy, ain't it?" He breathed deep, taking her essence, all the way inside him. In his jeans, his manhood swelled. He had all night to explain...and explore. "Nice to meet you, Trinity." If she didn't have to dance another set, he would have already had her in a private room. Naked. Filled with his length and screaming his name.

She turned, and they followed her along a dark hallway, her long, straight, platinum blonde hair swaying. At a red door, she turned, her gaze locking with his. "I've been excited to meet you ever since Tara told me about your video project." Her skimpy lavender lingerie top cupped her large breasts.

Liam's mouth watered. Were they real? Did he care?

She smiled through her shiny lips. “I’ve been waiting for this all day.” She glanced at Tara.

Tara blushed. “We’re all going to have such a wonderful time.”

He looked at Tara, who gave him a half-smile. What did she mean, *all*?

“That’s my music.” She opened the door and pointed to the far stage. “I’ll be over there, by the double poles.”

Liam didn’t move. He wanted this woman, urgently and primally. Could he talk her out of dancing, and convince her to get right to the horizontal stuff?

Tara grabbed Liam’s hand and tugged. “Come on, Casanova. Let the girl work.”

He reached for Trinity’s cheek, but the woman put two hands on his chest and pushed. “Later, sexy.” Her smile nearly knocked him out.

Liam let Tara pull him with her to the stage, and strangely, since meeting Trinity, the strong obsession for Amanda had dulled a bit. They found two chairs together and ordered beer. Tara reached into her pocket, pulling out a roll of one-dollar bills. “Here. Trinity will like it if you get the other guys started by tucking a lot of money in her G-string.”

The cash felt warm in his palm. Could this night get any stranger? “How do you know Trinity?”

Tara shifted in her chair and pointed to the curtain at the back of the stage. “Here she comes!”

The music blasted for a second, then paused. Trinity, in clear platform shoes, a black leather vest that pushed her breasts high and full, and a short, red leather skirt, strolled onto the stage, a thick length of chain in her hand. She’d pinned her hair up on her head, leaving hunks sticking out at wild angles. “Any bad boys here tonight?" She mouthed the words along with the singer, then the music blared, heavy and thumping.

She writhed and danced, using the chain to rub herself between her legs. After a few tricks on the pole, she flung the chain to the back of the stage and turned her back to him, unzipping her skirt.

The skirt came off, revealing a ruffled, hot-pink thong. When she dropped the vest, Liam's shaft lurched in his jeans. She wore a ruffled bra to match the panties.

Hell, who knew that pink fluff under raunchy leather would be such a turn on?

The music changed to slow and seductive, and Trinity released her hair and worked the pole, doing gravity-defying turns and sensual poses.

As their stares deadlocked on each other, Liam's body connected with her so intensely, he could almost feel every sexy gyration of her muscles as if she was pressed tight against him.

His mind flashed with visions of positions, the choices overexciting him, like a kid given free rein in the candy aisle. Missionary, reverse cowgirl, doggy, and oh shit, anal like he'd never had it before. And she'd suck him, too, on her knees, hard and strong.

When Trinity went down on her knees, then sucked her thumb, he momentarily imagined she'd read his mind, had listened to his command.

Men leaned forward, cash in hand. She slithered along the edge of the stage, paying attention to each man, letting them tuck bills in her bra, in her panties.

Why didn't it bother him to see other men sneaking touches? Bother? Hell, it juiced him harder, hotter, with each stolen stroke. When she reached him, she leaned over, nearly brushing her breasts on his face. He pressed a bill between her round orbs, wiggling a finger in the moist heat there. She lapped at his lips, so quickly, he barely had time to react. But a tightening of his groin told him his body had noticed.

Turning, she pressed her ass close to him, wiggling and circling her hips to the music. One by one, he tucked the bills into her panties, sneaking a feel of the seductive wetness between her thighs with each dollar. In seconds, a bulking man in black stood beside Tara. “Trinity.”

She looked up at him, blinking as if she’d been in a trance. She immediately got to her feet and danced to the back of the stage, removing the money from her clothes.

The bouncer looked at Liam and Tara for a few seconds, then moved on.

“She really likes you.” Tara gave him a goofy smile.

“She’s hot. When can we get out of here?”

“One more song, then she’s done.” Tara watched his face, looking like she wanted to say something more.

Then the music changed to fast and techie, and Trinity strolled forward, ripping off her panties to reveal a black leather thong. When she slowly removed her bra, those ripe breasts were bare. She cupped them, pointing her nipples toward Liam.

“It’d better be fast.” He gripped the edge of his chair to keep himself from leaping on the stage and taking her.

Chapter Fourteen

In the seedy motel next to the strip club, Liam unlocked the door with an actual metal key on a red plastic tag, swung the door open, and switched on the light. The smell of disinfectant leached into his nose as he stood back to let Trinity into the room.

Tara followed.

He'd been damn near speechless when he'd tried to hand Tara his car keys so she could wait for him, and Trinity had pulled her along with them to the motel, saying, "Let's all three have a good time."

A fucking threesome? Holy shit. His day had gone from crap to perfection in less than three hours.

As he followed them in, he shut the door and looked around at the 1970's wood paneling and industrial brown carpet. Scouting for the perfect place to set up his camera, he spotted a tall, narrow dresser next to the bathroom door.

Tara and Trinity stood in one corner near the queen-size bed, whispering. Tara clenched her hands in front of her belly, and Trinity looked like she was lecturing the shorter girl.

Liam put the camera on top of the dresser and snapped a picture. The viewfinder confirmed it was a direct shot to the bed, covered in a dull green comforter. No shitty tripod to worry about this time. He switched to video and pressed record, then set the camera in the sweet spot. He'd forget about it this time, and focus on these beauties.

The girls stared at him.

He smiled. "Are we ready, ladies?" He reached in his jeans pocket and pulled out the seven condoms he'd purchased at the vending machine in the strip club's bathroom. His blood sailed through his veins double-speed, swelling his shaft and flashing ideas into his mind of how to please two at once.

"Are you ready, baby?" Trinity had changed into a red sundress and high-heeled sandals before she'd met them outside the club. She struck a pose. "I bet you never thought you'd get to sleep with two hot s—"

"Hot sexies," Tara nearly shouted.

Trinity looked at her and shook her head. "He'll think it's kinky."

Tara scowled at her friend. "No. I told you he wouldn't."

Just perfect. The way his life was going lately, he should have known this would fall apart. Liam stuffed the condoms back into his pocket. "If either of you has changed your mind, I'm—"

"We haven't." Trinity led Tara forward. "We want to do this, but Tara is a little shy. She hasn't done a threesome before."

Tara's face turned bright red and her eyes looked rabbit-scared.

He grinned and pulled her in close. He'd never admit he hadn't either, but with all the porn he'd watched, he had no doubt he could make this good for all three of them. "Tara, sweet girl, I'll take care of you." Pressing his lips to hers, he slid his hand down her back to cup her butt, squeezing gently.

Her lips opened for him, and his tongue tangled with hers, tasting beer and mint. Heat pooled low in his groin, then he ended the kiss. "We'll take it slow, girl. You'll love it."

Liam looked at Trinity. He hadn't touched her yet, but her impact on him, just from looking into her eyes, was a thousand times stronger than Tara's.

Sliding a hand to the nape of her neck, he pulled her in for a kiss.

Pulse beats flared through him like alarm bells ringing, blood raced south to fill and stretch him, his brain lost touch with his logic, and sexual energy took over, turning the kiss ravenous. The animal in Liam broke loose.

He took the girls by the hand and had them sit on the bed. He looked at them both, seducing them with his gaze.

"Look at his eyes, Tara. They're a different color."

Tara squinted. "Yeah, weird."

Hadn't Kaylee said the same thing?

Trinity smiled, her eagerness seemed genuine as she shot the same hot look back at him. Tara's eyes showed confusion, an uncertainty he couldn't quite put his finger on. He stared at her, willing her to calm down.

Heaving a long breath, Tara's body visibly relaxed and she gave him a slight smile.

Liam chuckled, loving having two sets of eyes directed at him. "I guess I'll start. As he took off his shirt, he kept looking at both women. A sense of unreality dizzied him. Was this going to happen right now?

As if reading his mind, Trinity shouted, "Hell, yeah!"

Tara smacked Trinity.

Trinity rubbed her arm and glared at her. "Ouch."

Liam couldn't help but laugh out loud. It almost seemed that the two were bickering like sisters. The girls talked quietly for a few seconds. They seemed more wrapped up in fussing with each other than paying attention to a man getting naked in front of them. Liam yelled, "Hey, I'm over here," as he unbuttoned his jeans and let them drop to his ankles, making sure this time not to slip and fall.

They glanced at him, but had a few more words to spit at each other.

Which of them would he dive into first? How would he start? He tossed the condoms on the bed between them and tucked his thumbs in the waistband of his briefs.

Now he had their full attention.

Once he'd pulled his briefs free of his body, and his pulsing manhood throbbed at their eye level, the room went completely silent. So silent that it became almost awkward for Liam.

The girls just sat there and stared, looking like they might be in awe of his hefty package.

Tara opened her mouth. "I...I don't know if that will fit."

Trinity said nothing but immediately got up off the bed and knelt, taking him into her mouth.

Her technique was so flawless, Liam's knees instantly buckled a little as he threw his head back in ecstasy. "That's what I'm talking about."

The mouth pleasure she gave him was so euphoric, he instantly felt high. He motioned with one finger to Tara to come in his direction, keeping his eyes closed and his head thrown back.

Meanwhile Trinity was working him so good, his shaft had never gotten so hard so quickly. He placed his hand on the back of her head. Softly, his palm moved with the motions of her mouth and her head bobbing up and down, over and over.

Listening to her sucking sounds sent sharp spikes of pure ecstasy through him.

Tara hadn't made her way over to take his hand yet. He opened his eyes and looked at her.

She stared at Trinity, her eyes narrowed, her lips tight. Was it jealousy?

Liam motioned for her again, and this time, Tara stood, as if she was under his control, her shoulders rounded, her head down, as she slowly walked toward Liam's hand. After a few seconds, she straightened her back and looked into his eyes.

The thought of both these women sent his passion raging out of control. Once Tara was within reach, Liam pulled her to him, shoving his mouth onto hers, fishing around for her tongue. Once he found it, he sucked it ferociously. He mimicked the rhythm of the sexual euphoria happening between his legs as he drew on her tongue.

The kiss was so strong and passionate, it must have taken Tara's breath away, and she pulled back, gasping in air.

As Trinity continued to please him, Liam's hand cupped the warmth between Tara's thighs. Her juices moistened the fabric there. His finger found its way inside Tara's shorts. She was so hot and wet, Liam imagined his fingers had just dived into a pool of steaming water. Tara's gaze locked with his as he continued to kiss her, and he could almost read her mind. She wanted him, and she wanted him bad.

As he found her clit and rubbed it between two fingers, he could feel her heartbeat pulsing there. Her panting grew intense, her eyes and mouth opening wide in surprise, almost as if no one had ever gone there before.

In the back of his mind, in his lust-drunk state, he tried to piece together clues. Was this her first time? He moved in and kissed her again, plunging his tongue alongside hers.

Liam's body tightened with the overstimulation of pleasures all happening at once. He had to cool down, and he had to cool down fast before he exploded down Trinity's throat. He grasped Trinity's hair and pulled her back.

As his member popped free from her mouth, he released Tara's tongue. It was almost as if the erotic clock stopped ticking for a moment. Both girls looked at Liam then looked at each other and giggled.

"You guys have seen what I got, now it's time for me to see what you've got." Liam's voice came out low and hefty.

Lust drove him, sexual desire had completely overtaken him. The southern gentleman inside him was lost for now.

Tara lifted the hem of her shirt, and Trinity stood and dropped one dress strap.

"Stop." A flash of perversion gave him wicked ideas. "I want you to take each other's clothes off."

Both girls stopped mid-motion and stared at each other for what seemed like an eternity. Liam wanted to be their master, demanding that his submissives obey. "I said, take each other's fucking clothes off."

The girls awkwardly moved toward each other. Trinity with more confidence than Tara. Trinity pulled off Tara's top, and Tara slid Trinity's shoulder straps down, peeling the top of her sundress to her waist. They stopped.

"Keep going." Liam made his command firm, unquestionable.

As they moved to each other's bras, it was a little more awkward, but quickly both women's large breasts bounced free, their nipples tightening. Trinity peeled Tara's shorts down, exposing the girl's round hips and ample booty. Tara's hands shook as she pulled Trinity's dress to the floor. As they stood in their panties, both of them staring at each other's faces, Tara's whole body started to shake. Liam could barely watch their discomfort, so he stepped forward. "I'll take it from here."

With one hand on each of their thighs, he grabbed the fabric of each pair of panties and ripped them off. Both girls let out a surprised sigh at the exact same time. He grasped the backs of their necks and lifted a brow, impaling them each with a stare. "Kiss each other."

Tara seemed to be near tears. Trinity's eyes fixed on Liam's, her smile telling him without words that she would do anything he told her, without question.

As the girls leaned in to kiss each other, just as their lips were about to touch, Tara, whimpered and looked at Liam. "I...I got an idea. Why don't we both please you at the same time?"

Liam, drugged with his desire for them, immediately lay down on the bed. "Let's do it." The girls looked at each other, then turned toward him. There was no mistaking the looks in their eyes. They both wanted to please him, and Liam wanted nothing more than to see himself pleased.

Tara lightly grabbed the base of his shaft, clumsy, almost as if she'd never touched a man that way before.

Trinity, on the other side of him on her knees on the bed, immediately took his head into her mouth and began sucking ferociously.

Liam reached for Tara's hand, which jerked

up and down the bottom of his shaft, and placed his hand around hers. “No, darlin’. Like this.”

With Trinity sucking hard, and Liam and Tara working together to slide her hand up his shaft, massive surges of heat began to flood his lower torso. Again, he grabbed Trinity by her hair and pulled her off his cock. “I want you to kiss Tara.” He wanted it all, everything a three-way allowed them to do, and they had all night to fulfill every one of his fantasies.

This time, the girls lightly pecked each other’s cheeks.

He shook his head.

When they saw that wasn’t good enough for Liam, they pop-kissed each other’s mouths.

Even thorough his euphoria, Liam sensed something strange was going on. But he didn’t give a shit. Nothing was going to stop him from taking Trinity.

Liam sat up on the bed. “Trinity, on all fours.”

She scooted to the front of the bed to do as he bid, and he got up to stand behind her. “Tara, on your back next to her.”

His goal was to please one with his hand and one with his raging manhood.

Kneeling behind Trinity, Liam placed the head of his shaft at the base of her sweet opening, and as he barely dipped himself in, said, “Jesus, you’re crazy wet.”

Trinity responded with a devilish laugh. “Then do something about it.

Tara lay awkwardly, as if she didn’t want to be there. She stared at Liam, her frown almost bittersweet, as if she was making a sacrifice in order to please him.

Trinity wiggled her hips, trying to push him

inside her further.

"You got it, baby." Liam slipped on a condom and rammed half of himself inside her in one motion.

"Holy shit." Trinity's voice squeaked.

"Relax, darlin', I got this." He squeezed her ass cheek as he held himself there for a moment, pulsing inside her. Running his hand up Tara's leg, he found his way between her thighs with his two middle fingers.

Her slick passage felt so tight, there was no way two fingers would fit. Even though she was creaming, insanely wet, the circumference of her canal was barely penetrable. Could she be a virgin? No way, not crazy, freaky Tara.

As Liam slowed, gently pushing one finger in, Tara instantly began to moan, almost screaming. She grabbed handfuls of the blanket beside her, and her whole body tensed

Liam looked into her eyes and gave her a soft smile. "Just relax.

Without a word, she nodded.

Liam continued to move his finger in and out of her, while placing his thumb on her clit, massaging it gently.

As Tara started to relax, her hips began moving in the same motion of his finger and thumb.

He still pulsed inside Trinity, her wetness becoming so ridiculous that it dripped down the length of his thick base.

In that moment, he felt like he was two men, one, a deranged sex wolf waiting to devour his prey, and the other a person, as kind, gentle, and respectful as he could possibly be. In that moment, Liam did not know which one he wanted to be more.

Tara gently placed her hand around Liam's

thick wrist. It was a loving embrace, nothing sexual, nothing lustful, just sweet and gentle. Her panting started to increase, and what had already been tight became almost impossible now, clenching around his finger. She squeezed his wrist tighter. He knew exactly what would happen now.

Like the devil on his shoulder, a mischievous voice popped into his mind. Could he make them both come at the same time?

Immediately, Liam's ego answered the challenge. He knew he didn't have much time by Tara's reaction, so he had to get Trinity up to speed very quickly.

He began to jackhammer in and out of her with massive force. Her thighs shook as his engorged member completely rearranged her inner core. At the same time, he kept the same motion going, pleasing Tara.

Both girls began to moan, then their moans turned into hard, broken sounds.

The sexual energy in the room hung so thick, it felt like an all-consuming fire. The bed squeaked hard, emulating the sounds that could only be pure sex.

As Liam continued to pound and Tara's grip on his wrist became tighter, he knew the moment was rapidly approaching. He could feel Trinity intensifying. She got closer to orgasming, panting like a bitch in heat. Suddenly Tara's grip tensed, nearly cutting off his blood flow, then she immediately started staring at what was happening between Trinity and Liam.

She'd orgasmed, but hadn't taken the time to enjoy it, instead, looking shocked as she watched him service another woman.

Liam continued to jackhammer in and out of Trinity, his movements jerking both their bodies, feeling borderline insane as he let the heat and waves of shivers race through his body. The sounds coming out of Trinity's mouth echoed like the cries of a wild woman, and her hair tossed around crazily.

Tara sat up and pounded her fist on the mattress. With tears in her eyes, she yelled, "Liam stop. Please Liam, stop."

Chapter Fifteen

Liam watched Tara shout at him, her fist pounding the bed. He squinted his eyes to try to focus on her as his body continued to pulse even harder into Trinity.

Tara kept pleading with him to stop, but his body wouldn't obey.

Her face broke into a pathetic frown. "Fuck you, Liam." She stormed off in a rage, screaming and repeating those words at the top of her lungs.

Trinity, now in full frenzy, thrust herself back onto him, impaling herself on Liam's turgid length.

For a moment, Liam surfaced from his haze. He should pull out and go to Tara, figure out what had happened. But suddenly, Trinity's rain scent caught him so intensely, it seemed as if his body was possessed. Instead of pulling out, he drove so deep into her that she shouted, "I can feel you in my fucking stomach."

Liam stared, completely entranced. He pounded and pounded and pounded. In what seemed like echoes in the far distance, he heard Tara kicking the bathroom walls and screaming, but he couldn't make out what she said. And right then, he didn't care. Somehow, knowing that he could pleasure one woman while breaking another one's heart was so debauched, it sent his climax rocking through him, ready to shoot from his groin.

With one last pump into her, Liam heard Trinity gasp. "I'm coming."

All at once, every inch of him slid out of her as she raised up on her feet while her head was still on the bed. The surge of rain flowed free from her, so strong and thick, the words "tidal wave" popped into

Liam's head. The bed was completely soaked, then another huge rush flowed out of her.

Liam stayed on his knees, his world spinning wildly as he watched this magnificent miracle of ecstasy. Still in the throes of his orgasm, his thoughts began to whirl out of control, and he faded in and out of consciousness.

Trinity collapsed on the bed, shaking, a smile of pure satisfaction curled her lips, but things went black for Liam.

He didn't know how long he was out, but when he opened his eyes, he lay flat on his back on the bed, as Trinity patted his cheek, her face drawn in worry. "Liam? Liam?" She gasped, her eyes rolled back in her head.

Liam reached for her, then everything went black again.

****

Trinity had never had a man pass out on her. She had watched Liam kneeling behind her, his body shaking, his head wobbling. She'd fallen to the bed, exhausted, then he'd landed like a rock beside, out cold. Or was he? She'd rolled him onto his back, patting his cheek. "Liam? Are you not talking to me because of what I did here? The fluid that came out of me?" Sucking her lower lip, she held in a cry.

She swung her gaze toward the bathroom door. Tara had stopped shouting and now bawled like her heart was broken. Damn, Trinity hadn't wanted it to be like this.

"Beautiful. Rain is..." Liam murmured something else she didn't understand. It sounded like another language, repeating over and over. "U-to-hi-yu." His body convulsed as if he was having a second orgasm. Or was this still his first one?

Trinity gathered her things, needing to calm Tara down and get her home.

Then Liam's eyes opened, his gaze locking with hers, and in that instant her world turned upside down. Her eyes rolled back as visions of a future appeared so clear and vivid, she couldn't stop from calling out in excitement. She saw clearly how the world she had been living in wasn't where she should be. Working at Sugar Cherry, dating men for money; wasn't right. This life was slowly killing her inside. A vision of her holding a baby flooded her mind. She rocked the little one as she looked out the window onto a backyard where a man played with a toddler. He looked up at her and smiled, his mouth forming the words, *"See? There's Mommy and your little sister?"*

"Trinity!" Trinity's beautiful dream was interrupted by a voice loud in her ear. As Tara continued to speak, her hands guided Trinity, pulling her clothes on her naked body, but Trinity didn't want the present to interfere with her vision of the perfect future. She became aware of riding in a car...her car? Then Tara put her to bed as Trinity's vivid dream continued. Even after the lights went out and everything grew silent, her life—what could be her future—played like a three-dimensional film.

This was pure heaven!

****

Liam woke shivering, lying on the bed, which was wet with his ejaculate and Trinity's precious rain as the air conditioner blew frigid air over him. All at once, full consciousness came back to him and he sat up. The bathroom door stood open. Both Tara and Trinity were gone.

When he'd looked into Trinity's eyes after

they'd shared ecstasy, that thing had happened again, like when he'd made Kaylee squirt. He'd locked gazes with Trinity and sorrow had clenched at Liam's soul. Screams from long ago, and a language he didn't understand, had reverberated in his head, accompanied by visions of fire, pain, death. The same hallucination, but clearer this time. Then his world had gone black.

Now, his emotions played havoc with him. Despair sucked at him even as he exulted at having made two women come at the same time. He could almost cry at the downswing of his emotions.

He glanced around the room and when his gaze fastened on the dresser, excitement hit him, dispelling the darkness lurking inside him. "I got it!" He stood, still wobbly, and stared at the video camera. "Solid gold."

An hour later, Liam lay on his own bed, rewinding the video. He'd watch just the last piece, the part where he'd blacked out. Stopping it at a spot just before and hitting "play," Tara's voice screeched like an angry raven and he quickly plugged in his earbuds. The walls were thin in the house, and he didn't want to risk waking his grandparents.

The small picture in the viewfinder showed him with Trinity, and he watched himself pummeling into her, her face a mask of pleasure. Growing hard again, he shifted to relieve the pressure.

Something Tara screamed caught his attention, and he rewound, listening this time instead of watching.

"...hired a prostitute to prove how much I loved you..."

He sat up, his bed springs squeaking. "What the hell?" Rewinding the video to when Tara ran into the bathroom, he turned up the volume and listened.

"...wanted to give you my virginity, you bastard."

"Oh, hell." He'd known something was off. Why did he never trust his gut instinct? Liam huffed out a long breath. He had been gentle with Tara, but there was no way he would have not followed through with Trinity.

His heart thudded, thinking of the stripper, the exact same way it had for Kaylee after they'd made love. An ache settled in his chest. He'd call her, or stop by Sugar Cherry some night.

The video played to the spot where Tara's words had first caught his attention. "...hired a prostitute to prove how much I loved you..." She sobbed for long moments. "I even let you screw my sister."

"Sister." Liam pressed pause. Holy shit, that was majorly twisted. What was Tara thinking? No wonder she'd gone completely freaky and locked herself in the bathroom. Running through the foreplay in the motel room, he should have seen the signs. "Sisters. Damnit."

Shaking his head, he pressed play and watched, listening closely. Trinity straightened her legs, her rain spraying the most amazing proof of her pleasure, then his own orgasm surged and his lips began to move but... "Shit!"

Tara's cries from the bathroom drowned out what he was saying.

Trinity had rolled him over on the bed, trying to wake him, while his mouth had moved in the same pattern, over and over. She'd dressed, then their gazes met. He'd thudded back onto the bed, dead weight, and Trinity's eyes glazed over and closed. She started mumbling, laughing, smiling, as if she'd been transported to another dimension.

Tara came from the bathroom, drying her tears as she pulled on her clothes. She tried to snap Trinity out of her daze, then gave up and helped Trinity dress.

The women...sisters...walked out together, Trinity making joyful noises, and Tara staring at her as if she thought her sister had lost her mind.

Liam shut off the camera, stuck it in the nightstand drawer, and lay back on the bed. He'd been on this crazy-ass journey to seek the truth, but every attempt to get the evidence had failed. Was he doing this all wrong?

He took inventory of what had been happening to him, thinking about why certain women turned him into a raging lunatic, while others just made him horny.

Kaylee, Trinity, and Amanda were an obsession. Maureen? Made him horny. Grace? She sure as hell made him horny. Her tale of the legend replayed in his mind. Something made him starved for more of the story. How could he feed the part of him that hungered for forbidden knowledge?

> *Dear Me, what a holy pile of shit this has turned out to be. Needless to say, my exploration into videography gets an epic fail. But in some ways, my failure has become a success. There seems to be a pattern; the scent, squirting, my obsessive behavior. But I still have unanswered questions, and it seems I'm definitely not going to find the answers in sex,*

lies, and videotape. True love?... Maybe I should consider the source and find out more from the library? Search the internet? Maybe go to the reservation. But something, without a doubt, is happening to me. What, I don't know.

The next morning, Liam drove into town, hours before his shift at the gas station started. The library had computers he could use. He set down his notebook and plopped onto a hard wooden chair, moving the mouse to wake the monitor. His fingers hovered over the keyboard. What should he type? Grace had said *Rain Ceremony*. He typed it in.

Nothing.

He tried adding the names of local indigenous tribes, but still didn't find anything. He sat back with a loud huff of breath, pushed back until the chair balanced on its hind legs, and stared out a window, brainstorming what to type next.

"Something I can help you with, Liam?" The whisper came from his left. The librarian, Mrs. Fieldhouse, had been his English teacher the first year he'd attended Liberation High.

"Yes, ma'am." He eased his chair back onto all four legs. "I'm…researching some of the local lore."

She pulled out the chair next to him and sat, her brown eyes sharp but kind, as she tucked loose gray hairs back into her tight bun. "Which ones in particular?"

Did he really want to talk about sex legends with the town librarian? "Uh, ceremonies performed by Native American tribes?"

She touched her index finger to her lip and squinted off into the distance. “Nothing online?”

“No, ma’am.”

She stood. “Let me show you what we have in print.”

Liam followed, the squeak of the soles of Mrs. Fieldhouse’s gray shoes on the old linoleum floor the only noise in the building.

“This section, these five shelves, are everything we have from the local area and…” She reached for one book and flipped open the first page. “This man still lives on the reservation.” Pointing to his picture, she handed the book to Liam. “He might be a good place to start asking your questions.”

Blinking a few times, Liam imagined driving onto the rez, a place his grandparents had warned him to stay away from. “Thank you. I’ll see what I can find here, first.”

She nodded and squeaked her way back toward the checkout desk.

For an hour, Liam lost himself in researching the faces, customs, ceremonies and tragedies of the local tribes. Pages had been ripped out of each of the volumes, though, and he couldn’t piece together the entire story without them. With five books checked out and tucked under his arm, he left the library, slid into his car, and headed to work. Would Tara stop in tonight? Would she burst into the Pump and Run hot with anger? Or would his tires be slashed when he went outside after his shift?

And Trinity. His heartbeat galloped when he thought of her. He’d like to see her again, have a repeat performance—without her sister present.

Liam pulled into a parking spot next to Amanda’s old blue sedan. Yeah, of course she’d be here, hopefully, training with Ray or one of the afternoon girls. He didn't want to be alone with her.

Liam tugged his phone from his pocket and dialed Travis.

"Hey. What's going on?" Travis's voice sounded tense.

"Nothing." Things had been cool between the two of them since the baseball game. "Working tonight. Stop by?"

Travis was silent for a few seconds. "Okay. Yeah, I'll come by later."

Liam wanted to get things back to normal. "Did you know Amanda's working at the station now?"

His friend cleared his throat. "Yep. She called me yesterday and told me she'd transferred there."

After a few seconds, Liam cleared his own throat. "You gonna ask her out, or are you still too lazy to drive up to Rogers Corners?"

Travis chuckled. "Yeah, I'm gonna ask her out. I just gotta finish this goddamn summer school so I can officially graduate."

Liam got out of his car and locked the door, leaning back on it to enjoy his last minutes of freedom. "If you need help…"

"Yeah, smart man, I'll ask. Gotta go, my dad's yellin' about something."

"Later." Liam trudged along the sidewalk, pushed open the glass door of the Pump and Run, and walked in. The room turned instantly hot, the scent of rain swirling through the air, his mind nearly forcing his body to turn in her direction. "Hey." He said it to whomever stood behind the counter and walked straight through to the back room.

Leaning one hand on the wall, he dropped his

head and caught his breath. He was stronger than this. He could push past it, learn to deal with it.

Instantly, the scent, the pull, grew stronger.

"Hey, yourself." Amanda leaned against the doorframe. "What's your hurry?"

"Gotta clock in." He typed his code into the computer then turned and grabbed the vest with his nametag pinned on it.

She sighed, straightened, and took a step toward him. "You mad at me or something?" In the small room, her essence became overpowering.

As he pulled on the vest, he imagined it being lined with kryptonite, the only thing that would keep this superwoman away from him. Liam spun and faced her. "No, Amanda. I'm not. But I do need to remember we're co-workers now."

Her green eyes widened and she let out a quick laugh. "What does that mean?"

"It means we work together, and that's it." Travis had claimed her, and Liam was not the kind of a friend who'd betray a buddy.

"You're seeing someone?" She made a sexy little frown and tossed her red hair over her shoulder.

"Yeah. I'm seeing someone." Liam brushed past her into the store. He'd make a call later, once he was alone here. Maureen had told him to call anytime, and this was just about the perfect time.

Amanda left the store a few minutes later, and once the air cleared of her powerful aura, his head realigned from sex-fiend to human. Thoughts of Trinity slowly started creeping into the back of his mind again, but he ignored the nebulous thoughts.

Six hours later, as the sun set, he called the number Maureen had typed into his phone.

"Hello?" She sounded unsure.

"Maureen?"

"Yes. Who's this?"

"It's Liam. Liam Jackson." He smiled. He'd almost said "Jackman," like she'd called him.

"Liam, hi." She sounded excited. "I didn't think I'd hear from you again."

"Why not?" He watched a customer pumping gas, hoping they wouldn't come into the store.

"I don't know. It just didn't seem like you..." She let out a breath. "Are you calling to ask me out on a *date*?" Her voice rose, filled with a teasing note.

"Yes, Miss Maureen, I am." He smiled. Things with this woman seemed so easy compared to the rest of his life.

They talked a few minutes and arranged to meet at the drive-in Friday night at six, and decide what to do from there.

As he ended the call, Travis pulled in, his pickup loud and flashy. Strolling into the store, he nodded to Liam and went straight for the beer cooler.

When Travis returned to the counter, they made a show for the camera, Liam checking his ID, then Travis ducked behind the chip display in the camera's dead spot. A hassle, but Liam didn't want to risk getting fired.

Once Travis sat in his chair sipping a cold one, Liam struggled for something to talk about. The only thing on his mind was the resin bullshit at the baseball game. Then his thoughts jumped to the books he'd checked out from the library. "Wanna go to the rez with me?"

Chapter Sixteen

Travis swallowed beer and coughed. "What? Seriously? Why?" He wiped a few drops from his chin. "No fucking way. The Hackers are like goddamn moving targets on the…" He shook his head. "Never mind. Why the hell do you want to go there?"

Liam leaned back on the counter of the Pump and Run. Strange statement about his friend's family's friction with the rez. "You know *that thing* I told you about? With Kaylee?" He lowered his brows.

"Yeah." Travis's brown gaze fastened on his.

"I want to talk to a guy who might know something about it." Liam wasn't ready to tell Travis that *that thing* had happened again. With an exotic dancer. And if Liam couldn't control himself better, it might just happen one more time. With a girl Travis wanted to date.

"You sure you want to do this?"

"Yeah. I'm going to record it, make it like a documentary. Say I'm doing research on history and folklore."

"Jeez." Travis stood, hauling his five remaining beers with him. "I guess I could. When?"

"Thursday? We can take my grandpa's truck. It'd be less flashy."

Travis walked toward the door. "Sure, I'll go with. You know I got your back, bro." He looked back at Liam. "Next to you, man, my life seems so fucking normal."

Liam laughed. "You have no clue how true that is."

****

Thursday, Travis had to cancel because of

some crisis on their farm, so Liam picked him up late Friday afternoon and they made the two-hour drive to the reservation.

Tribal law enforcement signs marked the entrance to the community even before the tribe's name and logo appeared on a carved wood sign.

"You ever been here before?" Travis's head swiveled as he took in the forested area. As if he expected to see ancient ruins or something.

"Nope. I'm not sure why, but the grandparents warned me off of the place. They said it's almost like sacred ground to the tribe."

"I got the same warning from Dad, but he said it was because they were violent."

Liam snorted. Classifying a whole tribe based on a few members… "Your old man." He stopped himself before he made a comment that would fuck up their friendship.

"Yeah, I know what he is. He's a paranoid bigot." Travis's phone started beeping. The GPS feature that Liam's old phone didn't have. "Says to go right at this road."

Liam slowed, checking out the rutted dirt trail veering off the blacktop. "You sure?"

His friend shrugged. "It's been wrong before. Guess we can only try."

They bounced along the path for a few miles until they came to a grouping of houses. Trailer homes, small ramblers, and a couple of nicer two-stories.

"No addresses on the houses." Liam didn't even see mailboxes. "Guess we have to stop and ask someone."

Dogs barked but he saw no other sign of life.

"Good luck with that." Travis's gaze shot in

every direction. "Looks deserted."

A door opened on one of the trailers, and a young man stepped out, his dark hair blowing around his shoulders and reddish skin the only noticeable clues to his lineage. Barefoot, his white T-shirt and worn jeans were nearly identical to Liam's.

Liam unclicked his seatbelt and reached for the door handle.

Travis grabbed his arm. "What're you doing?"

Liam shook his head and stepped out of the truck, walking slowly toward the man. "Hi. I'm looking for Ernie Crow."

"What you want him for?" The man's dark eyes narrowed.

"I'm doing research on some of the history and legends of the area."

"For what?" The man crossed his arms.

"I'm a student at Mortonson and I—"

"He won't want to talk to you." He looked past Liam into the truck.

Liam hoped Travis hadn't done anything stupid, like bring a pistol.

"You and your friend can leave now." He turned and grasped the door handle.

"I have a copy of Mr. Crow's book. I'd like to ask him about a ceremony." When the man stopped walking, Liam continued. "The Rain Ceremony. The Giver, The Flower…"

The guy swung around. "That's not in Ernie Crow's book."

"I know. And I want to find out more. You can be there if you want. Make sure we don't pressure Mr. Crow in any way, or overstay—"

"He don't need anybody to run interference for him, but he won't want to talk to you." As the man pulled open the squeaky door, Liam grasped at his last option.

"Buck Waya? Does he live around here?"

The man froze then turned slowly. "You don't want to talk to that crazy fucker." He paused as if thinking, then nodded toward this left. "Ernie Crow's is the last house on the left, the gray one. I'll call him and tell him you're coming. If he doesn't open the door, leave. Got it?"

"Yeah. Thanks." Liam nodded and walked back to his truck.

"Are we going?" Travis sat stiffly, watching the trailer house the man had disappeared into.

"No. We're going to see a man about a legend."

Four minutes later, a gray-haired man in bib overalls and a flannel shirt silently let them into his house. He gestured to the worn green couch as he sat in a matching recliner across from it, muting the volume on the soap opera playing on a small television.

"My grandmother watches that one, too." Liam clamped his mouth shut. Probably not the best icebreaker.

The man stared into Liam's eyes. "What do you know of the Rain Ceremony?"

Liam held up his camera. "Is it okay if I record this?"

The man shook his head. "No video. Just sound."

Liam set the camera on the table and pressed record, aiming the lens toward Travis. "Thank you." He sat forward. "This is going to sound strange, but I believe I might have the power to perform the ceremony."

The man's black eyes stared into Liam's but he didn't speak.

Travis shifted, his breath hitching.

"Who are your people?" Mr. Crow's voice came out clipped, almost angry.

"I don't know, sir. My grandmother doesn't mention any Native American lineage, though."

He nodded once as if reading the doubt in Liam's tone. "Tell me why you think you are The Giver?"

Travis let out a quiet groan. Had he been hoping the man would laugh at Liam and tell him he was imagining things?

Liam spoke about the scent, the connection with certain women, the after-effects of bringing the rain from a woman. The fact that the man didn't kick Travis and him out—that he listened to Liam—caused the most empowering feeling Liam had known in his life.

The man took it all in silently.

When Liam finished, they all sat quietly for nearly ten minutes.

"You'll go now, and come back in four days."

"Four days?" Liam looked at Travis.

His buddy shrugged his brows.

"Okay, thank you. I'll be back." He picked up his camera, letting it continue to record in case the man said anything else.

Mr. Crow picked up his TV remote and raised the volume, effectively dismissing them.

Heading outside as the sun slid below the horizon, Liam let his camera capture some of the area, then shut it off. "What do you think, Trav? Freaky weird that he didn't tell me I was full of shit?"

"That's 'cause he doesn't know you as well as

I do." Travis laughed. "And 'cause you look like you could be related to him."

"What?" Liam stopped and looked at his friend.

Travis got into the truck. "Just giving you shit, man."

Liam slid into his seat. His brow did look similar to Ernie Crow's, but that's where the similarities ended. He glanced at his reflection in the rear view mirror. That and their skin tone.

"Waste of time?" Travis pulled out his phone and started typing.

"I don't know." Liam got them rolling. "I guess I'll find out in four days."

"Man, I'm supposed to be out of town on a delivery run." Travis adjusted his seatbelt, still looking around like there would be an ambush. "You should find someone to come with you. You don't want to be alone here."

Maybe the old man would speak more freely if Liam was alone. "Yep." They headed out of the rez and toward home. "Wanna stop and eat?"

"You payin'?" Travis finally relaxed back in his seat.

"Yeah, if you don't mind fast food."

"Don't mind at all."

A half-hour later, they sat inside a McDonald's, eating fries and washing them down with shakes.

"Anything new with Amanda?" Liam wanted her dating Travis, and completely off Liam's radar.

Travis paused with a fry halfway to his mouth. "Why so concerned about her and me?"

Liam sat back, swirling his straw through the thick strawberry shake. "I don't know. You seemed to really like her, but aren't doing anything about it."

When Travis was silent, Liam wrapped up his trash. "Let's go." A light rain fell, shining off the cars in the drive-through, and he wanted to get home before… "Shit. The drive-in." Maureen. He was supposed to meet her there at six.

"What?" Travis dumped his trash and carried his shake outside with him, following Liam as he rushed to the truck.

"I screwed up, buddy." He slid his phone out of his pocket as he jumped into the truck and dialed Maureen's number. No answer.

****

Travis grinned as he listened to the pitiful excuses Liam left on some poor girl's voice mail as they raced toward Liberation. His buddy was up to his ass in alligators.

"Mind if we stop at the drive-in?"

Travis choked back a laugh. "Nope." Liam had better haul his butt to wherever the girl was and do some major begging. Standing up a woman was a major fuck-up. He should know. He'd forgotten to meet his lady at a party last weekend, and shit had hit the fan.

That woman. She was more than Travis could handle, but he loved every minute of it. He'd run into her after the party at Cousin Grace's farm had fallen apart, and had immediately asked her out. She'd accepted on one condition—that no one could know they were dating.

She said it was her parents she worried about, but Travis didn't believe it. Something was going on with her, but as long as they found stolen hours to fuck each other into ridiculous orgasms, he'd play by her rules

She worked in Liberation now, and shared rent with a girlfriend who worked nights. Travis stayed there too, most nights. He had to park blocks away, and she made him sneak out by four in the morning so nobody would see him.

Whatever. Whatever she wanted. He was just glad to have her for his own at night. His groin heated, knowing she waited for him right now, dressed in some kind of slinky nightgown, her hair wild, her eyes dark with lust. Hell, he did *not* want to leave her for a week to ride with his dad to deliver horses.

He grabbed his phone. "Know what? I don't want you going back to that place alone."

Liam looked at him for a second. "How'd you know I was going alone?"

"I saw the look in your eyes." His buddy had some wicked-freakish shit going on inside him. If he could help Liam through this, he had to go all-in. Travis dialed his dad's phone. "I'm not going on the delivery with you." He waited until his old man finished shouting. "I gotta take some tests or I won't graduate." It was a lie, but Travis had so many of those built up right now, one more wouldn't hurt. "Yeah, I'll be home later." He disconnected the call.

"You don't have to do that, Trav." Liam gripped the steering wheel. His voice sounded soft, almost grateful.

Guilt rushed through Travis for a few seconds, then disappeared. Yeah, it was his woman's smokin' hot body that had made the decision for Travis, but he'd let his friend think it was all about him. What the hell did it matter?

****

The next morning, Liam helped his

grandfather hook up the old irrigator, setting the intake filter in the river. Travis's words about his father dumping in it came back to him. "Grandpa, have you ever had the river tested for pollutants?"

He straightened, one hand on his lower back. "Yeah, a few times. I thought that might be what's ruining the crops, but the county says it's all good."

By the time they got it running, they were both pretty damn wet.

"Nearly dinner time, son." His grandfather carried a pipe wrench and it clattered as he set it in the bed of his truck. "Your grandma made pies this morning."

Liam's mouth watered as he ran his fingers through his wet hair. "She sure can cook."

"Yep." Grandpa got into his truck and fired it up as Liam plopped down in the passenger seat. "That's why I married her." He winked at Liam.

With a laugh, Liam rolled down his window. The rain he'd driven through the night before hadn't reached the farm, and things looked dusty. "How's she feeling?"

"Better." Grandpa pulled up in front of the house. "Doctor says she's just getting' old."

Liam shook his head. "And how many teeth did he lose when she punched him?"

Grandpa laughed. "He didn't say it in so many words, but he did give her a shot that perked her right up."

They got out and walked up the mudroom steps. "How's work at the gas station?"

Liam shrugged as they took off their boots and washed up in the utility sink. "Not too bad." He'd called that morning, asking Ray for Tuesday night off. He couldn't stop thinking about what Ernie Crow might tell him in three days. "Can I use your truck Tuesday?"

"Sure." Grandpa grinned. "Friday when you used my truck, I took your Grandma for a spin in the old Malibu. Just like old times."

"Don't you be telling stories, old man!" Grams's voice carried from the kitchen where the scent of hamburger frying drifted in the air.

Liam stepped into the kitchen. Two pies sat near the open window and he pinched off a piece of crust and popped it into his mouth. It nearly melted on his tongue.

"Stop that." Grams wiped her hands on her apron. "You can have a whole slice after you eat. If you finish your vegetables."

Grandpa was the first to groan, then Liam joined in.

Laughing, Grams set two plates on the table, laden with hamburgers on homemade whole wheat buns, green beans, and thick, wedge-cut oven fries.

Grandpa sat and squirted ketchup on his fries. "As long as potatoes count as vegetables, I'm a happy man."

As Grams sat and dug into her own plate of food, Liam finished his beans first. "Heard the doctor gave you good news."

She smiled as she dredged a fry through ketchup. "He did. I was just low on iron, and he gave me a B-12 shot, too." She leaned over, tipping her bottom to one side. "The young twerp actually pulled down my pants and stuck the needle in my butt!"

Liam opened his eyes wide. "Grandpa, you let him get away with that?"

With a mouth full of burger, Grandpa just laughed. They ate and talked for a while before

Grandpa yawned and got up, heading for the bedroom and his nap.

Liam stood and stacked the plates. "I'll do the dishes."

Grams touched his forearm. "Sit a minute, sweetie."

He sat and looked into her pretty eyes. "When you call me sweetie, I know I'm in trouble."

She rolled those hazel eyes. "When have you ever been in trouble? No, I just want to make sure you're doing okay…you know, after Kaylee and all."

"Yeah, I'm good." As good as a guy could be who had weird powers that ended up making his soul feel like it was shriveling. "No trouble forgetting her."

Grams looked skeptical for a few moments. "Speaking of trouble, what were you doing with your grandpa's truck last night?"

Her habit of keeping track of him hadn't stopped when he'd turned eighteen. He'd rarely lied to her, and he didn't feel right doing it now, despite her prior warnings.

"I went to the reservation to do some research."

Her face paled.

Chapter Seventeen

"And I'm going again Tuesday night." Liam set his hands on the kitchen table, watching his grandmother's face flush red. Why would she have this reaction to his going to the reservation?

"Oh Liam, why? What do you need up there?" Her voice sounded so small.

"Just research, Grams. Nothing to worry about. And I'm taking Travis with me."

Grams made a flapping sound with her lips. "That one." She picked up the plates, looking like she wanted to say more, then she turned and set her load in the sink. Walking back to him, she stared into his eyes. "You be careful. Things aren't always what they seem, and sometimes it's better to just skim over the surface."

"What exactly do you mean?" He stood, looking down at her.

"Someday, we'll have a talk, but not yet." She walked away, down the hall, and her bedroom door closed.

Liam filled the sink with hot, sudsy water as he stared out the window at the irrigator inching its way along the hard ground, spraying life-giving moisture in every direction "Why isn't anything easy?"

Last night, they'd arrived at the drive-in just as it closed. He and Travis had split up and asked if anyone had seen Maureen, and they'd got conflicting stories. She'd been there, that was for sure, but someone thought she'd left with a man.

She wasn't returning his calls. He didn't know where she lived. He just had a gut feeling that she could help him through all the stupid shit going on right now.

After he finished the dishes, he took a huge slice of peach pie to his room and ate it quickly. He wanted to spend more time at the library before work that night. He'd spotted some possibilities in the books he'd checked out, and wanted to search more online.

> *Dear Me, I'm quite optimistic right now about Eddie Crow. He didn't reject my speculations about the Rain Ceremony. Needless to say, I can't wait to get some answers. Somehow, though, in my mind, I feel like I'm stretched. The moments that I'm not thinking about Amanda or obsessing over her, I'm definitely thinking about Trinity. I can't put it all together yet, but I know there are clues right in front of me that I just can't see. Sometimes I'm just tired, want to give up everything, and be just plain old Liam. But something inside of me says, in order to find the answers, I need to understand true love...*

The next three days dragged by. His research hadn't yielded anything. All he could focus on now, was getting back to the rez and hearing what the old man had to say. The few minutes that his shifts overlapped with Amanda's each day were pure torture. She'd only have to say his name to get his body roaring like a jet engine.

And she knew it. She could tell what she did to him. Her satisfied smile, the way her hips swayed and her nipples puckered, showed him she knew he wanted her as much as she wanted him.

Every day, Amanda made an excuse to get him alone. To deflect her, he'd pull out his phone and dial Maureen as he walked away from the redhead. But until she left the store, a power struggle raged. Their bodies craved relief, their minds demanded the release of an orgasm, and their souls called out for each other like lost spirits looking for the light.

She wanted it. He didn't.

And Trinity, shit, he hadn't had time to contact her. Hadn't heard a thing from Tara. That whole mess loomed like a ticking timebomb. It was just a matter of time before it blew.

Tuesday afternoon, as Liam and Travis drove in silence toward the rez, Liam repeated in his mind every question he wanted to ask Ernie Crow.

Travis sat silent, texting and checking his social media.

They pulled up to the gray house and Ernie Crow walked out his front door. Standing on the porch, he didn't appear ready to sit and chat a while.

"Sir." Liam walked up the steps but Travis stayed back a ways.

"There is a place. Once you find it, it will tell you what you need to know." The old man handed Liam a scrap of paper. On it, a hand-drawn map showed a river, a tree, and some other landmarks with scribbled handwriting next to them. Liam looked up.

A movement inside the house caught his attention. Someone in dark clothes.

"Go there and come back to tell me what you've learned." Ernie Crow turned toward the house.

"Now?" They had only hours of daylight left, but the way he'd drawn the map, it might take a few hours to get there.

"If you have the power inside you, it will be but a simple task." The man disappeared inside the house.

Liam trotted down the steps and handed the map to Travis. "If you want to wait in the truck, that's fine."

"Hell, no." Travis led the way to the truck where they grabbed bug spray and a couple of bottles of water from the backseat. "Did you see the guy in the house? It was that Indian from the trailer house."

Liam should have figured as much. Was he there to protect Ernie Crow, or was he part of the answer Liam sought?

Whatever test or quest or mission the old man was sending him on, it was important for him to succeed. "Let's get going." He pointed to a trail starting behind the house. "Looks like that's it."

They walked through the worn path until they came to a circular clearing with a fire pit in the middle.

"Weenie roasts?" Travis slapped at a mosquito then sprayed more repellant.

"Or ceremonies." Liam checked the map. An arrow drawn on the clearing pointed to a downed tree. He looked in the general direction and saw a huge tree, white with age, laying at the edge of the woods.

"That's it." They climbed over the tree then headed north, using the sun as a general compass. The brush grew thick, as if it hadn't been disturbed for generations. Thistles tore at their clothes and skin, their boots slipped through muddy bogs, and they detoured around areas where the kudzu created an impenetrable green curtain.

The heat closed in like bad breath, the scents

of rotting vegetation and old growth becoming nauseating.

The rocky bottom of the river forced them to hold on to each other as they crossed. On the other side, as they sat to empty water from their boots and wring out their socks, Travis chuckled. “Now that we’ve held hands, are we officially going steady?”

“Yeah, something like that.” Liam checked his phone. No service. They’d already been walking an hour and a half.

“How much further?” They checked the map.

“Not far.” Liam got to his feet and squatted at the river, splashing water on his face and through his hair.

“Ha. Ha.” Travis stood. “That’s what my dad used to say on road trips.”

“Seriously, Trav, if you start asking *Are we there yet?* I’m gonna clock you one good.” He stood.

“Shit’s getting serious now.” Travis grabbed the map and led the way.

After another half hour of fighting their way through the woods, they emerged onto a blacktop road.

“What the fuck?” Liam looked both ways. It was an old lay of asphalt that stretched as far as he could see.

“Yeah, look here.” Travis lifted the map and pointed to the words, *White man’s trail.*

“You’ve gotta be shittin’ me.”

“We could’ve driven here.”

“Maybe it doesn’t go anywhere.” Liam hoped to hell that was the case.

Travis pointed to his left. “Says to go that way.”

They ran as far as they could, walked, then ran

again until they came to a cutout where three cars and a pickup truck were parked.

"So your theory about this being an abandoned road…" Travis folded the map and put it in his pocket.

As they walked past the vehicles and made their way along the path, an old wooden sign announced, *Ancient Caves*.

"This is it." Liam's heart jumped a couple times.

Ahead of them, the sound of men's voices and laughter drifted on the air.

"What's going on?" Travis stopped and squinted, trying to see through the woods.

"Let's find out." Liam walked around him and into a clearing surrounding the high mouth of a cave. Beside it, seven men sat on lawn chairs, cans in their hands.

"Welcome." The guy from the trailer lifted his beer in a mock toast. "Ernie Crow told us you'd be coming, so we're holding a party in your honor."

From the mocking tone of the man's voice, Liam didn't guess they'd be offering him and Travis a beer anytime soon. "We just want to look around. Okay?"

The man made a face and gestured around them. "Free country." Then he tsked. "No, wait, it's not, is it. Sovereign nation. Sorry."

Travis let out a breath. "You're saying we can't?"

"Ah, let 'em look, Boner." One of the men smacked the guy's arm. "They won't find nothin'. At least, nothing they'll understand."

The man called Boner spat onto the ground next to his chair. "Go ahead, boys. See if the spirits talk to you."

The group laughed as Liam and Travis walked a wide path around the men and headed toward the cave.

"Should've brought a flashlight." Liam stepped into what looked like a cave, but turned out to be just a rock shelter.

"Doesn't look like we need it." Travis poked around. "Nothin' here." He locked gazes with Liam. "You think this was some kind of a joke or something? To see if we would actually do what the old man said?"

"Hell, I don't know." Liam looked back at the men sitting in a semi-circle. They didn't seem like they had much respect for the ancient site. "Yeah, probably." As his eyes adapted to the darkness, scratches on the cave wall caught his gaze. "Here's something."

Travis came closer. "Oh, hey, our phones." He pulled out his phone and turned it to a white screen.

Liam grunted. "Kinda slow, ain't I." He used his own phone to add light to the spot on the wall.

"U-to-hi-yu." Travis read the words.

Liam repeated them as he typed them into a note on his phone. He waited a few seconds, hoping they'd conjure up feelings or images. Nothing. "We'll ask the old man what that means." He used the light to search the rest of the opening, and Travis did the same. "Nothing else?"

"Nope." Travis tucked his phone into his pocket and turned toward where the men sat. "What now."

"Now, we figure out how to get back without going through the jungle."

****

Forty-five minutes later, they reached Liam's truck and each downed two bottles of water. One of the men had taken pity on them and told them how to get back to Ernie Crow's using the roads.

The old man came out on the porch and stood silently.

Liam motioned for Travis to stay at the truck and walked to the foot of the steps. "We found the cave. Was that it?"

His black gaze stared into Liam's eyes, unblinking. "Do you believe that was it?"

"It was a test? To see if we'd follow your directions, right?"

"It could have been."

Liam scratched a mosquito bite. "I did what you said. Will you answer my questions now?"

The old man threw back his head and laughed. "Your questions have been answered. You need to go back to your world and forget this one."

Hours of mucking through the woods, putting up with those punk assholes, searching a non-cave for nothing. "I'm not leaving until you tell me what I came to find out." Liam cooled his anger, shaking his head. "No disrespect, but I passed your challenge and I want—"

"You. Want." The man lifted his arm and pointed one gnarled finger at Liam. "You do not have the right to want anything. You have been given. And that, you have wasted."

Travis stepped up beside Liam. "Stop talking the witch-doctor bullshit. We're not leaving until you answer his questions."

The old man's face tightened and he turned and walked to his door.

"Hey." Travis stepped forward, but Liam

caught his arm.

"Let it be." Liam was just as pissed as Travis, but harassing an elder wasn't how he wanted this to end. Before he walked away, Liam would play his trump card. "I will find Buck Waya." He made his voice loud enough for the man to hear. "He is wise where you are just confused."

Ernie Crow stopped, reached beside the door, and turned, a shotgun in his hand. "Confused old men get away with killing trespassers." He leveled the gun at Liam's chest.

Chapter Eighteen

Liam froze. Would the dark hole of a single-barrel shotgun be Liam's last earthly memory? He looked into the black depths of Ernie Crow's eyes.

The old man's trigger finger twitched.

Liam's body jerked to the side as Travis body-slammed him.

The roar of the shotgun blast deafened Liam as he hit the ground, Travis on top of him.

"Fucking hell!" Travis jumped up, ran up onto the porch and pulled the gun out of the old man's hands, throwing it off the side of the porch. "You crazy fucking shithead!"

Ernie Crow laughed. "Crazy? That's my alibi." He wandered back into the house and shut the door.

"You okay, Trav?" Liam's voice came out high, panicked. He got to his feet and stumbled up the steps toward his friend. He had to have taken some of the shot.

Travis held his shoulder where his shirt was shredded, but there was no blood. "Rock salt." He picked a piece from his shirt. "Liam, you seriously owe me one, buddy." Travis's knees wobbled and Liam helped him down the steps and into the truck.

"I owe you a big one." He looked into his best friend's eyes. "Thank you, brother." Never had anyone risked their life for him. The knowledge that Travis was willing to do it made Liam's heart thud, and his eyes burn.

Travis flexed his shoulder. "Don't even think about hugging me, asshole. Just get me home in one piece, and don't ever haul me back to this shithole again." He sat back and closed his eyes, a chill shaking him for a second.

Liam got them off the rez and raced toward Liberation. Shit, he could have been killed. Travis could have been killed. All for what? To prove that he was somebody? That he was something special?

Fuck the Rain Ceremony. Fuck the whole legend and the bullshit idea that he had a gift. He was just plain white trash, not worth the rock salt it'd take to blow him to hell. Hadn't his stepfather said as much a hundred times?

All Liam had wanted was one thing that he could call his own. Proof that the talent he had for making women feel beautiful was unique and a part of a legacy Liam could claim. It would have been so amazing if Ernie Crow had been sane, had seen a special talent in Liam, had given him a history to hold on to. He gripped the wheel tight.

The cost of his stupid dreams had come at too high a price. He'd been made a fool of in front of Travis. Liam looked at his friend who had his eyes closed, either asleep or not wanting to talk to him. He didn't blame him for that. Liam had fallen for a stupid prank and Travis was paying for it.

He'd imagined his life would be a lot different from this, once he'd started having sex. This turned out to be more screwed up than pleasurable. He needed a break, time to step back and pull himself together.

Dear Me, in a word, done. If there is any link between me and this legend, it's not worth searching for anymore. I just want to be normal. I guess, reflecting upon the course of the past few weeks, I realize one important thing—being me is the best thing I'll ever be. I have good friends, well, one good friend, a great family, and I don't need to be any more extraordinary than that. Apparently the forces of the universe are telling me that, no matter what the answers are, I should just stick to what I know. It's strange that even as I sit here with the determination to put my investigation to rest, after coming up empty-handed, after meeting these particular women: Kaylee, Trinity, plus this crazy obsession with Amanda, my soul feels…ah, never mind, it sounds crazy. Anyway, I'm going to try just being normal for a while. True love?... Who gives a shit?

Three days later, after dozens of unanswered calls to Maureen and unreturned voice messages, Liam took an early shift at the Pump and Run when the regular guy called in sick. A woman pumping gas caught his attention. Her dark blue four-door looked like someone had kicked in a dozen spots on the passenger side.

Tall and curvy, her blonde hair was pulled up into a super-short ponytail. Her big sunglasses sat on her long nose… "Maureen." Liam locked the cash register, vaulted over the counter, and shoved open the glass door.

She jerked when he skidded to a halt in front of her.

"Maureen." He had a hundred things he needed to say to her, but he just grinned and replaced the nozzle on the gas pump for her.

Her lips tightened. "You work nights. What are you doing here?"

She'd kept track of him? "Taking an extra shift." He inched closer, tipping his head down. "I'm so darn glad to see you."

The words he spoke didn't match the feelings inside him. Why couldn't he find the urge to hold her close or kiss her? It wasn't like him to have a physical urge without some kind of emotion attached to it. Kaylee had overwhelmed him. Trinity had, too. And Amanda—hell, it nearly killed him to not touch her.

Why, with this girl, who he wanted to love, did the emotion just seem foreign in some way? He wanted this, wanted to connect with her, heart and soul. She would be his grounding wire, his anchor, his guide through the sorry mess that had become his existence and out the other side.

He revved up the determination that no matter how long it took, even if he couldn't feel it inside right now, he was going to like Maureen. A lot.

"I have a zero tolerance rule, Liam." She opened her car door, not meeting his gaze. The entire driver's side was banged up, too. "You stand me up once, you're done."

"I'm really sorry, darlin'." He had to get this right and do it quick. "It was an emergency, I was out of cell range, and I—"

"Yeah. You told me all that in the three hundred messages you left." Tossing her purse into the car, she shifted, ready to get in and leave.

He wanted to see her eyes, needed to know if he was getting through to her. "I think I sent three hundred and one. And the one you missed was me telling you how much I've been thinking about you."

She sighed and looked up at him. “Liam. I can’t.” She turned to get into her car.

He put his hand on her shoulder. “I’ve been imagining how good we’d be together. How much fun I’d had with you, just talking and getting to know you.” He would work on the rest of it, work on trying to conjure up the feelings for Maureen that he’d felt for Kaylee, and still felt for Trinity. But he needed her to let him into her world.

Her head swiveled and she faced him. “I’ve got that one rule, and you broke it, honey child.” One corner of her mouth turned up in a smile.

“What would it take for you to give a guy one more chance?” He reached up and slid off her dark glasses.

Her left eye was swollen and bruised. She looked away.

“What happened?” Gently he took her chin and turned her to face him. “Was it your boyfriend?”

She nodded.

“And your car?”

“He was mad that I moved out.”

Liam’s gut clenched. She’d been living with him? “When did this happen?”

Maureen leaned into him just an inch.

He took it as a sign and held her close.

“Friday. I packed my things that day, thinking he’d be working the weekend, but he came home and saw my note. He found me at the drive-in. I tried to drive to the sheriff’s office, but he cornered me.”

“That bastard.” Liam could see himself beating the shit out of the guy. Hell, he should beat the shit out of himself for not showing up Friday.

She shrugged. “I suppose I deserved it for—”

“No.” He took her shoulders and moved back,

looking into her eyes. "No one deserves to be hurt. It's ignorant people who can't control their anger who think they make themselves feel better by striking out."

"I know you're right, but deep down inside, I'm just too afraid to look at what I let him do to me."

Liam wanted to be the one to get her through this. "Did you call the sheriff?"

She shook her head.

"We should. Right now. I can—"

"No. He's related to a few of the deputies, so I can't see anything coming of it." She went back into his arms. "Oh, Liam. You're so good for me."

"Hey!" A man stood holding open the door of the convenience store. "Anyone work here?"

"Come inside?" Liam kissed the top of her head and backed away, watching her face.

"No, I've got to work. I'll call you later."

He stopped and lifted a brow.

She smiled. "I promise."

****

After Amanda drove into the lot and parked that afternoon, Liam watched her drag her fingers across the hood of his car as she walked past it. Why the hell did that simple action set his teeth on edge and his blood heating?

The minute she stepped into the building, it was like the air conditioning quit. And a solar flare filled the room.

"Maureen. Maureen. Maureen." He repeated the mantra silently as he rang up a line of customers.

When the store emptied, Amanda came up behind him at the register. "Liam." The word oozed from her mouth, slow and sexy.

"Hey, Amanda." He punched the buttons on

the cash register, logging himself out. "It's all yours." He turned.

She stood right there. Her green eyes widened as she stared at him, and her nipples hardened through her shirt and uniform vest. "I wish it was. All. Mine." She licked her lips and did a slow scan of his body. Not very subtle.

Whatever it was that ziplined between them felt stronger today, more enticing. What mortal man could resist this? Why should Liam? He was single, she wasn't with Travis yet. She evidently had seductive intentions toward Liam…

Travis. No, he couldn't rationalize his way clear to having sex with a woman his best friend wanted.

His body vibrated with need, his hands shaking as he held them up in surrender. "I'm not interested. Don't you understand that?" Harsh, but he had to fight dirty.

Amanda's face turned red and she glanced away.

Had he hurt her? Liam made a wide path around her and nearly ran to the back of the store, clocked out, hung up his vest, and left without giving her another glance. It took him a few tries to get the key in his car door, and he sat for a couple minutes before he felt stable enough to drive.

If he could capture the desire he felt for Amanda and combine it with the softer emotions he had felt for Kaylee and still felt for Trinity, then direct all that mojo toward Maureen…

He willed Maureen to call. Before he fucking lost his mind.

****

At exactly seven that night, Liam arrived at

the River Point Apartments carrying a big pizza box and a fistful of wildflowers snipped from his grandmother's garden, with her blessing. He knocked on the door to apartment 305.

"Who is it?" An odd-sounding male voice croaked the words.

"It's Liam, I'm looking for…"

The door swung open and Maureen stood grinning at him, holding a baseball bat. "A girl can't be too careful." She gestured for him to enter. Her blue T-shirt curved temptingly over her round breasts, and her cutoff jean shorts showed long, graceful legs and bare feet with purple-painted nails.

"You know how to use that thing?" He glanced down at the bat as he passed her.

"I sure do, and I'm not afraid to take a swing or two, sugar." She set the bat aside and closed the door, locking them in.

Liam admired the way she'd turned her life around, and was standing up for herself. He handed her the flowers. The mixed scents of sweet and earthy matched Maureen's personality. "They're not as beautiful as you are, but you deserve to be surrounded by pretty things."

She took the bouquet, her eyes opening wide. "Wow, flowers *and* a poem. All for me?" She almost seemed like she didn't feel deserving.

"For you, darlin'. And I have a lot more wonderful things planned for you. For us."

"Oh, Liam." She blinked a few times and he moved in, setting the pizza box on the entryway table. The scent of pepperoni and hot tomato sauce had taunted him during the drive over here, but now, her hot, sexy body drew him like a magnet.

His lips captured hers as his arms went around

her, pulling her to him, careful in case her asshole ex-boyfriend had gotten in any body punches. "I'm glad I finally found you again." He whispered the words against her lips.

She laced her fingers in his hair and tugged him closer, kissing him with an enthusiasm that rocked him, building his hunger for her as a low heat deep in his belly. Her tongue lapped at his, teasing him as he ran his hand down her spine, splaying his fingers wide at the curve of her ass.

Pulling back, she caught her breath and looked at him with her sky-blue eyes darkening. "Eat first?"

He could tell she would be willing to lead him to the bedroom that very second, but he didn't want to fuck this up. Didn't want to do things the way he'd done with Kaylee and Trinity, leaving him deflated and aching after they left him. "Yes, let's eat. I want to hear why you're living in Liberation, now."

"Okay." She smiled and walked toward the kitchen. "Grab a seat on the couch, and bring that pizza with you."

The furniture looked fairly new, a blue couch and matching chairs around a coffee table, where he set the box. The TV was small, but a good brand. "Is this all your furniture?"

"Nope. You know I can't afford shit. My roommate's. She's out of town on a job interview. Won't be back until late tomorrow."

Through the kitchen door, he saw her smell the flowers then arrange them in a vase. She carried them out, her other hand balancing a stack of plates, napkins, and two cans of beer. She set everything on the coffee table.

He opened the pizza box and waited for her to sit.

Plopping onto the couch, she patted the spot beside her. “You’re going to have to keep me awake, Liam. I had a rough fucking day today.”

Liam sat and loaded their plates with slices of pepperoni pizza, the only thing she’d asked him to bring when she’d called him that afternoon.

“You never said.” He handed her a plate. “Where are you working?”

“At the Pooch Palace. I’m a dog groomer.”

“Really? That’s cool.”

She rolled her eyes. “La-de-fucking-da.” She bit into her slice.

The shop she named was in a strip mall on the highway between here and Schaefer, near the drive-in. “How’d you get into that?” He popped open both their beers and sat back, taking a couple big gulps. The hoppy beer cooled his throat and he stifled a burp.

“I blew the manager.” She grinned. “Just kidding. I took a class in school.” She shrugged. “I was good at it, and started working when I was a junior, and now I’m full-time.”

Liam didn’t know much about her. “When did you move out of your parents’ house?”

Maureen froze, the slice halfway to her mouth. She set it back on the plate and put it on the table. “I guess I should tell you everything about my redneck, white-trash family so we can get it out of the way.”

“Not if you don’t want to. But I’m glad to listen.” Fact was, he was curious as hell, but he wouldn’t push her.

She snuggled in close to him, so he wrapped his arm around her, and offered her the pointy tip of his pizza slice.

Grinning, she took a bite. "Boy, you're smooth." She mumbled it around the food in her mouth.

He had no response to that, so he took a big chomp of his slice.

"I moved out after graduation last year and moved in with Brody. My parents…" Taking a long uneven breath, she stared at her hands. "They didn't really care what I did. I wasn't their smartest kid; that was my sister. And I wasn't their most talented kid; which was my brother, the football star." She looked at him. "So I got attention in inappropriate ways. Such as getting fucked-up and making really bad decisions. Ha ha."

He nodded. He could pretty much imagine how a girl known as The Sub-Maureen would get her parents to notice her.

"It was good at first, Brody and me. But he liked things rough, and after a while, it got too rough, and left bruises. A few months ago, I started stepping out on him with other guys, hoping to meet someone I could…" Her tongue traced her bottom lip as she stared at the wall. "I was being stupid. I thought I had to have a man to take care of me. But a woman at work helped me get my head straight, and I finally left that motherfucker."

Maureen smiled at him. "Valuing myself by relationships with men was selling myself short. She told me that." Blinking a couple times, she picked up her beer. "That's when I saw what I was doing and decided to make a change. I called every girl I knew, girlfriends, cousins, even a few bitches I'd been nasty to in school. Sissy, that's whose apartment we're in, was on the dance team with me in high school, and was looking for a roommate, so I thought, hell yeah, and here I am."

Gesturing around the room, she sighed. "I am free of Brody and making it on my own." Her brows knitted together as if she couldn't believe it.

Liam's breath caught. He set his plate on the table and kissed her. "I'm glad for you, darlin'. I'm really proud that you found your way here. That you're doing what you want."

She laughed. "Yeah, it's like a cheesy TV movie, huh? But besides always looking over my shoulder for Brody, I'm pretty happy."

Liam could do this with her. Be happy. Work through their separate shitty issues together, support each other, maybe find something real and lasting. The excitement of finally finding something that could be all his, had his breath coming fast and his heart thumping. In his jeans, his excitement grew in the form of a denim-stretcher.

Maureen stared into his eyes, her own turning dark as her pupils dilated. She set down her beer without breaking eye contact. "Maybe we've had enough to eat?"

Chapter Nineteen

Liam and Maureen were alone in her apartment. All night. And Maureen was offering him heaven in her bed. But wouldn't it just turn out like Kaylee and Trinity? With him alone. Again. "Let's watch a movie."

Maureen's brows shot up. "I don't think Sissy has any porn channels."

He laughed. This girl was trying to change her behavior, but it didn't seem to be working too well yet. "No, just a movie. Something on HBO or Netflix or something."

She looked away and her lips turned down. "Okay."

He'd insulted her. "Darlin', it's not that I don't want you." He glanced down at the rise in his Levis.

Her eyes locked on his bulge.

"But I want this to be more." He tipped up her chin. "I'd like to take it slow, get acquainted, really work at it and see if we can make something lasting happen." He'd work his ass off making himself feel what he needed to feel for her, even though it bore all the signs of a rebound relationship.

"Oh, Liam." Her voice sounded choked and she buried her face in his neck.

He pulled her onto his lap. Big mistake. Her lush booty pressed hot and soft along his manhood. Liam forced down his baser urges. "Oh, Maureen." He tried to sound just like her, and it earned him a laugh from her.

"You're amazing. You actually heard what I said about not measuring my value by the man in my life. And you're respecting that."

True, he'd heard what she'd said. But his motives weren't that altruistic. But they weren't all that far misaligned from hers either, so no harm in letting her see him in a glowing light. "You know it, darlin'."

They found a movie just starting, dimmed the lights, and settled in, sharing pizza and beer until Maureen fell asleep.

The knock on the door woke Liam, and Maureen blinked awake in his arms.

"What time is it?" She whispered the words.

He checked his phone. "It's after eleven."

"Shit." She jumped up and peeked out the curtains. "I don't see his car."

"I know you're in there, Maureen. I hear the TV." The man's voice carried through the door.

She spun, her eyes shifting wildly. "It's Brody."

Liam stood and took a step toward the door, but she held out her hand to him.

"I just want to give you the money I owe you." The man's voice sounded quieter. "And I want to apologize for…you know. Stuff."

Her body sagged. "Hang on." She shouted the words at the door as she gestured for Liam to go into the bedroom.

Liam stiffened and shook his head. He'd like to show the woman-beater what it felt like to get punched in the eye by someone bigger than him.

Maureen pressed her palms together like she was praying. She tipped her head and gave him a puppy-dog face.

Hell. As he walked past her, he whispered, "He touches you, I'm gonna kick his ass."

She nodded quickly and shoved him into the

room, closing the door.

The queen-sized bed was covered by a pink, frilly quilt. The headboard was nearly invisible behind a dozen pillows in multiple hues of red and pink. He didn't picture Maureen as the princess-type.

"No, you can't come in. Just—" Her voice dropped. "Hey, I said no. Now, get out."

"You left our nice apartment for this?" Brody's voice passed the bedroom door.

Liam reached for the handle, then stopped. He'd let Maureen do this herself. Up to a point. Then it'd be his pleasure to connect his knuckles with the guy's face.

"Brody, it's over. Just give me the envelope, say you're sorry, then get out of my life forever." She sounded strong, confident.

"I don't want it to be over." Brody's voice sounded close. "Give me another chance, baby-girl. It'll be better this time."

"Take your hands off me and go." Maureen didn't sound afraid.

Liam's hand grasped the handle. He'd give her another few seconds.

"If you won't give it to me, I'll take what I want." Brody spoke quietly, like a snake about to strike.

"You're hurting me, Brody."

Liam heard a crack in Maureen's voice and ripped open the door. "Get your fucking hands off her, boy."

Brody's beady eyes shifted toward Liam. His black faux-hawk and dark scruff matched his ripped clothing. Maureen liked the bad-boy type, huh?

Liam didn't wait for the man to comply. He swung low, catching Brody in the gut. Fuck, that felt good. After everything in Liam's life that spiraled out of control, taking charge here seemed nearly orgasmic.

The man released Maureen and bent over, his arms wrapped around his waist. "You're fucking another man already? You skanky whore."

Liam pulled Maureen behind him. "Not another word, white trash." He punctuated his words with a fist to Brody's mouth.

The man stumbled sideways, banging his shoulder against the wall and cracking the sheetrock.

"If I see you anywhere near her again…" Liam strode up to the shorter man, tightening his fist in the guy's shirt and pressing his knuckles against his windpipe. "I'll make sure you won't be walking out."

Blood leaked from the guy's mouth as he shrank, bracing for another hit.

Liam wasn't one to take advantage of a coward. "Get the fuck out." He shoved Brody toward the door. "Forget you ever knew her."

Maureen opened the door and Liam shoved the guy out.

Brody limped down the hallway. "This ain't over."

Liam stepped out and took quick strides toward him. "Okay, fucker. Come back and let's finish it."

The asshole actually ran away, scurrying like a rat.

Liam walked back into the apartment, closed the door, and took Maureen into his arms. "I don't think you'll be seeing him again."

"I hope not." She didn't sound too sure.

"When's your roommate coming back?"

"Tomorrow." She shivered. "Stay with me tonight?" Her voice was so small, he couldn't help but want to protect her. Was that the first step in training his heart to love?

"I'll stay." He kissed the top of her hair. "How can I resist that big, pink bed?"

She laughed. "That's not mine. This is a one-bedroom, so I get the sofa sleeper."

"Hm. Good. All those pillows in there might have drowned me."

Maureen looked up at him, her hand pressing softly over his heart. "You're my hero, Liam." Moisture sparkled in her eyes.

"I want to be, Maureen." And he actually meant it, intellectually, but his heart still didn't know how to embrace the experience.

Slowly, she kissed her way from his neck to his chest, then lower, and her knees bent. "I want to thank you for…"

He grasped her arms and tugged her up again. "No, darlin'. A hero doesn't need a reward." There wasn't much he'd like more than to have her lips wrapped around his manhood again, but he had to stick with his plan. He kissed her softly, breathing in her floral scent. "C'mon. Let's get that hide-a-bed pulled out and get some sleep."

"Whatever you want, Liam." Maureen wiped a tear from her cheek. "Hey, you know what? I'm glad you found me again, too."

****

The next morning, Liam woke feeling better than he had in weeks. Maureen lay next to him, sleeping on her back, her hands up over her head, and the soles of her feet touching. He smiled. She looked like a big pretzel, but she was the best thing that'd happened to him in a heck of a long time.

When he rolled away to get off the bed, she reached for him, her hand gliding along his ribs. “Are you sneaking out?”

“Hell, no!” He pounced on her, pinning her hands to the bed and kissing her with every ounce of desire he had for her. “Never. You’ve got me, darlin’. There’ll be no shaking me loose.” The words came from his mouth, but they didn’t evoke any emotion in him. He felt almost empty.

Under him, she wiggled, her smile showing both the angel and the devil inside her. “Are you sure I can’t change your mind?”

His manhood swelled, growing hard, pressing his briefs against the little pajamas she’d changed into last night. “Let’s wait. Let’s see what happens between us before we jump each other.” He rolled them onto their sides, their bodies still pressed together.

She didn’t say anything.

“Okay?”

She nodded, her eyes unblinking as she stared into his. “I’ll wait if you want to, but I have to tell you, I’ve never come like I did that time in the car with you.” Swallowing, she paused, then cupped her hand on his cheek. “I’ve always had difficulty reaching climax. Until you. And I’m greedy, Liam. I want that again.”

He’d heard of women who couldn’t orgasm. What were the statistics on that? And on the number who had wet orgasms, like the rain he was able to coax from women? He’d have to hit the library again and do some research. “I’m glad I can give you pleasure.”

“Pleasure?” Her hand slid down his stomach,

just brushing the tip of his hardening length before she guided her palm up to his chest. "It's so intense, Liam, don't be surprised if I tie you to the bed to keep you from leaving this morning."

He kissed her, long and deep. "Maureen." This was what he'd hoped to have with Kaylee. What he'd never imagined finding so quickly with someone else. Now he just had to find the emotion to match this physical perfection.

She snuggled on top of him, her lips nipping at his skin.

"Girl, you don't need to tie me up to keep me here." He couldn't help but visualize it, though, and he could almost feel the way her hot mouth would please him. Soon. Very soon.

****

That evening, Maureen stopped by the Pump and Run on her way home from work. "Hi hun." She leaned across the counter to give him a kiss.

Liam hesitated, knowing the security camera was running, but went for it anyway. "How was work?"

"Uh." She half-sat on the counter. "They double-booked me, so I didn't have a break the whole eight hours." She looked up at him from under her lashes. "A foot rub would feel amazing."

Liam laughed. "Are you inviting me to your place tonight, or are you asking for a rub right here on the checkout counter?"

"Um, can I have both?" She grinned and shook her head. "No, I want your complete attention, so let's wait until tonight."

He showed her where she could sit so the surveillance camera didn't spot her, and they talked and ate a supper of junk food. When she got up to leave, he sent a six-pack of beer with her. "I'll be there in about an hour."

"Okay, hun, and thanks for supper." She winked and walked out the door.

He watched her put the beer in the trunk of her car and slide into the driver's seat. A black car raced into the lot and pulled up right behind hers.

"Ah, shit." Liam jumped over the counter and ran out just as Brody pulled open her driver's door and hauled Maureen out by her arm. She yelled at her ex, and the guy shouted back, shaking her.

Liam ran straight for him. "Get your hands off her."

He looked up but didn't release her. "This ain't none of your business any more, vest boy. Maureen called me. She wants to move back home with me, so go back inside and you won't get hurt."

"He's lying, Liam." She struggled to get out of Brody's grip, but the man held her between Liam and himself.

Anger rose hot and wild in Liam's chest. "You son of a bitch. You slunk away last night like you had no balls at all." He stopped a foot from the little shit. "Tonight, I'm gonna finish you off."

"I'd like to see you try." The asshole shoved Maureen aside and squared off with Liam. Where had Brody gotten all this confidence all the sudden? Liquor? Drugs?

"Listen up, Bro-dee, you little fuck. Maureen is my woman now." Liam gestured for her to get into her car, then he shoved her ex back a few feet. "And nobody touches my woman. You hear?"

"Liam, let's go back in the store and call for help." Maureen tried to step between the two men, but Liam turned, pushing her behind him. Before he could turn around again, the guy punched him in the kidney.

Liam went down on a knee. He let the pain fuel the anger and he sprung up and slammed a fist under Brody's chin.

The man stumbled back a couple of steps then shook his head and came after Liam. Brody grabbed him around the waist and ran him back into the wall. Something inside Liam made a popping noise.

"Stop it." Maureen's voice sounded full of tears.

Liam lost his breath, but shoved his hand on the man's face and pushed backward.

Then the front passenger door of the black car opened, followed by the back door. Two men got out and rushed toward them.

Liam knew he was fucked. If he could take Brody down quickly, he might have a chance with the other two. He gut-punched the guy, and when Brody was bent over, thrust his knee into his face, sending him back on his ass. But he wasn't out.

Brody's friends came at each side of Liam.

"Hold him for me." Brody's nose leaked blood as he scrambled up off the pavement.

"No." Maureen was still trying to stop this. "You get the hell out of here. I've called the sheriff and told him there was an armed robbery in progress."

Brody's friends stopped and looked at each other.

"Don't listen to her. She's a fucking liar." Brody shoved one of his friends toward Liam.

Stepping back, Liam drove his fist into the guy's neck and tripped him, letting him fall to the ground.

The other guy lunged at Liam and caught him with two punches, one to his eye and the other to his mouth.

Liam's world tipped as he stumbled back.

Brody gut-punched him and kicked at his knee, missing and hitting his calf.

The pavement came rushing up at Liam's face and he rolled to avoid another kick.

Maureen's cries faded in and out of Liam's brain, alternating with buzzing and darkness. "Hear the sirens? Derrick! Joe! You guys get out of here right now, or I'll give them your names and addresses."

The two men looked at her then at each other and headed for the car, the one pressing a hand to his neck and clearing his throat as he slid into the driver's seat. "Brody, let's go, man!"

Liam got to his hands and knees.

A booted foot caught him in the ribs and sent him rolling.

Behind him, Liam heard a thud and Maureen screamed. "Please don't, Brody. You're breaking my hand."

Chapter Twenty

Struggling to see through the black fog in front of his eyes, Liam pushed himself to his knees, but his stomach heaved and he found himself back on all fours, hurling up a mix of beef sticks, potato chips, and red raspberry slushy.

The screech of tires sounded, then loud running, like boots on pavement.

"Fucker!" A man's voice reached Liam's ears, then the sound of a fist connecting with flesh sounded over and over again.

"Help me, you assholes!" Brody called to his friends between the punches he took.

"Travis, stop. You're killing him." Maureen screeched the words.

"Motherfucker deserves to die." Travis's voice. Jeez, he'd never been so glad to hear his buddy's rich-boy southern drawl. "You guys want some of my shit, too?"

"No," one of Brody's friends said. "Let him alone. He's on the ground, man."

"Get this piece of shit out of here." Travis sounded like the big-shot he was.

And Liam felt like the weak punching bag he'd ended up being.

Maureen's arms came around Liam, and she kissed him, crying softly. "I'm so sorry, Liam. Please forgive me. Oh, hun, this is all my fault."

"Not your fault." It hurt to talk. His gut ached, his ribs burned with each breath.

"Liam, buddy." Travis sat on his heels next to him, well away from the puke. "You need an ambulance?"

"No. Grams can fix this." Liam tried to push

himself up off his hands and knees but nearly blacked out.

"Hold on." Maureen and Travis hauled him to his car. Fishing the keys from his pocket, someone got the passenger door open, and folded Liam into the seat. They stood there with the door open, looking down at Liam.

"Think you can drive, Maureen?" Travis sounded so fucking in control, it made Liam feel like a wuss.

"I can drive." Maureen's voice came out strong.

"I'm going to stay here, have a couple friends come, and one of them will drive your car out to the farm. Just in case those punks come back to get their revenge on your sorry-looking sedan."

Maureen gave a half laugh. "Thanks, Travis."

"Any time. Glad you called me, and glad I was in town."

Liam couldn't grasp the significant of that last piece of information.

Travis gave Maureen directions.

"The store…" Liam couldn't leave it open. "Ray's number is—"

"I'll call him, let him know what happened, but I've seen you close down a dozen times. I'll figure it out and lock up if Ray doesn't get here right away." Travis leaned closer. "But no way in hell am I going to clean the slushy machine after seeing that gross shit you spread all over the parking lot just now."

Liam laughed and pain tore through him. "Thanks. You're…"

"Yeah. Just like your first day of school, huh? I can't leave you alone for a minute." Travis closed the car door.

Liam woke when his grandpa and Maureen pulled him out of his car and helped him to his room. Pain surged through his foggy brain every once in a while as his grandmother wrapped his ribs and put cold packs on his bruised face. She pushed a pill through his lips, lifted his head to hold a glass of water to his lips, and commanded him to swallow.

The next time he came around, he heard women's voices. Maureen and Grams sat talking. Maureen said something about the bad choices she'd made, and how she had valued herself by the men she was with.

Liam smiled. Grams would love this girl. He drifted off again.

****

Maureen didn't want to leave Liam's side, even when his grandparents offered to make up the couch for her. She felt better being close to him. He'd taken a beating for her. For *her*. No one had ever done anything like that before. He could have let Brody take her—either time—but he'd stood up to the man.

Liam's cough woke her and she jumped from her chair and stood at his side. His pretty blue eyes opened. "Hey." The word croaked from his throat.

"Hi. Want some water?" She brushed his soft hair back from his face.

"Yeah." He started to sit up but moaned and eased back down.

"Don't move, I have a straw." She let him sip water then offered him a painkiller. Something in a prescription bottle with his grandmother's name on it, guaranteed to knock him out, Emma had said.

Liam grabbed her hand. "Lie next to me."

She glanced toward the door that the older woman had left open a crack. Would the grandparents be upset if she did? While she had very little respect for her own parents, she would do just about anything to gain Liam's grandparents' approval.

"With your clothes on." Liam smiled, his split, swollen lip distorting his usually charming smirk.

"Of course." She carefully climbed in next to him and tried to find an unbruised spot to rest her hand. She settled on his hip as she pressed her lips to his shoulder. "Heal quickly, Liam. I want to wrap my arms around you and hang on tight forever." A tear snuck from the corner of her eye. She could see being here by his side, maybe even here on the farm someday.

"What happened…?" Liam cleared his throat. "With Brody and his boys?"

That man's name still sent her into a fit of anger. "Ray called the sheriff, who wants to talk to you, but with the security camera and the information I gave, there should be no problem charging them."

"You gave up those two guys? Even when you told them you wouldn't?" His voice held laughter.

She pressed her cheek to his shoulder and held in the sob that threatened to erupt. "After what they did to you? Those three are lucky if I don't put out a contract on their lives."

Liam laughed once, then groaned with pain. "I like a redneck woman."

Maureen pulled the sheet up to cover them both. "Good thing, 'cause you got one."

His breathing grew slow and steady.

She snuggled as close to him as she could, contorted her body until it touched as much of him as possible. In the warmth of his skin, and with the sweet emotion swirling through her, she fell asleep, letting herself dream of a future.

Liam's muffled shout woke her. The sun peeked over the horizon and he was sitting up, trying to get out of bed.

"What are you doing?" She sat up, wishing she had a toothbrush in her purse.

"I've got to get up."

"Whatever you need, I can get for—"

He swung one leg over the side of the bed then paused. "No. I mean I've *got* to get up and go."

"Oh." Nature calling. "Let me help."

He got his other foot on the floor before she'd come around the bed and stood in front of him. Liam breathed heavily, his face tight with the pain he had to be enduring. "Not exactly what you'd imagined our second date would be, huh?"

She put his arm around her shoulders on his less-injured side. "Best date ever." Something she'd never forget, and would talk about for years to come. "Ready?" Maureen dropped him off down the hall and went into the kitchen where Emma stood looking out the window with her hands in dishwater.

"Hi." Maureen padded toward the older woman.

"Good morning." She dried her hands and gestured to the full coffee pot.

"None for me, thanks." The smell of fresh brewed coffee made her a little nauseous. It had ever since she was a kid and took a dare from her older brother, swallowing a huge gulp from her dad's cup. Piping hot, it'd burned its way down her throat and into her stomach. "Does Liam drink coffee?"

"Not too often." Emma looked down the hall. "Is he awake?"

"He is, and he's using the bathroom."

Liam's grandmother pulled a pan from a cabinet and set it on the stove. "How's his pain level?" She went to the refrigerator and hauled out a carton of eggs.

"Not bad, I guess, since he's walking." She looked around the room. "Anything I can do to help?" She should really get home and shower, get ready for work, but she hated to leave.

Emma's face lit with a smile. "Sure. Let's cook up a big old-fashioned country breakfast. Something that'll get him healed up in no time."

Maureen jumped right in. She hadn't known her own grandparents, and she'd sure like to find out what all the fuss was about.

****

A half an hour later, Liam held his protruding stomach as he eased himself down into his bed. The women had cooked all his favorites. He'd eaten like a man on death row, and now, feeling the blur of the pain pill taking effect, he settled in for an all-day sleep.

Maureen seemed to like his family. She'd kept up a conversation with his grandparents, and was helping with the dishes now.

"All settled?" Maureen's voice came from the doorway.

"Yep." He held out a hand. "You gonna lie down with me for a bit? I've got the crazy need for one of your awesome kisses."

She held her hand over her mouth. "Breath."

"You can use my toothbrush if you want. It's the red one."

She hesitated, then smiled and ran down the hall. When she returned to the bedroom, she cuddled in next to him. "I have to work in an hour, so I can't stay long." Running her fingers over his bruised cheek, she sighed. "I'm so sorry this had to happen, Liam. I'd give anything if I could undo it. Take away your pain."

Compared to some of the beatings he'd taken as a kid, this was barely noticeable. "I just wish I hadn't let you walk out to your car alone. I should have known dipshit—"

"No." She touched her fingertip on his lip. "It's not your fault. And if everything goes right, dipshit will spend some time in jail, and will be out of our lives."

"Mmmm." Liam smiled and tugged her closer, kissing her as best as he could with half his mouth swollen. "I like the sound of that." He concentrated on the woman in his arms, willing himself to grow soft emotions for her. "Our lives."

"Sounds nice, doesn't it?" Her phone gave off a ping.

A memory intruded, reminding him of something… Grams's pain pills made his eyelids heavy.

"I should go." She kissed the uninjured side of his mouth then slid out of the bed.

Her phone.

Travis.

"Maureen, why do you have Travis's phone number?"

She hesitated, then smiled. "I have a lot of phone numbers. I don't remember how I got his in my phone." She shrugged. "Maybe his cousin Jesse?"

He could barely stay awake, much less conjure up more questions for her.

"Liam." She tipped her head. "You need to

trust that the only time I'll be calling another man is to have him come save your life."

She'd turned that around, and unintentionally made him feel like an idiot. "Have a good day at work."

"I will. See you later." She waved and left, quietly closing his door.

Liam nodded off. The woman had a past, that's for sure.

****

That night, Maureen stopped by after supper. Liam lay stretched out on the couch watching a baseball game with his grandfather.

Herschel stood when Maureen entered the room. Behind her, Emma clicked her tongue. "When was the last time you stood when *I* came into the room?"

"Just an hour ago, when you told me supper was on the table." His grandfather gave Maureen a wink.

Maureen smiled, then pointed at Liam. "Don't you get up."

He patted the spot in front of him on the couch. "I would if I could, darlin'. You deserve all the gentlemanly deeds I can give you."

Maureen's cheeks turned a sweet shade of pink as she walked toward him.

"Hersch, don't sit down. I need you in the kitchen." Grams gave her husband a look.

"But the game's on." He deflated. "Okay. Kitchen it is." His grandfather followed her out of the room.

"They're so sweet." Maureen brushed back Liam's hair. "How are you feeling?"

"Somehow it got worse all day, but now that

you're here…" He laced his fingers in her hair and tugged her down for a kiss.

She avoided his bruised lip and pulled back too quickly for his liking. "I have some news."

"Oh yeah?" The deputy sheriff had been out that morning to take Liam's statement, and dipshit and his stooges had been locked up since early this morning. Had she heard more about that?

"Sissy, my roommate?"

He nodded.

"She got that job. She's going to be moving to Indiana in less than a month."

"So, what does that mean for the apartment?"

Maureen's brows lifted. "It means, I can take over the lease, and I make enough to afford to pay the rent on my own. That's the good news."

"And the bad?"

"I don't own any furniture, and Sissy offered to sell me most of hers."

Liam liked everything in the apartment. Except the bed that looked like a cotton candy machine exploded on it. "And that's the bad news?"

"I have zero savings. What she's asking, I'd have to get a loan for, and I have zero credit, too."

His paychecks from the Pump and Run went into an account for his college expenses. He didn't want to jeopardize that by withdrawing money. But… "I could get a second job." It'd be his third, counting his farm chores, but he'd gladly work more hours to keep Maureen happy.

"Really? That's so sweet. Then maybe in a month, when she moves out…you could move in?" Maureen blinked at him a few times.

"Yeah. In a month." He could move in. It'd relieve some of the expense his grandparents had, feeding a bottomless pit, as Grams called him. This could work. He and Maureen, they could be something special for each other. "And let's wait, Maureen." He glanced around, but didn't see either of his grandparents. "Wait until the place is ours before we're together." He whispered the words and waited to feel excitement at the prospect, but it didn't come.

"You mean, not be *together* together, until then?" Her voice came out quiet, too."

"Yeah, you know. Spend the next few weeks really gettin' to know each other before we have s-e-x." He whispered the last word as desire grew inside him at the thought of having her alone in their own apartment.

"Okay, Liam. Whatever you want is fine with me." She kissed him and moved to the end of the couch, taking his feet onto her lap and rubbing them. "You can tell your grandpa it's safe to come back in now."

Her touch warmed him, her thoughtfulness made him smile, and her beautiful lips begged for his kiss. It wouldn't be long now before his heart followed his body's lead. Wouldn't it?

****

After three days at home, Liam was incredibly bored and ready to get back to work. "Doctor" Grams announced that he might be well enough to work the counter at the gas station, but no lifting for at least another week.

When he walked into the Pump and Run, Ray greeted him at the counter with a handshake. "Glad you're back, Liam."

Amanda came out from the snack aisle and smiled at him.

Liam's brain jerked to a stop as his body took

over, gorging on the scent, the pheromone, the link between the two of them.

"We need to have a talk, though." Ray came out from behind the counter and gestured toward the back room.

Liam followed, not caring what Ray had to say, as long as it got him away from Amanda.

Ray leaned on the old desk. "I saw on the videotapes that your girl was here for quite a while."

"Yes sir, sorry." He couldn't lose this job. He'd contacted a few local schools and colleges to put his name on the list of tutors, but he was realistic about the slim chance of getting any business from it. He had to keep this job, maybe put in a few more shifts each week. "I'll be sure to follow the rules from now on out."

"Well, since you're my best employee, I'm not going to put this in your record, but I'd appreciate your promise to be respectful of the rules."

"Yes, sir, I will." It occurred to Liam that if he'd been defending any other customer besides Maureen in the parking lot, the store would be responsible for his medical bills and lost wages. But saving his girlfriend from an attack by her ex-boyfriend was a different story.

"Okay." Ray stood. "Take it easy, though. I've asked Amanda to stay and finish stocking the shelves this afternoon."

That was the last fucking thing Liam needed. "That's not necessary. I can handle—"

"Nope." Ray shook his head. "Mizz Emma called me yesterday and laid down the law." He walked out of the office. "You're on light duty until she says so. Don't do anything to get me in trouble with her." He laughed and strolled through the store and out the front door.

Liam braced himself for Amanda's usual back-room cornering trick, but she didn't appear. He clocked in, vested up, and wandered to the counter.

"Feeling better?" Her voice came from the personal items aisle.

Just the sound of her talking juiced him up. "Better. Not one hundred percent yet."

She stood and peered at him over the shelves. "I saw the tape. It was brave of you. What you did to defend her."

"Maureen is my girlfriend. I would have given my life for her." He recited the words he'd read in a book at some point in high school, but the emotion that should have accompanied them didn't register.

"Actually, you almost did." She disappeared again, and worked steadily for another hour before she went toward the back room, lifting her phone to her ear.

Liam finally took a deep breath. Which burned like fire through his ribcage. The tension between him and Amanda seemed to be controllable as long as he couldn't see her, smell her, or hear her.

Looking out the window, he spotted a woman jogging by the store, and all that well-tempered control inside him turned to heartbreaking need.

"Trinity!"

Chapter Twenty-One

Liam raced out of the Pump and Run as fast as his aching body would allow him.

Trinity had already made it to the middle of the block. Her white-blonde hair, pulled up into a ponytail at the back of her head, bobbed and shimmered with each step she ran.

There was no way he could keep up with his ribs burning with each breath and his bruised calf throbbing at each step. "Trinity!" He shouted at the top of his lungs. Longing poured through him. How had he ever let her slip out of his grasp?

The woman turned slightly, watched him trotting along behind her for a few seconds, then turned and kept running.

"Wait, please." He sucked in painful breaths and slowed.

She stopped moving forward but ran in place. "Me? Are you talking to me?"

"Yes." He leaned against a tree to keep himself upright.

Slowly she walked toward him, her eyes narrowed on his face. "Do I know you?"

When she came within ten yards of him, he saw it wasn't Trinity. Just a woman with the same hair, same body, but not Trinity's face. His chest tightened, this time not from the bruising, but from his heart aching for the woman he didn't want to be without. "Sorry. I thought you were my friend Trinity."

Looking him over, she backed away. "Looks like you could use all the friends you can get." She smiled and turned, resuming her run.

He did look like hell on Earth, with his

bruises, swelling, and clinging to the tree to keep upright.

Damn, if he didn't feel more excitement at merely the possibility of seeing Trinity than he ever felt when Maureen walked into a room. Why was everything so screwed up?

He got his legs under him and walked back to the store.

Amanda stood outside the doors watching him.

He nodded and pushed past her into the building.

"Someone you know?" She followed him in.

"Nope." He took his spot behind the counter.

She looked at him for a few minutes, then went to the back of the store. She came out without her vest and gave him a brief wave as she walked out the door.

Had Amanda given up on him? Had seeing the videotape of him getting the shit kicked out of him for another woman made her realize Liam was serious about Maureen?

Why did the thought of never having Amanda make Liam want to break down in tears?

****

Maureen sat at the kitchen table with Liam's grandparents, enjoying a slice of the best peach pie she'd ever eaten, as they waited for Liam to get home from work. She'd come a little earlier than the time Liam had said he'd be home, just so she could spend time with Emma and Herschel.

They were so kind to her. The last few days, she'd been at the farm every chance she could, keeping Liam company and helping Emma with the kitchen chores. Taking a deep sniff of the homey scents of pie, Emma's floral perfume, and something spicy in the oven, Maureen knew she could easily adjust to the country life.

"Here he is." Herschel stood, as the headlights from Liam's car shone brightly in the window.

Maureen picked up her plate and empty milk glass, but Emma shooed her away. "Go see your sweetie. Dishes will wait until morning." She gestured toward the oven. "There's a plate in there for him, if he's hungry."

"Which he usually is." Herschel winked and took his wife's hand, leading her into the living room where the voices on the TV reported the day's news.

Maureen had the odd urge to put on an apron to welcome her man home. She took her dishes to the sink and opened the door for him.

"Hi." His face showed pain as he navigated the steps, but he walked in and took her in his arms. "It's nice to see you here."

"I came a little early." She looked up into his blue eyes. "Because I knew there'd be pie."

He laughed. "Grams makes the best ones in the county." He sniffed the air to his left. "Do I smell meatloaf?"

"Yes, sir. Sit down and I'll get your plate."

She fussed over him while he ate, and they talked about their day. He looked tired.

"I'll go so you can get some rest." Maureen set his dishes in the sink.

"No way." He walked up behind her and pulled her against him. "Let's go sit with the old folks and watch the news."

The feel of his hard body pressed against hers made her want to suggest going to his bedroom instead. But she'd play by his rules and wait until they had the apartment to themselves before letting him give her another one of those wild orgasms. "I can stay a few minutes."

"C'mon." He took her hand and brought her into the living room where his grandparents were watching a documentary on the Vietnam War. Emma dabbed at her eyes with a tissue, and Herschel looked pale and sat rigid in his recliner.

Liam sat on the couch, and when Maureen went to sit a distance from him, he pulled her down right next to him and cautiously put an arm around her. They watched the last ten minutes of the show in silence, respecting the sacrifice made by so many Americans.

After the show ended, Herschel turned off the TV and pushed out a long sigh. "I served in Vietnam." He looked at Maureen.

She nodded. "Thank you for your service, sir. Which branch?"

He nodded graciously. "Army. I have a reunion coming up in a few weeks." He sat quietly for a few minutes, then put the footrest of his chair down. "Come to think of it, I should get my trunk down from the attic." He stood and hefted up his jeans. "Where's the flashlight, Em?"

"Tonight?" Her voice squeaked. "You want to go up and get it tonight?"

"No time like the present." He walked into the kitchen.

Liam stood.

"Oh, no. You're not helping him." Emma got up and pointed at Liam. "You'll reinjure yourself and end up in the hospital."

Maureen got to her feet. "Let me help." She flexed up her biceps. "I'm pretty strong."

"Good Lord." Emma tossed up her hands as if in surrender. "The lot of you." She seemed very upset.

After ten minutes of searching the hot, dusty attic, Liam and Maureen found the small trunk. Herschel lifted it himself. "See, it's only some clothes and a few medals." He and Liam got it down the steps with no problem, and set it on the floor in front of the dark television.

Herschel sat on the coffee table and flipped the side fasteners, then tried to open the middle lock. "I don't remember locking this. Emma!"

"Right here, don't lose a lung with your shouting." She nudged her husband aside and sat on the table next to him.

Maureen smiled up at Liam, and mouthed "Cute!" as they looked at the older couple sitting hip-to-hip.

Liam grinned down at her, his lip almost healed. "Sometimes they do actually seem *cute*."

"I put my mother's shawl in here." Emma unlocked the chest and opened it, grabbing out an old white cardboard box.

"So you felt the need to lock my trunk because you were afraid someone would break in and steal an old shawl?" Herschel didn't sound very compassionate just then.

"Oh, go polish your brass buttons." Emma stood, taking the box with her, and walked into the kitchen.

Maureen would love to see the shawl, and as Liam sat next to his grandfather, she walked toward the kitchen. Through the door, she saw Emma set the box on the table and open it, unfold the cream-colored lace shawl, and take out a necklace. It looked to be some kind of beaded chain with a large, flat stone hanging from it.

Maureen backed up a step, hiding beside the door.

Emma put the necklace over her head and tucked it down inside the front of her shirt. She grabbed a sweater from the chair in front of her, and pulled it on, buttoning it to cover her neck.

Now Maureen was really intrigued. Why wouldn't Emma want to share the jewelry with the rest of the family? Or was it just Maureen she hid it from? She shrugged and tiptoed back into the living room and sat on the couch, listening to the men talk about the treasures in Herschel's old Army chest.

Emma came back into the room, carrying the box, and sat next to Maureen on the couch. "This was my mother's. She'd made it herself and wore it at her wedding." She opened the box and reverently touched the aging lace.

"It's beautiful. Tell me your mother's story." Maureen settled in to hear about Liam's great-grandmother, when all she could think about was that intricate old necklace around Emma's neck, and why the woman had gone to so much trouble to keep it hidden.

****

The next morning, Liam woke feeling nearly healed. The bruises had turned green, and he could almost bend over without the pain making him squeal like a baby pig.

There'd been some ruckus during the night, voices and water running, but Liam had been under the influence of his grandmother's pain pills, and hadn't had the clarity of mind to get up and see what was going on.

He dressed in old jeans and a long-sleeved shirt, ready to help Grandpa with chores.

"Morning." Liam picked up the coffee pot and offered a refill to his grandpa. "Where's Grams?"

Herschel looked up at Liam with red, tired eyes. "Still in bed. She had a…an episode last night."

Liam nearly dropped the pot. "What kind of episode?" He poured coffee for them both, then sat across from his grandfather.

"Hard to breathe. Couldn't catch her breath." Grandpa looked worried.

"Why didn't you wake me? Did you call the doctor?" Liam could barely catch his own breath.

"Why do you think I wouldn't wake you? *She* told me you needed your sleep to heal."

Damnit. "Don't listen to her when she tells you shit like that." His grandma treated him like one of the hothouse flowers she loved seeing in the conservatory in Indianapolis.

His grandfather gave him a look that said Liam wasn't too old to be spanked. "If it had been serious, I would have woke you, but it only lasted a few minutes. She blamed that dusty old chest for it."

"Sorry, Grandpa." Liam sat back in his chair. "I'm just worried about her. And I know you are, too, so I won't make you give me that Vietnam War hero death stare again.

Grandpa cracked a half-smile. "I let her sleep in, but now we have to fix our own breakfast."

Liam stood. "I got this." He pulled eggs and bread from the refrigerator, butter and sausage, and in fifteen minutes they were eating. He made a plate for Grams, and Grandpa took it into the bedroom for her while Liam made sandwiches and packed a mid-morning lunch for them.

Grandpa came back reporting that she seemed much better. "You sure you're up to working today, son?" He pulled his seed cap over his head and walked out the door.

"I'm good." He'd favor his side, but he could work. "You think we should leave Grams alone?"

"She swears she's back to normal. And she'd be mad as hell if we stuck around to stare at her all day."

After a few hours of clearing brush from along the fence, they heard an animal cry from a thicket of woods.

"What the hell?" Grandpa picked up the blade he'd been using, Liam grabbed the chainsaw, and they walked into the wooded copse.

The cries grew louder, almost like a wolf howling. From beneath a thick bush, blue eyes stared out at them from a furry, brown face.

"What is it?" Liam prepared to start the chainsaw if the thing lunged.

"Well, sons of guns, it's a dog." Herschel untangled a chain from the undergrowth, and led out a tall, painfully skinny dog. His brown hair was matted and full of burrs, and his ribs showed so prominently, it might be too late for the poor guy.

"Grab those sandwiches we brought with us." Herschel handed the dog's chain to Liam.

"Hey, little guy, you hungry?"

The blue eyes that looked up at him hit Liam right in the heart. "Yeah, let's get you something to fill that belly, okay?" Pointy ears cocked as if he knew what Liam was saying.

The dog's legs wobbled, and Liam walked slowly to the truck. He pulled out the bag he'd packed with sandwiches, chips, and cookies, and laid it all out in front of the mutt.

The dog waited, watching Liam closely.

"Go ahead, boy." When Liam backed away, the dog lunged and inhaled every bite.

"Lucky we decided to tackle this corner today." Grandpa poured water from his jug into a pan, circled it to rinse it out, then set it on the ground by the dog and poured as the animal lapped at the water. "He might not have made it another day."

When he'd had his fill, the dog sat, then crumpled to the ground with a long sigh, his eyes closing.

Liam stepped closer, talking calmly to the animal, but the mutt was out cold. He checked his collar for identification, then shook his head at his grandpa. When he stood next to the older man, Liam spoke quietly. "You recognize him?"

"Nope. He's not from any of the farms around here. They don't chain their dogs, anyway."

"Can we fatten him up, then let him go? See if he can find his way back home?"

Grandpa cocked his head. "I'm gonna say that this animal ran away from home for a reason. And he probably doesn't care to go back."

Liam knew the feeling. When he'd run from his step-father's house, he had no intention of going back. Until he was caught.

"You know how your grandmother feels about dogs." Herschel walked back toward the bush. "You'd better find a home for that old fella fast, before she realizes he's around."

Liam would keep the mutt in the barn, fix him a bed, get some dog food. He followed his grandpa, firing up the chainsaw. *If* the dog was still by the truck when they got back there.

****

Two hours later, Liam lifted the revived animal into the bed of the truck, pricking himself on the burdock and thistles imbedded in the poor fella's fur. He drove to the house, but didn't shut off the engine. "I'm going to take him to town. See if anybody knows him."

"Good idea." His grandpa gave him a ten dollar bill. "Get yourself some lunch." He gestured to the back of the truck. "And a burger for the mooch, too."

"Mooch." A fitting name.

Instead of driving toward Liberation, Liam turned the truck toward Schaefer. The mutt's health came first. When he walked into the Pooch Palace, Maureen and her three co-workers swarmed on Mooch, pushing Liam out of the circle.

"We found him out in the woods, his chain got wrapped around a bush."

The ladies set up a ramp for Mooch to walk up onto the grooming table, and coaxed him up. The animal behaved well, Liam had to give him credit there.

"We may have to sedate him." Maureen looked at Liam, her eyes filled with tenderness. She was one sweet woman.

The dog lay down and immediately began snoring.

Laughing quietly, Maureen shrugged. "Or maybe not."

"You want me here, or…" Liam didn't want to see what they'd have to do to clean up the poor old guy.

She walked to his side. "This'll take us a couple hours, and I'm going to have the vet next door take a look at him."

"How much is all this going to cost?" He didn't want to be cruel, but his resources were limited.

"No charge for the primping, and I'll see what the vet will do for you. He owes me one."

Liam didn't want to even think about what she'd done for the veterinarian to have him in her debt.

"Hey." Maureen frowned. "I groom his dogs for half-price. Get your mind out of the gutter."

Had his face been that easy to read? He pasted on a smile. "Darlin', you gotta forgive this country boy for bein' a dumbass sometimes."

She gave him a sideways look. "Don't pull that good-ol'-boy BS with me, Liam." She went up on tiptoes and gave him a kiss. "I'll call you when he's ready." She turned to walk away.

Liam smacked her butt and waved to the women gathered around the dog. "Thank you. And Mooch thanks you, too."

"Mooch?" The ladies cooed his name and talked sweet to him. The lucky mutt.

****

Liam spent a couple hours in the Schaefer library. They had a few books on indigenous peoples that he hadn't seen before, and their computers were newer and faster than the ones at his hometown library.

While searching the name of the man he'd met on the reservation, as well as Buck Waya, he came up with a few sites that had interviewed them. Taking notes, he barely registered his phone ringing. Maureen's face popped up on the screen.

"Hey, darlin'."

"Liam, you won't believe what the vet told me about Mooch."

Chapter Twenty-Two

Liam stood so fast, the library chair tipped over. "Is he okay?" Panic ripped through him.

"Yes, he's fine." Maureen's laugh came through the phone. "Come get him any time. I'll be here 'til three."

Damn, he'd only had the dog for half a day, and already he'd gotten attached? He could empathize with the dog, being as how both of them were runaways, and lucky enough to be saved by a kind human.

After gathering up his notes, Liam cleared the search memory from the computer. He didn't need anyone looking into what he'd found. While Ernie Crow spoke in circles no one could understand, Buck Waya had some interesting ideas about heredity, legacies, and mysticism. When things planed out in his life, he'd have to go looking for the man.

At the Pooch Palace, Liam didn't recognize Mooch. The guy looked nearly bald, dark gray instead of brown, and his tail wagged as he ran to Liam. Crouching down, Liam looked into his eyes. "Look at you, all cleaned up. You are one handsome dog."

"He is." Maureen bent to pet the dog. "And he's more than just any old dog, too."

Liam stood, pulling her up with him and tugging her close for a kiss. "Is he royalty?" Liam had imagined Mooch being a lost showdog with a hefty reward posted for his return.

"He's half wolf." Maureen's eyes watched Liam's closely.

"Wolf?" He looked down at the scrawny thing. "You sure?"

"The vet is sure. The coloring, the blue eyes,

the shape of him, those big paws."

Strange coincidence. Liam had looked up the meaning of Buck Waya's last name. *Wolf.* And hadn't Grace said something about Liam being like a wolf cub? "Son of a gun. Grams is gonna love this."

"She won't make you turn him in, will she?" Her brows drew together.

"Turn him in?"

"Like to the Humane Society." She blinked up at him.

"I'll see what she says, and if she says she wants him gone, I'll let you turn those sad eyes on her to change her mind." He smiled and kissed her. "No one can resist that face."

Maureen laughed, kissed Liam, kissed Mooch on the head, and backed away. "I've got a couple more dogs to do. I'll stop by the station later to see what Grams said."

Liam loved that Maureen called her "Grams" already. Loved? Just thinking the word was a good sign. Wasn't it? "See ya, darlin'."

****

"If I didn't want a dog on the farm, what—in the name of all that is holy—makes you think I'd want a wolf here, instead?" Grams stood staring at Mooch through the screen door.

The dog sat on the porch, watching her with wide eyes.

"Just until we can get him back in fighting shape…wait, let me rephrase that." Liam laughed.

Grams glared at him.

Grandpa sat across the kitchen table from him, eating his sandwich. "We'll get some chow from the mill. It won't be too expensive, and like the boy said, Mooch has all his shots and was wormed and…" He rolled his hand. "Whatever else they do with dogs nowadays."

"I'm looking for a second job." Liam hadn't mentioned it to his grandparents since he'd made the decision to job-search just a short time before he ended up being three guys' punching bag.

"You have enough to do here on the farm." Grams pulled out a chair and sat. "And you already work more than forty hours a week at the Pump and Run."

"I'm not talking about taking another full-time job. Just enough to help…" He almost mentioned Maureen, but he didn't want to bring her into this. "Help around here, and save more for college."

"Hersch, will you talk some sense into him?"

His grandfather shrugged. "I don't see what it can hurt."

Liam stood, kissing his grandmother on the cheek as he passed by on the way to set his dishes in the sink. "I've got to get ready. I'll pick up some dog food from work tonight, but if you have any leftovers, Mooch would be mighty appreciative." On the way home from the Poodle Palace, they'd driven through a fast-food place, and Liam had ordered ten dollars' worth of hamburgers, no pickles. Liam had eaten one, and Mooch had wolfed down the other six.

"Mooch. At least the name is right." Grams stood and went to the refrigerator, bending over with a sigh to peer into the lower shelves.

"Thanks." Liam winked at his grandpa and went to his room.

****

It took nearly an hour for Liam to get his body under control at the Pump and Run. Amanda stood behind him restocking the cigarette bins, and taking forever to do it. The proximity charged the air with electricity and he held on to the countertop, focusing on what to do with Mooch, hoping that would bring his desire to a normal level.

When Maureen walked in the door, he grinned, never feeling so glad to see anyone in his life. Leaning over the counter, he slid his hand around the back of her neck and gave her a long, hard kiss, putting all his sexual energy into it.

When the kiss ended, she blinked, her eyes sparkling. "I thought we're supposed to behave for the cameras?"

"Darlin', with you in the room, that *was* me behavin'."

Her cheeks turned red. "Well, aren't you the sweetest thing." She whispered the words.

Behind him, Amanda dropped a box.

"Oh, hey, Maureen." He moved to the side. "This is Amanda."

"Hi Amanda." Maureen smiled and looked at the redhead. "Have we met before?"

Amanda strolled up to the counter right next to Liam. "Maybe. When I saw the videotape of the other night, I thought you looked familiar."

The smile left Maureen's face.

Liam walked out from behind the counter.

"Where do you go to school?" Amanda leaned a hip on the cash register and stared hard at Maureen.

"I graduated from Schaefer last year. I work at the Pooch Palace." Maureen took the hand Liam offered her. "How about you?"

"I graduated this year from Rogers Corners, and I'll be attending Mortonson College this fall." Amanda sent a smile his way. "With Liam."

"That's nice." Maureen didn't sound too sure

of it. “Do you live here in town?”

“Yeah, I’m staying with a girlfriend.” She tucked her hair behind her ear. “Were you on the cheer squad?”

“No. Danceline. Maybe that’s where we’ve seen—”

“Oh.” Amanda made it sound like danceline was a big disappointment. “Could be. I was captain of the cheerleaders my senior year, and I’m trying out for the Mortonson squad next month.”

“Good luck.” Maureen almost nailed sincerity. She turned toward Liam. “Can we talk somewhere, hun?”

“Sure thing.” He looked toward Amanda. “Can you watch the register for a few minutes?”

Her mouth turned down, but she nodded. “Sure thing.”

Liam ignored the sarcasm in her voice and led Maureen to the back room, closing the door behind them. “Is this something serious, or did you just have the urge to get me alone in a small room?” He wagged his brows at her.

“I wanted to get away from Amanda.” Her eyes went wide. “Wow, she really doesn’t like me.”

Liam had picked up the subtle bitchiness.

“And I think she likes you too much.” Maureen poked her finger into the middle of his chest.

He grabbed the finger and kissed it. “No, we’re just co-workers. And Travis has the hots for her.”

Maureen froze. “Travis? Travis Hackers?”

“Why’s that so strange?” Was it just paranoia, or was something going on with those two?

“It’s not, I guess.” She looked completely

confused. "I just can't imagine Travis with someone like…that."

He opened his mouth to ask what *that* meant, but snapped it shut. "No accounting for taste. Look at you, beautiful, talented, and sweet as my grandmother's pecan pie—liking a rough bumpkin like me."

She laughed and they sat and talked about Mooch for a few minutes before he felt the pull of guilt. "I'd better get back to work."

"Okay. Want to stop over on your way home tonight?"

"Sure." He walked her to the front doors.

"Nice to meet you, Amanda." Maureen gave a little wave.

"Same here." The girl didn't even look their way.

Maureen gave him that *I told you so* look.

He shook his head and pulled her out the door with him. Keeping one hand on the hunting knife in his pocket, he looked around the parking lot.

"See you in a few hours." Maureen kissed him and slid into her car, speeding out of the lot.

Liam did not look forward to spending another minute inside, next to Amanda. But he cowboyed-up and got back to work.

****

Three days later, Liam parked the tractor next to the barn and shut it down. Travis's red truck stood in the driveway. His buddy always seemed to stop by the farm close to lunchtime, but Grams's cooking was a damn sight better than Travis's housekeeper's.

Travis sat on the porch steps, petting Mooch. The animal couldn't get enough attention. "Heard you had a dog out here." He cocked his head toward the door behind him. "Grams okay with that?"

Liam wiped his shirt sleeve across his forehead. "It's temporary, until we can get him fattened up and find a home for him." Liam would miss the mutt. He'd never had a pet in his whole life, and he'd already grown used to the companionship. Liam sat on his heels and the wolf trotted over to him, nearly knocking him over with his excitement. "How'd you hear about Mooch?"

Travis shrugged. "Talk in town." The guy wouldn't meet his eye. "Hey, want to ride up to Millersville with me after lunch? I gotta go pick up some parts for the electric fence."

"After lunch?" Liam stood. "Does that mean you're inviting yourself for another meal?"

"Hell, yeah. That's providing Grams has a pie made."

Walking up the steps, Liam sniffed the air. "Smells like it. I'll shower now and let her know you're gracing us with your presence for lunch."

Travis held the dog's face close to his own, turning his head to one side then the other. "What kind of dog is this, anyway? He looks a little off."

Whoever was gossiping about his dog didn't know all the facts. Liam stepped inside the screen door and let it shut. "It's part wolf."

Travis immediately released Mooch's face and scrambled up a step. "No shit?"

Liam laughed. "No shit."

An hour later, they jumped into Travis's truck and headed toward the freeway.

"I haven't seen you in a while." Liam hadn't even talked to Travis since the night he'd gotten beaten up. "What have you been doing?" Liam adjusted his seatbelt.

"Been busy finishing summer school, and the farm has been jumping lately." Travis swiveled his head to look at him. "How about you? What's keeping you busy? Besides Maureen?"

"I'm looking for another part-time job. I'm gonna need the money."

"Oh yeah? For what?" Travis pulled into a gas station.

"School. Life. Stuff."

Travis got out and shoved the gas nozzle into his truck.

A corner of a plastic bag stuck out from under the passenger seat. "Is this trash?" Liam reached down and opened it.

Travis looked in the driver's window then opened the door. "Gimme that."

Condom foils, used condoms, tissues. "Holy shit. What have you been doing? Or who have you been doing?" He handed the bag to his friend.

Travis's face turned red. "No one. Just some girls I picked up."

"Who?"

Trav slammed the truck door and walked away, tying the bag handles and tossing it in the garbage can.

Why was his buddy having one-nighters when he was so damn hot for Amanda?

Liam got out of the truck. "You want anything from inside? A Dew? Some junk food? A bottle of lube?"

Glaring at him, Travis lifted his middle finger.

With a chuckle, Liam went inside and came out with some road-trip food.

Travis sat in the driver's seat, texting, and Liam handed him a bottle of Dew and stuck the junk food he'd bought in the middle console.

"You don't have to tell me who you're seeing. Or why you're having sex in your truck. Or why my finding out about it makes you so damn mad." It wasn't like Travis to be so pouty.

Travis started the truck, turned the radio on, and cranked up the volume.

After a few miles, they were both singing along and had chowed through the food selection.

During a commercial, Travis lowered the volume. "I'm in a tough place right now."

They rode in silence for a few miles.

"Is it your farm?" Liam wanted to be there for his buddy.

"It's that, and my grades, and tryouts for the baseball team next week."

Liam had nearly forgotten about the tryouts. "Did you get your diploma?"

"Yeah. With a D-plus average. I should have taken your help when you offered it."

Liam understood pride. Some men could afford to have it.

"Dad's pissed that I might not be able to play until I get my grades up." Travis slapped the steering wheel. "I told him to make a donation to the college, and they'd let me play. He didn't think it was funny."

Liam could see Old Man Hackers bribing his son's way onto the baseball team.

"You're not laughing." Travis turned onto the highway to Millersville.

"You probably gave your dad ideas." What would it be like to have money like that? Buy your way into whatever you wanted.

"Yeah, probably did. So, what kind of job are you looking for?"

"I put my name in at a few schools as a tutor. Haven't heard back yet."

"Oh yeah?" Travis bobbed his head along with the song on the radio. "I'll spread it around that you're a pro tutor."

"Great, thanks. A recommendation from a D-plus student should help." Liam smirked at his buddy.

Travis gave him a glare. "I've said it before, and I'll say it again now. Fuck you, Liam." He laughed and turned up the radio, singing along and playing drums on the wheel.

Liam belted out the song right along with him, hitting a sweet harmony, and resting his brain from the crazy thoughts that ran through it.

They pulled into the parking lot of the electrical equipment supply in Millersville and both went inside the store. Travis went right to the counter and Liam looked around at the new technology he hoped to afford for their farm someday.

"No. I don't want to take that." Travis's voice carried through the store.

The man behind the counter spoke quietly, and Liam couldn't hear what he said.

A few seconds later, Travis stomped out of the building carrying a large envelope, stuffed full.

Liam followed, hopping into the passenger seat of the truck. "What's up?"

"Asshole dad of mine. Shit." Travis backed the truck out of the parking space and laid rubber across the lot toward the loading docks at the end of the building. After the boxes were loaded in the bed, Travis headed back to Liberation.

"Something you want to talk about?" Liam turned down the radio volume.

Travis snorted. "Why the hell does he have to

get me involved in his business?"

"You're going to take over the farm someday. He probably wants you—"

"Not that business." Travis's jaw tightened. "Never mind. Just… Tell me what's going on with those assholes who jumped you."

Liam reported all he knew, they talked about the baseball tryouts, then Travis pulled into the driveway of the Hackers Farm. "Let me get rid of this shit, then we can cruise through town before I drop you off."

"Yeah, that's fine." Liam had nowhere to be this afternoon.

After they unloaded the electrical equipment, with the help of the hired hands, Travis asked where his father was.

They drove out past the grain silo and found Jarvis Hackers leaning on a split-wood fence watching a man lunge a horse.

Travis circled the truck, shifting into park with the front end facing away from his dad. "I'll be right back." He grabbed the thick envelope from under his seat.

"Take your time." Liam pulled out his phone and stared down at it.

As Travis walked away, Liam watched Jarvis in the side mirror.

The older man turned to Travis smiling, but his son threw the envelope at him. It bounced off his round belly, and hit the ground, tearing open.

"What the fuck?" Liam leaned forward to get a better view. Green bundles spread on the ground. Cash?

Both the Hackers looked toward the truck and Liam focused on his phone.

What were they into? This was not good.

Their voices carried, loud and angry as Travis stormed back to the truck, jumped in, and sent dirt spraying from under his tires as he drove off. He didn't say a word.

If his buddy didn't want to talk about it, he wouldn't push. Liam held up his phone. "How the hell do you get five-bar service out here?"

"Dad had them put in a tower. Dad can buy whatever he wants."

Liam sat quietly, waiting for more. When it didn't come, he pressed buttons on the radio. "You wanna get a couple six-packs and go hang out in your treehouse?"

Travis almost smiled. "I wish I could. I need to be somewhere in a couple hours."

They rolled through Liberation, their windows down, nodding to people they knew, and Travis whistled at a couple girls.

Maureen's car sat at a pump at the gas station.

"Hey, pull in. I wanna say hi to my girl." His girl. It sounded so perfect, but felt like absolutely nothing.

Travis pulled up to the pump behind Maureen's car and Liam got out and walked up to her. "Hey beautiful."

"Hi handsome." She leaned in for a quick kiss.

"Hi." Travis shoved his credit card into the pump next to his truck.

"Hi, Travis. What are you two up to?"

When it clicked off, Liam pulled the pump handle from Maureen's car and replaced it. "Went to Millersville to get some parts. Now we're cruising."

She laughed. "Cruising? You two are such boys."

"Thank you." He winked. "I think."

"Come inside with me." She tugged his hand. "I have to pick up a few things."

Liam let her drag him along, and looked at Travis. "Think she's using me for my employee discount?"

"Yep. Why else would she be with a gomer like you?" Travis smiled for the first time since Millersville. "I'll be right in."

Amanda stood glowering at them as they laughed and acted like an old married couple filling a handbasket with groceries.

Maureen announced that Liam was coming home with her and she was cooking them supper.

As Amanda checked them out, Travis walked in, took one look at Amanda, and turned away, heading toward the back of the store.

****

Maureen hated to see Travis so miserable about a girl. Had she turned him down? Is that why he avoided Amanda that way?

Liam paid for her groceries, even though she had her wallet out. He was such a gentleman.

While Amanda bagged their things, Travis wandered to the counter with two six-packs of beer.

"Travis, have you met Amanda?" Maureen could get away with playing the dumb blonde matchmaker.

"Ah, yeah." Travis frowned at Liam, who just shrugged. "We've met. Hi, Amanda."

"Hi Travis. Good to see you again." Amanda gave him a half-smile.

Maureen could see that Amanda liked Travis, but they transacted the purchase in silence.

Liam tried to guide Maureen out of the store,

but that didn't seem like enough of a manipulation of the situation. "You know what would be fun?"

Everyone looked at her.

Maureen took Liam's hand. "Why don't the four of us go out together one night? Just as friends."

"No." Liam started pulling her toward the door, and Amanda seemed to be glaring at him.

"Yeah, okay." Amanda turned her stare on Travis. "How about it, Travis?"

He stood frozen for a few seconds. "Okay, sure."

Liam seemed to shrink a few inches. "C'mon, let's get your milk in the refrigerator."

"Our milk, hun." Maureen gave Travis and Amanda a little finger wave and let her boyfriend help her out the door. "You don't seem too enthusiastic about a double date."

"It's fine. I didn't want Travis to be put on the spot." Liam opened the passenger door for her and she handed him her keys. He wouldn't look directly at her.

Something about Amanda and Liam just wasn't right. She'd make sure they double-dated so she could figure out exactly what it was.

****

The next afternoon, Liam pulled into the gas station and parked next to Amanda's car. "Only five minutes, Liam. You can do this." After Liam had pestered Grams for an hour, she'd called Ray last night and told him he could lift the restrictions. Hard to believe an eighteen-year-old man let his grandmother control his life to that extent. Only for another few weeks, though.

He slid out of his car and headed into the building.

Amanda rang up customers and Liam went to the back room and clocked in. After the last customer left, he walked up behind her. "Did Ray let you know you don't have to stay and finish stocking the shelves?"

She logged out of the register and turned toward him. "He did. I'm glad you're all healed." Her smile lifted her face.

Everything inside Liam went jittery and hot. "Okay. Thanks, then." He stepped aside so she could pass, but she stayed where she was.

"I have something to tell you, Liam." Her eyes narrowed. "And don't run away like you usually do. You're going to want to hear this."

Chapter Twenty-Three

Liam's knees wobbled a bit as he stared at Amanda. His body flushed then shivered as he fought the physical desire for her that clung heavily to the very air he breathed.

A customer came in and laid a bill on the counter. "Gimme a pack of those generic menthols."

Liam reached up and plucked the pack out of the dispenser, brushed past Amanda, and logged into the register. After he gave the guy his change, Liam was alone with Amanda again. "What is it?" He wanted to rush this along, get her gone.

"I signed up for tutoring." Her smile looked more like a smirk. "With you. Eight hours a week."

"Why?" He couldn't handle any more hours with her. He'd go completely insane.

"I really want to ace the first-year classes. I took a look at the curriculum, and I know I can't do it without help."

It sounded reasonable, but there was another purpose for this forced time together. Something to do with the roaring river of lust that swept through them, trying to push them together.

"Where did you hear about my tutoring?"

"I don't know." She leaned just a little too close. "Around town, I guess."

Who the hell was talking about him all over town? He stepped out of the employee-only area and made himself busy straightening a display of lighters. "I don't know if I'll have time."

"Grow up, Liam."

His head jerked up so fast, something in his neck popped.

She puffed out a breath. "It's just tutoring.

We'll meet at the library. I'll sit across the table from you. You can have your *girlfriend* monitor us on your phone if you want."

Suddenly, he did feel childish. "I want to help you, Amanda, but that's all. Just help, nothing more, okay?"

With her hands raised in surrender, she walked past him toward the back room. "I won't even bake you brownies as a thank you."

Liam needed the money. Maureen was counting on him. He and Amanda would be in a public place.

Amanda strolled past him, swinging her purse. "You still have my number? The one I gave you that first day?" With her hand on the glass door, she gave him a neutral look.

Just meeting her gaze shot him into orbit, making him hard in his jeans.

When he didn't answer, she laughed. "Yeah, I figured you'd still have it." She walked out the door.

"Shit." Why couldn't he have lied? Said he'd thrown it out the window the day she gave it to him.

That night, he lay in bed knowing he needed to man-up and tutor Amanda. It was his only option. He flipped on his light and spotted the wrinkled receipt she'd given him. Her phone number wasn't clear from where he lay. But he knew it. Had somehow memorized it over the weeks since he'd found it in his bag.

He'd be damned if he'd give her his number, though. He'd talk to her at shift change the next day. Turning off his light, he flopped onto his stomach. Just when he started drifting off, he remembered Maureen and her stupid double-dating scheme. He'd tried to talk her out of it while they cooked supper at her house, while they watched TV, and when she gave him a ride home.

She was set on it. *It's the best way to get Travis and Amanda together,* she'd said.

Liam didn't believe it, but he'd do whatever she wanted.

Dear Me, I am absolutely losing my mind over this Amanda girl. Whenever we're next to each other, I am completely at her mercy. It's taking everything that I have to not cash in on the lustful signals she gives me more than daily. I'm trying with Maureen. She seems like a really sweet girl, my grandparents think the world of her, but for some reason, inside, the connection just isn't there. We've decided to wait until we move in with each other to have any kind of sex. As strange as it sounds, I'm kinda over sex. Ever since I lost my virginity, life has been no picnic. I'm so confused about who I am, inside and out. Thinking back to the first part of the year, I felt so confident, so assured in everything I did, it was the one thing I had going for me. But nowadays, since Kaylee, and even more so after Trinity, I'm second-guessing everything I do. I feel like I'm writing checks I can't cash, but my back's against the wall, so I will do this tutoring thing with Amanda, and God help me, I can't help but think it will be the death of me. Why am I so uncertain? Obsessed? True love?... Whatever, man.

Two nights later, Liam sat opposite Amanda at an old wooden table in the town library.

"What does this mean?" She pushed her trigonometry book toward him, turning it so he could read the caption under the diagram. She'd signed up for some advanced classes, and it had been easy for the two of them to fill three and a half hours of tutoring time.

The problem was his body. Shocked at the constant proximity to her, he could barely speak for the flashes of pure lust that blasted from his subconscious when he wasn't vigilant in keeping his mind on the textbook.

As he explained the symbols and concept, she stood and leaned on her elbows on the table, her ass thrust into the air behind her, round and tight.

Liam's eyes closed for a second, but when he tried to open them, it was like they were sealed shut. He could almost feel his body rising from his chair, stepping behind Amanda, lifting her skirt and sliding his hands up her toned, cool thighs. Her thong covered just centimeters of her sweet, pink womanly heaven.

Sliding his fingers along her warmth, they immediately slicked with her juices.

She cried his name and levered her hips to give him better access. "Now, Liam. Don't wait."

He ripped off the button on his jeans in his haste, pulled out his long, throbbing length, and pressed it deep into her…

"Liam?"

His head jerked back, his eyes opened, and he stared into her eyes. He was in his seat. She was leaning on the table. His shaft was 50 shades of hard. Had he just daydreamed sex? It'd been so real.

She leaned closer. "You okay?" Licking her lips, her hand reached for him.

Liam leapt out of his chair. "I've got to go. Maureen…" They didn't have plans, but he needed to see her, touch her, clear his mind of whatever had just happened.

"Okay." Amanda packed up her books, keeping a close eye on him. "I don't work Saturday. Can we meet here at eleven?"

"I don't know." He backed away as his body and mind coordinated to derail his willpower. If he had just stayed focused, this vision, or whatever it was, wouldn't have happened. He'd have more Dew Saturday, keep his mind sharp, on task. He needed the income. "Yeah, okay. Eleven." He turned and walked away.

"Thanks, Liam." Her voice, library quiet, carried, echoed, and cut through him like a razor.

What did he need to do to turn off the electricity that hardwired between them?

Outside the library, he called Maureen, but she worked until seven that night.

"Go grab Mooch and bring him to the apartment. See if he'd be a good town dog."

Liam imagined he would. He barely left the porch at the farm, and begged for attention from everyone. Strangely, he'd never heard Mooch bark, or even howl again, the way he had in the woods the day they'd found him.

"Is Sissy going to be there?"

"Yeah, but she'll stay in her room. Especially

when I tell her you're bringing a freaking wolf with you." Maureen laughed. "Gotta go, I'll see you real soon."

"Can't wait, darlin'." Liam disconnected the call and watched Amanda pile her books in the back seat of her car and slide into the driver's seat. The pull between them was strong, even from a distance, and it seemed to be gaining momentum, taking on a life of its own.

How far would he have to be from her to get her completely off his radar?

****

"Get out of here!" Liam's own shout woke him. He sat bolt upright on the sofa sleeper.

"Hun?" Maureen touched his back. Mooch lumbered up and laid his head on Liam's shin.

Sissy's door opened. "What's happening?"

"He just had a nightmare." Maureen turned on the lamp. "Sorry we woke you."

Liam knew she had been here. Amanda. Standing at the foot of the bed, butt naked, ready to crawl in between Maureen and him.

It'd been so real.

The chain lock hung on the door. All the windows were closed and locked. He could smell her—rain and pheromone, sexy, musky woman.

Maureen kissed his shoulder. "Were you dreaming about…Brody?"

He shivered as the sweat covering his body cooled. "Yeah, Brody." He checked the room one more time. She really wasn't here?

"Do you want a sleeping pill?" Maureen got up and padded toward the bathroom.

Liam scratched behind Mooch's ears. "Did you see her, boy?"

The dog just blinked and enjoyed the attention.

"Can you tell if I'm going insane? Do wolves have that ability?" Because something crazy was going on inside him. Something one sleeping pill wouldn't cure, but thirty of them would. Permanently.

****

Liam made it two hours through the tutoring session with Amanda before the biology lesson switched to tongues. His mind began to drift and when he closed his eyes, he could almost feel his body drop from the chair and land on all fours under the table. Crawling toward Amanda's legs, he could smell her sweet, heavy rain scent, and his mouth watered.

In his torrid delusion, she spread her legs. No underwear today, and her short-trimmed red curls glistened with her nectar. Licking a trail from her knee, along the soft skin of her thigh, he ran his tongue in circular patterns, getting her flavor on every taste bud. He lapped closer, all the way to her soft lips. He sucked them into his mouth, teasing each one with his tongue.

"Now, Liam. Don't wait." Her fingers gripped the hair on each side of his head and held him tight against her.

Plunging his tongue into her soft heat, he rolled it, slowly at first, then faster.

"Where did you go, Liam?" Amanda's voice jarred him back from the other reality. "Is this too boring for you?"

He opened his eyes.

Whatever she saw in them made her gasp.

Liam couldn't speak. His desire roared through him, seeming to take on a life of its own, making him desperate to grab her and have her.

"Why are we fighting this?" Her breath panted, her pupils widened, and the sparks between them flared and snapped. She stood. "Not here. Follow me to my apartment."

Her demand turned off something inside him, and he shoved back his need. "No." He stood, letting the chair fall back. "This is not right."

She reached for him and he scrambled away. "I can't."

"Why? Maureen?" Amanda gestured between them. "Does she do this to you?" She took a step toward him. "Liam, no other man has ever made me feel this way. This out of control."

"That's the thing. I can't lose control. Travis likes you, Maureen likes me, and I will not betray either of them." The last words came out nearly a shout.

Shushing sounds came from the other room.

Amanda touched her throat, dragged her fingers down to the spot between her breasts. "No one needs to know. It'll be our secret. I promise."

Liam's eyes slowly closed as a vision of him taking her up against the door in her apartment flooded his brain. He forced his eyes open. "I don't live like that, Amanda. I pride myself on my integrity." Tarnished though it was, lately. He turned to walk away, but had to make this sink into her head. He sent her a glare over his shoulder. "You might want to look that word up in the dictionary."

Her eyes narrowed. "Fuck you, Liam." It came out a hiss.

He left as fast as his jittering legs would carry him. He had to get away. The word "fuck" coming from her lips revived the flaming lust he'd nearly been able to snuff.

No more tutoring. Liam jumped into his car and sped away. No more tutoring Amanda. No more time alone with her. He should ask Ray if he could transfer to another of his gas stations, get himself out of her line of fire.

He drove around for a half hour until the world came back right again, then headed to the Pump and Run to talk to his boss.

****

"You're a good worker, Liam. I trust you implicitly, and I can't say that about any of my other employees." Sitting on the other side of the desk in the back room of the gas station, Ray cleared his throat. "You don't have to tell me why you want to avoid…a certain employee, but I've seen the way she looks at you, so I'm willing to accommodate your request."

Instead of letting Liam transfer to another store, Ray had insisted Liam chose his own days, his own shifts, and he even gave him a few extra hours each week. Avoiding any shift changes with Amanda required a lot of rearranging, but Ray just set up the new schedule and emailed it out to the employees.

"Thank you, sir." Liam stood. "I really want to make it work with Maureen." He knew he was probably sharing too much, but he valued Ray's confidence in him.

"You're a good boy…man, Liam." Ray grinned. "Now get out of here and enjoy this nice weather."

Liam stood beside his car, watching the slow parade of vehicles pass down Main Street. Farm trucks covered in dirt, townies' sedans, shining from the carwash, the occasional beater driven by one of

Liam's schoolmates.

The chances of him running into Amanda were good. He'd have to stick close to home, or make sure he was with Maureen when he went out.

Just thinking of Amanda made him feel wired, making him feel like he was starring in a B movie, fighting the whole demonic possession thing going on inside him, needing an exorcist to purge her from his system.

Or maybe another one of his grandmother's pain pills.

"Just to take the edge off." Liam headed home, knowing it would be a temporary fix, but wanting to drift a while, not have to wrestle with the beast inside him.

****

Three days later, Liam drove to Maureen's for supper. He'd spent five hours that morning tutoring a set of twin girls who would be in high school that fall. He'd driven to their big house on an acre of land on the outskirts of town where the wealthier Liberationaires lived.

Whenever their mother left the room, they'd practice flirting with him, and it felt so easy, so normal, compared with every other woman in his life.

The twice-weekly sessions with the twins plus the extra hours at the Pump and Run would bring in enough cash to buy Sissy's furniture for them.

He pulled into the parking lot at the River Point Apartments and spotted a red truck in the lot that looked just like Travis's. "Ah, crap." He parked and headed up the stairs to Maureen's place, and knocked.

His lady opened the door, a sweet smile on her face. "Look who's here!"

Chapter Twenty-Four

Liam didn't have to guess who waited for him inside Maureen's apartment. The air hung thick with the unique scent of Amanda. He waited for Maureen to open her apartment door all the way before he looked into the room.

Travis sat slumped in one of the chairs, and Amanda turned to smile at him over the back of the couch.

The intensity of her presence hit him like a semi-truck and he nearly turned and ran.

"Hun?" Maureen's smile faded. "Are you okay with this?" she whispered, as she stepped closer to him. "Amanda and I bumped into each other outside the Pooch Palace, and she suggested tonight would be a good night to get together.

"Why didn't you let me know?"

She blinked a couple times, as if offended. "When I called Travis to see if he was available, he said we should surprise you." She shrugged. "Kind of a joke, I guess, but maybe I made a mistake?"

He could either turn into a complete asshole and walk away—maybe throw Amanda out—or he could deal with this. Pulling Maureen into his arms, he kissed her and backed her into the room, kicking the door closed with his heel. "It's fine." He whispered into her ear. "I'm just not feeling very good, so let's end this early, okay?"

Maureen gave him a pout. "Poor baby. Do you want an ibuprofen or something?"

Liam had dropped a couple of Grams's pain relievers in his pocket, just in case. Damn glad he did, too. "I have one. Let me get a beer to wash it down."

As she backed out of his arms, her smile lit

her face again. “You sit down. I’ll get you one.” She headed for the kitchen.

The scent of spicy red sauce hit him for a moment before Amanda’s powerful pheromones drilled their way into his nerve endings.

“Hey.” Travis lifted one booted foot and rested it on the opposite knee. “Surprise, huh?” The guy did not look happy.

“Yeah, it is.” He sat in the chair opposite him. “Hi Amanda.”

“Liam.” The smirk she sent him told him the whole story. She was not going to let this thing go, no matter what she had to do to spend time with him. “Haven’t seen you at work lately.”

Liam nodded. She would never see him at work. He’d be sure of that.

Maureen brought an iced mug of beer for him, and she sat on the arm of his chair.

He popped the pain pill into his mouth and washed it down with half the beer. Wrapping his arm around Maureen’s waist, he caressed her softly as she laid her hand on his shoulder.

“What smells good, darlin’?”

“I made my aunt’s spaghetti recipe.” Her voice carried excitement. “This is like our first dinner party.”

“Aw, isn’t that cute?” Amanda’s voice sounded more snarky than sincere, but she covered it with a near-perfect smile.

Maureen’s body stiffened for a second, then she relaxed. “Did Liam tell you?” She looked at Travis. “He’s moving in when my roommate moves out.”

Travis slowly shook his head. “Hadn’t heard about it. He gave Amanda a quick glance, then looked at Liam. “Congrats, man. You deserve happiness.”

“Thank you.” Liam took his friend’s words and let them replace some of his anxiousness. He would be happy. He’d make sure of it.

Once in a while, Liam thanked the universe for a friend like Travis. Then there were the times that he could curse his buddy to hell—like when he’d talked Maureen into having tonight be a surprise for him.

Silence stretched. Neither Travis nor Amanda spoke, didn’t look at each other, and looked like they hated being in the same room together. Great. This would be a lot of fun.

A timer beeped.

Liam patted Maureen’s butt. “Want me to help in the kitchen?”

“No. You stay and talk with our guests.” When Maureen walked out of the line of sight of everyone but Liam, she gestured between Travis and Amanda.

So evidently, Liam was supposed to get them together? The beer had dulled his senses a bit, but until the pain med kicked in, he didn’t even want to look at Amanda. “I got a call from Mortonson. I made the baseball team.”

“Hey, good for you.” Travis downed a few swallows of beer. “I got on the team too, but I’ve got to keep my grades up the first semester, or I’m out.”

Liam opened his mouth to offer to help him, then snapped it shut and just nodded. The room went deathly silent again. “Trav, I’m tutoring the Poytras twins. Their mom said you recommended me. Thanks.”

Travis nodded. “They’re friends of my parents. I slipped it in when the four adults were talking about how dumb their kids were."

Liam didn't understand why Travis would say something that critical about himself and his parents in front of the girl he wanted to date. And his body language; slunk down in the chair, tipping back his beer like he was bent on getting drunk.

"What about *our* tutoring, Liam?" Amanda slid along the sofa until she was right next to Liam's chair.

Tingles raced along his skin, heating, swelling, shaking everything inside him. "I won't have time now that—"

"You're getting tutoring from Liam?" Travis's brow wrinkled. "Since when?"

Amanda glanced at him, then immediately back at Liam. "Since a week ago, but I haven't seen you to arrange another time." She pulled her phone from her bra. "Give me your number so I can call you."

Something clattered in the kitchen.

Liam jumped up, turning to hide the stretched denim at his zipper. "Can't. I'm all booked." He walked into the kitchen.

Maureen picked up a large metal cover from the floor. Her eyes narrowed on Liam's. "Why didn't you tell me you were tutoring her?" She whispered so quietly, Liam had to read her lips.

"I didn't think of it. Sorry." He hadn't wanted to poison the few hours of time he had with Maureen by bringing up Amanda's name. Turning to the stove, he stirred the bubbling red sauce. "We always met at the library. We were never alone, but it's done now."

She didn't move, but she let out a sigh.

Another timer went off, and they got busy filling bowls with noodles, red sauce, and salad, and a plate with toasted garlic bread.

"Come and eat." Maureen set everything on the table as Liam poured red wine into glasses. His girl had thought of everything, and he'd have to remember to ask her where she got the wine.

Amanda took a seat at the small table, and Travis plopped down opposite her, leaving Liam and Maureen to sit opposite each other. And forcing Liam into close proximity with Amanda.

As they ate, Amanda chatted with him, practically ignoring Travis and Maureen.

He gave her monosyllabic replies, and tried to join in the chatter Maureen kept up with Travis, but as the pain pill numbed Liam's mind and body, he just didn't care to try any more, and enjoyed relief from the torture of Amanda's invisible lure.

As Liam shifted his legs to the side to keep Amanda from touching him under the table, Maureen and Travis laughed and carried on a conversation.

Why the hell were those two so close? They always had fun together, had each other's phone numbers, maybe knew each other better than either of them admitted?

Anger, fueled by the frustration of all the shit going down tonight, had him ready to scream.

"Liam, hon? Are you okay?" Maureen got up and walked around the table, pressing her fingers to his forehead. "You're really hot."

"He is." Amanda forced a laugh, then cleared her throat. "I guess the party's over." She stood, chugged down her wine, then set the glass on the table. "Thanks for the meal."

Maureen attempted a smile.

Travis got up, too. "It was delicious, Maureen. You did a great job." He winked at her. "Liam, I didn't think you could do it, but you found someone who's as good a cook as Grams."

Maureen blushed and smiled. "You're welcome any time, Travis."

Liam pushed back his chair.

"Don't get up. You do look like you're about to keel over." Travis followed Amanda to the door, they left, and closed it behind them.

"Let me open the bed so you can lie down." Maureen fussed around him.

Liam's chest finally filled with oxygen that didn't contain Amanda's venom. His head cleared, his body cooled, and everything settled back down. "Let's lie on the couch together for a while, then we'll clean up, okay."

"Sure." She hovered over him as he got up and walked to the couch. He lay on his side, and in seconds, was out cold.

****

He woke to Maureen's sweet, off-key humming in the kitchen. Joining her, he dried the dishes she washed. "What were you and Travis talking about?" He tried to keep suspicion from his voice, but it lurked in the back of his mind.

"Oh, just filling the void. That awful Amanda. She wouldn't say a word to him. Isn't that strange?" Maureen handed him a dripping wine glass.

"I guess. I know Trav likes her. Doesn't seem like she likes him back, huh?"

She tsked. "I know. But when I asked him here, and told him Amanda would be here, too, he said he wanted to come."

"Did Trav say why he thought it would be a good idea to surprise me with this?"

Maureen shook her head. "No. And I didn't

stop to think about it."

Was it some kind of test? What kind of response had Travis expected from Liam? With his head still muddled from the liquor and pain medication, he couldn't grasp his buddy's intention.

"Do you think Travis keeps asking Amanda out, and she just keeps turning him down?" She pulled the sink stopper and soapy water drained away.

"Maybe."

"Is there another guy she likes?" Maureen looked at him, complete innocence in her eyes.

"I wouldn't know. We don't talk at the store, and it was all business when I tutored her."

Maureen paused. "You don't think…" She let out a breath. "No, you'd know if she had feelings for you."

"Yeah. She's never said." Technically, the statement was true, because Amanda had never used the word "feelings."

"Well, you just watch out for her, Liam." Maureen threaded her thumbs through his side belt loops. "Something's going on with her, and after tonight, I just don't think I can trust her."

"Okay, darlin'. Whatever you say." He tugged her close. "But don't think you have to make me jealous by paying all your attention to another man, either."

Her eyes widened. "You were jealous? Of Travis?" She gave a quick laugh. "I was just keeping a conversation going so he didn't feel so left out, being ignored by Amanda."

That made sense to Liam. He wanted more than anything to trust Maureen, love her, feel the need to spend forever with her, but it'd take more time for his heart to get into this thing.

"I'd never do anything to make you jealous." She batted her eyes at him. "He did swipe that yummy bottle of merlot from his parents' wine rack for me, though." She laughed. "But since you drank it too, you can't be jealous."

"You are a tease." He kissed her forehead.

"Let's go back to the couch and get cozy."

"Whatever you want, Maureen." With the exception of "the truth" and "his heart," he really meant it.

****

Maureen sat on a stiff folding chair in her third cousin's huge yard, somewhere in the middle of Alabama. She'd driven down two days ago with her sister and nephews, since her brother-in-law was not much for the annual Beauregard Family Reunion. Her parents had arrived days before for the preliminary get-togethers.

Today was the big day, when descendants of the pre-war Beauregard family came from four states to talk about who was still married, who got divorced, and who was no longer among the living. She sat in a circle of elderly aunties listening to all the gossip.

A puff of smoke off behind the gazebo caught her attention. A head with spiked black hair moved back and forth along the length of the railing. *Peyton?* It had to be her cousin.

Not wanting to be rude, Maureen faked a few sneezes and excused herself, running to catch the only relative who would dare break the no-smoking rule.

As she ground out her cigarette, Peyton looked up at her. Her crazy green eyes brightened as she smiled. "Cousin Maureen." She laid on the southern accent as heavy as a pecan pie.

"Cousin Peyton." Maureen grabbed the petite

woman close for a hug, then backed away and looked at her. "I didn't know you were coming."

"I got recruited to drive my aunt and uncle at the last minute." She gestured to the gazebo. "Let's sit and talk."

"Where are you living now?" Maureen knew her cousin had tried some unconventional careers, and shifted residences often.

"I'm still in Nashville. How about you?"

"I moved to Liberation. I've got an apartment and my boyfriend is moving in next week."

"Good for you. Still working at the dog thing?"

"Dog grooming. Yes, and I really enjoy it." Maureen almost hated to ask. "What are you doing for work now?"

"Wait, Liberation?" Peyton lit another cigarette and hid it over the edge of the railing. "I was with a guy there just like a month ago. Holy fuck, was he a freak."

"A freak?" Was it somebody she knew? "What do you mean?"

"He lived out in the country, he had to be like twenty or so, but he wanted to record it."

"It?" Maureen rolled her eyes at how slow she was sometimes. "Oh, yeah. I bet a lot of people do." It would be fun to watch it afterward.

"I walked in, got naked, and bang, just like that, did it without knowing each other's names."

Maureen nodded. She'd heard her cousin sometimes did *it* for money.

"It was pretty hot at the end." Peyton stared at the roof of the gazebo. "He was this big, scarred guy with a huge schwanker." She laughed. "I thought it was going to be wild, but he couldn't keep his eyes off the damn camera. Worst sex ever, until he went for…" She shook her head. "You don't want to hear all this."

"I don't mind. I'd like to get kinda kinky with my guy." She'd seen a nice camera that recorded too, in Liam's room when he'd been passed out after the attack. "Do you think guys like to be recorded?"

"Some of them do. You can set it up next time you have sex. If he says no, then just don't turn it on." Peyton pulled a flask out of her purse. "Whiskey? Makes the whole reunion go smoother."

Maureen laughed and took a sip. When she looked across the lawn, she saw her sister gesture at her. Maureen just ignored her. Let her take care of her own kids for a change. "I'd love to have you come and meet Liam. That's my guy. Do you still have the same phone number? I'll call you once we're all moved in together."

"Yeah, I'd like that. For sure, I'll come and visit." She pulled out her phone. "Let's set a date right now."

Chapter Twenty-Five

Liam and Maureen stood in the middle of her bedroom—*their*—bedroom. The air hung so thick with sexual tension, it was almost as if the oxygen had been sucked out of the room. Liam stared into her eyes and she stared back, her sky blue eyes darkening with each breath.

Liam wanted so much to just love her, to feel even a part of what he felt like when Amanda was in the room, but somehow inside, his heart just wouldn't play ball. Being as stubborn as he prided himself in being, he was bound and determined to find a way, even if he had to make one up. And this would be that moment.

For the first time in his life, Liam wasn't having sex, wasn't being yanked around by his lust. He would attempt to make love to a girl who had stood by his side, had met his grandparents and of whom they'd approved. He'd finally get to make love to a girl who deserved it, who needed to feel his complete attention on her, and Maureen needed to know that, no matter what. But even though he hid his true feelings from her, and he couldn't "feel" that special feeling inside him, in this moment, he'd seal the deal, and show her he'd always be by her side.

He rested his big farm-calloused hands on her neck, and slid them slowly down to her shoulders, letting the fabric that slipped from her skin fall down her arms.

Just that one little area, that line from where her neck began and her shoulder ended, Liam yearned to taste her there. Softly, gently, almost as if she were a porcelain doll, something, that if he wasn't careful with, would shatter into million pieces.

This was such a different experience for him. This time, no words were spoken as he leaned forward to claim her neck with his mouth, sucking gently, massaging with his tongue. Her body began to quiver, her breathing becoming heavy and deep. So responsive, and he hadn't done anything yet. But the way that he touched her would make her feel loved, cherished. Liam knew that, on this night, Maureen would be making love for the first time, too.

Her hand glided under his shirt, slowly, pressing hard as if her fingertips sought her destiny.

Liam kissed her shoulder, softly, gently.

Her hand traveled all the way up under his shirt to his shoulder, the palm of her hand pressing deep into his muscle.

He could almost read her mind, knew by the way her hand dug into him, she teetered on the edge of love and lust.

Even though his hands traced her body, sculpting her beautiful curves with his palms, mentally he stood at a crossroads.

Her breath came heavily as the smell of pure sex became so thick in the air, he could rip all her clothes off right now. He could ravage her right now, and she would accept every moment, every motion, every drop.

But instead, he would make this different for them. He took off his T-shirt.

Maureen's palms dug into his shoulders, squeezing tightly.

Liam tucked his finger under her chin, tipping her head up to look into his eyes. "Maureen." The word came from his lips like a song he'd just written, the perfect melody. "I want to make love to you." He sighed, as if he'd just confessed his deepest, most tender desire.

Maureen's cheeks became rosy red, and a small tear slid from the corner of her eye. She reached to wipe it away.

He grabbed her wrist, placing her hand on his chest. "No, let it fall."

Silently, she nodded, looking at him with such devotion, he wished once again he could feel deserving of her.

Liam placed his hands around her waist, picking her up, her body pressed along his. He had to look up to see her face, and she smiled with a joy so free, it was as if he'd unchained her from some cold, dark, meaningless place.

This embrace symbolized unity. Now, with her up in his arms, hugging her close, it wasn't their shared sexuality he honed in on, but the strong beats pounding from his chest onto her flesh.

She placed her warm, soft hands just below his jawline.

Liam looked up at her and she kissed his lips.

Fire lit inside him as she caressed his lips with hers, and it drove him absolutely insane, but at the same time, the kiss felt so soft, so caring, he asked himself if this could be love.

With her wrapped up in his big muscles, he moved her legs, encouraging her to wrap her legs around his waist.

This was it. He walked toward the bed.

With each step, their lips changed focus, going from soft and gentle to a deep press of tongues, creating that signature sound that Liam associated with lust before sex. Only this time, it would be making love.

Laying her gently on the bed as if on a cloud,

her body seemed to float out of his arms' embrace. She waited, soft, vulnerable, wanting.

Her pupils dilated and she watched him slowly unbutton his jeans, gradually let his zipper down.

With almost excruciating deliberation, he exposed his body to her, feeling more naked than he ever had in his life.

As if in a dream, the world before this moment slipped away, all his past sins forgiven.

He took a moment to really look at her. She didn't see him as only a sexy hunk, or stare like she wanted to devour him. The look in her eyes said he was beautiful to her.

For first time since he could remember, he didn't just feel like a man, he felt like a valued human being.

The anticipation built between them in slow motion. Maureen shifted, grasping her shirt to take her clothes off.

He placed his big hand on her chest and locked his gaze with hers. "No."

Slowly he glided his hand to her shorts, then unbuttoned them, taking his time, making sure that if something happened to stop this wonderful night—if their lovemaking did not occur—he'd remember every moment of it until it ended.

He smiled at the negative train of thought going through his head. Why, recently, did he always assume the worst would happen?

Liam slid his hands into her shorts, his palms massaging her hips, sliding the shorts and panties off her, caressing her thighs with his palms, careful not to miss one curve as he gently released the fabric, letting it fall on the floor.

He took off her shirt the same way, touching her as he slid up her body. As his palms pressed past her ribs, she inhaled as if she had completely stopped breathing so she didn't miss a moment of his touch.

Pulling her top and bra free, he exposed her beautiful body.

All this time, their gazes never lost contact. Maureen's eyes darted from left to right as if she was nervous. Hadn't she ever been here before? Truly making love, and not just having sex?

Liam slid onto the bed and Maureen scooted over, lying flat on her back. He looked deeply into her eyes, memorizing this moment as if he stared at the most beautiful painting that had never been painted.

She placed her hand on his cheek and Liam leaned in, kissing her passionately, soft, lovingly, letting his body become fully aroused from her touch.

The scent of her juices perfumed the air. This wasn't about sex, yet he became more turned on than he'd ever been before, and he prayed that she was, also. This was about innocence, about sharing that one certain moment.

Liam ended the kiss, letting his need for her show in his eyes. He would not withhold their complete pleasure one more second. Slowly, he rolled onto Maureen's body, pushing her into the brand new mattress they'd purchased and hauled home that morning. It amazed him that they were a couple, and this was their life, now.

The feel of her, hot and soft, pressed along his body, nearly snapped him into rutting mode. Caressing her cheek with the outside of his hand, he drew an unsteady breath. "This may hurt a little, but I'll be gentle."

With a little smile, she opened her legs for

him, her eyes filled with emotion, silently inviting him in.

The knowledge that she trusted him, that she knew his size, yet was not afraid that he'd tear into her, sent ripples of gratitude through him. With his hand around his base, he placed himself against her soft warmth, gently parting her lips as he let his head slide in.

A tightness around her eyes showed that it did hurt, but her quiet moan and the goosebumps that rose on her skin told him she loved it.

"Are you okay, darlin'?"

She responded by sliding her hands down his back to his buttocks, pulling him in even deeper.

Intense heat rose from her body. "Why do I love the pain, Liam? Why do I want more?"

With one last pull from her hands on Liam's buttocks, he finally seated himself completely inside her.

He stopped, waiting for her body to adjust to his length and width. He kissed her neck, kissed her cheek, then ran his fingers across her forehead, moving her hair back behind her ear. "You're so beautiful."

She giggled a little, and then, in her satirical way, responded, "You're not so bad yourself."

They both grinned, and the lighthearted moment cut through the intensity, allowing their comfortable relationship to return.

He imagined them somewhere far away from all the responsibilities and hazards of their real lives. Sliding his hand to the back of her neck, he kissed her passionately. Against her lips, he drew in oxygen. "I'm going to start moving now. I'm going to make love to you, Maureen."

She nodded, her eyes were no longer darting around, but looking straight into his. "Liam, please don't hurt me, you have all of me."

He sobered for a second. She wasn't talking about the physical pain, because she enjoyed the ecstasy that came from rough loving. Liam knew exactly what Maureen meant. *Don't break my heart.*

He'd given that look to somebody before, and it had nearly killed him when that was exactly what she'd done.

Thrusting slowly, he opened her. Liam rotated his hips to the left, right, then pushed in deep.

She inhaled as his thickness slowly expanded her inner walls.

With each movement, each thrust, he glided into her, not with ease, but definitely with satisfaction for both of them.

A moment of clarity diverted his attention. He was doing it, he was actually making love. He reached out to massage her arm, rub her ribcage.

Left, right, out, all the way in, and his eyes rolled back with the dreamlike pleasure.

Maureen's body shuddered, as if she was having one big, long multiple orgasm.

Liam looked deep into her eyes as his physical motion increased. "I'm going to go faster now."

Her hands slid along his neck, her eyes focused on him with the intensity of fire. "Yes." Her words came out in a slow, broken tone.

Each time he thrust hard, she said, "Yes," in that sexy tone.

Both of them needed more. He started pumping in a rhythmical motion, in and out.

After only a few minutes, her voice grew stronger, still a broken sound, but more determined.

Liam quickened his strokes, sliding into her harder. Looking into her eyes, he increased the moment's intensity.

"Yes, yes, yes." She ground out the words with each thrust.

Liam's body tingled as each stroke pulled him halfway out, then he drove his shaft all the way in.

Her small body took the jolt with ease now, and, judging by the look on her face, with pure ecstasy.

Liam drove all the way into her and held himself there for long moments.

Maureen sighed. "I can feel you inside me, so deep, Liam."

"Are you okay?" He craved release, but felt an intense need to cocoon her in satisfaction.

"Absolutely."

They both smiled.

"Are you ready to come for me?" He touched his nose to hers.

She kissed him, biting his lip. "I've *been* ready, Liam. Forever."

Even though he had a green light, he wanted Maureen to realize this was all about her.

Gently he placed his arms around her neck and put his lips next to her ear. "Hold on to me tight."

Maureen followed his instructions as Liam began to pummel into her, over, and over, and over.

She went from saying yes to letting out the most beautiful cry of pure bliss, her moans filling every corner of the room.

The bed pounded into the wall so loud, it sounded like a wrecking ball hitting wall after wall.

As they looked into each other's eyes, Liam could see by her soft expression that she knew it was anything but sex.

Feeling her clench around him, almost pushing him out, he nearly imploded with the tight slide of his length inside her.

Liam knew she was going to come. Instinctually, he wanted to slow this, make it last, but he'd do just the opposite, making this first time unforgettable for both of them.

Looking into her eyes, he pistoned his hips in and out as she began moving frantically under him.

As their hips rotated and moved in opposite directions, meeting in the middle, their sensitive skin heated and engorged, getting so close to their release.

Liam's pumping intensified, driving in quick, deep jabs, pushing the limits of her inner walls.

Her moaning became louder, and the sounds coming out of her fueled him for more, more, more.

She cried, "Oh my God, I'm going to come."

Before the last word came from her mouth, he pulled her tight to him and pushed hard and deep inside.

Giving her every ounce of energy he had, he let himself release inside her. Within himself, his fever broke, cooling him with sweat, tingles cascading along every nerve ending.

The way she sucked him in, it felt as if her insides were eager, hungry for what he'd given her.

His pumping slowed, and with every easy movement in and out of her, he silently thanked the universe for this moment. He stared at her face, savoring the bliss in her expression

After she slowly fell back to earth, Liam kissed her forehead, cheeks, and lips. His body shook. He'd never done this before, had never come inside any woman before, never had sex without a condom before.

They melted into each other, their hearts beating as one. A bead of sweat trickled off his brow and traced along Maureen's shoulder. He nestled his head above her breasts.

She caressed his back as if to say, I love you. Although he didn't feel deserving of it, he mirrored her motions, willing himself to feel the same way toward her.

They lay in each other's arms for what felt like an eternity. As if neither wanted the moment to end, though truth be told, Liam fought a slight fear that it could never be this good again.

Her breathing became louder, and he realized he was too heavy for her.

Liam rolled off of her, kissed her forehead, and ran his knuckles down her cheek.

There were no words that could express his hopes, his fears, his deep need for this to last.

****

Maureen could barely contain herself until she made it into the bathroom. After closing the door, she giggled and spun in circles. Liam was everything she'd ever dreamed of. For a while after he'd suggested waiting to make love, she'd been afraid there might be something wrong with him—or her—sexually.

But after the sweet way he'd loved her just now, there was nothing but happiness ahead of them. "Oh my gosh." She stared at her reflection in the mirror. "I love him." The tiny ache just behind her heart confirmed it. This had to be love. True and pure and shared so freely between them.

To prove how much she wanted their relationship to work, she'd planned a surprise, thanks to her cousin Peyton's idea. Liam's camera was set up on his tripod in the bedroom closet. She'd pull it out and let him know that whatever he wanted to do, no matter how kinky, she was willing.

"I love him." Saying the words sent tickles of joy across her skin. When would she tell him? Maybe catching the moment on camera would be fun, something they could keep and look at for years and years.

Oh, gosh. She was planning a future already? Finishing up, she walked out of the bathroom, gave a lazy, sleeping Mooch a quick pet, and padded into the bedroom.

Liam lay exactly where she left him, stretched out on their new sheets with a smile on his face. "Where you been? I missed you." He held out his hand.

"Hold that thought." She wanted nothing more than to scooch in next to him and cuddle up for more afterglow and a new round of hot loving, but she wanted to see what he thought of her video idea, first.

Opening the closet door, she glanced back at him.

He'd stacked his hands under his head and watched her with a sexy half-smile on his lips; one she wanted to kiss and nibble at for hours.

She pulled out the tripod, spread its legs, and set it on the floor. Stepping to the side, she watched for his reaction.

His smile disappeared, replaced with a frown and narrowed eyes. "What's that for?"

Her nerves jangled. "I hope you don't mind, but when I stopped at the farm this afternoon, I grabbed this along with the other things you wanted." She swallowed.

Liam's eyes shifted nervously.

"I thought it would be fun…you know…to record. Just for fun." At his silence, she knew she could talk him into it. "You don't think it's ridiculous, do you?" She grabbed the tripod and adjusted the legs to lock them in. "If *you* don't mind, I really don't think it's such a dumb idea."

Liam forced a smile. Without saying anything, his expression softened. "If you want to, I want to."

Peeking at him, she expected more of a reaction. With the way he sat up in bed, she couldn't tell if he was eager or taken aback. She forced her nervousness away, replacing it with a determination to make this fun and sexy for both of them.

"Liam, I—" She almost said it. Almost told him she loved him. But she needed to save it for a more tender time.

She winked at him. "You ready to do this, big boy?"

He sat straighter. "Let me show you how—"

Maureen raised her hand. "No. I can handle pressing the 'record' button." She positioned herself behind the camera and pressed the button, leveling the camera so it faced…

The video that played on the small screen made her feel instantly empty inside. Instead of record, she must have pressed play. She shook her head. *No, it couldn't be*. The back of the man's naked body moved rhythmically forward and back. Who was this man on Liam's video camera? The horrible reality set in as she watched the woman on her hands and knees in front of him on a bed. *Oh my God, it's Liam's bed.* She saw the face of the debaucher. It was Liam.

Was this a sex tape of him with another

woman? Of course it was. She wasn't his first. But the way he kept looking back over his shoulder…

The woman lifted her head. Spiky black hair, green eyes. "Peyton?" Her lungs stopped working. Out of the corner of her eye, she watched Liam on the bed, looking confident as he flexed his muscles for his big film debut. "Hurry up, darlin'. Get back in our bed so I can show you how much I want you. He shot her a sexy look.

The sight, his words, made her stomach churn. Her fucking cousin? The part-time hooker! Liam had hired her for an anonymous fuck so he could videotape it?

Sucking in a breath, she tried to fight back the tears, even though her heart was beyond broken.

Maureen's legs started shaking as she fast-forwarded and stopped when she saw another disgusting display. He was fucking one woman and fingering another. The man she'd thought was perfect for her suddenly turned disgusting in her eyes.

"What's going on, Maureen?" In her peripheral vision, Liam's confidence began to fade, his face showing confusion.

She had to be tough. She'd been walked on, beaten, manipulated, and she'd compromised her integrity her whole life. She would be damned if she'd give Liam Jackson the satisfaction of seeing her cry.

Before she completely fell apart, before Liam could say a word, Maureen turned and walked out of the room, closing the door on their life together.

Chapter Twenty-Six

As sunrise lit the sky, Liam stood outside the closed apartment door, regret shadowing his soul.

Maureen had sent him a text early this morning; *Come to the apartment, but don't come in, just knock and I'll hand you your things and take the key back.*

He lifted his fist for the third time, but let it drop again. Strange how he hadn't been able to feel love for Maureen when they were together, but now, somehow, it was like a boulder sat on top of his heart. Even though Liam was vacant inside, his mind told him he was losing a really good thing.

Scratching sounded on the lower part of the door, followed by a low whimper.

"Aw, damnit. Mooch."

Last night, Maureen had kicked Liam out, wouldn't let him explain, and threatened to call the police when he'd refused to leave without talking it out. He'd gone home and lay in his cold bed all night, waiting for a call from her, then the text came at around five this morning.

The door opened.

Maureen's face looked ghost-white, her eyes red and puffy, and Mooch stood staring at him, looking as confused as Liam felt.

As Liam opened his mouth to say something, anything, Maureen shoved her finger in his face, and shouted, "No!" She lifted an open box filled with his things and handed it to him. "There's nothing, Liam Jackson, absolutely not one goddamn thing you could ever say, that would fix this."

Liam wanted to retort, but he knew she was right, there was no sense in his pride showing up today. Taking the box under one arm, watching the tears of the end of their relationship flow down her soft cheeks, he pulled a check from his jeans pocket and handed it to her along with the key to their apartment, their future.

Fighting back his own tears, and turning to walk away, he said, "For the furniture." His words came out broken. He'd promised her he'd help her buy it. And right or wrong, he always kept his promises.

He walked down the hallway, then stopped to look back at her. A silent cry shook her body as hard tears flowed again. She slowly pushed the door to close it.

Mooch stuck his head out, staring at him as if he was being abandoned, too.

Liam looked into the wolf's eyes, silently communicating, *Take care of her, wolf.* As Liam headed down the hall, it was as if life moved in the wrong direction in slow motion. This was the right place for the dog. After all, Liam could barely take care of himself. How could he keep a big, hairy—

A piercing howl filled the space. Mooch knew they'd never see each other again, and loneliness yawned like a chasm in Liam's soul.

In his car, Liam set the box on the seat next to him and let the pain of loss batter him. Was this better than feeling nothing?

A small sticky note was attached to his camera. *I recorded something.*

Liam pressed play.

Her blotchy red face appeared. "You're into keeping a video record of the high-points in your sex life, so you'll appreciate this. I'm a better person now, Liam, thanks to you and your grandparents. You showed me how good I could be, and I'm really proud of myself." She swallowed and dipped her head for a second. "I'm letting you go because you don't deserve me. You're on the wrong path. Liam." She stared right at him. "Be careful which you feed—your love or your lust. It'll come back to haunt you in the end, and you'll be the one with a broken heart."

It would take a while, but he would convince himself that she was right, that he didn't deserve Maureen, that she'd be better off without him. He tried to work up emotion, tried to feel hurt by her rejection, but nothing came. He felt worse about abandoning Mooch. Abandoning? His regret came from his sense of responsibility. But why wasn't anything aching inside him for Maureen?

On the screen, she groaned as she pressed a bunch of buttons before she hit the right one, then the screen went blank.

Be careful which you feed. Hadn't his grandparents told him essentially the same thing over and over? *Be careful which side of your personality you cultivate.*

When the hell would he learn?

****

After he sat for a while and tried to connect all the pieces of his life, he called Travis for help getting him through the most urgent cluster fuck he'd created. "Hey, buddy, you got a couple hundred cash I could borrow right now? I just wrote a check, and it's going to bounce." He didn't want to take it out of his college fund since his grandparents were listed as co-owners.

"You? Wrote a bad check?" Travis laughed, but stopped abruptly. "Oh shit, what happened?"

"I'll tell you when I get there."

"No, meet me at the bank. We'll get the money transferred, then hang out a while."

Liam needed someone to talk to right now, and as always, Travis came through. "Okay. Thanks."

When the money was in Liam's account, they grabbed a booth in the café and ordered breakfast.

"Maureen?" Travis gulped down half his coke.

"Yep. I fucked it up, and she's done with me." He ran his finger along the rim of his coffee cup. "Kept my dog, too."

"Can she do that?"

"She needs him more than I do. For protection, and company."

He stared into the black liquid. Memories of last night flooded his thoughts. Why hadn't he jumped up when he saw Maureen with his camera? He could have sent her to lie on the bed while he erased the videos. Was this karma coming back at him? Telling him to get his life straightened out?

"…reading about the toxic water downstream. There's an investigation…" A man's voice sounded in the booth behind them.

Travis's face paled as he met Liam's gaze, then he stared down at his fork.

Liam leaned forward, keeping his voice low. "Is your dad involved?"

Travis shrugged. "Nothing he can't buy his way out of."

Damn that asshole. Liam constantly tripped and fell his way into deep shit, but Jarvis Hackers jumped right into it and kicked it onto everyone he came in contact with. Their food came and Liam struggled to find a subject. "What's going on with you and Amanda?"

A bark of laughter came from Travis. "Did you see her at your apartment? Treats me like shit even when I…" He shook his head. "I can offer her everything."

"Maybe she doesn't need everything. Maybe just a walk by the lake."

Travis snorted. "Like I'd take relationship advice from you."

Liam felt his face heat.

"Ah fuck, I'm sorry, man. That was really shitty."

"Yeah, but true." Liam had no talent for relationships.

They ate the rest of their meal in silence.

"I work this afternoon." Liam could use some sleep, but it seemed like he and Travis needed to hang out and talk more. "Come out to the farm for a while this morning, stay for lunch."

The waitress brought the bill and Travis grabbed it. "Can't. Got too much to do." He slid out of the booth. "But, thanks, you know. For understanding." He glanced sideways at Liam. "Besides, you look like you've been dragged through the bushes backward. Go home and take a pill. Get some sleep."

Liam ran his hand through his hair. He'd need a pill to be able to even close his eyes without seeing Maureen's shattered expression in his mind.

Travis left, paying their bill on the way out.

Liam owed the guy more than just money, but money was the one thing he could pay back. And there was only one way he'd be able to get enough cash before school started.

****

The next afternoon, Liam walked into the

library and spotted Amanda. In a short, red skirt pink halter top, and high-heeled sandals, she looked like a foldout page from a men's magazine.

The day before, he'd stopped at the station and apologized to her for acting so strange, and offered to resume tutoring.

Now, he regretted it. The air sizzled between them and the pill he'd taken to dull his senses didn't kill any of the ache below his waist. Plopping down on the chair across from her, he gritted his teeth and focused at a point just off her shoulder. "What are we working on today?"

She reached for him and her fingers skimmed his forearm for a second before he pulled back. "Liam, I heard about you and Maureen. I'm so sorry."

That slight touch pounded through him like a jackhammer. He had to take a few breaths before he could form words. "How did you hear?"

"That doesn't matter. But if you'd like to talk about it instead of jumping right into chemistry, I'm glad to listen." She sounded sincere, but her eyes looked dark, her pupils large.

They both fought this thing between them, and if Travis didn't make his move soon…

"No, let's get right to it."

They spent a couple hours going through the basics, then she leaned closer. "What is *our* chemistry? You know, whatever's going on between us? Why don't I feel this way about anyone else?"

Huffing out a long sigh, he dropped his head. "I don't know. I don't get it. But…"

"But?" Her sweet breath brushed over his face, starting a rapid chain reaction of desire building inside him.

He blinked but couldn't open his eyelids. He

braced for another daydream, which would be more like a sexmare.

He saw himself rising from the chair and grabbing her, pulling her soft, hot body along the length of his. Her breath panted at his neck, and he needed to make her completely breathless, completely his. Grabbing the hem of her skirt, he yanked it up, baring her lacy black panties. Cupping her ass cheeks, he walked her backwards until her thighs hit the table, then he sat her on it. Pushing her upper body back, he kissed her neck, bit a path down the middle of her chest, across her breast to suckle at her nipple through her clothes, then down her belly.

His fingers pushed aside the musk-dampened lace of her underwear, and he slid two fingers inside her, his other hand pressing down on her belly. He'd make her come hard, let her sweet rain coat his hand, wet his shirt.

"Now, Liam. Don't wait." Her cry echoed up to the high ceiling.

Heat throbbed in his thigh, radiating along his leg and through his body.

A loud boom rattled the windows.

Liam opened his eyes.

Amanda had moved and her hand rested on his leg, but she stared outside. "I think we were just hit by lightning."

Through the thick muck slogging his brain, he knew he had to get away from her. He stood and nearly toppled sideways.

The librarian stepped into the room. "I'm sorry, we're going to have to evacuate the library."

Liam helped Amanda gather her books and they followed Mrs. Fieldhouse's squeaking shoes out through the back door as a fire truck pulled up, lights flashing.

The few clouds crawling across the sky didn't look like they'd produce thunder, but a tree near the building was split in half and smoldering.

He set Amanda's books in her back seat. "Divine intervention."

"Meaning you want to come to my place?" She gave him a wicked smile.

"No, Amanda." He opened her car door and stood behind it. "You work tomorrow?"

"No."

Still feeling dazed from the aftereffects of his supernatural vision, he searched for the reason he'd asked the question. *Tutoring*. "How about noon? We'll finish the chem chapter."

"Liam." She ran her tongue over her full bottom lip. "I'm not interested in Travis."

"Yeah, but he's interested in you." He couldn't make a move on her. Not until Travis gave up on Amanda, then there was the bro-code waiting period, then Liam would need to ask his friend for permission.

"He doesn't have to know." She grabbed his arm. "I can be your rebound from Maureen. I don't care."

Where she touched, flames seared through his bloodstream. He somehow found the strength to walk away. "I care." He made it to his car and sat in the driver's seat for long minutes, hearing her voice echo in his head. *He doesn't have to know*. Temptation pulsed through him like Amanda was the last woman on earth. He could let this fire burn them both, satisfy them as he knew it would…but could Liam live with himself if he did something that desperate?

He headed home, and when he pulled up to

the farmhouse, he let himself reconnect with reality. He had a family. He had a piece of land that he loved, that would be all his one day. If he could reconnect with the best things in his life, he'd be able to fight off the marginal stuff.

Liam walked into the house. "Grams, do I smell pie?"

Dear Me, you are a dumbass. You are stupid, and you make all the wrong decisions. There, now that I got that off my chest... I feel nothing inside my heart for Maureen. But yet, there's a part of me that's vacant, that I can't explain without her. There's one thing I'm good at: fucking things up. I fear my friendship with Travis is in jeopardy if I don't escape the devil's daughter, Amanda. She's everywhere. Why am I "obsessed?" Why do I smell spring rain every goddamn time she's around, and there's not a cloud in the sky? My mom was sick in her head...I wonder if I'm losing my mind. I don't know what's up, I don't know what's down. Every single choice I've tried to make, I've failed at. But, Grams always says, when you get knocked off the horse, dust off your britches and get back on. Just between you and me, having sex with Amanda is inevitable. I think Travis is or was sleeping with my girlfriend, and at this point, I'd trade in the smell of spring fucking rain for a whole barn full of manure.

True love?... Maybe in the movies. Afterthought (but definitely not in my movies.)

Amanda crawled naked onto his bed. "It's going to happen, Liam."

"No. Get out! Get away from me!" He sat up and tried to push her off him, but his hands went right through her, as if she were a ghost. He blinked. His eyes were open, but the vision continued, like an overlay on reality. "Stop. I can't take any more."

Her scent filled the room, he could feel her pressing her body against his, her forked tongue lapping a path over his pecs. His heart thundered so hard, he couldn't get a full breath.

In his mind, the covers were stripped away, he was naked, his shaft standing tall and hard, and she bent and took it into her mouth. All of it.

The overhead light popped on. "Liam?" Grams tied the belt on her old pink robe as she walked into the room.

He pushed a pillow over his lap to cover his privates. "Can you see her?" He knew it was an insane question, but he had to know.

"See…who?" She looked around the room. "Is Maureen here?"

"No." The vision slowly faded, the heaviness in the air lifted, and his blood pressure dropped. "No one's here. Just a dream."

Grams sat on the bed and patted his hand. "You're missing her, huh?"

The three of them had talked about the breakup after supper, and Liam had seen the sorrow in both his grandparents' eyes.

"I'm having nightmares, daydreams that seem

so true, it's like something is taking over and I have no way to resist it."

His grandmother watched him for a few seconds. She reached for the prescription bottle on his nightstand and shook it. It was nearly empty. "I think it's these, sweetie. Why don't you give yourself a few days to let them clear out of your system. Things will look better then."

The pills. Could it be? Were they making him wonky? "I think you're right." He lay back and she tucked the covers under his chin the way she'd done when he'd first arrived and was still having nightmares.

"Sorry I woke you, Grams." He held her hand for a couple seconds.

She leaned over and kissed his forehead. "I love you, son. You can wake me up anytime you need anything."

"Love you, too."

Walking through the doorway, she shut off the light and closed the door behind her.

Liam almost called her back, asked her to hold him, but he was a grown man, now. He needed to do this on his own. He curled into a tight ball and prayed for dreamless sleep.

The next morning, Liam called Amanda at the Pump and Run and postponed his tutoring lesson with her for two days. That'd give the drugs time to work their way out of him, and give him time to find perspective.

He and his grandpa worked around the farm the first day, then Liam tutored the twins the next two mornings and worked at the station both evenings.

But each night, a vision of Amanda haunted his dreams. He learned not to scream at the apparition, to turn on the light, then take a cold shower to pull him back from the edge of…insanity? Is that what was happening? He was finally becoming certifiable?

That morning, he drove into Liberation for the scheduled tutoring session with Amanda. He felt more stable than he had in a long while. He could control this. He had complete charge of his body and his mind.

Then he stepped into the back room of the library, and realized how wrong he was.

Chapter Twenty-Seven

Amanda stood as Liam walked toward her. Her jean shorts showed her sexy legs, and her green, frilly blouse was unbuttoned too low.

On the library table in front of her, the chemistry book's pages flapped as the force of their attraction collided like two storm fronts.

The taste of her pheromones landed thick on his tongue, and her body seemed to shimmer in the artificial light.

She looked at him as if she were seeing the same thing happening to him. "What is going on?"

The rays of sun that had been streaming in the windows faded, the world around them darkened.

The days without pain pills had cleared his mind, which had evidently released his sex drive full-force. Hard as granite, he throbbed down low, and his hands came up of their own volition, reaching for her, his lips formed her name over and over.

Amanda's arms shook, then her legs, and finally her torso quivered as she took halting steps toward him, looking like someone was pushing her from behind. "I can't resist."

He shook his head. "Have to." He fisted his hands, but his knuckles ached with the effort to keep them from reopening.

A flash lit the room. Lightning. Followed by the boom of thunder.

Locking his knees, he kept himself from going to her. Everything inside him rebelled at his stillness. Unseen forces promised exquisite release once he had her under him, naked and writhing.

His eyes closed. He saw a vision of her lying on a wooden bench, spread and waiting for him in a room made of concrete, with a brown metal door, locked from the outside.

Lighting flashed, thunder roared, and a burst of wind whipped tree branches against the windows as airborne dirt peppered the glass.

"It's a tornado." Amanda pointed out the windows, her voice coming out panicked.

Liam forced his brain to function and looked behind him. The sky had turned as black as night, and the tree threatened to break the glass.

"Here." Amanda pointed to a door marked with a storm shelter logo by the bathroom doors.

"Go." He pushed her toward it and ran the other way.

"Liam!" Amanda followed him. "You have to—"

He turned her around, bodily, and pushed her toward the door. "I'll be right behind you, gotta see who else is in the building.

She ran, and Liam bolted through the small building, shouting for Mrs. Fieldhouse. No one else was in the building. He ran through the room he and Amanda had been working in and the windows burst inward followed by a roar that sounded like a locomotive.

He covered his head with his arms and kept moving, his feet crunching on broken glass.

Yanking open the door to the shelter, he came face-to-face with Amanda. "Go."

She shook her head and clung to his arm.

"Come on." He jogged down the steps, leading Amanda into the dimly lit basement.

The building creaked over their heads, as he stepped onto the concrete floor. To their right, a light shone on a metal door. Brown, just like in his vision.

"Shit."

Amanda scooted around him and opened the door. "It's so weird. It's like I've seen this before." She reached up and pulled a string which turned on a low wattage light bulb that hung from the ceiling by a chain.

Liam stepped in behind her. Benches lined the walls and one ran along the middle of the room, just as he'd envisioned. Yeah, this was too much. He couldn't be here. It felt like his life was replaying from a dream.

Above them, wood cracked, followed by a gust of wind that swirled through the room.

Then the door blew closed.

They faced each other and his vision narrowed, as if he looked at her from inside a tunnel. All sounds disappeared, replaced by the thudding of blood through his veins.

Her head bobbed on her neck. "We're meant to be together." She wobbled as her knees gave out.

Liam grabbed her to hold her upright, and everything imploded. All at once, panic had his heart pounding harder than it had ever with anyone before.

He knew he stood on the doorstep of pure lust. He had to run.

Frantically, he placed her on the bench and went to the door. The handle wouldn't turn, and he grasped it with both hands, straining to force it, but knowing it wouldn't open. Something stronger than him was at work here.

Liam's nostrils became intoxicated with the scent of rain. Almost as if in a hypnotic trance, his hands dropped from the handle.

His mind went dead-calm as he turned around.

The dank room had sealed his fate, as if they

were in a tomb buried deep below morality and loyalty. He didn't care about anything but now, this instant.

Thoughts rushed through his mind, frame by frame. How many times had he resisted her? How many times had he walked away from Amanda with his heart throbbing?

Veins filled in his manhood like someone held it and squeezed it, as if it were about to burst. He'd never had an erection like this before.

Liam thought about nothing but the scene in front of him. All he could feel was physical insistence.

He immediately ripped down his pants, unable to stop himself.

He had to free the lustful desire that physically hurt from the fabric pushing so tight.

Once he sprang free, he stared, transfixed, as the light swung over where Amanda lay on the bench, like a pendulum, back and forth.

One second, her skin shone, then in the next moment, she plunged into darkness. The swinging repeated over and over until he wondered if he'd finally lost his mind. Had he pushed himself over the edge? He had no idea what he was doing.

His body had tightened so hard, his muscles were engorged, as if he was a ravenous bear about to devour a soft doe, lying in the grass.

The light swung, flashing off Amanda's skin, then sent the room into darkness. A pendulum over what would be the end; the end of anything that made him a gentleman. The end of innocence, the release of his inner beast.

The room became hot, and Liam pictured himself standing at the gates of hell. Humidity hung so thick, it rolled off the dank walls.

His skin perspired, his raging beast stood so engorged with blood that the head of his cock looked two sizes bigger than normal. No way could her frail body fuck him, but he didn't care. He felt only the need, the drive to complete this sinful union.

Amanda began writhing on the bench, as if drunk with ecstasy, her arms moving in slow motion, grasping for something, holding on as if he was on top of her, his length already inside her.

"Please, take me. Now, Liam. Don't wait." Her hips pumped up and down onto the bench, over and over. She moaned, primal sounds he'd never heard before, a foreign tongue that called to him with words that shattered all that was left of his willpower.

His eyes locked on his prey, sweat dripped off his brow, his muscles rippled as his cock pulsed, huge and rock-hard.

Amanda's eyes rolled around, as if she wasn't there anymore, not present in her own body, she kept crying out, showing him that all she wanted was to be fucked.

Liam gripped her arms, sat her up and ripped her blouse open, exposing small, firm breasts and dark, pebbled nipples.

Amanda tore the blouse free. "I'm ready Liam, ready right now."

He placed his hand over her mouth, afraid that if she said more, this moment would be gone. As if he was an addict, and she was his heroin, addicted to have her as his high.

His hands trembled as he ripped open the button of her shorts. One tug freed her shorts and panties from her legs, and they hit the wall as he cast them aside.

He straightened, standing naked over her as he straddled the bench.

She panted as she stared at his bulk, her gaze touching every inch of him, stopping when they reached his heavy shaft.

He took her in as well. It was as if the devil himself had made her to incite his lust. Her body, completely shaven, her toned abs, her chest rising and falling with her breaths.

Bending, Liam took both her legs, laying her back on the bench and pulling her ankles to his shoulders. He straightened, so her sweet ass and her back lifted, leaving just her shoulders on the bench.

As if by mystical decree, their bodies aligned perfectly and he shoved every inch of his hard length inside her inferno.

She screamed his name, but he pressed his palm over her mouth. “Shut up.” He said it not in a commanding way, but in desperation that they wouldn’t be caught, like a junkie making sure no one could take away his fix.

He could feel her inner walls ease wider as he drove in, balls deep.

When she went silent, he grasped her hips, holding her where he wanted her. He began tearing into her, her juices flowing from her entryway, making slick, wet sounds that increased his feral need to fuck.

Liam thrust hard, pistoning like a well-oiled machine.

Amanda’s eyes widened, and her pupils completely dilated, making her eyes black.

Over and over he sank into her and withdrew, his mind flashing frames of lust-skewed encounters with her, bending her over the counter at the Pump and Run, taking her against the glass door at the gas station in Rogers Corners, dragging her into the bed he shared with Maureen and fucking her doggy-style.

The crazy flashes only made him piston harder and harder as if he could expel every bit of resistance he'd ever had.

The bench rattled left and right, its steel mountings barely handling their manic movements.

Amanda's eyes rolled back. With each thrust, he pulled her higher, her neck barely on the bench as he held her and pummeled into her.

The heat thickened in the room, sweat from his brow dropped onto her, running along her skin and shimmering in the light.

As his mind and body prepared to climax, he had a second of panic. He had no idea what had happened. How he'd slipped from humanity into this animalistic rage.

Nothing that Earth had to offer could compare to this intense, all-encompassing, immoral perfection. Liam was dealing with the devil, and would gladly pay his dues.

Along his thick beast, intense pressure built in her insanely tight canal, increasing until he roared, "Now, woman!"

Her arms went limp, her eyes rolled as if she were possessed. He lifted her up, pulling his beast out of her.

"Oh my God!" Her voice sounded like it came straight from the depths of hell as her unholy spray from her slick core hit him hard in the throat, dripping down his chest as he held her thighs, her body convulsing, her head rolling back and forth on the bench.

Liam didn't want to stop, his head started

spinning, plunging him into a black hole where his mind tunneled to a place that was all too familiar. But his body, seeming not under his own control, grabbed the back of her neck, pulling her up and impaling her body onto him.

Her head fell hard onto his shoulder, bobbing, and her arms went limp.

Liam grasped her ass in his big hands, holding her mid-air, positioning her so she wouldn't fall. Pistoning into her over and over, a vision of fire, buckskin, and people running, filled his thoughts. He didn't care. Nothing was going to stop him from claiming every drop of Amanda's hellish rain.

"Oh my God, I'm going to fucking come again." Her shout rang in his ears as she arched her back and shot her rain three feet along the bench.

With his heart pounding so hard, visions flashing in his brain, his body pulsing, the room shaking, the light swinging like a pendulum guiding him from this life to next, he jackhammered into her, seeking his own release.

Light, dark, Earth, Hell. He didn't care where he ended up, as long as he drained her of every drop.

A need to taste her, to gorge on her mouth overcame him, but instead, he pulled out, setting her on her back on the bench, and stood over her, his beast at her head, his mouth at her gates of immorality. He dove his face into her harlot cunt, tasting the sweet rain mixed with her musk. Somewhere deep inside, he knew what he was doing was wrong, but he didn't care. This was his addiction.

He rolled his tongue over her clit, sucking it into his mouth.

Amanda grasped his beast, pushing it into her mouth, bobbing onto it, sucking and licking.

Everything went hazy in his head. He didn't care if he was losing his mind. The physical pleasure was worth everything he'd lose.

She sucked hard, really hard, her head bobbing, her hand jerking on him firmly.

He tasted her like it was the last thing he'd ever eat.

Her legs quivered with each lick on her swollen lust.

Liam felt himself surge, his climax close. Pumping his ass, so worn out from thrusting, he fought the desire to come this second. No way he'd come like this, when her sweetness tasted hot and hungry.

He turned around and lifted her, placing her on the bench on all fours. Her body shook, her breath sucked in hard, releasing with tiny cries.

Liam bit her ass then shoved his tongue into the crack, licking all the way down her lips, taking all her juices.

She turned her head, looking back at him, her eyes showing pure lust, an animal rage.

He knew exactly what she wanted, crouched there with her perky ass beautiful, and welcoming.

The light swung wildly.

Liam shoved every inch of himself into her, hard and fast, damn near pushing her inner walls beyond their limits.

Her hands white-knuckled the side of the bench, but if she felt pain, she didn't show it.

He knew she loved every fucking minute of it. Uncaged, the wild animal in him found a carnivorous burst of energy. He pounded into her doggy style, slapping her ass with his palm so hard, the sting on his hand almost became a distraction.

He moaned loudly, animalistic sounds bursting from his throat. He didn't care. Lust-drunk, he knew he'd already sent himself to hell, so why not enjoy every depraved second of this.

All morality escaped him, replaced with savage instinct. They were animals, devouring each other. In the back of his mind, he heard a wolf call, and a vision of golden eyes in a wolf's head flashed for a second.

The image, the sound, coming as if from the walls, made his head spin, his body rocking off-balance, but he pushed everything aside, never missing a beat as his thick, heavy balls swelled and tightened.

He gripped her hips so tightly, he knew there'd be bruising, but the darkness had overtaken him.

White flashed as a surge in the lightbulb's filament blinded him, then all went black.

Liam woke, sitting on the floor, his chest on the bench.

Amanda lay limp on her stomach, naked on the bench.

What had happened? He couldn't remember anything but the echo of their footsteps on the stairs.

The light was on, but not swinging any longer. The room felt cold, and goosebumps rose on his skin.

Liam pushed himself to his knees, looked down at his naked body, and let tears fall from his eyes.

He'd finally lost the fight.

The scent of rain which had filled the air, the strongest he'd ever smelled, was now gone. The sweet liquid puddled on floor, on the bench, and dripped out of her. Had he seen a vision? Did he speak at all? He didn't remember anything but the sudden impact of giving in to his obsession, and being consumed by Amanda.

Her red hair covered her face. His chest ached as he realized how much he loved her. All this time, he'd resisted for Travis's sake, but now that they'd consummated their feelings through this lustful exchange, he'd love her forever, with every breath he took. He would gladly give his life for her.

Amanda started mumbling as she lay on the bench.

Liam was so weak, he could barely move. He should cover her, she'd be cold. It was his job to take care of her now.

His cell phone rang, startling him.

He couldn't move just then if he was offered a million dollars. His text message chime went off next. He closed his eyes, confused by the mix of joy he felt for his new relationship with Amanda, and the strange ache that tempered his enthusiasm. His phone rang again. Struggling to his knees, he dug his phone out of his jeans.

Travis. Shit, he didn't want to deal with this now.

Liam let the phone go to voice mail and checked the text message.

It was from Travis, too. *911 – your farm is on fire.*

Chapter Twenty-Eight

Liam's body snapped into panic mode and he dialed. "Travis what—"

"I was driving past and saw smoke. I'm halfway down the driveway, and it looks like the downstairs is…just get here. I've called the fire department." Travis hung up.

His grandparents were home. Gut-wrenching panic threatened to incapacitate him, but he firmed his resolve and said a quick prayer for them. "Amanda, I've got to go." He stood and pulled on his jeans.

She lay on the bench, naked, staring as if she hadn't heard him.

"Amanda." He shook her arm.

She started talking, incoherent speech flowing from her mouth.

Damnit, he couldn't leave her like this. He stuffed her underwear in her shorts pocket and tugged her shorts onto her, zipping them most of the way up. Holding her in a sitting position, he got her arms into her blouse and buttoned four buttons before he saw he'd started wrong. "Fuck it." He grabbed her shoes and slung an arm around her, hefting her up the steps and out the door.

Amanda laughed and chatted with whatever unseen force had taken over her mind.

The storm had passed, and sunshine poured through the broken windows. No water? It hadn't rained?

Liam picked her up in his arms and carried her through the library, outside, then got her buckled into the passenger seat. He raced around to the driver's side, jumped in and cranked the Malibu to life, roaring out of the lot toward home.

Would there be volunteer firefighters close to the farm who'd be able to help Travis get Grams and Grandpa to safety?

Amanda continued to ramble on about nothing. The same way Kaylee had. When he'd watched the video of him with Trinity, hadn't she gone on like this, too?

Hell, he didn't give a damn. His home was on fire, and his grandparents were in danger. "Fucking priorities." He'd screwed up again, and it might cost him everything this time. He brushed a tear from his cheek.

****

Travis skidded his truck to a stop and jumped out. Liam's farmhouse billowed smoke out of the lower level windows on the right side.

The sound of coughing came from the house.

He ran and jumped up onto the porch then pulled open the screen door. "Grams? Herschel?"

Smoke wafted in layers, burning his eyes and choking him.

A quiet cry came from the left.

Dropping to his hands and knees, he crawled until he found a foot. "Emma." She lay on the floor, but her wrist was tied to a wooden chair.

Travis found his pocket knife and flipped it open, cutting at the rope until it broke loose. He stuffed it in his pocket with his knife. After sucking in a breath, he lifted her in his arms, and ran out the door but stumbled down the steps, sending her rolling on the gravel driveway with him slamming on top of her.

"Emma. Grams. I'm so sorry."

She was barely breathing.

What did he do now? His dad was a volunteer

firefighter, which was the reason Travis hadn't joined.

"Liam." Her voice sounded gravely and weak.

"Grams." He arranged her so she looked comfortable. He didn't have anything to put under her head…

"Liam, I have to tell you before I…" She coughed and gasped for breath.

Travis's whole body went cold. Grams couldn't die. She just couldn't. Over the crackling of the house fire, he couldn't hear sirens, but he prayed they were on their way.

"It's your legacy." Her shaking hand went to her stomach. "Not the wolf's."

Liam's dog? Now she was talking crazy. "Just relax." He rubbed her arm. Her skin felt cold. "Help will be here any minute."

"No. Help me." She lifted her shirt an inch, exposing a small buckskin pouch tied around her waist. "Take it."

Travis untied it and put it in her hand.

"Take this, Liam. For the ceremony."

He looked into the pouch. A beaded necklace with a stone pendant. "What is it for?"

"My grandmother was one of The People."

His mind flew to everything that'd happened on the rez, everything Liam had told him. Had it been true? He shoved the bag in his pocket. "

"The wolf came here, trying to get the necklace."

The wolf? Was that a person? Is that why she'd been tied to the chair? "Did he start the fire?"

Grams didn't inhale for a few seconds, then gasped in a breath. "Not on purpose. The lightning. Herschel…" She lifted her hand toward the house.

"He's upstairs."

A rattle came from her chest, her hand dropped, and she went limp.

Tears poured from Travis's eyes. "Grams. No, please. No." He hugged her to him, rocking her. It was like a nightmare. This couldn't be happening.

He should go in and get Herschel.

An explosion sounded from inside the house and flames burst from the windows on the right side.

Shaking with fear, Travis tried to force his mind to function, to direct his body to get up and go in there, but it was more than he could manage.

Liam's car raced up the driveway and slid to a halt. He jumped out of the vehicle and ran toward Travis.

"Grams." Liam's face was white, his eyes frantic.

****

Liam skidded to a stop next to where Travis sat holding Grams. She wasn't moving, and Travis's cheeks were wet.

Liam fell to his knees. "Grams?" He touched her cheek.

"She's gone." Through his tears, Travis's voice squeaked like a girl's.

"No." Liam pressed his face against her neck as his eyes filled and overflowed. She was warm, she smelled like her floral perfume. How could she be gone?

He should pick her up, move her further away… He looked at Travis. "Grandpa?"

Travis shook his head. "Grams said he was upstairs, but there's no way…"

They both looked at the house. Smoke clouded the second floor windows.

"He could still be alive. Come on." Liam stood and ran toward the house. At the door, he turned, but his friend was still sitting, holding Grams.

This was too much for Liam to expect from Travis. To walk into a burning building with very little chance of walking out again.

Liam rushed in. The smoke hung thick, scorching his lungs and eyes, and the heat coming from the burning rooms singed his skin. He felt his way along the wall until he stumbled into the door to the stairs, banging his head hard.

Ringing filled his ears and the world tilted a little, but he climbed the stairs, crawling along the floor when he reached the top.

"Grandpa!" He coughed and shouted as he crawled.

It took too many minutes, but he found his grandfather lying face down on the floor, the back of his head bleeding.

What had gone on here? He didn't bother checking for a pulse. Grandpa was coming with Liam, whether he was alive or…

He dragged the limp weight to the top of the steps, then lifted him onto his shoulder in a fireman's carry.

Bracing his hands on the walls on each side of the steps, Liam went down slowly, stumbling more than once, but catching himself. Dizzy and choking, he had to close his eyes against the burning smoke.

Feeling his way along the wall, he reached the front door and burst out through the screen.

In seconds, Travis had Grandpa on his shoulder, wrapped his arm under Liam's, and helped both of them down the steps.

Opening one eye, Liam saw trucks racing

down the driveway followed by the town's fire truck, lights flashing. Then everything went black.

****

Travis had to let Liam fall, but he cushioned the drop by sliding his friend down his leg. He hauled Herschel further from the house. In seconds, people took the heavy man from Travis and others rushed past him toward Liam. Toward the fire.

Collapsing to the ground, Travis cursed his own cowardice, wished—for the thousandth time—he could be more like Liam, and fought back tears for what a shitty life he had created for himself.

Another explosion blasted from the house.

Travis looked back. The whole place was engulfed in flame. If Liam had been two minutes slower…

"Anyone know this girl?"

Travis stood, stumbling a little. He looked to where the voice had come from.

"Amanda?" Holy shit, how had she gotten here? He staggered to where one of the volunteer firefighters stood holding her arm.

"Amanda?" Travis looked into her unfocused eyes.

She mumbled and smiled and laughed as if she'd been hit in the head.

"Where did she come from?" Travis asked the man.

He gestured toward Liam's Malibu. "Just got out and started walking." The guy released her and backed up a couple steps. "Can you keep her out of the way until the ambulance gets here? Have her checked over?"

"Yeah, sure." Travis took her hand. "Amanda? Baby? What's going on?"

She tried to pull out of his grasp, still chattering incoherently.

He walked with her, guiding her away from the fire.

Barefoot, she didn't seem to feel the gravel under her feet. Her shorts were only partially zipped, and her blouse was buttoned wrong. Something black and lacy stuck out of her pocket.

Anger ripped through him. Had she been attacked? Who had done this to her? Her hair was wild, snarled, and she smelled like…it was a scent he didn't recognize, except that he'd smelled it before.

He stepped in front of her, halting her ambling. "Amanda, talk to me."

She stared through him.

He wrapped his arms around her. "Baby." They'd been seeing each other since he'd met her at the gas station in Rogers Corners, the day he and Liam were on their way to his cousin Grace's farm.

And they'd been having sex every day since, sometimes twice a day, if she could sneak away with him in his truck.

But she'd sworn him to secrecy. At first, she'd said it was because of her parents, but she finally admitted she had a fiancé in the service who she didn't want to break up with until he came home. Or at least, that was her story. He'd never found any evidence of this soldier when he'd gone through her things.

The ambulance arrived and the crew ran toward the house carrying a stretcher.

"Oh, Travis, I love you." She was still looking dazed, but those words had to be for him. She'd never said them before, and through the pain and uncertainty of what had happened to her, he felt his heart fill with the emotion.

"Amanda." He put his hands on her cheeks, directing her to look at him. "It's me. Travis. Talk to me. What happened?"

Her words jumbled together and she laughed and gestured. What was going on inside her head?

The ambulance workers walked past with Herschel on their gurney. The blanket was not covering his face. Another man had Liam's arm over his shoulder and helped him toward the ambulance.

When Liam saw Travis and Amanda, he stopped, said something to the man, then broke away and shuffled toward Travis.

"What the hell happened to her?" Travis glared at Liam.

His friend's eyes filled with guilt.

In that instant, Travis knew how total betrayal felt.

"I'm sorry, man." Liam stepped toward Amanda. "It just happened." He took a breath and coughed it out. He reached for her.

It just happened? Travis smacked Liam's hand away. "I hate you for doing this to her. I won't forgive you for it. Ever." Tears rolled down his face.

Liam stared at him. "What? You two barely spoke to each other. It's not like you were serious about each other." He moved closer to her. "Amanda, I love you, girl. Come with me."

"Why is she acting like this?" Travis put his hand on Liam's chest and shoved. "Did you drug her?"

"No I didn't drug her." Liam rubbed his head, his body swaying from side to side. He shook his head, looking really confused.

"You had sex with the woman I've

been…trying to go out with." Hatred burned so fierce, Travis felt like he could strangle Liam, pick up his body and throw it into the burning house.

"I'm sorry. She and I…" His former friend coughed, bending over.

Travis shook with the force of his revulsion. He vowed Liam would never lay another hand on his woman.

"Hey, we're ready to go." The ambulance driver tapped Liam's arm.

"Amanda, come with me to the hospital." Liam held her shoulder.

Travis pulled her out of his grip. "I'll take her in. You go with your grandfather." He needed time alone with Amanda. Away from Liam so he could curb his desire to murder him.

Liam looked back toward the house, where a white sheet covered Grams. He seemed to be near collapse. Then he walked, stumbling sideways a few times, and someone helped him climb into the ambulance.

Travis would miss Grams. He hoped Herschel made it. But in that moment, he swore that Liam would pay for everything that he'd done. It had finally happened. Travis Hackers, who had fought so hard against becoming like his father, would now take Jarvis's place as the prince of darkness.

With pure rage burning inside him, he said, "Amanda, baby." He kissed her temple as he guided her toward his truck. "We're going to make this right." Travis's lips curled into a snarl as he touched Emma's leather bag in his pocket. "Liam Jackson, I will have vengeance."

Chapter Twenty-Nine

Liam didn't see Travis or Amanda at the hospital, but after a doctor checked him out in the emergency room, Liam sat next to his grandfather's gurney most of the night. Just before sunrise, they transferred Herschel to a room in intensive care with glass walls facing the nursing station.

Emotionally, he was as close to numb as he could get. Grams was gone, and according to the doctors, Grandpa didn't have much of a chance.

Herschel's heart rate was slow, his blood oxygen dangerously low, and he hadn't regained consciousness yet. He stayed the same for three days.

For those three days, Liam ate whatever the nurses brought him and slept on a recliner in his grandfather's room until one afternoon, a nurse pulled him out of the room, brought him to the doctors' lounge. "We've been getting complaints." She smiled and handed him a stack of green scrubs. "Here, change into these and I'll wash your clothes, Liam."

He scratched his chin. He had to look like hell. He hadn't shaved, wore the same grungy clothes he'd been wearing that day, and smelled riper than a manure spreader on a hot Sunday.

"Thank you."

She directed him to a small room the doctors used, he showered and changed into the scrubs then lay on the bed, but he couldn't sleep. Amanda hadn't even shown up. After what they'd experienced together, with his feeling the way he felt for her, how could she stay away? He pulled out his phone to call her, but slid it back into his pocket. Later. He needed to focus on Grandpa.

When he woke hours later, his clothes sat

stacked neatly on a table.

He dressed and went right to his grandfather's room. Everything was the same.

A nurse outside the room caught Liam's attention, gesturing for him to come out into the hall.

"Everything okay?"

She nodded. "The sheriff is in the waiting room. He wants to talk to you."

"Thanks." He glanced back at his grandfather lying so still, so chalky-white.

"I'll keep an eye on him." She patted his arm.

Liam opened the door into the small waiting room. The sandalwood aroma of the sheriff's aftershave hung so thick it almost knocked him on his knees.

Liam stood in the doorway looking out the window, wishing he could be out there right now. He knew what the sheriff wanted.

The man sat at a small table in the corner. Without turning, he said, "Well boy, are you going to come in or aren't you?"

When he sat, he felt a hundred years old, but his heart raced as if he'd run a marathon. He had to tell the story of that day, and it would be one of the most difficult things he'd ever had to do.

The sheriff didn't speak, but looked into Liam's eyes, his black, soulless stare almost seeming to see right through him, as if looking to find answers without saying a word. He didn't introduce himself, but placed a small black tape recorder on table, pressed the record button, and slid his hand away.

"Son, why don't you tell me what you remember about what happened a few days ago."

A movie flashed inside his mind. Where should he begin? What would he say first?

So many thoughts rushed at once, all he could say was, "I don't know."

The sheriff's lips curled into a mockery of a grin. "Take your time, son, it'll come to you."

Liam tried to focus, but all he could think about was how much he loved Amanda, how confused he felt about Travis, and how he prayed his grandfather would recover.

He'd start at the beginning. "I…I…I was in the library when the tornado came through."

The sheriff's eyes narrowed. "Hmmm."

He hadn't heard? "Yeah, it was around noon."

The sheriff's expression didn't change. "Go on."

Liam rubbed his temples. "I saw lightning, heard that train sound, then went down to the cellar." Words stumbled out of his mouth as the man stared at him. This didn't feel right. As if he was on trial. But why would he be on trial? It was his family that had suffered. His grandmother who had died, and his grandpa who lay in a hospital bed grasping for life.

"Ask Mrs. Fieldhouse. Ask Amanda…" Heck, he didn't even know her last name, and he loved her? Things blurred inside his brain, almost as if Liam's mind and heart were tangled in a battle of wits.

"Amanda…" The sheriff lifted his brows.

"She works with me at the Pump and Run."

The sheriff wrote in a small notebook. "This Amanda gal." His deep southern accent seemed to thicken. "She was at the library too, huh?"

It seemed almost as if the man was interrogating him, but he was the victim. Maybe he just misread the sheriff's demeanor. Liam explained how he couldn't find the librarian, the windows broke, and they headed downstairs. He skipped ahead thirty minutes. "Then my buddy Travis called and said that my farm was on fire, and I had to get home."

"So what you're saying to me is..." The sheriff paused, not breaking eye contact. "You weren't at the farm, is that correct, boy?"

The tone of the sheriff's voice sent chills up and down Liam's spine. He knew this wasn't a concern visit. It was an interrogation.

****

Liam dug in his pocket and took out his phone with a shaking hand. "Look, look here." He held the phone toward the man, showing him the log of two calls from Travis, then he searched through his messages and showed him the text. "See, this proves I wasn't there."

The sheriff raised his hand then lowered it. "Just calm down boy, let's start from the beginning."

Liam didn't know what the beginning was, why he was the one on trial. Did the sheriff think he'd actually harm his grandparents?

"Sheriff, just call Travis Hackers and Amanda. They'll both support my story, they were both there."

Raising one eyebrow, the sheriff tapped his finger on the notepad. "You know, son, showing me your phone don't mean nothing. What I mean is, you could have gotten your phone calls and texts, but still be at the fire."

He didn't know how to respond. Swallowing hard, he tried to calm his frantic mind. "Well, I suppose, but when you talk to Travis, he'll tell you the exact same thing I said."

For the first time since Liam had sat across from him, the sheriff's stare moved off him and the man looked out the window. "Seems here, boy, we have conflicting stories."

Liam didn't say a word, just focused on the man.

For long minutes, the sheriff sat silently, staring outside. "You know what would be something strange. If you were saying one thing, and your buddy and his girl were saying the other. The whole town might start thinking you were covering up something, or trying to get attention."

The sheriff swung his head and his black eyes stared right into Liam, almost as if he could see his exposed soul. "Do you read the paper, boy? The special edition?" The man's voice was too polite.

It had been a simple question, but Liam couldn't find a thought to answer with. "I don't know." He had to swallow to keep tears from overtaking him. "You have to believe me. Travis was outside when I got to the farm, and I went in for my grandfather."

The sheriff leaned back and lifted a brow. "What if I told you that the people you're telling me will corroborate your story, they have something totally different to say than what you're sayin'."

Liam laid his hands flat on table. What was he telling him? Why had he asked about the newspaper?

The sheriff's lips curled into a sneer as he stared at Liam. "Now son, I'm on your side. I understand you've had a rough life, how your grandparents took you in, how a damaged boy like yourself could get confused, maybe need a little extra attention, have to give in to some type of mischievous behavior in order to seem bigger. Did you set it, son? Just tell me. I promise you we'll figure out a way to bring this around to be less damaging for you."

Liam's mouth dropped open, and he couldn't

speak. Without realizing it, his hands had turned into shaking fists, then his eyes narrowed, anger burning white-hot inside him.

The sheriff didn't look intimidated. He winked. "Now that's the face that could start a fire."

Liam stood, looming over the man like a grizzly about to attack. "I wasn't even there." His voice thundered through the room. Pain shot through his chest. Tears ran down his face. "I love my grandparents. I would never harm them or the farm."

Grief choked him. His Grams's ashes were in a box somewhere, his grandpa could be on his deathbed, and hateful lies were being spread about him, now. "Look sheriff, I don't know and I don't care what you're getting at, I just want my grandfather well, and I want to rebuild the farm that has become my home."

"Well, boy, first we gotta address all this arson suspicion, now, don't we." His voice carried sarcasm.

Liam stalked to the door. "My friend Travis will vouch for me, I know that." He could feel the sheriff's eyes boring into him, but when he turned around, the man wasn't even looking at him.

"Now son, why would a rich boy like Travis Hackers take up with, or vouch for, a kid with your past? Assault, vandalism, juvenile hall. You think the Hackers want to be affiliated with anything like that? Now granted, son, your grandparents are…were, upstanding citizens. So my question is, after they took you in, is this how you repay them?"

His words froze Liam's rage, turned him cold and he swung to look at the door. It didn't make sense. Why would Travis betray him? The guy had been willing to take a bullet for him.

Liam fought the urge to run, fought the fear of the sheriff pulling out handcuffs and arresting him for arson. He turned to face the man. "I haven't done anything wrong."

The sheriff nodded slowly as he picked up the tape recorder, held it to his lips, and stared at Liam. "Don't leave town." He turned around, looking out the window again.

Liam had to get out. He opened the door to leave. Wanted to hide from this cold, frightening reality.

"Just two more things, boy."

Liam waited, staring at the back of the sheriff's head. "There was no tornado that day, and you really should read the paper." The sheriff, still facing the window, pulled their town's newspaper from his back pocket. He held it up, not bothering to look at Liam.

Liam grabbed the paper from him and read the headlines. *Travis Hackers Risks Life to Save Farm Family. Grandson Suspect in Possible Arson*. Liam's heart stopped beating for a moment.

The sheriff crossed his arms, staring out the window. "We'll be seeing you, boy."

Liam headed back to his grandfather's room. He had to talk to Amanda, Travis, get this sorted out. But first things first; he just wanted Grandpa healthy again. Wanted this nightmare to end.

Chapter Thirty

That night, the nurses shooed Liam out of his grandpa's room and down to the cafeteria for sustenance. Instead of eating, he sat in the outdoor garden and called Amanda. He'd start with her, then call Travis.

"Hello?"

She sounded happy, and a half-smile curved his lips. "Amanda, it's Liam."

Silence.

"Amanda?"

"Why are you calling me?"

"Honey, I love you, I miss you. I need you beside me." How could she be so cold? "I think something strange is happening. The Hackers. I think they might be setting me up. For some reason, they want to blame me for the fire." He looked up at the stars. "When the sheriff calls, you have to tell him we were together."

"You have a lot of balls, asking for my help after what you did to me."

Liam's brows dropped. "What I did to you?"

"You took advantage." The words came out choppy.

"Girl, you've been after me for a month. At the library, it was—"

"You have no right to talk to me that way. I'm the injured party here."

"Injured…what the hell are you talking about? You jumped on me the minute we got into that storm cellar."

"Travis explained what you did to me. How you have some kind of mind manipulation, or you drugged me to make me feel the way I did."

"Travis, huh." Liam took a long pause. Every still frame ran through his mind, from the time they'd met and every moment they'd shared together as best friends. Liam's reflection turned to anger. "Well, maybe Travis needs his ass kicked, then. Where are you? Let me come and talk to you, darlin'." He hated to leave Grandpa, but this was the woman he loved, or he felt like he loved. Come to think about it, why did he love her? Why was he suddenly compelled to feel, that she was his future?

"Don't you come anywhere near me. I love Travis, and he loves me, and you are just fucking lucky I don't press charges against you."

"Love…Travis? That's a fucking joke. What the hell are you talking about?" Even though his words were sharp, he felt too vulnerable inside. "You and him barely talked."

"You're so clueless, Liam, and obviously dense. Travis and I have been seeing each other since the first day we met. He's the only reason I moved to Liberation."

Liam stood, clenching his fist. "You're kidding me, right? All this time I've been trying to do the right thing by you and him, and you've been fucking my best friend while you were offering yourself to me every goddamn day?"

"Hello? Hello?" The connection broke. He dialed again, but the message came back saying he was blocked. "Fucking bitch."

Behind him, a man cleared his throat.

Liam got up and walked past a smoker. The man, wearing scrubs, faced away from Liam. "Sorry. Woman trouble."

The gentleman chuckled. "When is a woman ever *not* trouble?"

He couldn't make out his features, but the man's voice resonated inside him somehow.

****

Travis watched Amanda throw her phone onto the couch. "Who were you talking to?"

She jumped and turned toward him, her hands going to her stomach. "My doctor. I'm not feeling well."

She sat in the western-print chair his mother had made especially for their guest house. Amanda had been staying here, close to Travis, since he'd taken her from the Jackson farm.

"What are your symptoms?" He felt her forehead.

"Dizzy, sick to my stomach, tired."

Travis almost added, "*irritable*," but that wouldn't go over well. The symptoms sounded familiar. "Have you spent a lot of time at Liam's farm?"

She gave him a glare. "No. I've never been there."

"Sorry." Since Liam had put his curse on her and had taken advantage of her, she'd been on edge. His anger threatened again, but he shoved it back. They'd make Liam sorry for what he'd done to her. To him. But he needed to think about Amanda, now.

Since she'd admitted she loved him, Travis had swung between elation and despair. Why had it taken her being used by Liam for her to realize she loved him? It was too fucking bizarre.

"Have you been swimming at all? Like in a lake or river?" On the days his dad's crew dumped into the river, people were getting ill.

"I went tubing with the girls last weekend." She narrowed her eyes. "Why?"

He leveled his gaze on her. "I've been hearing about people having problems after being in the river. You need to get checked. I can bring you to my doctor…"

She shook her head. "I'll go to mine." She got up and picked up her phone. "I'll make an appointment now." As she made the call, Travis thought about what he'd do if she'd contracted the sickness from the water. Was it time to stop covering up for his father, and take action to stop him?

"Okay, I'll be there in ten minutes." Amanda hung up. "They had a cancellation. Want to go with me?"

Travis stood and pulled her into his arms. "I want to, but Dad and I have to go talk to the mayor about the award I'm getting."

****

"Emma? Where are you?" Grandpa's voice sounded like a ghost's, and Liam froze, his heart double-pumping with fear. Then he saw Herschel's eyes open.

"Grandpa." Liam jumped up and took his hand. "It's Liam, Grandpa. You're in the hospital. I need you to tell me what happened"

The old man's eyes flickered. "What happened?"

Liam could barely breathe with the hopefulness filling him. He pressed the button for the nurse, and saw her head pop up over the counter. Liam gestured for her to get in there.

He looked down at his grandpa.

Herschel's gaze landed on his. "Where's your grandma?"

Liam swallowed. "She's gone."

"Ah." The pain in that single word sliced

through Liam's soul.

He hated to bring more pain, but he had to know. "What happened? At the farm, how did the fire start?"

"Fire? I don't know." His grandpa squinted.

The nurse came into the room. "Mr. Jackson. How are you feeling?"

Grandpa turned his head toward her voice but didn't speak.

She smiled. "I called for the doctor. She'll be here in a minute." She busied herself with monitors and tubes.

Liam needed a witness. "Grandpa, what happened at the house?" He caught the nurse's eye.

"Last thing I remember, I was upstairs, napping."

Urgency set in. He had to clear his name. "Grandpa, the newspaper is saying the fire was suspicious. They said that…that I might have set it."

Herschel groaned and gave a feeble cough.

The nurse looked at Liam, pity in her eyes. She touched her patient's forehead. "Now just you relax, Mr. Jackson. Everything will work itself out fine."

His grandfather's eyes closed and his breathing went back to normal.

When the doctor arrived, he was unconscious.

****

A few hours later, his grandparents' pastor and two of the church ladies stopped by. The women looked at Liam with suspicious eyes, as if he shouldn't be allowed to roam free.

The pastor took him aside. "The church has arranged a small trailer for you. Some of the men are setting it up on the farm right now."

Liam didn't know what to say. Their kindness brought a fresh threat of tears.

The man held up his hand. "It's just until you get your feet back under you, but you keep it as long as you need."

"Thank you, sir." Liam felt a stab of guilt for the many, many, many Sundays he'd slept in instead of worshiping with his grandparents.

"You call if you need anything else." The group prayed and left quietly.

The weight of everything that had happened, everyone who had betrayed him, everything he'd lost, came down on him until it was almost too difficult to breathe.

He let bone-chilling quiet surround him and just sat for nearly an hour.

****

That evening, when the doctor assured Liam his grandfather was stable, he begged a ride from one of the nurses who lived out his way. She chattered on about all the miraculous recoveries she'd seen in her career.

When she turned into his driveway, the car behind them slowed and crawled by. It was a sheriff's department cruiser. Shit, would this nightmare never end?

She headed down the long driveway, and her headlights shone where the house used to be.

He let out a low cry.

"Oh, Liam. I'm so sorry." She petted his arm. "You tell me if I can help with anything, won't you?"

"Yes, ma'am. Thank you for the ride." He slid out of her car and walked toward the black hole that had once been his home.

When her headlights disappeared, he stood in

near-complete darkness. The yard lights weren't on, and there was no moon. He moved his car to face the charred remains and turned on his high beams. Pieces of wood had been dragged out and lay on the grass around the foundation. Was that from the fire department's arson investigators?

He sat on his heels. Was there anything left? Should he sift through it all for pieces of metal that hadn't burned? Goddamn it, his journals were gone. And his video camera. He touched one of the broken foundation blocks, and looked at the black covering his fingers. The scent of burnt wood made him gag. "Poetic justice."

For a moment, he felt heavy guilt for everything he'd done, for everyone he'd hurt over the last few months. He shook it off. His time was better spent figuring out how to rebuild the house, where to live when Grandpa was released, and how to handle the insurance claims. He stood looking around him at the few things he had left. The clothes on his back, his wallet, his car, Grandpa's truck, the implements, the barn, and the land.

He could start over, skip ag school and become a man his grandfather would be proud to call his grandson. Plans formed in his mind. He'd figure out just what Jarvis Hackers had been pouring into the river, get that asshole in jail, make a new start on the farm, and do his best to get Amanda back. With her by his side, he could be a very happy man.

He shut off the car lights and wandered toward the trailer.

Hours later, the nightmare struck and despite trying desperately to wake himself, he stayed deep in his own private level of hell. Dream Liam laughed as he tipped over a can of gasoline in the kitchen of the farmhouse. With a sickening smile, he walked backward until he stood on at the screen door.

Then he lit a match.

The flames shot up, licking at the ceiling.

Grams's face appeared behind them. "No, please." She reached for him, her hand shaking.

He turned and strode across the porch and down the steps.

From above him, his grandfather's voice called out. "Help us." He pressed his hands against the second window, looking down on Liam.

A banging woke him.

Chapter Thirty-One

He sat up, screaming, his body covered in sweat. He looked around the small bedroom.

A voice called from outside the trailer. "Anyone here?" Another car door slammed. Was it the sheriff? Fire investigators? He scrambled into his clothes and stepped out of the trailer.

A county ag service truck sat behind the Malibu, and a man in a cowboy hat stood holding a clipboard and a box that looked like it should hold fishing tackle.

"Hello?" Liam strode toward him.

The man turned, and a grin broke out on his face. "Liam, thank God. I've been stopping by looking for you." He set down his box and took off his hat. "I'm deeply sorry for your loss."

"Thank you." Liam tried to recall the man's name. "What can I help you with?"

He set his hat back on his head. "I'm Zeke Fillion. I'm one of the volunteer firefighters."

"Right. Thank you." Liam waited. Was he the arson investigator?

"When I was here, I noticed how your corn looked strange. And there should have been…" Zeke gestured. "Come over here, I'll show you."

They walked to where the corn field came to within yards of the house.

"See here?" Zeke pointed to black chunks amidst the corn. "These were flaming boards that burned here in the corn."

"Okay." Four years of living with his grandparents hadn't given him a great deal of agricultural knowledge.

"See, the corn should have gone up." He

waved his arm out over the field. "It should have burned like a son of a bitch." He looked briefly at Liam. "Excuse the expression."

Liam nodded, not sure where this was headed. "But—"

"Look at this stalk. It's normal on the surface, but when you break it, look at that. Isn't that amazing?"

White liquid oozed out. "I'm really not up on corn shucks."

"Not a problem. What I need from you is your permission." He pointed to a line on a paper on his clipboard. "I took the liberty of coming back the day after the fire and took some soil samples from points all around the farm. In the corn, the beans, by the river. I started running tests, but…" He shoved the clipboard at Liam. "I need your approval."

Liam signed. "What do you think you'll find?"

The man set down his box and opened it. "I don't know, but I have a suspicion." He pulled out a small trowel. He started to walk away.

"Wait, can I give you my phone number so you can call me with whatever you find?"

"Sure. Write it on the form." The man disappeared into the corn field.

Liam set the clipboard on the hood of the ag truck, and walked back toward the trailer. Leaning against the door, was a large brown envelope, thick and heavy. He looked around. He hadn't heard anyone drive up.

He turned the envelope over. Scribbled in pencil on a post-it note, he read, *Don't open until you get the results from the county man.* Under the note, the envelope was addressed to the Environmental

Protection Agency, and it even had postage on it.

Liam looked around the trailer again. He hadn't heard a car pull up. He went inside and checked the small table next to the bed. His phone and wallet were still there.

As he sat on the bed, he hooked his finger in the flap and tore. He leafed through the papers. Reports, graphs, recommendation papers stamped in red with *Environmental Hazard*, all from the county ag service. Why hadn't his grandfather seen these? The only paperwork he'd gotten had reported normal levels in the soil and water.

His phone rang. The hospital's number. Fear choked him. Liam dropped the papers on the bed and picked up the phone.

"My grandpa? Is he okay?"

"He's okay, Liam." The nurse's calm voice soothed him like a caress. "He's awake, and he wants to see you."

"On my way." Liam ran faster than he ever had in his life.

****

Skidding into his grandfather's room, Liam nearly bawled when he saw his grandpa in a semi-sitting position.

"Well, there you are. Had a hot date last night, and just waking up?"

Liam looked at the clock. Almost noon. "Yeah, I slept in. You know what a slacker I am." He pulled a chair next to the bed and sat. "You look good. How do you feel?"

Grandpa lifted the cup in his right hand and sucked at the straw. "Hungry." He shook the cup. "They've got me on some liquid old-folks food."

"That won't last long. By tomorrow, you'll be

eating ribs and fries."

Herschel held his stomach and moaned. "Don't tease me." Grandpa looked at his ring finger. "What I wouldn't do for one more piece of your Grams's pie."

Liam let emotion well up. "God, yes."

When his grandpa tried to set down the cup, Liam took it from him and placed it on the table. "I'm sorry I wasn't there."

"You couldn't have been there to watch us twenty-four hours a day, son. Don't blame yourself."

The doctor walked it. "Look who decided to wake up." She held his wrist, taking his pulse. "How are you feeling?"

"Like ten pounds of ache in a five pound bag."

She laughed. "We're going to try to fix that, Mr. Jackson." She used her stethoscope and listened to his heart and chest, had him breathe fast and slow for her.

"I'm going to get a few tests ordered for you. We'll get you up out of bed later, if you're up to it, and if all goes well, we'll move you out of ICU tomorrow."

"Head hurts like a son of a…" He closed his mouth. "Like heck."

The doctor took a look under the bandage. "Did you fall? It looks like it's heavily bruised."

"You know, ma'am, I don't know. I keep having these strange visions of seeing someone else in the house, but I can't know for sure."

Liam stood and looked at the wound from his side of the bed. "He was lying face down when I found him. And the blood was running forward, toward his face."

"Hm. Odd." The doctor looked closer. "Were

you struck, Mr. Jackson?"

He gave a long sigh. "Wish I could remember." Herschel tossed up his hand. "It just won't come back to me. But if I was a bettin' man, my gut would tell me someone else was there, and it wasn't Liam."

"That's all right." The doctor placed the bandage back on his head. "It'll come to you in time." She looked at Liam. "But you might want to let the sheriff know about it."

The sheriff. Liam hated to push his grandpa, but he needed to clear his own name. "Grandpa, in the paper, they're saying I started the fire." He looked at the doctor.

She met his gaze for a second, frowning, then looked at Herschel.

"Doc, give me a few minutes with my grandson. And have a nurse call the deputy sheriff to come and take my statement, would you?"

The doctor patted Herschel's hand. "I'll be right outside." She left.

"Thank you, doc." Herschel made a shooing motion.

Grandpa's brown gaze locked with Liam's. "You've got to get the hell out of this town, son."

Liam could only blink.

Herschel pressed a button on the bed's safety rail and the top part of the hospital bed moved, sitting him up straighter. "I read that damn newspaper. They're blaming you for starting the fire? That's just rubbish. You wouldn't start a fire in your own home any more than I would."

"I can prove I didn't do it. I don't need to leave town." Liam rested his forearms on the safety rail. "I have some plans, Grandpa. For the farm."

"The farm." He shook his head. "It's not going to be ours much longer."

His brow furrowed. "What do you mean? You've sold it?"

Grandpa gave a sad laugh. "I wish I had, all those years ago when Jarvis Hackers made me an offer." He reached for his cup, and Liam helped him. "No, with the crops doing so poorly, I haven't been keeping up with the bills, son. I've even borrowed on our life insurance…" Moisture filled his eyes. "Bottom line is, the county is ready to take possession of the place for back taxes."

Liam sat down hard. "The farm is…" What about his future? He couldn't work at the gas station all his life.

"Yep, son, it's gone. We never carried enough crop insurance, and when things started turning bad, it was too late to buy it."

"Did Grams know?"

Grandpa shook his head. "I didn't want to worry her. And with her feeling so badly lately, I didn't want to burden her." He swiped at a tear that had leaked from his eye.

"Maybe we can take out a loan. When you get out of here, I wanted to—"

"No. There is no loan money for us. And when I get out of here, they'll send me to an old folk's home to 'recuperate,' but we all know it's just the next step closer to the grave."

"Grandpa, don't talk like that." Liam wanted to hurl himself onto the bed, hug the old man close.

"It's time we face facts, son." He pierced him with a stare. "You've been living your life like you didn't care about tomorrow. People in town talk, Liam, and some of the things you do, I blame on your bad childhood, but some of them I blame on lack of discipline by me and Grams."

Liam couldn't imagine what people were talking about. His life had been straight-and-true until he'd gotten caught up with Kaylee, then Punk Rock Girl, then Tara and Trinity, then… "Yeah, okay, I've had a few bad months, but—"

"What you need is a structure for your life. The same as I did when I joined the Army, and it made all the difference. I became a man who could be proud of himself."

"Army?" Liam didn't know where he was going with this.

"Go today. Tonight. Get out of this town and drive to Nashville. There's a recruiting office there. Sign up and get yourself into boot camp as soon as you can."

Liam couldn't leave his grandfather. "I'm staying. You'll need me to help get back on your feet."

"No. Listen to me." He focused on Liam so intently, Liam had to look away for a second. "I'll be fine. There are plenty of folks in this town who can help me, and if I'm lucky enough to not need a nursing home, I'll get into a senior apartment."

"I want to be—"

Herschel banged his hand on the safety rail.

Liam jumped.

"Listen to me." He nearly shouted. "I love you, son, more than breath itself, but I need to know your life won't be wasted. Promise me you won't come back here until you're wearing an Army uniform. Promise me, Liam."

Liam's breath came fast and shallow. Could he do this? Could he leave his grandfather alone? Or could he promise it, but not follow through, and stay here in town to help him. "Yes, Grandpa, I promise." The weight of those words nearly broke him, but he'd deal with his choices later.

A buzzer started on one of the machines.

"Your promise is your oath, Liam. Don't disappoint me." The cup dropped out of his hand.

"Grandpa?"

A beeping noise filled the room, and a nurse rushed in.

Liam stood. "Grandpa?"

His eyes rolled back in his head and his body shook.

"Grandpa!" He shouted as he grasped the old man's strong shoulder. "Stay with me."

The room filled with people.

Liam was pushed back a few steps as a man dropped the side rail and lowered the head of the bed.

"Grandpa?" He stepped back until he bumped into the wall.

A half-dozen people in scrubs and uniforms worked on him, pumping oxygen manually, pressing their hands into his chest, shocking his heart, and checking his eyes. After only minutes, it was over. One by one, the machines were shut off, and people left the room.

A man in green scrubs walked over to him. "I'm sorry, son. We did everything we could."

Liam nodded.

The man turned and walked out, leaving the door open.

Liam took the first few steps, then ran to his Grandpa and lay next to him on the bed, pressing his face into his shoulder. "Don't leave me alone, Grandpa."

****

Three hours later, after what seemed like an eternity sitting on the bench outside the hospital entrance, all Liam could hear was that final flatline sound. Everything he'd ever loved was gone, and that sound just seemed to be the punctuation at the end, but it didn't seem real. How could he have lost everything so quickly?

The heat and humidity played heavily on his mind, scenes of last few days running like a horror movie. Travis. "*You'll never lay a hand on her again.*" The sheriff. "*We'll be seeing you around, boy.*" Grandpa. "*You've got to get the hell out of this town, son.*"

The words spun like a tornado, as out of control as his life was.

He heard a woman's voice.

Her silhouette in front of a ray of sun bouncing off a statue blinded him.

He shifted to side and looked up at her, sweat tricking down his brow.

She wore some kind of gray uniform.

He stood, woozy at first but then starting to focus. Trinity? Or another look-alike?

This woman had soft golden-blonde hair, cut straight along her chin, and wore minimal makeup.

"Liam? Is it you? I can't believe it." Her smile lit her face. She held out her hand to shake his.

It was her. He shook her hand, shocked that she acted as if nothing had happened between them. "Hi, Trinity."

She gave a joyful laugh. "It's just plain old Teresa now."

He looked her up and down. "Are you in the service?"

She rolled her eyes, almost glowing. The darkness she'd once had was gone.

Liam wished his darkness was gone, but the gloom just continued to press closer.

"I'm a flight attendant." She gave him a proud smile as she touched a small pin in the shape of wings on her collar." She sobered. "After that night at the hotel…" She paused and seemed to drift away. "Something just snapped inside me and I knew I needed to go after my dream. I'm so happy. I'm seeing the world, and it's everything I wanted to do but had never taken the chance.

Liam tried to find a smile. "That's great." It took all his breath and the last bit of his strength to do what he needed to do now. "Trinity, I'm so damn sorry. I—"

"Stop, Liam. It was the lowest point of my life." Her frown, the shine in her eyes, nearly broke what was left of his heart.

Liam knew that would be his burden to bear. He looked down at his feet. There were no words to apologize for being the worst thing that had ever happened to someone.

She hit him on shoulder. "No, silly, not you. I was the one making a mess of things. You just happened along at the wrong time." She shook her head. "Anyway, enough talk about that. I have to hurry. I'm here to see a friend before I fly out again."

He couldn't believe she'd absolved him so quickly.

"I saw you sitting here and wanted you to know that it's great seeing you, and…" She blushed. "You know, when I woke that next morning, it was like…" She patted a spot over her heart. "Like a chain had been taken off of me and I could finally move on with my life, or actually have a life. I know it sounds corny, but whatever went on, I owe you." She tipped her head.

He could almost reach out and touch the positive karma she exuded, wanted to harness the energy she possessed.

"Goodbye, Liam." She walked away.

Liam wished he had the right to ask her to stay and help him through the hell he was going through. But he would take the karmic brain smack she'd given him and do what he needed to do, now.

Chapter Thirty-Two

Liam parked the Malibu right over the oil spot that marked the car's usual resting place. He took the car keys from his chain and set them on top of the registration form in the glove compartment, and closed the small door with a firm push.

Running his hands over the steering wheel one last time, he could almost imagine his grandpa at Liam's age, driving this baby around town, showing off for Grams, before she even agreed to date him.

Thanks to Ray, the Malibu would have new home, and in return, his grandparents would have a respectable funeral and dignified headstones. With a half-smile and a pat on the dash, he opened the door. "See you, Cherry."

His smile faded and turned into a frown when he saw what looked like Amanda's car coming down the churd rock driveway.

He was not ready to hear what she had to say. He exited the Malibu and shut the door as her car pulled up next to him. For a moment as their eyes met, he felt all-consuming passion, love, lust, obsession. But judging by the way she looked at him, he knew none of that was real.

She got out of the car holding papers.

Liam raised his farm-callused hands to stop her. "There's nothing I want to hear you say." He smelled the air. There was no rain scent any more.

She started talking, but Liam walked toward the trailer. He had to focus. He needed to grab the envelope, make sure there was nothing else he needed to do, and leave. Leave before the sheriff or the Hackers pinned the burning of the family farm on him, leave before Amanda said one word that would set him in any direction but what his grandfather had directed him.

He stepped into the trailer and slammed the door behind him. He'd leave behind his heartache, the disappointment in himself that would haunt him for the rest of his life. Where was he when his family needed him? In a basement room, giving in to his darkest urges.

The trailer door swung open, banging against the outside wall, interrupting his thoughts.

Liam walked into the bedroom, shoved the papers in the envelope and sealed it, then tucked it under his arm.

Amanda stood in the tiny kitchen with papers in her hand, shaking. She looked sick, her face pale, perspiring more than normal.

Why was she there? What more did she want from him? Hadn't she taken enough from him?

Liam shot daggers with his stare, trying to scare her away. "I told you, I have nothing to say to you."

She cried out, started mumbling words that didn't make sense, then stopped. "You'll want to hear what I have to say."

Her words echoed inside Liam's ears. "No, I don't." The truth was, he wanted to hear everything she had to say. He wanted her to run up and kiss him, hug him tight, make love like they had in storm cellar.

Of all the sins he'd committed over the last few months, he knew that would be the worst one.

He set her small body out of his way and left the trailer.

"Wait, damnit." Behind him, she tripped, sending her papers flying.

He hesitated, wanting to stop and help her, but

he turned away and strode toward the pickup that had belonged to his grandfather. He had to do this quick, before something she said made him change his mind.

"Liam." Her cry sounded weak.

He turned, watching her pick up the papers. She looked confused, stumbling, saying something too quietly for him to hear.

His heart hung on every word, even though his brain told him to bolt.

When he was almost to the truck, she ran ahead of him and slapped her hands with the papers onto the hood of the truck. She breathed hard, moving her lips as if she couldn't say what she'd made the trip all the way out here to tell him. "Just read the papers."

He wanted to care, wanted to know what was going on. But he'd made an oath, and he wouldn't be detoured from it. He had to end this now, before he weakened. "Go tell it to Travis." He slammed the door, and rolled down the window to release the heat trapped inside.

She smacked her hand on hood several times. "You don't understand. I'm…I'm…sick."

Travis had money for doctors, hospitals, medicines. He'd take care of her. Liam turned the ignition key. The truck fired up on cue, a testament to his grandfather's care of everything in his life. A diesel truck with 250,000 miles that sounded like brand new.

She moved to the front of the truck, blocking him.

He revved the engine and could see her mouth moving over the noise.

When he popped the clutch and shifted into first gear, the truck rolled forward, and she walked backward.

She kept smacking her hands on hood, screaming crying, looking pale and frantic, like she was on her death bed. There was definitely something wrong with Amanda.

But Liam had no choice. He would honor his grandfather's dying wishes, and God forgive him, whatever was coming out of her mouth was the last thing he needed to hear.

He stared coldly at her, and said nothing as he drove forward slowly, but his heart melted for her, and gave the truck one last rev to get her to move out of the way

She moved to the driver's side of the truck and he accelerated past her.

Looking in the side mirror, he saw her raise one middle finger. "You son of a bitch." She fisted the papers in her hand and shook them at him.

He felt…broken. Everything he loved was gone. He rolled up the window, shutting her out of his life permanently.

In the rearview mirror, he watched Amanda running down driveway screaming at the top of her lungs. As she fell to her knees, the dust from his tires blew over her, finally obscuring her, absolving her from his view.

Liam slowed the truck. He wanted so much to just stop and turn around, but he remembered the words echoing in his mind; *Get the hell out of this town.*

His phone rang, breaking the moment of indecision.

****

Travis ran behind the trailer catching his breath as Liam drove away. When he'd followed

Amanda here, he'd thought he'd be walking in on them fucking, but the words she'd yelled at the tailgate of Liam's truck were nothing close to what he'd expected.

"Liam, I'm pregnant."

How in the hell could that be? They'd always used double protection. And why would she come out here to tell Liam? They were together just four days ago. Unprotected sex, from what Travis could piece together. Too soon to know, wasn't it? Or was she afraid Liam would try to claim the baby? Make trouble for them?

Travis would marry her, raise the baby no matter who the kid ended up looking like. He loved Amanda and would risk everything for her.

Her car engine started, and he saw Amanda just sitting there, her hands covering her face. He'd give her the life she deserved. A nice car, a big house, money, vacations, the best of everything.

And all he'd had to do was sell out his best friend.

"No, I didn't betray him. He seduced Amanda." Travis reminded himself of that fact each time he softened toward Liam. The next few weeks held a lot of surprises for the bastard. Travis's dad helped make sure of that. The fucker would wish he'd never come to Liberation, and would learn to hate the day he first heard the name Hackers. Travis knew Liam's secret. He did have powers. The legend was true. But Travis would die before he ever let Liam know his birthright after taking from him what Travis valued so much.

He took out the buckskin sack Grams had given him. He'd throw the cursed thing in the river, let it sink to the bottom, burying Liam's legend forever.

He grinned as he removed the necklace from of the bag and held it up to the sun. The beads sparkled like multi-color lasers that hurt his eyes. The stone pendant was round in front, and flat in back. He turned it over. There was some kind of carving on the flat side. A circle, half dark and half light, two lines with circles on the end, opposite each other almost like yin and yang, and below it—

Something cracked behind him, and Travis jerked around.

The man had long, dark hair, reddish skin.

Travis swallowed around the lump in his throat. "Hey, I know you."

"Evil heart." The words came slowly out of the man's mouth, but the fist that caught Travis under the jaw came like lightning from out of nowhere, and sent him flying, landing hard, and slipping away into blessed darkness.

****

Liam pressed the green light on his phone. "Hello?"

"Liam, it's Zeke Fillion from the Ag Service. You're never going to believe what we found."

Liam pulled the manila envelope from his pocket and stared at it. "Yeah, I think I will believe it."

As Zeke spoke, Liam headed down the driveway, over the rise and down the other side. Travis's red truck sat empty on the side of the driveway. He'd help Amanda. Liam let go of the guilt clutching his stomach and pressed harder on the accelerator. The quarter-mile stretch seemed endless today.

Zeke finished the quick, excited explanation

of the soil's harmful chemical signature, and promised to get back to him later with more results.

Liam thanked him and hung up. He stopped at the mailbox and jumped out of the truck, the manila envelope in his hand.

Everything Zeke said was confirmed by the papers in the envelope.

"Jarvis Hackers, you're done."

He shoved the package in the mailbox, lifted the flag on the side, and shut the mailbox door. "Grandpa, this is for you."

He stood for a moment, listening to the silence, smelling the patch of earth that was no longer his future. To the right was town. To the left, Nashville.

Should he go right? Try to fight for his place in this town? But there was nothing left for him. To his left was his future. Would it be anything like his past?

He slid into the driver's seat and made a left turn toward Nashville. He would follow the destiny his grandfather had envisioned for him. "Life can only get better from here, right?"

No one answered.

And the legend begins.

~~*~*

How Will the Legend End?

Connect With Me

Both Leo and I appreciate that you took the time to read Legend Awakening. True stories are often the hardest to tell, even through fiction. It was a privilege and an adventure working with Leo. His knowledge of the subject continually inspired and awed me. We hope that our series of books will open channels of discussion on the subject of the ultimate female orgasm.

It's a difficult and often taboo subject, but women owe it to themselves to take on the tough stuff in order to love everything about their bodies. You can make a difference. Imagine if your comments unlocked the courage of every woman to step forward and say, "I deserve the ultimate female orgasm!"

We encourage you to grow with us, discuss with us, and be proud of your bodies and all its pleasures.

All my best,
Randi

Website: http://randialexander.com/
Newsletter: http://randialexander.com/subscribe-to-my-mailing-list/
Facebook: https://www.facebook.com/RandiAlexanderAuthor
Facebook Fan Page: https://www.facebook.com/RandiAlexanderBooks/
Twitter: https://twitter.com/Randi_Alexander
Goodreads: http://www.goodreads.com/author/show/4885056.Randi_Alexander
Randi's Blog: http://randialexander.com/blog-3/
Wild and Wicked Cowboys Blog: http://wildandwickedcowboys.wordpress.com/

About the Author

USA Today Bestselling Author Randi Alexander knows a modern woman dreams of an alpha cowboy who takes the reins, and guarantees they're rode hard and put up satisfied.

Published with Cleis Press, Wild Rose Press, and self-published, Randi writes smokin' hot romance with heroes who'll have you begging to ride off into the sunset with them. When she's not dreaming of, or writing about, rugged cowboys, Randi is biking trails along remote rivers, snorkeling the Gulf of Mexico, or practicing her drumming in hopes of someday forming a tropical rock-band.

Forever an adventurous spirit with a naughty imagination, Randi is also family oriented and married to the best guy in the world, her own cowboy, Kick. Give in to the allure of erotic passion, strong but vulnerable heroines, and irresistibly seductive cowboys, as Randi's emotional love stories sweep you off your feet and leave you breathless with passion.

Saddle up! And prepare yourself for the sexier side of happily ever after.

~~*~*

~~*~*